THE Breaking POINT

FALLON
GREER

THE BREAKING POINT
Edited by: Castle Walls Editing, LLC
Proofreading by: Jenny Sims
Cover Illustration by: Mayhara Ferraz
Cover designer: Sommer Stein
Formatting: Elaine York
www.allusionpublishing.com

The *Breaking* Point

Grace Kensington has been my secret crush since we were kids.

Though she is definitely all grown up now.

Long blonde hair, big blue eyes, and curves that could bring even the toughest hockey player to his knees. She's the full package, too—smart, funny, and as real as they come.

One might go as far as to say perfect. Except for one tiny detail: Grace is my coach's daughter.

And she just walked back into my life. Apparently she's doing an internship for the team.

The last thing I should do is get close to her again.

So the plan is to keep my distance.

But that plan flies out the window the very first time we run into each other...and I'm naked in the locker room.

Chapter 1

Grace

Are you still in the office?

I glanced at the text from my best friend Kelly Wright and rolled my eyes. Kelly was obsessed with hockey, and she'd burst my eardrums squealing when she'd heard I'd gotten an internship with the LA Blades.

Because you should go find some hockey players already, was Kelly's follow-up message.

I typed back that I was still busy working and that she should maybe finish her work, too. I could just see Kelly scoffing and telling me I was boring as fuck, but in a good-natured way.

I had a lot to prove with getting this internship. Everyone assumed that I'd gotten it because my dad coached the Blades. Sure, nobody had said that to my face, but I felt it in the air when I'd first come into the office a week ago.

My supervisor, Julia, had also seemed hesitant to give me any real work. Where the other marketing interns were being given assignments and coffee runs, I was relegated to liking positive comments on Facebook.

"Only likes," Julia had reminded me for the millionth time. "No sad or angry reactions. And no replies. Got it?"

I'd nodded, annoyed but knowing I couldn't complain. I'd done the assignment within a half hour and then had tried my best to find something to occupy my time.

Now I was the last one in the office. Even Julia had gone home, considering it was a Friday. She'd told me to lock up when I was done.

She might not trust me with the work, but I guess she's not worried about security, I thought wryly.

I'd decided to write up a few different social media posts and present them to Julia on Monday. Maybe she'd see that I was serious about giving this internship my all.

My phone sang again, and I stuffed it into my bag. But it kept ringing, and ringing, and ringing.

I finally picked up, exasperated. "Kelly, seriously? What is it?"

"You have to tell me everything," she said.

"Tell you *what*? I'm going home. There's nothing exciting to report."

"You're telling me you were in the stadium all day and didn't run into one hockey player? Your dad is the coach. Come on, now."

Kelly was about to start grad school, so she told me she needed the 411 on my internship before she got too busy to demand daily updates.

"My dad might be the coach, but that doesn't mean he has anything to do with marketing or PR," I pointed out.

"Ugh, you're boring. At least tell me you'll go to the rink tomorrow and watch them practice."

"If I have time, maybe."

Kelly just sighed like I'd told her I was about to die of an incurable disease. "You really need to have more fun. When's the last time you went out on a date?"

"I told you about Will, right?" Will and I had just started dating. We'd only gone on two dates, but he was a nice guy.

"That guy? Has he even tried to kiss you yet?"

"No," I spoke over Kelly's interjection, adding, "Because he's a gentleman."

"Or he's just not that into you."

Okay, Will wasn't the most exciting guy ever. I knew that. He tended to talk about *Minecraft* a lot, and the one time I'd tried to hug him, he'd acted like I'd tried to put a bug in his shirt.

"I need to finish up here and head home," I said before saying goodbye.

At the end of the day, I didn't need Kelly distracting me—or tempting me with finding some of those hockey players she was obsessed with.

Because I was all too aware that there were sexy hockey players not far from me. The offices were within the stadium, and I'd heard the guys practicing when I'd gone to the bathroom. It'd taken every ounce of my self-control not to go watch.

Not that anyone would care. I'd been around hockey my entire life. But I also hadn't been around much in the past four years since I'd been away at college.

I wasn't that naive little teenager who'd left. I was a woman now. And I knew that I had to grab life by the horns if I wanted to achieve anything of value.

I yawned, closed my laptop, and decided to call it a day. It was already past five o'clock. But I needed to take a few photos first before I went home.

One of my ideas had been to give an inside look at the team's locker room. Okay, yes, it didn't sound that exciting, but die-hard fans like Kelly loved that kind of stuff.

I went downstairs to where the locker rooms were and listened. I didn't hear any voices, so everyone had likely already gone home. I knocked on the locker room door, then called, "Anyone inside?"

No answer. Shrugging, I pushed the door wide open and started taking pictures.

I was so immersed in taking photos that when a man stepped into the view of my phone, I nearly threw it straight at his head.

That was when I realized the man was naked. Wet, dripping, and naked.

I froze. And then I wanted to die right then and there because the man was none other than Brady Carmichael.

LA Blades defenseman. Playboy. Sex magnet. And my childhood crush, whom I'd never actually gotten over.

"What the hell?" Brady exclaimed. Then his eyes widened, recognition filling his expression. "Holy shit, Grace? Is that you?"

It was too late to run. Besides, I was frozen to the spot.

Brady Carmichael was a magnificent specimen of a man: his entire body was delineated with muscles. From his pectorals to his biceps to his abs to his—

I forced myself to look away. Because he was naked, and his dick was right there. And it was just as impressive as the rest of him.

He laughed. Laughed!

"What, you come in here to take dirty photos and then get shy? Come on now," he teased.

I blushed so hot that I was sure my face was on fire. "I didn't think anyone was in here," I squeaked out.

Brady just stood there, arms crossed, not a care in the world. And then when he started to walk toward me, I did the only thing I could: I ran.

Sprinting toward the door, Brady shouted after me. I hurried to the elevator, but to my immense annoyance, it was too slow. He caught up to me and grabbed my arm.

"Hey, wait!" Brady said.

His skin was still damp, water dripping from his hair. But now he at least had some sweatpants on, even if those pants only emphasized the delicious V-cut of his hip bones. I forced myself to look anywhere but at him.

"Sorry," I mumbled. "I really didn't think anyone was in there."

Brady let me go—I could still feel his touch like a brand—and he chuckled. "Oh, I believe you. Everybody knows Grace Dallas follows the rules."

I wanted to scowl. I wanted to tell him he was wrong, but he wasn't. I was a good girl. I'd never done anything to upset the apple cart. I did as my parents wanted. I'd never even gotten drunk in college.

In other words, I'd always been too much of a Goody Two-shoes for a man like Brady.

"Hey, come on." Brady held out his arms. "A hug for old times' sake?"

I hesitated, but I wasn't made of stone. I let him give me a hug even though he got my shirt damp in the process.

"I didn't know you were back," he said.

"I got an internship with the team."

His eyes widened. "Since when?"

Was he surprised? Or worse, annoyed? I couldn't tell. "Uh, I just started."

Brady looked like he was going to say something but then thought better of it. He just asked instead, "So you're back in LA for good?"

"At least for the time being."

Silence fell. I could tell Brady felt awkward around me.

And why shouldn't he? I'd been the girl who'd thrown herself at him back in high school, and he'd rejected me. After that, he'd kept his distance. I hadn't seen him since I'd moved away for college.

Brady cleared his throat. "You look different."

I cocked my head to the side. "Says the man running around without shoes or a shirt on."

"Sorry, I mean, you look—" Brady hesitated. "Older."

"I mean, I am older than when you last saw me. So that tracks."

He grinned, and that stupid grin went straight to my heart like an arrow. "You always were a little spicy."

"I thought you just said I was boring?"

"Boring? You? No." Something crossed his expression, but I didn't know what it was. "No, you've never bored me."

I wanted him to explain that comment, but unfortunately for us both, my dad interrupted.

"Carmichael! Go put on a goddamn shirt!" Dad barked as he approached us.

Brady grimaced. "Yessir," he said, saluting ironically. He winked at me and returned to the locker room.

My dad had always been a big, gruff man, but inside was a gooey marshmallow center. He'd only ever shown that side with his family, though, and with me especially. I'd known since I was a kid that I had my dad wrapped around my little finger.

"What the hell was that about?" Dad barked.

I forced myself to stop gazing at where Brady had disappeared to. "What? Brady? We were just saying hi."

"Why was he shirtless?"

I wasn't about to explain that one, so I just shrugged. "Maybe a dog ate his shirt and shoes."

Dad narrowed his eyes at me and then sighed. "Come on. Your mother texted me to say we better be home in time for dinner tonight."

Dad and I both knew how much Mom hated when anyone was late for dinner. Although Dad had assured Mom that she didn't need to cook every night, she'd done it since before I could remember.

When Brady had joined our family as a foster kid, he'd been confused that we'd always eaten together in the dining room.

"You guys don't watch TV?" he'd asked.

My older brother, Ben, had just laughed. "Don't say that out loud, or our mom will tell you off."

Brady, though, had asked our mom point-blank why we never ate in front of the TV. Our mom, who wasn't the type to get ruffled by a fourteen-year-old boy, had simply informed Brady that those were the house rules, and he could either follow them or see what happened if he didn't.

"Cat got your tongue?" Dad asked me, forcing me back to the present.

I hadn't even remembered walking out of the stadium with him. We were almost to my car, which I'd parked next to Dad's.

"Uh, sorry," I hedged, feeling a blush crawl up my cheeks. "Just a lot on my mind."

Dad narrowed his eyes at me, his bushy eyebrows almost coming together into one judgmental line.

"Stay away from him," he said suddenly.

I stopped in my tracks. "Who? Brady?" I let out an incredulous laugh. "Dad, he's practically family!"

"He's not your brother. Never has been." When I was about to protest, Dad put up a hand. "I'm not saying he isn't family. He's like a son to me and your mother. But as far as being your brother . . ." Dad grimaced. "You know what I mean."

I blushed harder. Mom and Dad had been all too aware of my unrequited crush on Brady back in the day. But I wasn't a teenager anymore. I was an adult.

"I'm not Brady's type," I said, even as my own words made my stomach sink.

Dad snorted. "You're a woman. You're his type. Which means you need to be on your guard."

"If he's such a bad guy, why did you even let him on the team?" I snapped, annoyed now.

To my irritation, Dad just shook his head. "He's not a bad guy, but he's not the guy for *you*. You're a smart girl, Gracie. I don't want you to throw yourself away on a guy who doesn't deserve you."

"Well, Brady didn't even know I was back in town, so I doubt he's been dying to jump my bones."

Dad scowled. "Enough of this talk. I'll see you back home. And don't drive too fast, and be careful merging onto the interstate—"

I held up a hand, laughing now, then gave Dad a kiss, leaving him grumbling as I drove away.

Since I'd only just moved back to LA and rent was absurdly expensive, I'd decided to move back in with my parents for a time. Although I didn't love being under their roof—and their rules—it was better than living with five roommates in a two-bedroom apartment just to make rent.

But being back in my old room, which hadn't changed since I'd gone to college, felt strange. I'd only been in it for about a year and a half before I'd left for college, but I'd still left a lot of stuff behind.

The walls were still a bright magenta that my mom had surprised me with. I hadn't had the heart to tell her that that was no longer my favorite color when we'd moved in.

Worse, my bed still had the ruffled duvet set I'd begged Mom to get me when I'd been fourteen and living at the old house in Las Vegas. It'd come along to the new house, but by the time I was sixteen, I'd felt like I'd outgrown it. The overall color scheme and ruffles made the room look especially childish, and I winced a little as I took it all in.

Old makeup and hair accessories filled the vanity I'd used as a teenager; the bookcase was similarly filled with romance novels I'd inhaled at the time. I even found my old MP3 player in my nightstand and had been pleasantly surprised to discover it still worked. I'd listened to a few of my favorite songs from back then until the walk down memory lane became too much.

Thinking about my adolescence meant thinking about my older brother. And it meant thinking about Brady Carmichael.

The first time I saw Brady—I'd been twelve years old—I'd known he'd change my life. Perhaps not in the way that I'd expected, but I'd known, even at a young age, that Brady was special.

It'd helped that, even at fourteen, Brady had been handsome. When many of the other boys in his ninth-grade class had yet to go through full puberty, Brady looked older than his age. He'd been tall and muscular; he'd even had patchy facial hair, which I'd thought made him intimidating at the time. Even Ben hadn't had much facial hair despite being older than Brady.

Oh, Ben. I wish you were here right now. You'd know what to do.

Kneeling on the rug in front of my old bed, I rummaged underneath to find a shoebox that I'd decorated in junior high. Inside was a collection of drawings, letters, sticker books, and even an old BFFs FOREVER necklace that my best friend Heather had given me in eighth grade.

The letters were all ones I'd written to Brady but had never given him. I read the first one, chuckling at the excessive use of hearts in dotting my i's.

I even signed the letter as *Yours for all eternity, through every lifetime, until the sun goes dark and the stars fall from the sky.* I laughed aloud at that one. I had a flair for the dramatic, that was for sure. Then again, I tended to imagine Brady as a dashing knight who'd someday whisk me away to his castle.

I found the letter I was searching for at the bottom of the box. It was folded into a thick but tiny square that you only ever did when the information inside was top secret.

Dear Brady, I'd written, *you're probably surprised that I'm writing you a letter instead of just talking to you.*

But I don't know how to say what I need to say. Do you know how I feel about you?

Sometimes I think you do know. But other times, it's like you don't see me as anything other than a little sister. I'm not your sister, though.

I'm in love with you, Brady Carmichael. In LOVE. With YOU!

And I wanted to ask you something . . . would you be my first?

My first . . . You know what I mean, right?
Love,
Grace

Chapter 2

Brady

An hour after running into Grace, I sat at a bar, waiting for my teammate and friend Mac to arrive. Mac had always been the one to arrive before me until he'd fallen in love with Elodie.

I had a feeling the two of them had gotten busy before Mac was about to leave. I grimaced thinking about it. I was happy for my friend, but I was also unbelievably jealous—not that I'd ever fucking admit it to him.

I was fond of this dive bar off Sunset Boulevard, mostly because nobody bothered us here. Nobody gave two fucks that I was a hockey player. People kept to themselves. Even the dreaded paparazzi left us alone here. Or maybe they just hadn't figured out that so many of us from the Blades came here on the regular.

How the fuck did no one tell me Grace was coming back? I thought for the millionth time.

Running into her had given me the shock of my goddamn life. Running into her when I'd been totally naked? Christ, I'd been torn between laughter and arousal just from her being a few feet away from me.

Grace Dallas had grown up. As a kid she'd been chubby, with braces and glasses. She'd lost the braces, gotten tall and slim, and wore glasses only when she thought no one would see her.

At least, that was how she'd been as a teenager. The woman standing in front of me in that locker room was a stranger.

A fucking gorgeous and sexy blond woman. She had a self-confidence she hadn't had the last time I'd seen her.

Then again, Grace had always confused me. One second, she'd been shy, then the next, a vixen who Satan himself must've sent to tempt me.

It didn't matter that Grace was an adult now. She was still off-limits. When he caught me talking to her, Coach's reaction showed me that nothing had changed.

"Sorry I'm late," Mac said, slapping me on the shoulder. He sat down next to me, smiling like an idiot. "Elodie needed me to do something for her."

I cocked an eyebrow. "Is that code for 'I was banging my girlfriend'?"

"Surprisingly, no. She needed me to fix something with her car."

I stared at my friend, unconvinced. Mac just chuckled and ordered a drink.

We chatted about the upcoming game against the Tsunamis, the latest play that Coach had had us practicing, and why our teammate Zach was a gigantic douchebag. I'd started in on my second beer, the alcohol relaxing me.

But when Mac brought up Grace, any relaxation I might've felt instantly fled.

"Yeah, I ran into her," I said.

Mac stared at me. "What? When?"

"After practice."

"Huh. I've only met her once, years ago. I'd always thought Coach would never let her work for the team. I'm pretty sure if he could've locked her up in a tower, he would have." Mac chuckled. "I met her at a party at the Dallases'. She was home from college. And Coach gave her an earful because she tried some of the wine even though she wasn't twenty-one yet. I think her birthday was a week away or something."

I hadn't gone to that party. I'd wanted to, but I'd steered clear when I heard Grace would be there.

"Her birthday was the day after," I said without thinking.

Mac stared at me. I scowled at him when he gave me a look that said, *Tell me more.*

"I know the Dallases pretty well," I finally hedged.

Mac just waited.

I sighed, but I also knew that I'd rather tell Mac all of this myself than have him hear it from a third party.

"You know my mom was messed up, right? Well, I was put in foster care starting when I was just five. My mom would get sober for a bit, I'd go home, then she'd relapse, and back to foster care I'd go. When I was fourteen, the state finally terminated her parental rights when . . ."

I shook my head. "Never mind. But you should know that Coach and his family were my foster family until I turned eighteen."

Mac didn't say anything for a long moment. I hated waiting for people's responses to my pathetic childhood. More often than not, people would either say they were sorry and give me a pitying look, or they'd change the subject because they didn't know what to say.

Mac, though, just squeezed my shoulder. "Sorry, man," was his simple but sincere reply.

I shrugged. "It was a long time ago. But I grew up with Grace and her brother." The thought of Ben made my throat close, and I had to clear the lump that formed there. "She's just two years younger than me. Anyway, we used to be close."

Until you wanted her for yourself, my brain reminded me. *And you fucked everything up right afterward.*

"How did I not know you lived with Coach?" Mac asked.

"I mean, it's not something you just bring up in the locker room." I made my voice sound higher. "'Hey, guys, do you have a minute to talk about how my parents were assholes?'" I dashed a fake tear from my eye.

Mac, though, didn't laugh. "That sounds tough. Is your mom still around?"

"Shockingly, yeah. She's still drinking. Last I heard, she'd moved in with a guy named Weasel out in Bakersfield."

"And your dad?"

I gestured at the bartender to pour me a third beer. "Prison for selling drugs and a little incident where he shot a police officer." When Mac swore under his breath, I added, "The cop survived, at least. And this all happened when I was a baby. I never knew my dad. A blessing, really."

"So did you know Grace was coming back to LA?" Mac asked.

My stomach knotted. Considering I was a pseudo family member, you'd think Coach would've told me. But no, he hadn't said a fucking word. As far as I knew, he hadn't intended to tell me at all. I had no idea how he thought I wouldn't run into his daughter when she'd gotten an internship with the team.

"Nope," I replied.

But even as I was pissed at Coach and confused about my reaction to Grace, I couldn't stay mad. Not when I remembered all that the Dallases had done for me.

"They saved me," I said quietly, staring off into space, remembering. "I'd been a fucking mess. I was angry. I pushed them all away because it was easier than believing that somebody might not abandon me for once."

I let out a humorless laugh. "Did you know I was adopted? Before I was sent to live with the Dallases. But after a month, they changed their minds. Said I was too difficult."

Mac looked incredulous. "What the fuck? You can do that?"

"Yep. They needed to 'rehome' me. Like a fucking dog."

"Jesus. I'm so sorry."

"So I was waiting for the Dallases to do the same thing. I pushed all their buttons. I broke their rules. I was an asshole, but they never gave up on me. And then Ben introduced me to hockey, and my life changed forever."

"Ben?" Mac asked.

Shit. Why the fuck am I running my mouth like this?

I shook my head. "Never mind. Coach doesn't want me hanging around his daughter, anyway."

I'd always suspected Grace had a crush on me when we were younger. And then there'd been a time when that suspicion had turned into a certainty . . .

"Can you blame Coach?" Mac was saying, forcing me to stop reminiscing about the past. "You have a reputation."

I was offended even though I couldn't disagree with Mac. "I'm not going to do anything to the coach's daughter," I protested.

"Dude, you'll fuck any woman who you think is attractive. Pretty sure you have way more notches in your bedpost than even I do."

"Nothing wrong with wanting to have fun." But the alcohol flowing through my veins ended with me adding, "But I'm getting kind of bored of it all, to be honest. It's too easy. Women just throw themselves at you. I miss the chase, you know?"

Mac nodded. "I get it." He paused, then said, "Maybe you need a change of pace."

"Like what, exactly? Catfishing women on Tinder?" I joked.

"I went to this club often." Mac gave me a pointed look. "It caters to lots of different . . . tastes. You might like it. I haven't been going since Elodie and I started dating, and Zach has been wanting an invite, but if you want it instead . . ."

We both knew our teammate Zach was even more of a horndog than I was. But he was the worst kind: he collected women like trophies and then crowed about his exploits to the team afterward.

"Different tastes?" I repeated. "Now I'm intrigued."

"You can do a trial run. They know me there. Let me know if you want an invite."

A sex club wasn't normally my cup of tea, but maybe it'd relieve this ever-present boredom I was feeling lately.

"Maybe it'll get my mind off Grace Dallas," I muttered.

"Were you guys close?"

I thought about the question, then shrugged. "Sort of. But like everything else in my life, I fucked it up."

Mac and I talked for a bit longer, but Mac had to leave. *Probably to "fix" something else on Elodie's car,* I thought in amusement.

I finished off my beer and was about to call for a ride when a woman approached me. She was just my type: gorgeous. Dark hair, dark eyes, big boobs, and a nice juicy ass that you could bounce a quarter off.

"You're Brady Carmichael, aren't you?" she asked, her eyes widening in shock.

I nodded. "The one and only."

"That last game you guys played . . ." She shivered. "It was amazing. I love watching you play."

I wasn't immune to her charms. She was totally the type of woman I preferred to take home.

"Thank you," I said.

The woman reached out to pick something off my shirt. She giggled. "Sorry, but you had a bit of fuzz."

She didn't remove her hand, though. She made a point to run her fingers across my chest, her eyelashes fluttering. I didn't stop her from moving her hand to my shoulder and then down to my biceps. She squeezed one, and her eyes widened.

"Wow. You must work out a lot," she remarked.

"It's kind of part of the job." I winked and then made a point to flex my arms.

The woman made an ooh noise, like I'd just performed some amazing party trick.

"What's your name?" I asked her.

"Theresa," she replied. "But my friends call me Tess."

"Then should I call you Tess, too?"

Tess licked her lips. "Sure."

I gestured for her to sit down with me at the bar, an invitation that she accepted eagerly. My brain, though, kept demanding to know why the hell I was wasting my time with this woman.

Even worse, I couldn't stop thinking about Grace Dallas. As I stared into Tess's eyes, listening to her talk about the most inane subjects, I could only wonder what Grace would think about this entire situation.

"One time I drank five Jell-O shots in a row," Tess was saying, "and you know what happened next?"

I forced myself to smile. "What?"

"I fell flat on my face trying to run after Aidan Miller. You know, the basketball player? But he helped me up right after. I wish he hadn't, though. I ended up puking all over him."

I had to restrain myself from rolling my eyes. "Does this story have a happy ending?" I asked.

Tess giggled. "Well, yeah! Aidan took me up to his room to help him clean up." She leaned closer to me. "And he invited his friend. We had a great time, the three of us."

"Ah."

"How about we go find somewhere else? Somewhere with a little more privacy." Tess traced a hand up my arm, her long, red nails scratching at my skin like a cat's.

I seriously considered her offer. She sounded like she'd be a fun time, at least. I had a feeling she'd be up for anything, too.

But something was stopping me. The words that I should say somehow wouldn't come out of my mouth. It made zero sense.

What's stopping you? I was suddenly disgusted with my hesitation.

Hadn't I just been complaining to Mac about being bored? Tess would definitely relieve my boredom for a bit. It was clear she wanted me.

So what was the fucking problem?

"Let me buy you another drink," I said, turning toward the bar to get the bartender's attention.

I managed to extricate myself from Tess's claws before she dragged me into a dark alley to have her way with me. She wasn't happy at me not taking her home, but I didn't care.

I made a point to give her an autograph, told her who to contact for some free tickets to the next Blades game, and then headed home.

And I was going home alone. No Tesses to distract me tonight. I told myself it was because I was tired when I knew, deep down, it was because I couldn't get Grace Dallas out of my head.

As if by fucking magic, I got a text from Grace herself. *Is this still your number? It's Grace.*

I stared at my phone screen. But my jumbled, tipsy brain couldn't put together a coherent reply. So I stuffed my phone into my pocket and ignored the problem, like I always fucking did.

But by the time I arrived home, it felt like my phone was burning a hole in my pocket. I couldn't stop myself from responding.

Yeah, it's me, I sent.

Grace replied quickly. *Did you not want to text me back or what?*

No, I was just busy.

Bullshit. I know you.

I chuckled. She *did* know me, damn her.

Our conversation over text continued as the evening wore on. I admitted that it'd been weird seeing her out of the blue like that.

Weird, bad? Or weird, good? she asked.

Weird good. It was a surprise.

Oh good. Glad it was good for you, then.

I could hear the sarcasm. I laughed. *You know you look good,* I replied.

The three dots of her typing appeared on my screen. Then they disappeared. Then reappeared. At last, she sent, *You look good, too.*

When we finally said good night, I'd forgotten all about the woman I could've been fucking.

I could think only about the woman I knew I could never, ever have.

Chapter 3

Grace
Ten Years Ago

The boy my dad had brought home earlier that morning was acting weird.

It wasn't the first time my parents had fostered kids. They usually fostered younger kids, though. This time, they brought home a boy who they said was only two years older than me, but he looked way older than that.

Dad said his name was Brady. When I'd introduced myself, Brady had just looked at my outstretched hand like I'd tried to give him a bomb.

Now, I watched him from my bedroom window on the second floor. Maybe because he seemed so mysterious. Or maybe because, even at twelve, I found something about him fascinating.

My bedroom overlooked the back of the house, where our pool was, where Brady was now. Normally, Ben and I would be swimming all day, every day, during the summer, but Ben was too busy to hang out with me anymore.

And I wasn't about to wear my swimsuit around this new boy. The mere thought made me blush in humiliation.

Brady was big for his age. When Dad had said he was fourteen, I'd been shocked. He looked so much older!

"He's never lived with a family longer than six months," Dad had said to me quietly when Brady was unpacking in his new bedroom. "So he might not know how to act around us."

Brady had stayed in his room the entire morning. I'd listened outside his door until Ben had told me to stop being a pest.

Now, Brady sat at the edge of the pool with his feet in the water, but that was it. After a few minutes, I was about to go back to reading my book when Brady started wading into the water.

Then he kept dipping his head down, like he wanted to go for a swim. But then he'd stand back up. He kept doing this. Was it some strange exercise routine?

Dad had said Brady might act weirdly around us. But as far as Brady knew, nobody was watching him.

When Brady bent down one last time, hesitated, and then slapped the water like it'd personally offended him, I jumped. I must've made a noise because somehow Brady turned to see me sitting in my window. He scowled up at me and then pointed at me, yelling, "Stop staring at me!"

I was used to Ben, so boys getting annoyed with me wasn't new for me. I opened the window and yelled back, "I'm coming down!"

I changed into my swimsuit—a boring blue one-piece—and hurried to the pool. Brady sat on the edge again, and he didn't even acknowledge me when I sat beside him.

"Why were you watching me?" he finally asked.

I folded my arms around my knees. "I wasn't watching you for that long," I said.

"Bullshit. I saw you."

I stared at him. "You knew I was watching you?"

"It's not like you were trying to keep hidden," he said mockingly.

"You know, it's not nice, how you're talking to me." I lifted my chin. "And this is my house."

Something dark crossed Brady's expression. "Whatever. Do what you want."

I waited for him to explain himself, but I could tell he wasn't going to unless I prodded him.

"Did you want to go swimming?" I asked.

He snorted. "I don't even have swim trunks."

"But you were in the water."

"Yeah, so?" At my look, he sighed. "Fine. I was trying to swim."

"Trying?"

"Yeah, trying. Because I don't know how to fucking swim."

I flinched at his swearing. Even Ben wasn't brave enough to say the f-word around our parents. Dad would kill him.

"You shouldn't say that word," I admonished.

"What, *fuck*? Seriously?"

"You'll get in trouble. My parents won't like it."

"If they try to hit me, I'll just hit them back." He cracked his knuckles.

I gaped at him. "My parents would never hit you!" I was outraged at the mere suggestion. "They aren't like that."

Brady laughed at me, confusing me entirely. "I've been in enough homes to know that's bullshit."

"They aren't like that."

I could tell Brady didn't believe me. It made me feel sad for him. Had his other foster parents hit him? Did he expect that now, no matter where he went?

"You said you couldn't swim," I said.

"Yeah. So?"

I felt my cheeks heat but pushed through to reply, "I can teach you."

Brady didn't say anything. I had a feeling he was going to tell me to go to hell, but he didn't. He just stared off into the distance, almost like he hadn't even heard me.

"You don't have to do that," he mumbled.

He wouldn't look at me. I didn't know why. But even though he was a big kid and seemed intimidating, I had a feeling it was all for show. I moved into the water until I was standing waist-deep.

"Come on. I'll show you how to float," I said.

To my surprise, he agreed. He wore shorts and a T-shirt, but he didn't take off his shirt.

"Uh, you shouldn't wear your shirt," I said, wanting to die.

"What? Why?"

"I mean, you won't drown, but the fewer clothes, the safer it is. More clothes mean you'll get dragged down easier."

I remembered my swim instructor telling me and the rest of my class that we shouldn't jump into the water fully clothed. We especially shouldn't do it wearing shoes.

"But if you do fall into water wearing street clothes and shoes," she'd said, "there are ways to keep yourself safe so you can get out of the water."

Brady finally took off his shirt. I couldn't help but stare at him. He had a sprinkling of hair on his chest already. How was this boy only fourteen? I'd never seen another boy his age look like him.

He was tan, too, and muscular. He also had bruises on his ribs that I wanted to ask him about, but I bit my tongue just in time.

Brady then went to the last step and just stood there, the water up only to his knees.

"Come on. You can't float in the shallow end," I said.

"Why not? It's all water."

I snorted. "Fine. Here, watch me."

I'd taken swimming lessons since I was little. I'd even swum a few times in swim meets, although I'd gotten bored with the sport after a few years. I preferred to read inside most days.

But the muscle memory remained. I began floating on my back, staring at the bright-blue sky. There was nothing like the blue sky of the desert. The world was always bright and illuminated here—no rain, no clouds, no cold.

"Come on." I waved Brady over.

He finally waded toward me. When his arm brushed me, I nearly came out of my skin. I couldn't look at him as he tried to start floating.

I had to help him the first few tries. He got frustrated easily, and I didn't know how I managed to keep him from stomping inside after his third attempt resulted in him kicking and flailing.

"Don't! You'll make it worse," I said.

"This is stupid," Brady just kept saying.

But on the fourth try, he floated. I could tell he was uncomfortable, but he didn't say as much.

After that, he let me show him how to dog paddle. He was better at that, but when his mouth dipped below the water, he burst upward and returned to the steps.

"That's enough," he said, breathing hard.

I went to stand next to him. "Good job. You'll get better the more you practice."

After we got out of the pool, Brady's gaze took in my wet, swimsuit-clad body, and I wanted to melt into the ground. I instantly regretted doing this.

He probably thought I looked like a silly, chubby baby. I hadn't even gotten my period yet like some of the other girls in my grade. People tended to think I was younger than I was, and maybe Brady did, too.

"I'll see you later," I said and hurried inside, not caring I was dripping water throughout the house as I ran upstairs.

That evening, I braided my hair and put on some lip gloss and eye shadow. I knew I couldn't put on too much or Dad would freak out. I was almost late to dinner. By the time I came downstairs, everyone sat at the table, waiting for me.

Brady didn't even look my way. Ben stared at me, his forehead creased like he didn't recognize me.

"You look nice," Mom said as I sat down. "Are you wearing makeup?"

"Makeup? Since when do you own any makeup?" Dad responded.

I turned bright red. "Dad . . ."

"She's too young for that kind of thing," Dad kept saying to Mom. "Did you buy her some?"

"Honey, she got some in her stocking for Christmas. It's just for fun." Mom looked over at me. "You look very pretty, sweetheart."

I felt even more embarrassed at my mom's kindness. I wished I'd never put on the stupid stuff. And it wasn't like Brady was even paying attention to me.

"You look weird," said Ben as he leaned closer toward me. "Babies don't wear makeup."

I was close to crying when Dad told Ben to knock it off. Ben shrugged, unfazed.

What was worse was that Brady ignored me the entire dinner. I wanted to tell everyone about me teaching him to swim, but I bit my tongue. I could tell Brady didn't want to talk about it.

Was he embarrassed he'd let a girl help him? Or worse, was he just embarrassed of me in general?

I probably looked like an idiot, with my hair all braided and with all this makeup on. I swiped at a tear, but I refused to let any boy see me cry.

I went straight to my room after dinner, despite Mom trying to get me to stay downstairs to watch TV. I lied and said I wanted to read my book.

Instead, I flopped onto my bed and hugged my pillow close.

Boys are stupid, I reminded myself. *Don't let them ruin everything.*

I must've dozed off, because when I woke up, it was almost dark outside. I heard someone open a door and then walk down the hallway. I usually could tell the difference between my family members' footsteps. Mom was quick and light; Dad was slow and heavy; Ben was a combination of them both.

But these footsteps . . . they sounded like somebody didn't want to be noticed.

I waited but didn't hear anything else. I eventually went to my window that faced the part of the yard where our tree house was located. I watched as Brady tried to climb the tree and then fell on his butt.

I stifled a giggle. Didn't he know there was a ladder you could pull down? I watched as he tried a second time and failed.

When I approached him at the tree, Brady was wiping dirt off his backside.

"Why do you keep following me around?" he said, annoyed.

"You know there's a ladder, right?"

He just stared at me. I reached up and pulled said ladder down. It clicked when it reached the ground.

"Huh." Brady shook his head. "I didn't see it."

"It's dark out." I wanted to make sure he didn't feel embarrassed.

He didn't protest when I climbed up after him into the tree house. He didn't say much, either. We sat in silence, listening to the sounds of twilight.

"I come up here to write," I said. "In my journal."

Brady looked around. "Is your journal in here?"

I laughed. "No way. Ben would read it if he could. And I'd never let him."

Brady just grunted.

"Do you want me to leave you alone?" I asked quietly.

Brady, to my surprise, shook his head. "It's fine. It's your tree house after all."

"I'm not a scaredy-cat," Brady said suddenly. "About swimming, I mean."

I blinked in surprise. "What?"

"I mean, I'm not afraid of the water. Not exactly. But every time I try to learn how to swim, I think about how my mom's boyfriend threw me into the ocean. A riptide caught me, and I thought I was gonna drown."

"Your mom's boyfriend threw you?" I was horrified. "How old were you?"

"Uh, three? Four?"

"What!"

Brady shrugged. "I mean, it's whatever. I didn't die. But ever since then, I can only take showers. I don't swim."

"Did anyone try to help you?"

Brady was incredulous. "What, like Rick? Rick was laughing when I got to shore. My mom was drunk, passed out somewhere. Rick told me he'd never seen anything funnier."

I felt so sad for Brady right then. Had no one ever protected him? Loved him? No wonder he didn't know how to swim.

"Well, if you keep practicing, that won't happen to you again," I said.

"We can't practice again. Your dad told me to leave you alone." Brady grimaced. "You should probably leave before we get in trouble."

My dad had told Brady to leave me alone? I was outraged. He didn't even know Brady!

"That's stupid," I said. "And besides, my dad is gone by eight o'clock Monday through Friday. Tomorrow's Friday, so we can keep swimming after my dad is gone."

Brady just stared at me; then he let out a laugh. "Seriously? You don't care about getting into trouble?"

"I wouldn't get into trouble. You would."

That made Brady's expression close. "Right."

"But I'd tell Dad to leave you alone. Anyway, we're not doing anything wrong. I'm just teaching you how to swim."

Brady smiled at me, which made me blush and feel warm and fuzzy inside.

"You know, you're not as annoying as I thought you'd be," he said.

I rolled my eyes. "Gee, thanks. I don't get why you'd think I was, anyway."

"Because pretty girls are always a pain in the ass."

The butterflies in my stomach turned into an entire flock. I didn't know what to say to that. And apparently Brady didn't know what to say, either.

When I returned to bed, I couldn't sleep. I stared up at the ceiling, my heart full, determined not to let anyone stop me from being around a boy like Brady Carmichael.

Chapter 4

Grace
Present Day

It was family dinner night on Fridays, and we all fell into our usual routine like I'd never left for college. Mom was in charge of the cooking; Dad was in charge of the cleanup.

I was in charge of everything else—setting the table, plating the food, and making everything look pretty. I also helped Mom with any cooking tasks. Dad usually tried to get me to help him with dishes, but as a kid I always managed to slip outside before he could rope me into that task.

I was pouring salad into a large wooden bowl and adding a few other toppings when Mom said, "When is Will coming?"

It took me way too long for my brain to register what she was asking. *Will? Oh. The guy I'm dating.*

I winced inwardly. I'd been so focused on Brady that poor Will had basically disappeared from my thoughts recently. It didn't help that I kept running into Brady while at the arena.

I didn't run into many of the other players. Just Brady. *Strange coincidence, that.*

Brady only ever said hello, maybe with a wink added on for good measure. Even that short salutation never failed to get my traitorous heart racing.

"Will. Oh, yeah. Um, six o'clock?" I finally answered, hoping Mom took the blush on my cheeks as me being excited to see the guy I was dating.

"Be sure to put out five plates tonight," Mom said before her attention turned back to the risotto she was carefully stirring.

Five plates. I grabbed the dishes before my brain realized five would be too many.

"Mom, isn't it just four of us tonight?" I called from the dining room.

"I invited Brady," Mom said offhandedly. "I saw him at the arena and invited him. I hope you don't mind."

I gritted my teeth. I eked out a vague response that tried to sound casual, but I was sure it didn't.

Brady, here. Tonight. When my new boyfriend would also be here.

Will isn't your boyfriend, I reminded myself. Will was just the guy I was dating. We hadn't even talked about making things official. We'd been on two dates. We'd only just kissed on the last one.

And if I were being honest, the kiss had been lackluster at best. Will's lips had been overly moist, and I'd had to surreptitiously wipe away the saliva he'd left on my chin after kissing me.

But I'd agreed to keep seeing him because I knew that sometimes chemistry took time to build.

Or you're just too nice to call things off, I thought morosely.

How would Brady react to Will? And why did I care? I shook myself. I had to play this cool. Brady was a brother to me. I just had to hope he wouldn't try to razz Will like an older brother would.

After I set the table, I took out my phone and googled Brady. It was rather masochistic but a good reminder of why we'd never work out. The top pages were all posts and photos of Brady out with various gorgeous women. There were multiple photos of his arms around two women, with other women following him like starry-eyed ducklings.

If ducklings had huge boobs, huge lips, and wore basically scraps of fabric that somehow equaled an outfit.

I scowled and returned my phone to my pocket. *Brady will never change. So you might as well get over him.*

I busied myself with finishing up dinner preparation, although Mom got annoyed when I nearly let the bread burn in the oven. She gave me a look that she'd perfected over the years, one of exasperation mixed with affection.

"Get out of here," she said, hitting me lightly with a dish towel.

Will arrived promptly at six o'clock. Brady, who'd told Mom he'd be there at six as well, was late. As per usual. Brady had never been one for punctuality.

"Hi there," Will said, forcing me to stop thinking about Brady.

Will was in IT, and he looked like it. He wore glasses, along with a button-down that was two sizes too big. He'd recently shaved, and I had to pick off a piece of toilet paper he'd left on his jaw.

"Don't be nervous," I said, taking him by the hand.

Will laughed awkwardly. "I might not be a sports guy, but even I know who Coach Dallas is."

When I'd first told Will who my dad was, he'd looked at me like I was an alien. I'd been surprised—and a little annoyed at myself for revealing my dad's identity.

I usually kept that a secret for a while longer. I'd been on too many dates with hockey bros who thought getting close to Coach Dallas's daughter would get them close to the hockey coach legend himself.

I'd never understood it. It wasn't like Dad would add a guy to the team because he'd bought me a drink. But when I'd pointed that out once, my date had gotten so defensive that he'd ended the date early.

I introduced Will to Mom first because she was nicer. Mom smiled kindly at Will and shook his hand. She asked him the usual questions that moms loved to ask: Where do you work? Did you grow up in the area? Is your family nearby? Will answered them all without breaking a sweat.

But when Dad finally came inside after mowing the lawn—because of course he had to mow the lawn before dinner—Will's calm exterior didn't last long.

"What are your plans with my daughter?" Dad asked after perfunctory introductions were done.

Mom rolled her eyes. "Mike. Don't scare the poor guy away."

"I'm not scaring him." Dad's intense gaze narrowed as he looked Will up and down. "Am I, son?"

Will swallowed. I was about to take Will into the living room for a reprieve when the doorbell rang.

"That must be Brady," Mom chirped.

I made a face, which Dad saw. He just raised an eyebrow at me.

And then Brady Carmichael, the man I couldn't escape, was in my parents' house again, taking up every bit of space he could.

Brady wore jeans and a black fitted tee, his hair was damp, and sexiness dripped from every pore. He didn't have any bits of toilet paper on his face, and his clothes fit perfectly.

Don't compare him to Will. It wasn't fair. Brady was on another level from any man I'd ever met. Poor Will could never compete with a man like Brady.

"Grace," Brady murmured before pulling me into a brief hug. "Nice to see you again."

I inhaled the scent of his cologne, my heart pounding, which only made me feel horribly guilty.

"Brady," I said hoarsely.

"I'm so glad you could join us," Mom said. "It's been too long since you've joined us for family dinner."

"Mr. and Mrs. Dallas. It's nice to see you," said Brady.

Mom waved a hand. "Call us Mike and Elise, won't you?"

"Or *Coach*. Since I'm still your coach at the end of the day, right?" said Dad with a raised eyebrow.

Brady's gaze landed on me. "It has been a long time since I've been over for dinner, though, hasn't it? Not since Grace left for college, right?" He shot me a look that spoke volumes.

I wanted to die. I'd been an idiot back then—a young, lovesick idiot. I'd hoped against hope Brady had forgotten about that night, but . . .

"And who's your friend?" Brady asked.

I blinked. Then I blushed scarlet, because poor Will had been forgotten entirely.

"This is Will," I stammered, "we're dating."

Brady's eyes narrowed. "Really?" he drawled.

Will, for his part, shook Brady's hand firmly. "Nice to meet you," he said.

"The feeling's mutual." Brady's tone dripped with sarcasm.

Thankfully, dinner was ready, and we all went to the dining room to eat. Brady made a point to sit on my right; Will was on my left. And I realized Brady had done that because he was left-handed, which meant his arm would brush mine throughout dinner.

"Do you want to switch with Will?" I asked Brady sweetly. I gestured to his left hand. "Then you won't feel so crowded."

"Oh, you never crowd me," Brady replied. "Don't worry about it."

I knew that was code for *Are you going to make a fuss about this?* I wanted to stab Brady with my fork. It didn't help that Will was watching the exchange with suspicion in his gaze.

Dinner was awkward, to say the least. My parents seemed divided on which guest to pay attention to. Mom focused all her efforts on Will, while Dad preferred to grill Brady. And of course Brady made a point to brush my arm with his every chance he got. He even made sure to "accidentally" pick up my water glass and drink from it.

"Oh, was that yours?" Brady winked at me. "Sorry. You can have mine. I haven't used it yet."

I wanted to dump the rest of the contents of the glass on his smarmy, arrogant head. Instead, I tipped the glass back and drank the rest of the water.

"Don't worry about it," I drawled, mimicking his earlier tone.

One side of Brady's luscious mouth curled up in a grin.

"Grace, how is your internship?" Will asked me.

It took me a long moment to find my answer. "Uh, it's good. I got to make copies today," I said jokingly.

Will frowned. "I thought you said this was a real job."

"It is—I mean, it will be. I'm still training."

"How much training is there to post on Instagram?" Brady asked, chuckling.

Now I was pissed. I kicked Brady under the table, which made him wince. Mom and Dad just watched the tableau with confusion on their faces.

Or, rather, Mom looked confused. Dad looked pissed, too. Except I couldn't tell who, exactly, he was pissed at: Will, Brady, or me.

"Will, where do you work again? Grace never mentioned that."

Now Brady sounded like we were talking to each other all the time. I could strangle him.

"I work in IT," replied Will.

"Oh, that tracks." Brady shook his head, grinning to himself.

It took every ounce of restraint for me not to kill Brady right then and there. I had a feeling even my parents wouldn't stop me.

We finished eating in awkward silence.

"Brady, can you help me clear the dishes for dessert?" I asked.

Brady knew a command when he heard it. He smiled, his gaze heavy lidded, and then saluted me.

When we were in the kitchen, I whirled on him. "What the hell is your problem?" I demanded.

Brady put up his hands. "Whoa there, sweetheart. Should I put the knives away first?"

"You're being a jerk. To Will, to me. To my parents, who invited you. Seriously, what the hell is wrong with you?"

I saw something flash across Brady's expression that I almost thought could be remorse. But it disappeared so quickly that I probably had imagined it.

Brady popped a grape into his mouth. "Baby, you do look sexy when riled."

"I am not your baby," I hissed.

"Well, you're definitely not Walt's, either."

"His name is Will."

Brady looked bored now. "Is it? Sorry. Seriously, that's the best you could find? He looks like he'd burst into tears if you stepped on his foot."

"So? Why do you care?"

Brady blinked. Then his gaze narrowed. "Because you and I both know that little IT guy isn't your type."

I started laughing because there was no other response to make. "My type? You don't know a damn thing about who my type is, Brady Carmichael. You also have no say in how I live my life—"

Brady pressed a hand over my mouth. "You're yelling."

I bit his palm—not hard, but enough to make him remove his hand.

"I'd forgotten how spicy you could be," Brady said, almost to himself. He looked at me now like he didn't recognize me.

I pointed a finger at him. "Behave yourself. You have to be boring. So dull that we'd all rather watch paint dry. Otherwise, I will never, ever forgive you."

"And you're still just as bossy as when we were kids."

"Only because you're a huge pain in the ass."

Brady just grinned lazily. "You enjoy this."

I stared at him. "What?"

He gestured vaguely. "This. Us. I just know Will doesn't get you going like I do."

I blushed to the roots of my hair. "You have no idea what you're talking about."

"Come on. That guy? Seriously?"

"I'd rather be with a guy like Will than a guy who constantly has women with fake boobs falling all over him. Have you ever been with a woman who hasn't spent thousands on plastic surgery? Do you even know what breasts without silicone feel like?"

Brady just laughed. "Baby, now you just sound jealous."

I didn't respond to that. Instead of decking Brady in the face, I returned to the dining room with a sweet smile plastered to my face. Dad raised an eyebrow as I sat back down.

"Everything okay, sweetheart?" he asked.

"Everything's great."

I realized a moment later that I hadn't returned with the promised dessert. I was about to get up again, my cheeks heating, when Brady came back, holding the cake Mom had made yesterday.

"Did you forget something?" he said to me, shooting me a wink.

Will managed to find me after dinner for a private conversation. "We should head out soon if we want to catch the movie at seven thirty," he said.

I'd completely forgotten he'd asked to go to a movie afterward. But the thought of sitting in a theater for two hours with Will just didn't appeal to me right now.

"I'm sorry, but can I get a rain check?" I asked, feeling horribly guilty. "I have a headache."

Will looked disappointed, but he didn't push it. To make me feel even guiltier, though, he made sure to ask whether I needed to take anything or if he should go to the store for something. I told him I'd be fine—I probably just needed to drink more water.

Will had gone to the kitchen to get me a glass of ice water when Brady came over. "What was that about? He looked like he was about to start crying."

"He did not," was my brilliant rebuttal. When Brady just waited, an eyebrow cocked, I sighed. "I told him I had a headache and didn't want to see a movie tonight with him."

Brady chuckled. "Poor guy. But I can't say that I blame you. Were you going to see a documentary? Like the history of computers or something?"

Will returned with my water. But I didn't even take the glass he offered. Instead, I wrapped an arm around his waist and kissed him—hard.

Will grunted in surprise. I felt water splash onto my arm. When I pulled away, I could see that Will had spilled half of the glass onto the rug.

Brady, though, was the person I was really paying attention to. He just stared at me, his eyes narrowed, his nostrils flared.

I was breathing heavily. I told myself it was because of the kiss, but I knew that, deep down, it was because of Brady's intense, jealous expression.

Some ten minutes later, I heard the front door open and close.

"Brady had to head out," Mom explained. She gave me a look. I chose to ignore it.

I was sitting in the tree house when Brady texted me.

The sun had just set, and it was starting to get cold. But I didn't want to go inside. I mostly wanted to avoid my parents' questions—about Will and Brady.

I was a dick tonight. Sorry, Brady's text read.

I snorted. I didn't reply because he didn't deserve forgiveness. I was still too mad at him right then.

Why did Brady care so much about who I was dating? He was the epitome of the dog in the manger: he didn't want me, but nobody else could want me, either.

What if he did want you?

I already knew he didn't. He'd rejected me when we were teenagers, and now that I was grown, he'd never shown any interest in dating me. It wasn't like Brady Carmichael didn't know how to ask a woman out. If he wanted me, he'd say as much.

I lay down on the wooden floor of the tree house, staring at the ceiling. I hadn't spent much time up in this tree house when I'd been younger. My parents had moved to LA and into this house right before I'd left for college. The previous owners had built this tree house for their kids, and my parents hadn't had the heart to take it down despite the annoyance of having to maintain it.

The tree house I knew best was the one at my parents' house in Las Vegas. The same house where Brady had become my foster brother. *That* tree house . . . it held a whole lot of memories, both good and bad. I'd spent so much time up there when I was a kid, but it'd tapered off when I'd become a teenager. It had felt silly and babyish, hanging out in a tree house.

Now, I wished there were more tree houses for adults in general. Why did kids get to hide away? Adults needed something like that just as much as kids did.

I must've dozed off because I was awoken an hour later by my phone buzzing. It was Brady texting again.

At least tell me to fuck off. Don't ignore me.

I laughed at his audacity. I took a picture of me flipping him off and sent it to him.

I nearly jumped out of my skin when I heard someone climbing the ladder. Then, to my shock, Brady was inside the tree house, gazing down at me with an amused expression.

"What the hell?" I groused, sitting up. I brushed dirt from my shirt, hoping that my hair wasn't full of leaves.

"I thought you'd be up here," he said as he sat down next to me.

I scooted as far from him as I could, which wasn't far, given how small the tree house was and how huge Brady was.

"I thought you went home?"

"I went to a bar down the street. And I could tell from your picture you were up here."

I sighed, rolling my eyes. "Okay. Do you need something?"

"Did you get my text earlier?"

"That you're a dick? Yeah. I already knew that. You didn't need to come back to tell me."

He chuckled. "Still spicy, huh? Well, I am sorry. I was a dick tonight. Feel free to punch me if you want."

I was sorely tempted, but I knew that I probably wouldn't even make a dent in his fat skull.

"I'm still mad right now," I said, "but I'll get over it. Eventually."

Brady put his chin on his palm. "So. How's it going with Will?"

I burst out laughing. "Seriously? Man, I envy your sheer audacity sometimes."

"I'm being for real!"

I rolled my eyes. "Will is great. Amazing. I'm so glad we're dating."

"I can't tell if you're being serious or not."

I looked away. "We're just getting to know each other," I hedged.

"Was that your first kiss?" Brady asked, his voice rough.

"We've kissed once before." I swallowed, my mouth going dry. "But we haven't had sex yet, if that's what you're asking."

Brady made a strange noise in his throat. "I don't need to know the details."

I knew that, but I also knew that talking about it bothered Brady. Why, I didn't know—or I didn't want to think too deeply about it.

"I'm thinking about Will being my first," I blurted.

I couldn't look at Brady. I waited in anticipation, my heart pounding. But when Brady said nothing, I forced myself to look at him.

The light was dim, but I could just see how dark Brady's eyes were. His jaw was tight, his fist clenched.

"I'm happy for you," he said finally.

He didn't look happy. He looked pissed. Why did he hate Will so much? Was he really such a bad choice for a boyfriend?

My gaze moved from Brady's eyes to his mouth. My heart leaped when he licked his lips.

And then I could feel his heated gaze on my own mouth, and suddenly, the air crackled with tension. The hair on the back of my neck rose.

Brady leaned forward—ever so slightly, but I saw it— and I couldn't breathe. *Was he going to kiss me?*

But then he just said, "Let me know if you need any sex tips, kid."

Then he was gone, almost like the entire thing had been a figment of my imagination.

Chapter 5

Brady

Since when did Grace have a boyfriend?

Lying in bed, I couldn't stop imagining Grace with that bug-eyed little guy she called a boyfriend. When I'd shaken his hand, I'd half expected I'd break his weak paper bones if I squeezed too hard.

I growled under my breath. I was being fucking ridiculous. But my mind was stuck on who this Will guy was. Maybe I'd missed something about him. Something that made Grace think he should be her first lover.

She's still a virgin. Fucking hell.

I didn't want to think about that. If I did, I'd lose my goddamn mind. Because the thought of another man kissing her, touching her, pushing inside her—

I got up and grabbed my phone, which I'd left charging in the living room. Then I proceeded to fall down an internet rabbit hole to learn everything I could about Will.

I didn't even know his last name. But it didn't take long for me to find his Instagram account, which followed

Grace's. He'd posted three photos in the past three years, all of which were pictures of the insides of computers.

I snorted. What a fucking dweeb.

I had nothing against nerdy dudes. Hell, plenty of my friends played shit like D&D and loved video games.

But Will just seemed fucking *boring*. Did he even know how to please a woman? Make her moan his name and beg to let her come?

I doubted it. He was probably a sad sack in bed. *I bet he cries when he orgasms,* I thought darkly.

I then went to Grace's profile, where I found a recently posted photo of her and Will. They were side-hugging. Will appeared vaguely constipated, while Grace looked stunning—as usual.

But they looked like siblings. Despite Grace's impromptu kiss, I hadn't detected any chemistry between them last night. Will had seemed like his head was going to explode when she'd kissed him suddenly.

How is she still a virgin? I couldn't believe it. She was gorgeous: tall, blond, with legs for days. She could have any guy she wanted. How had she attended college and never slept with anyone?

It made zero sense. I scrolled through her photos, going back to when she first left for college four years ago. She was the Grace I'd known best: the Grace I'd made a point to avoid as much as possible.

In one photo, she posed with duck lips. In another, she was making some goofy pose with a bunch of her friends from high school. But that goofiness had disappeared from her latest posts, which I found intriguing.

Then again, it'd been four years. Grace wasn't a teenager anymore. She was a grown woman, moving up in the world.

And I was some hockey punk who didn't deserve to so much as kiss the bottoms of her feet. No matter how much my body screamed to take her and make her mine.

I hated the thought of Will fucking her. But I also knew that I couldn't keep lusting after her either. Nothing could come of this attraction I had for my coach's daughter.

So I tossed my phone aside and forced myself to stop thinking about the woman who'd haunted me for too many damn years.

Practice later that afternoon was a joke. I'd thought I'd gotten Grace out of my head until the woman appeared in the arena.

We had a big game with the Blizzards in a few weeks,, and we'd lost the last time we'd played them. Coach had been drilling us hard. He told us if we lost again, he'd skin our hides.

"Carmichael!" Coach roared from the stands. "Did you hear what I said, or are you too busy daydreaming?"

I scowled. Mac shot me a grin, and I could tell he was stifling a laugh.

"Yeah, I heard you," I shot back, making sure Coach couldn't see me rolling my eyes.

Even though we were all grown-ass men, Coach Dallas never failed to make us feel like kids sometimes. There were some occasions when I half expected the old man to put us over his knee if we dared to sass him.

I passed the puck to Riley when I saw Grace. At first, I just saw a woman with blond hair, but when we stopped to regroup, I heard her laugh.

I'd know that laughter anywhere. It sounded like wind chimes. Which I knew was fucking bonkers, but it was true.

I couldn't help but watch Grace, who was with what looked like a small camera crew, as she pointed and gave directions. I thought she was supposed to be in some dim office, posting on Twitter or some shit?

"Dude, get into position," Mac said in a low voice.

It took every bit of strength to pay attention to practice instead of to Grace. It didn't help that whatever she was doing seemed to take fucking forever. She was still filming and talking to her group when we'd finished practice.

"You doing okay?" Mac asked me after we'd showered and changed. He sat on the bench across from me with a strange expression.

"Yeah. Why?" I made a point to stare at my feet.

"You were totally off your game today. Is there something going on between you and Grace?"

I whipped my head up, looking around. "Don't be so fucking loud," I hissed. "What if Coach heard you?"

Mac leaned back, crossing his arms. "What if he did? Is there something going on?"

I groaned. I did not need Mac to grill me, but I also knew that being cagey would only make things worse.

"Nothing is going on," I said. "I'm just messed up after I went to Coach's house for dinner. Grace brought her boyfriend."

"Ah."

That single syllable made me want to growl. "Ah? That's all you have to say?"

"Sounds like you're jealous."

I groaned. "It's so fucking stupid. The guy was a total wet blanket. The boyfriend, I mean. But I can't stop thinking about her. And him. What the fuck is wrong with me?"

"I still don't get why you can't just ask her out."

I snorted. "She has a boyfriend."

"Since when has that ever stopped you?"

He was right. If I wanted a woman, I never failed to get her. I'd pissed off plenty of dudes, but I'd never regretted it either. Besides, I'd only ever pursued women who obviously wanted me to pursue them. It was on them if they had shitty boyfriends.

"Nothing can happen between me and Grace," I said. When Mac looked like he wanted to ask why, I cut in. "I can't tell you why. It is what it is."

Mac frowned. "Well, if that's the case, you should get your mind off her. The invite to the Scarlet Rope is still open, you know."

I'd forgotten about Mac's invitation. I hadn't been all that interested, but now it sounded like a great idea. Anything to take my mind off Grace and her dull-ass boyfriend.

"Since Elodie and I got together, we haven't been going as much," Mac was saying. "It's kind of a waste not to have anyone use our membership. I know BDSM isn't your thing, but there are lots of other kinks to explore there."

Since Mac had "come out" as a Dom, he'd been more open to talking about his once-secret life. It'd caught me off guard the first time. Now it was like he was telling me about a new restaurant in town.

"And I met Elodie there," said Mac. "You might meet somebody even better than Grace."

I doubted it, but I wasn't going to admit that out loud. "I guess it can't hurt to try it once." I grinned. "Fuck it. Give me the deets."

Mac slapped me on the shoulder as we left the locker room. "I'll email over everything you need to know. You'll also need to sign some paperwork when you get there."

"Seriously?"

"The club doesn't fuck around. It also won't hesitate to kick your ass out if you break the rules. Remember that."

I held up my hands. "I do so solemnly swear I'll keep my whips and chains to myself."

"Probably a good idea until you get a lay of the land," Mac replied wryly.

That night, I honestly didn't know what to expect when I entered the foyer of the Scarlet Rope. I didn't expect it to look classy, I had to admit.

Maybe I'd expected a dingy, underground club with carpets older than I was and a sticky film on the walls and furniture. But this place? It was like some ultra-fancy hotel, except everybody wore next to nothing, and sex was on the table with just about anyone you asked.

Not that different from hotels I've been to, I thought with a grin. Mac had explained that I could wear a mask to conceal my identity, but I had nothing to hide.

Besides, I was just here to see what this place was all about. I didn't even know whether I wanted to partake yet.

Lush, scarlet carpets covered the foyer. A huge chandelier hung overhead, and sultry jazz made the entire atmosphere seem moody and intense.

Before I could begin to explore, though, a woman named Serena took me back to her office to sign my life away. When I joked about what would happen if I broke the rules, Serena told me in a serious voice that I'd forfeit my firstborn.

When I laughed but she didn't, I wasn't entirely sure she wasn't serious.

I went to the bar, where multiple groups were drinking and talking. I'd noticed a few couples making out on settees, but no actual orgies right in the foyer.

A woman with bright-red hair flashed me a smile at the bar. "I've never seen you here before," she purred.

She wasn't my type—too much like a saloon girl, with her huge breasts and even bigger hair—but she looked like she'd be fun.

"It's my first time. Popping my cherry tonight," I said with a wink.

She laughed. "Well, if you need any help, let me know."

I nodded and began to explore. Mac had explained the basic layout of the club, but when I came upon the first room, I had to admit I was a little stunned.

It was like a large, lush hotel room, except people could watch what was going on inside. This scene included three people—two women and a man—and the women were pleasuring the lucky guy. One woman had her hands tied around her back as she sucked the man's cock. The other woman was kissing and licking the guy's neck and chest.

I was riveted. I watched as the woman standing helped the kneeling woman up. Then the woman whose hands were free was kneeling and eating the bound woman's pussy. The man stood and watched.

I shuddered. I took a swig of my beer and kept walking.

The next room was a BDSM room: a woman was whipping a man, and his moans filled the air. His ass was already bright red. I wondered how long the woman had been whipping him.

Other rooms had group orgies, men only, women only, whips and chains and gags and ropes and sex toys of all kinds. I'd never seen such a vast array of depravity.

No wonder Mac had loved this place. Even if you didn't want to join the fun, watching it was fascinating.

My body was buzzed, my cock half-hard, as I noticed a blond woman. She wore a black mask, and when she smiled seductively at me, I couldn't help but notice her resemblance to Grace.

What would Grace do if I bound and gagged her? I shuddered at the thought, both aroused and disgusted with myself.

"You look lost," the blonde said to me, her tone caressing.

"Just exploring the place."

"Is this your first time?"

I was tempted to lie, but I had a feeling this woman already knew the answer. "Something like that."

"I'm Shayla." She reached out a hand. "You?"

"Michael," I lied, giving the woman my middle name.

"Michael. What do you like? Are you a sub or a Dom?"

I hadn't ever thought about it, but I knew instantly I wasn't a sub. "Dom. Definitely a Dom."

"Oh, excellent." She pressed a hand to my chest. "I'll do whatever you want me to do. Does that excite you?"

It did. It really fucking did. When I wrapped my fingers in Shayla's hair, pulling her head up and back, she let out a gasp of surprise.

"What if I told you to kiss my feet right now," I growled.

Shayla smiled. "As you wish, Master."

She kissed my feet, right and left, and then I hauled her up and pulled her into one of the nearby private rooms.

Before we got started, though, Shayla made sure to tell me her safe word and what her boundaries were. I gave her the safe word I'd thought up when Selena had asked me. I then told Shayla that since I'd never done something like this before, I didn't know yet what I didn't like.

"You mean I can peg you?" Shayla asked, grinning.

I snorted. "Fuck no."

I didn't want to have sex with Shayla. I wanted to see what it was like to dominate a woman. I had her strip and lie down on her stomach. I went to the wall of instruments, wondering which one I wanted to use.

"Do you have a preference?" I asked Shayla, curious now.

She looked at me over her shoulder. "The red whip. That's my favorite."

I grabbed the whip in question. I ran my fingers down the length of it. It seemed rather unassuming. Would this really give a woman like Shayla pleasure?

I tested it on her ass. She shivered, and I did it again.

After a few strokes, Shayla guided me on how hard she liked it. It didn't take long before I was whipping her ass until it was a bright, cherry red. With each slap of the whip, Shayla moaned.

And then she was begging me to stop, which made me hesitate. But she wasn't using her safe word. So when I kept going despite her feigned protests, I felt a strange sense of triumph.

I was also so turned on my cock was like an iron bar in my jeans. I'd never thought doing something like this would get me going.

Worse, Shayla's blond hair and long legs reminded me so much of Grace that it was easy to imagine it was her moaning and begging.

Marking Grace like this, her ass jiggling, her cries filling the room—God, the thought alone was intoxicating. I increased the speed of my hits until Shayla's yells turned to squeals.

My arm was tired by the time we finished. I hauled Shayla to her feet and gave her a smacking kiss.

"Thanks for that," I said, breathing hard.

"Great job for your first time." She kissed my cheek. "If you ever want a repeat, let me know."

I was on a strange high as I drove home. It felt like my entire body was vibrating, and it wasn't like I'd even fucked anybody. I hadn't even wanted to.

I understood now why Mac had been so obsessed with the Scarlet Rope. You could lose yourself in a club like that.

You could also discover lots of new things about yourself. Although I'd always been the alpha in my relationships, I'd never done anything BDSM-related beyond a blindfold here and there.

After I arrived home, my phone buzzed. When I saw it was from Grace, I froze. I had the stupidest thought that she knew that I'd been thinking about her as I'd flogged Shayla.

I shook myself. And when I read the text, I felt like I'd entered an alternate universe.

I've been thinking about you, it read.

Christ, if she only knew what I'd been thinking about her tonight. She'd turn around and run in the opposite direction.

I almost replied to her. I almost told her that I couldn't get her out of my fucking mind. I almost told her that I whipped a woman tonight just because she looked like Grace.

But I couldn't text Grace any of that. So I didn't reply at all, and I hoped this fever I had for this woman would go away.

Chapter 6

Grace
Nine Years Ago

The first time I asked about Brady's parents, Mom told me it wasn't any of our business. When I'd tried to ask Brady himself, he'd scowled and had refused to answer the question.

The mystery behind it all just made me want to know even more. But at age thirteen, I also understood when to keep my mouth shut. I wasn't a baby anymore.

Babies whined. I wasn't going to whine to get my way. I would just wait and hope that someday, somebody would tell me about Brady's past.

It was a hot, sunny day in the middle of summer when the phone rang. Mom was in the shower; Ben was in the yard. I was about to go pick it up when, to my surprise, Mom stepped out of the shower naked to answer it.

She was dripping water onto the carpet as she talked on the phone. Mom had never been shy about being nude around her kids, but she wasn't the type to get water everywhere either. She always got on Ben when he left puddles in the bathroom after he showered.

"Uh-huh. Okay. Well, then." Mom sighed and said something else before hanging up. She then turned and said to me, "Go get your brother."

I knew that tone. I did as she said, telling Ben Mom needed him. By the time we were both inside, Mom had put on a robe, her hair wrapped in a towel. She told Ben that he needed to drive over to where Brady was and bring him home.

"What happened?" Ben asked, crossing his arms.

"I'll tell you later. Just go get him," Mom said.

Ben glanced at me. Then he shrugged, grabbed his keys, and headed out.

Mom sat down heavily at the kitchen table. She looked exhausted.

"Why didn't you go get Brady?" I asked.

"Because I need to make some more phone calls. And Ben's a good distraction."

I waited for more of an explanation, but my patience was about to run out. What the heck was going on?

"Brady's mom is in the hospital," Mom said finally. "She's really sick."

"What happened?"

Mom just shook her head. "I can't tell you. I'm sorry. That's for Brady to decide if he wants to tell you and Ben. But I want to respect his privacy and his family's."

I wanted to argue, but the expression on Mom's face told me not to push my luck.

Brady arrived home with Ben, and then before I could ask any more questions, Mom was driving Brady to the hospital. Ben went upstairs to his room.

Dad was working all day, so he was useless. I tried to find something to do, but I just channel surfed and waited for Mom and Brady to come home. By the time I heard the front door open, it was close to dinnertime.

"Brady wanted to go back to the rink," explained Mom when I noticed she was alone.

"How's his mom?"

"Stable, but it'll be a long recovery." Mom sat down on the couch with me and hugged me. "I'm so proud of you, Gracie."

I blinked in surprise. I didn't understand where this was coming from. "Um, okay."

"You're a good kid. I know we've been busy with Brady and hockey and everything, but I just wanted you to know that." Then Mom kissed my forehead and went to start dinner.

Brady had started playing hockey earlier in the summer after getting into a fight with one of the neighborhood bullies. Brady had seen the bully pushing around a fourth grader, and Brady had intervened. Although I'd seen the whole thing, Mom and Dad hadn't been happy.

"Fighting never solves anything," Mom had said to Brady, exasperated.

"Trevor started it!" Brady had shot back.

"Doesn't matter," said Dad. He crossed his arms. "Violence never helps."

"You coach fucking hockey!" Brady replied.

Dad made sure to tell Brady to watch his mouth. I wanted to defend Brady but knew it was a losing battle.

Later, I heard my parents arguing in low voices in the kitchen.

"I still don't think it was fair to come down on him like that," Dad said.

I heard Mom sigh. "You know as well as I do that with foster kids don't get the benefit of the doubt. What happens if somebody calls the cops when he's in a fight? He could get sent to juvie. And given how big he is already, somebody could mistake him for an adult."

"So he should never defend himself? Or others?"

"He needs to learn to use his words, not his fists."

I peeked around the corner. Mom was leaning against the kitchen island; Dad had his back to me.

"Or maybe he needs to channel that energy into something productive," said Dad.

"I don't want him playing hockey."

"Why not? He'd be great at it."

"You don't know that."

Dad sighed. "Baby, come on. I know you don't like that hockey is more violent than other sports—"

"I hate it."

"But at least hockey lets Brady channel his anger. And if he hates it, then he can do something else. Besides, he's told me more than once that he's interested."

Mom's mouth twisted. Then she laughed a little. "Fine. Fine! I guess you're right. Better fighting on the ice than on a playground."

"That's my girl." Dad pulled Mom into a chaste kiss, which made her laugh again.

So Brady started playing hockey. According to Ben, Brady was a natural. He learned to skate like he'd been born on the ice. And when Dad handed him a hockey stick, everything changed.

Now Brady spent all his time at the rink. I'd been a little hurt, which I'd known was stupid. But it felt like Brady was rejecting spending time with the family over hockey.

Or it feels like he's not interested in hanging around a little kid like you, I thought. Even though I knew I wasn't a little kid, Brady didn't know that. He still treated me like a little sister on the few occasions he interacted with me.

Brady fascinated me. I wanted him to like me. I wanted him to think my jokes were funny. I wanted him to hang out with me like he hung out with Ben.

But despite my best efforts to attract his attention, it never worked. Despite me teaching Brady to swim when he'd first joined our family, our time together had been limited at best.

I noticed that when Brady found me alone, like when I was watching TV or inside the tree house, he always muttered something and let me be.

I then tried to watch TV shows I knew he liked. But no matter what show was on, Brady never stayed to watch. Even when I'd catch him watching the same shows later.

It made zero sense. But it must be because he thought being around me was embarrassing. That was what Ben had told me, at least. Boys like Brady didn't want to hang around girls like me.

Going to my room, I sat down in front of my mirror, gazing at my reflection. I'd grown two inches this year. Everyone always liked to comment how tall I was going to be. I didn't have chubby cheeks anymore. I was covered in freckles from being out in the sun, my blond hair lighter than ever. My breasts were bigger, although they were still shamefully small.

I didn't know if I was pretty. I wished I was. I wished I was tan and fit and that all the boys were in love with me.

I started putting on makeup. I braided my hair and then wore a top that was too small for me now. I put on some jasmine-scented perfume from the mall and waited for Brady to come home.

But when I went down to dinner, Dad was the one who'd come home, not Brady. He gave me one look and said, "Go take that off your face and put something decent on, young lady."

Brady didn't come home that night. It was weird because my parents didn't seem worried about it.

But I was worried about him. No matter how old he looked, I bet he didn't want to be alone right now.

I got out of bed around eleven o'clock. I listened intently, but I didn't hear anyone still awake. I got dressed quickly and managed to get out of the house without anyone noticing me.

Then again, I wasn't exactly the type of kid to sneak out of the house. Ben had done it once or twice before my parents had put the fear of God into him. But it was most likely because Ben knew he had to keep up his grades to graduate with a hockey scholarship.

I got on my bike and started riding to the rink. It was only two miles away, and despite it being dark out, I wasn't afraid. Our little suburban neighborhood was quiet. Boring, even. People didn't even lock their doors at night. The worst crime I'd heard about was when some kids TP'ed Mrs. Jenkins's house across the street on Halloween.

Dad had somehow gotten the rink owners to let Brady skate any time he wanted. I didn't know how Dad had managed that, but he had.

When I got there, there was one car in the parking lot. When the single person working there saw who I was, he just sighed and waved me on in.

"If you could get the kid to go home so I could go to sleep, that'd be great," he drawled, yawning widely.

I shrugged and didn't promise anything. Going into the arena, I saw Brady skating at the other end. He was passing a puck back and forth, completely focused. He then proceeded to slam into the boards, like he wanted to fight the arena itself.

I'd never seen Brady like this. Sure, I'd seen him fight Trevor at the park, but that'd had a purpose. This just seemed . . . self-destructive.

Only when he stopped to take a swig of water did he realize he had an audience. He scowled over at me.

"What the hell are you doing here?" he demanded, skating up to the door that swung open into the bleachers. He eyed me up and down. "Where's Ben?"

I stuck out my chin. "I came by myself."

"In the dark? What the hell is wrong with you?"

I wasn't going to let him rant and rave at me or intimidate me. He wasn't going to make me cry, either.

"I'm fine. See?" I waved a hand down my torso. "I almost got into a white van but decided not to when the guy didn't have my favorite candy."

Brady blinked. Then he shook his head, laughing.

"Dammit, you're crazy," he said. He came up and sat down next to me. "You shouldn't bike around at night by yourself, you know."

"Since when? This neighborhood is safe."

"Nowhere is really safe," was Brady's dark comment.

I looked especially broody. I stared at him from the corner of my eye. His eyes were red. Had he been crying?

"How's your mom?" I asked tentatively.

Brady's mouth screwed up. "She'll live."

"I'm glad." I meant it.

"I'm not."

I gaped at him. "You don't mean that."

"You don't know what you're talking about. You're lucky. You have nice parents who give a shit about you. My mom only cares about getting drunk and finding somebody to buy her more booze. Do you know she spent money on beer instead of diapers when I was a baby?" Brady let out a harsh laugh.

I didn't know how to respond to that. I'd been so curious about Brady's mom that it hadn't occurred to me that she was somebody like this.

"I'm sorry," I said.

Brady shook his head. "Why do people always say that? Why would you be sorry? She's the one who's a fuck-up, not you."

"But you said she'll be okay?"

"Oh yeah. She'll survive. She always does. Even though her liver is failing and her kidneys barely work. The doctors are always like, 'you should stop drinking.' And then she swears she'll stop. But she never does.

"Last time she was in the hospital, she got caught drinking hand sanitizer. Fucking hand sanitizer! Who does that?"

I didn't know what to say. I didn't even know people did things like that.

"You look shocked," Brady said. "You're so naive. It's cute."

I blushed to the roots of my hair. "What about your dad?" I stammered.

"My dad? He's in prison. Got caught dealing drugs three times, and now he's there for the rest of his life. My mom always told me that she kicked him out because he liked to take me with him on his drug runs. Made the cops less likely to stop him. Until one time they did, and they found bags of crack in my stroller."

Brady cracked his knuckles. "Yeah, so, my parents fucking suck. That's the whole story, basically. My mom keeps wanting me to come back home, but why should I? She drinks her money away. At least in foster care, I get to eat."

I felt like crying, hearing Brady's story. But I knew he wouldn't like me crying for him. I dug my fingers into my jeans, forcing my emotions under control.

"I'm glad you got to come live with us," I said.

Brady was silent. I felt myself blushing again. He wouldn't look at me, but then he said, "Yeah, your parents are decent, at least."

Then his expression darkened. "But I don't want to be a charity case my entire life. People always look at you different when they find out you're some punk-ass foster kid. They look all sad and shit. It's annoying."

"You're not a charity case," I protested.

"I'm living off your parents' dime when I'm not their kid. Pretty sure that's the definition of charity," he said wryly.

"They get paid for it."

"Barely. Believe me, I know it's a pathetic amount of money. My last three foster families never failed to tell me how little the state paid them to take care of me. My last foster mom always bitched that I ate too much food. So I'd have to sneak it and keep shit hidden from her."

Brady gazed out on the arena. "No, I'm not gonna be a charity case forever. I'm going to be a pro hockey player. I'll make so much money that I can swim in it. Everyone will know who I am. And it'll be because of who I am, and that I'm a hockey player. Not because I'm some pathetic kid with shit parents."

I could hear in his voice how serious he was. I had a feeling he was going to pursue his goal no matter what.

"Well, when you get famous, I'll sit right here in the stands wearing your jersey," I said.

Brady chuckled. "This isn't a pro arena, kid."

"Whatever. You know what I mean." I shot him a smile. "I'll be in the stands, cheering you on, until you get so embarrassed that you'll make security kick me out."

"Like I said, you're crazy." His expression turned somber. "But I bet you won't remember me by then."

"What? I'll never forget you. You're the crazy one."

Brady didn't say anything after that. But I could tell by his smile he was pleased.

Chapter 7

Brady
Present Day

Grace was here. Why was she always around, no matter where I went?

We'd won our game tonight. I should've been happy. I should've been celebrating with the team.

But I could only watch Grace laughing and flirting with my teammates.

It was all innocent. Grace wasn't the type to lead anyone on. I could even tell when she was uncomfortable, when the guys were too flirtatious with her. She had an expression that was a cross between embarrassment and annoyance. She'd look up at the guys from under her lashes, her pretty lips scowling.

She didn't know she made that face often. I'd pointed it out to her once, long ago, but she'd denied it. She claimed she had the best poker face when she'd probably lose at poker because she wore her heart on her sleeve.

We'd beaten our rivals the Blizzards with only seconds to spare. Coach hadn't been happy about the almost loss, but now, after a few beers in him, he looked happy again.

We'd gone to a nearby club with a huge private room upstairs. The music was blaring, the alcohol flowing, and I didn't know half the people in attendance.

There were probably more women here than actual hockey players or fans. I should be thrilled.

But here I was, standing in the corner, glaring over at where my teammate Riley was saying something in Grace's ear that made her laugh.

Look at me, I thought. *Look at me, Grace.*

As if she could hear my thoughts, her gaze met mine. Her eyes widened.

And then she looked away. *Damn her to hell.*

How much had I had to drink? I'd forgotten. Somebody kept putting glasses in my hand, and I wasn't disinclined to stay sober tonight.

Then I made eye contact with Coach Dallas. He'd been looking over at his daughter. Had he seen me staring at her?

His eyes narrowed at me, but then somebody caught his attention. I let out the breath I'd been holding.

I needed to get ahold of myself. I was being too fucking obvious. The last thing I needed was Coach getting on my ass for lusting after his virginal daughter.

I groaned inwardly. Christ, just the thought of her being a virgin, of giving in to temptation, of making her mine, finally—

"What crawled up your ass and died?" Mac asked me with a raised eyebrow. He punched me lightly in the arm.

I scowled. "Nothing," I growled.

"Why are you standing in the corner by yourself? That's not like you."

I finished off my drink and looked around for a server to refill it. "Maybe I'm not in the mood to celebrate."

"After scoring the winning goal? Okay, sure." Mac frowned at me. "What's up with you, anyway?"

"Nothing."

"Well, did you have a chance to go to the club? Because if you haven't, you definitely should. Blow off some steam."

The memory of my night at the Scarlet Rope and my time with Shayla improved my mood a little.

"I did go," I replied, forcing myself to stop scowling. "I had a good time, actually."

"You sound surprised."

"I mean, I've never been into whips and chains. I guess I'm just fucking vanilla at the end of the day."

Mac chuckled. "Everybody says that until they try it once. Are you going back again?"

"Yeah." I hadn't known whether I would until that moment.

But Mac was right. I needed to blow off steam. And what better way than getting my mind off the one woman I could never have?

"Well, a word of advice," said Mac. "Everybody signs NDAs, but that doesn't mean shit doesn't get leaked. Did you wear a mask? Because if not, I would, going forward. You never know who'll recognize you and snitch."

I shrugged. "I'm not worried about that."

"I speak from experience: you don't want this shit talked about in the tabloids. It gets twisted and complicated."

When the media had found out Mac liked BDSM, it'd been a whole fucking thing. It hadn't helped that Mac's parents were ultrareligious.

"This is where I'm glad my parents don't give a shit about me," I said, clapping Mac on the shoulder. "Unless they can get money. That's all they care about."

I said the words jokingly, but it still hurt, knowing that my family was fucking useless. Mac had always complained about his parents not understanding him. But at least he had parents.

God, I'm turning into such a sap, I thought. It must be the alcohol.

Right then I saw Riley say something to Grace. She shook her head, that annoyed expression of hers on her face.

"Excuse me," I said, handing Mac my glass.

I heard Mac mutter something under his breath. But I cared only about Grace because I could tell she wanted to get away from Riley.

Riley had his hand on her arm. She was laughing, but I could tell it was strained. Not because I could hear her: no, I could tell just by her face.

"Come on, baby," Riley said, "don't be a tease."

"I'm going to the bathroom," said Grace, her tone firm. She glanced at me, her jaw tight, and then she headed toward the back of the club.

"Bitch. She's not even that hot. No tits and no ass, either."

Riley didn't even have time to laugh at what he'd said before I punched him in the mouth. He went down hard, roaring and swearing.

I saw only red. I punched Riley again, but this time, Riley punched back. Then we were fighting, throwing punches and grabbing at each other until I felt hands yanking me away.

"Brady!" someone was shouting in my ear. "Brady! Let him go!"

I wanted to kill him. I could just imagine choking him until his face turned blue—

But then Riley was being dragged away, and my gaze landed on Grace. She was staring at the entire scene, her face pale.

"You're fucking drunk," Coach Dallas yelled at me. "Get him out of here," he said to Mac, who was the one who'd pulled me away.

"Jesus, Brady," Mac kept saying as he escorted me out. "What the fuck is going on?"

I wiped the blood from my lip. I winced as I felt my right eye. I was going to have a nice shiner in the morning.

"He insulted Grace," I said.

Mac let out a breath. "Be careful, dude. Go home. Sleep it off. And apologize to Coach in the morning because he looked like he was going to have a stroke."

I was inside a cab and on my way home before I realized what was happening. I got upstairs to my apartment without falling on my face, although I wasn't sure how I managed it.

I hadn't realized how drunk I was. I laughed under my breath as I struggled to get my key in my lock. What would Grace think of me, seeing me like this?

I finally got inside and saw that my phone was blowing up. Multiple texts included links to the fight that had already been posted on social media.

I don't have time for this, I thought. I was about to turn my phone off when Grace texted me.

Are you okay? Mac told me he called a cab for you before I could find you.

Yeah I'm home. Don't worry about me.

It took a second for her to respond. *Okay. Just be careful. There's been a lot of chatter online about what you've been up to lately. I know you don't care, but everything reflects on the team.*

Since when had Grace turned into PR? Then again, interns tended to be whatever the boss told them to be. Maybe she was shifting gears more from marketing to PR. But I knew she was right, even in my drunken haze. I also hated the thought that I was letting her down.

Noted, I replied. I knew she'd probably be hurt at my shortness, but I didn't have the energy to care.

But I also knew that Mac had been right. I needed to be careful. This Grace obsession was going to end badly.

So what if another guy insulted her? She wasn't mine. She could never be mine.

"It's all over the internet!" Julia, the Blades' PR lead, yelled.

If I'd known this meeting was just to chew me out, I would've skipped it. I didn't have time for Julia to rip me a new asshole.

But I also knew Coach was watching me closely. If I'd skipped this meeting, he would've taken me out back and broken my kneecaps.

"Yeah, I saw it," I drawled, crossing my arms. "What do you want me to do about it?"

Julia, who was normally the most even-keeled of people, looked at me incredulously. "That's all you have to say?"

"I was drunk. I shouldn't have done that. The end. But people are always going to post shit that gets the most interaction."

I glanced at Grace, who was avoiding my gaze. Why the hell was she here? What did Julia yelling at me have to do with her internship?

"Did you even have a good reason for punching Riley?" Julia asked, a hand on her hip. "Because at least if you do, we could spin this story into something better than 'drunken hockey player decks teammate for no reason.'"

I glanced at Grace. I watched as a blush climbed up her cheeks.

Would I throw Grace under the bus? Have everyone know that Riley was calling her a bitch because she'd rejected his advances?

Fuck no. Social media—the worst parts of it, at least—would pounce on that and say she deserved it. Or that she'd been insane to say no to a hockey player like Riley.

"I was drunk. I don't remember," I replied.

Julia sighed. She pushed her glasses up her nose and sat down heavily. "Fine. We'll come up with something. Or better yet, we'll bury this story with something else. Have you done any charity work lately, Carmichael? Hugged infants, played with puppies? Anything?"

I snorted. "Should I go find a random baby and get a photo with it?"

"It's not the worst idea," Grace muttered.

I shot her a look. Now she just raised an eyebrow at me, as if daring me.

Daring me . . . to do what? Was she pissed I hadn't been honest? Because I was saving her from humiliation here. The least she could be was grateful.

After Julia lectured me a bit longer, I finally managed to get out of her office. We didn't have practice today, so I had the rest of the day to stew.

I didn't really give a shit what anybody said about me online. People were going to be assholes, no matter how many babies I held.

But the thought of Grace being disappointed in me, or Coach thinking the worst of me . . . yeah, it fucking hurt.

I needed to blow off steam. So I waited until it was dark and went straight to the Scarlet Rope.

After an hour of searching, I couldn't find Shayla anywhere. When I asked a few people if Shayla was coming tonight, nobody had an answer for me.

It didn't help that, with so many blondes in the club, it seemed like every other woman could be Shayla. And, of course, when I saw blond hair, I didn't first think of Shayla but of someone else entirely.

"You need a fucking therapist," I muttered to myself, disgusted.

I considered finding another woman, but I couldn't bring myself to do it. Instead, I just wandered, watching various scenes.

The first that caught my attention was a scene with two women. They both had black hair, the red of their outfits contrasting with their dark skin tones. The woman with shorter hair was caressing the other woman, whose hair hung down to her ass. The short-haired woman kissed the other woman's neck and massaged her breasts.

It was a surprisingly tender scene, given the fact that they had an audience. The short-haired woman pulled her partner onto a lush couch and buried her face between her partner's legs. Moans filled the room, the receiver's thighs tightening as she started climaxing.

I moved on after that. The next scene was more classic BDSM with a Dominatrix. A man was bound, gagged, and hanging from the ceiling. The Domme circled him while whipping his torso. The man threw his head back when the Domme placed clamps on his nipples. The man already had a cock ring that seemed to be preventing him from coming too quickly.

The Domme played with her sub's cock, kissing and licking it until she returned to whipping him mercilessly. Welts covered his torso, back, and ass.

I'd never been interested in being someone's sub. Despite that, the entire scene was still strangely erotic. It also gave me some ideas on how I'd like to play with Shayla if I ever saw her again.

My imagination conjured the image of Shayla bent over a couch like before. But as I began whipping her, she turned her head—and it was Grace's face.

I nearly groaned aloud. Grace was begging me—to stop? to keep going?—and I could see her pussy dripping with excitement. When I plunged my fingers inside her, she screamed in ecstasy.

I knew Grace would be tight. That untouched, virgin pussy would struggle to take even one of my fingers, let alone my cock. I'd have to go slowly with her. Ease her into things. Bring her to orgasm until she was open and ready.

Would she bite her lip and keep quiet? No, not Grace. She'd be vocal. I just knew it, deep down inside.

My cock was hard just imagining this scenario. It didn't help that as I moved on to another scene, the woman inside had blond hair.

She was on the floor, her ass in the air, as a man pounded into her. The slaps of flesh against flesh were intoxicating. The man was digging his fingers into the thick flesh of the woman's hips, so tightly that it'd probably leave marks.

He fucked her hard, her face buried in the rug, her squeals getting higher and higher. The man then grabbed her hair and pulled her head up.

"You love when I fuck you hard, don't you?" he growled. "Ride you until you come all over my dick."

"Yes, yes, yes," the woman was chanting. Her face was red, her eyes glassy. "I'm going to come—"

She moaned and shook as her climax hit her.

I closed my eyes, imagining that was Grace coming on my own cock. At that moment, I didn't know where reality and fantasy ended.

I somehow managed to find a private room that was unoccupied. Locking the door, I took out my cock and rubbed one out before I lost my ever-loving mind.

It took only a minute for me to come. I groaned, imagining that I was coming all over Grace's pale back. My orgasm seemed to go on and on for eternity.

I leaned against the wall and took in deep gulps of air. My body was shaking. I'd never come that hard just from jerking off.

Christ, what the fuck is wrong with me?

I cleaned myself up and knew that I needed to get out of here. But as I was about to drive home, I got a text from Silas, the Blades general manager and one of its co-owners.

Adidas is threatening to cancel its sponsorship because of that video of you fighting Riley. We need to talk ASAP.

My high was killed instantly. I slumped in my seat, swearing under my breath.

Silas then texted, *Riley is saying online that you hit him because his brother came out as gay. Is that true?*

"What the fuck?" I stared at my phone, incredulous. I hadn't even known Riley had a brother, let alone that his brother was gay. And why the fuck would I care?

Riley was a piece of shit trying to make me seem like some kind of bigot. He was just pissed that he'd lost the fight and that Grace had had the gall to reject him. *Did his brother know about this?* Because if I were Riley's brother, I'd be pissed at being used like this.

I could come clean. I could tell the world why the fight had happened. But protecting Grace was more important than my reputation. All I could say was that Riley's allegations were false, end stop.

I also knew I needed to get my emotions under control. Sure, I'd wanted to protect Grace, but I had this anger burning inside me that I couldn't seem to tamp down.

And if people knew why . . . if they knew what I'd done . . .

Well, then they'd definitely hate me, wouldn't they? And Grace would hate me the most of all.

Chapter 8

Grace

Will frowned over at me. "Grace? Is something wrong?"

I jerked in surprise. Nothing was wrong—except that I hadn't been listening to him talk about his new job at all.

When Will had invited me out to dinner, I'd been reluctant to go. This annoyed me because he was my *boyfriend*, so why should I not want to go out to dinner with him?

"Wrong? No, no." I pasted a fake smile on my face. "I'm sorry, I just have a lot of things on my mind. But I do want to hear about your new job."

Will had recently gotten a position at a promising start-up that was making some kind of medical-related app. He proceeded to tell me about how he was struggling to code something or other, while I struggled to stay focused on what he was saying.

And it wasn't because coding didn't interest me. It was because I couldn't stop thinking about Brady. The look on his face when Julia had scolded him like a little kid. Or that he'd refused to say why he'd punched Riley.

I knew he'd done it to defend me. I'd nearly bitten my tongue in half not to say anything, but I could tell that Brady would've been pissed if I'd spilled the beans.

Why? I didn't know. Men were idiots.

"So what is his deal? Your foster brother?" asked Will.

I blinked. I stared at Will, confused. "My brother?" I'd never talked about Ben with Will before.

"The hockey player," Will clarified, his eyes narrowing. "The jerk at your parents' place."

"Oh. Brady. He's not my brother." I let out an awkward laugh. "I mean, he's part of the family, kind of. But he's not my brother."

Apparently, "the lady doth protest too much" because Will didn't look convinced. He cleared his throat and stared at his glass of wine.

Will had chosen a nice little Italian place that I'd always wanted to go to. I'd been impressed that Will had remembered because I'd mentioned this place only once, offhandedly.

It also made me feel guilty. Will clearly paid more attention to me than I paid to him.

"Okay, well, Brady. Whoever he is." Will waved a hand. "What was his deal? Is he always such a jerk?"

"He's not a jerk," I snapped. "He's got a lot going on, that's all."

"Okaaaay. But you have to admit, he acted like a Neanderthal. I know he's a jock . . . they're not known for being that intelligent—"

"Brady is smart. You don't know what you're talking about."

Will closed his mouth. A blush climbed up my cheeks. Why was I so defensive about Brady?

He *had* been an asshole at dinner. He'd acted like he had some right to order me around or that I was out of bounds for bringing my boyfriend to dinner with my parents.

"He has a lot of pressure as a hockey player," I explained, floundering now. "If the team does badly, they all feel it. They could lose sponsorships, and ticket sales could tank. It's a lot of money on the line. And then because he's famous, people always want something from him. He doesn't trust people. Would you, if everybody thought they could gain something if they got close to you?"

Will looked uncomfortable. "I wasn't born yesterday, babe. I know that a lot of people are shitty."

I was glad when the server came with our appetizers right then. I busied myself with eating the bread while Will gazed morosely down at the antipasto platter.

After that, Will avoided the subject of Brady and hockey. Which meant he didn't ask me about my internship. Instead, he asked me generic questions: my dream vacation, my favorite restaurant lately, my favorite authors, and whatnot.

I felt a bit like I was being interviewed. I nearly teased Will about it, but I stopped myself. For whatever reason, I didn't feel like I'd earned that right.

After our entrées, I mentioned that I could go for some tiramisu. But when the server asked whether we wanted to see a dessert menu, Will told him no.

I was about to call the server back when Will put a hand over mine.

"I have dessert for us at home," he said. His gaze was earnest now.

His hand felt overly warm on top of mine. "Oh. Really?"

"I made tiramisu." He cleared his throat. "And, um, no pressure, but I wanted to see if you'd like to stay. The night, that is. Not just come over for tiramisu. No pressure, though. We don't have to do anything you don't want to do."

Will knew I was a virgin. I'd been up front about that early on because I knew that it'd freak out some guys. Will had told me that he wasn't in any hurry.

So why the suggestion now? He said no pressure, but at that moment, I felt a little pressured. Then again, we were at the point in our relationship when a lot of people would've slept together already.

"You made tiramisu?" I replied awkwardly. "Like, homemade and everything?"

"I even made the lady fingers." Will sounded inordinately proud.

I'd attempted tiramisu only once as a teenager, and it'd been a failure. The mascarpone cheese had curdled (I still didn't know how I'd managed that), the lady fingers had been mushy, and even my dad, who ate everything, couldn't finish a piece.

So I knew how much effort that must've taken. Now I felt really guilty for being so distracted tonight.

"Wow," I said because that was all I could think to say.

"So how about it?" Will gave me a small smile. "I also got a few of your favorite things. You told me that you loved lavender. I got a candle, and I even got you a robe since you said you love to wear one around the house."

He was being so sweet that I nearly said yes to his proposal. But I hesitated. Because deep down inside, I knew that Will wasn't the man whom I really, truly wanted.

"That's really nice of you," I said, "but I'd rather not. Not tonight."

Will's face fell. To his credit, he just replied, "That's okay. Maybe next time."

I needed to bite the bullet. "I mean, there won't be a next time. I don't think I'm the right person for you. This isn't working for me."

Will was crestfallen. "Did I push too hard? You can just come over and have dessert. I won't do anything else. I don't want you to feel pressured. I swear—"

"It's not that." I put my hands up. "I'm sorry. You're a really nice guy. You deserve somebody who wants to be with you wholeheartedly."

Will didn't say much after that. He paid the bill, and then we were in his car, saying nothing. I wished I'd driven myself. But I hadn't planned on breaking things off with Will tonight.

"Is there somebody else?" Will asked quietly.

I stared out the window. I didn't look at him as I lied, "No."

He didn't say anything. He probably knew I was lying. But why be honest and hurt him further?

And why be honest at all, when I knew that Brady would never want me like I wanted him?

I felt like crying. I felt like an idiot for pining after a man who'd made it clear he wasn't interested in me.

Was I a masochist? Or just an idiot?

When Will stopped in front of my parents' place, he put a hand on my arm.

"If you ever change your mind," he began.

I shook my head. "I'm sorry." I gave him a quick kiss on the cheek. "You're a good guy. I hope you find somebody worthy of you."

After Will drove away, I stood outside, staring at the front door. I didn't want to go inside because Mom would likely ask me about my date.

The last thing I wanted to do was to try to explain myself. Instead, I got into my car and went straight to a local dive bar to forget this night entirely.

"Baby, come on, don't play me like that," a man in a red baseball cap said. He slid onto the barstool next to me, smooth as butter. "Give a guy a chance."

This guy had already bought me two drinks. I'd taken him up on both offers, not caring if he expected something in return.

Now, my bloodstream was pure alcohol, and all my inhibitions had disappeared.

Well, maybe not *all*. I didn't want to sleep with this guy, or any of the other guys who seemed ready to pounce if I so much as winked at them. But I didn't care much that they were circling me like vultures.

"I'm not playing you," I said, laughing a little. "You bought me a drink. I am drinking that drink. The end."

"Nothing in life is free, darlin'," he replied.

"Sure it is, if you really want it to be. And I'm not your darling."

He seemed unaffected by that answer. "Baby—"

"I'm also not your baby." I got up, but for some weird reason, the floor was way closer than I expected. I giggled, grabbing hold of the barstool as another guy grabbed my arm to help me up.

"I'm fine," I slurred, brushing the other guy away. "I'm fine. Why does everyone think something is wrong with me? It's annoying."

I staggered to a nearby booth. I then fell sideways onto the leather, laughing like a lunatic. The world kept spinning.

God, I was drunk. I never drank like this. But it felt nice. I was happy. I didn't care that I'd broken up with my boyfriend or that I wanted a hockey star who didn't give two shits about me.

Brady. What was he doing right now? He was probably fucking some girl. He did that a lot. It was annoying.

I pulled out my phone and texted him, telling him he should stop fucking all the girls. He'd probably get chlamydia. I giggled as I tried to spell *chlamydia*. My phone struggled to figure out how to autocorrect my spelling attempts.

wear a condam, I texted. *condem condom? what?*

Then I sent him a whole bunch of eggplant emoji because those were hilarious.

I kept texting Brady until he replied. Well, he called me. I picked up and said happily, "Brady!"

"Where are you?" he demanded. He sounded mad.

I pouted. "You sound mean," I accused.

He sighed. "How drunk are you? No, don't tell me. Just tell me where you are."

I told him even though I didn't understand why he wanted to know. Unless he was going to come buy me some more drinks.

"I really, really like vodka cranberries," I told him. "You should get one."

"Don't fucking move. I'll be there as soon as I can."

Then he hung up. I frowned. I didn't know what was up with Brady. He was acting so weird lately.

I must've dozed off because suddenly, I felt hands on me. I tried to jump up, but the table was in the way. I let out a little screech before I realized Brady was the one touching me.

"It's you!" I threw my arms around him. "You're here!"

"Jesus, Grace, what the fuck?" He sighed and then picked me up in his arms. "I'm taking you home. Wait, no, if your parents see you like this—"

"My parents aren't home." I'd totally forgotten that they were out of town for their anniversary. I could've been drinking at home. I started laughing like an idiot. "They're not home!"

Brady just shook his head. "I'm taking you home," he said firmly.

I didn't want to leave my car behind, but Brady assured me he'd take care of it. And it wasn't like I could drive it. I was *drunk*. Smashed. Hammered. All the adjectives.

Brady parked in the driveway. I opened my door to get out, only to find myself on the concrete, my knee suddenly hurting.

"Ow! What the—"

"Grace, are you okay?" Brady crouched next to me. "I was going to help you out, you idiot."

"Rude. You're rude." I poked him in the chest.

"Sorry. You're not an idiot. You're just drunk." He helped me to stand, but I was still wobbly. He proceeded to lift me into his arms again and carry me inside.

It was nice, being in his arms. He was so warm—and strong. He carried me like I weighed nothing. He also smelled nice.

"Stop sniffing me," he growled as he carried me upstairs.

"But you smell nice. I like it."

He groaned. I didn't know why he sounded so frustrated. I was just complimenting him.

He put me on my bed and then disappeared. I realized that I was still wearing my dress, along with some annoying shapewear and a bra. I hated wearing a bra.

I was able to toss my dress over my head, but I struggled to unhook my bra. I was all tangled up when Brady returned.

I froze. His eyes were narrowed, and his nostrils were flared.

"What are you doing?" he asked, his voice hoarse.

"Trying to get my bra off."

He rubbed his forehead. Then after he took a deep breath, he gently turned me around and unhooked my bra. I pulled it off and tossed it in the corner, sighing happily.

I tried to turn, but Brady stopped me. "Let me get you a robe," he said.

He handed me my favorite one, which I put on after a few tries. When Brady wouldn't look at me, though, I realized that the V was open to the point that he could see a decent amount of my chest.

I laughed. "Sorry. But they're just boobs. You're acting like a baby."

He scowled. "I'm trying not to embarrass you."

I collapsed onto my bed. "Whatever."

I was staring up at my canopy when I felt Brady's hand on my calf. I sat up straight, my entire body heating.

Brady was gazing up at me with something I couldn't define in his expression. "Your knee," he explained.

I'd forgotten about it. It still stung, but the alcohol had numbed much of the pain.

I nodded, my throat tight. I watched as Brady opened the first-aid kit—how had he known where it was?—and pulled out a packet of alcohol wipes.

"This'll hurt," he said, and then he began cleaning the wound.

I sucked in a breath. It did hurt. But I'd gotten my knee pretty dirty, so I understood why he thought he should clean it.

The room was silent as he worked. After he cleaned the wound, he leaned down and blew on it, his gaze still on my face.

I shivered. I'd never had a man so close to me like this. And seeing Brady on his knees while I wore only a robe—

Well, a robe and shapewear. I hoped he hadn't noticed those because that would be more embarrassing than just seeing me completely naked.

Brady caressed my calf, my thoughts scattering. "You okay?" he asked.

I nodded. He then put a bandage over the wound and stood.

"Are you going to be okay?" he asked.

I didn't know how to answer that. My mouth felt dry. I glanced at the water bottle that sat on my nightstand.

"I'll fill that up," he said, grabbing the bottle before I could say a word. Bottle filled, he then watched as I drank the entire thing, telling me it was the best way to get the alcohol out of my system.

"Keep drinking as much water as you can. It'll help. Although you'll probably still have a hangover in the morning. Do you ever drink like this?" he asked.

I shook my head, yawning. "No. But I was sad tonight. I broke up with Will."

Brady stilled. "You did? Why?"

"Because he wanted to be my first, and I didn't want that. I want you to be my first."

Brady didn't say anything. I saw his chest rise and fall, rise and fall, and it seemed like he was breathing hard. His pupils were wide.

But he didn't touch me. He just shook his head. "You should sleep," he said.

I yawned again. "I'm not sleepy. I don't want to be alone. Will you stay with me?"

His jaw clenched. "That's not a good idea."

I snorted. "I know you don't want me like that. I just don't want to be alone." I grabbed at his shirt, gazing up at him.

"Go to sleep," he said gently. He unhooked my fingers and made me lie down. He then tucked me in and brushed his fingers across my forehead.

"I'll watch over you," he said quietly.

I closed my eyes. And then, with Brady's touch dancing across my face, I fell asleep.

Chapter 9

Brady

I knew I should avoid Grace. I should never have gone to that bar and taken her home. I'd nearly let myself fall into temptation.

The only thing that had stopped me was the knowledge that Grace was drunk. If she hadn't been, she never would've acted like that. I told myself she was just lonely after breaking up with Will. She would've done the same with any guy.

I told myself that even though I knew it was a huge fucking lie. Grace wasn't the type to just throw herself at men.

Which meant she wanted me. She *still* wanted me.

But it didn't matter. It didn't matter what she wanted because I knew I'd only make her miserable. Especially if she knew the truth about me.

I'd done my best to avoid seeing Grace for the past week despite the fact that she worked at the Blades arena. It wasn't too difficult not to see her, considering how large the place was. It helped that Grace didn't seem to have any projects that involved filming in the actual rink.

So when I saw her on a Friday evening near the locker room, I nearly had a fucking heart attack.

"Are we going to film the guys inside the locker room?" a woman asked Grace, laughing.

"I wish," said another woman.

Grace rolled her eyes. "I don't think that's in their contracts."

I caught her gaze, and it felt like time stretched right then. Her eyes widened.

And then I walked right past her without saying a fucking word.

I hated myself right then, knowing I was being a huge douchebag. But it was better this way. And if it meant Grace hating me, all the better.

I wondered whether Shayla was at the club tonight. Maybe I could take all this restless sexual energy out on her. Even better, I could be with Grace without actually being with Grace.

You need a goddamn therapist, I thought with a bitter laugh as I got into my car.

I didn't have time to go to the club, though. I got a phone call on the way home that erased any thoughts of fun from my mind.

It was Marty, my mom's neighbor. Marty only ever called when Mom was really fucked up. He was one of the few people who checked on her. He'd attended AA meetings with her back in the day, and she'd stayed sober for about a year. Then she'd relapsed. Marty had tried to get her to go back to rehab, but Mom was stubborn.

"Is she dead?" I said, my tone flat.

Marty sighed. "No, but she's in the hospital again. I saw an ambulance take her away just now. So I guess the good news is that she was conscious enough to call 911."

I sighed. "Thanks for letting me know," I said before saying goodbye.

I knew I should call Mom or, at the very least, the hospital. I knew which one it would be. But even as I knew I should call and check on her, I didn't see the point.

We'd done this fucking song and dance so many times. Mom would fall, or get blackout drunk, or get beat up, and she'd end up in the hospital. Sometimes she stayed for a few hours; other times, it was days. She'd stabilize, they'd offer her treatment, and she'd refuse 99 percent of the time.

What was galling was that she could get sober if she wanted to. She'd done it before. The handful of periods when she'd managed to stay sober had shown that she could be a good mom.

But in the past ten years, she just couldn't even be assed to try.

As a kid, I remembered finding her passed out on the kitchen floor. Sometimes she wet herself. I'd clean her up and help her into bed. She'd always end up crying and apologizing. She'd swear she'd get help. But she never did.

Sometimes she did go to rehab. Then, after a few days, she'd check herself out, declaring that she didn't need help. I'd find her passed out at some sleazy bar. Or worse, making a scene where the cops would get called.

Mom had a long rap sheet: drunken and disorderly conduct, DUIs, assault, petty theft. All because she was obsessed with the bottle.

I thought again about calling Mom later that night, but then I decided that I'd try in the morning. Mom was probably asleep anyway.

I woke up to my phone ringing. Yawning, I groaned when I saw that it was Marty again.

This time, Marty had worse news. "It's her liver," he said. "The cirrhosis has gotten to the point that she needs a transplant to survive."

I sat up in bed, my brain trying to understand what Marty was saying. "How long does she have?"

"The doctors say maybe six months, especially if she keeps going like this."

"And there's no way she'll get a new liver if she keeps drinking," I said, disgusted.

Marty didn't contradict me.

After I ended the call, I lay back down and stared up at the ceiling. Mom had six months to live—maybe less.

I didn't even feel anything at that realization. Except guilt because I'd avoided talking to her last night. Her neighbor had been her only friend to tell the news to. Not even her son had cared enough to be involved.

That old feeling, that maybe if I just tried a little harder, I could get Mom to change her ways. As a kid, I'd done everything to get her to stop drinking.

I'd pour her liquor bottles down the sink, even knowing she'd rage and scream at me. I'd beg. I'd plead. I'd give her the silent treatment. I'd stage interventions when I was the only one present.

I thought maybe when I'd gone into foster care, she'd get help. I waited for that phone call from her—when she was finally sober, and she'd tell me I'd get to go back home.

Of course that call never came. Her drinking only got worse after I was taken away from her. She preferred drowning in self-pity over getting her kid out of the system.

I still hesitated to call her. When I finally did, I hoped she didn't pick up.

"Brady," she said when she picked up. "Why are you calling me so early?"

It was always strange to hear motherly concern in her voice. I wanted to tell her she didn't have the right to act like that, while the other, more pathetic part of me, lapped up the attention.

"Marty told me you were in the hospital," I replied.

She sighed. "I told him not to call you."

"Why?"

"Because I'm fine."

"Did you call 911 yourself?"

"Betty did. She was watching TV with me."

Betty—she was still around? Mom and Betty had been drinking buddies back in the day. Last I'd heard, though, Betty had been on the streets.

"Is Betty living with you?" I asked.

"Just for a little bit. She's getting back onto her feet."

Great. Two alcoholics living together. I gritted my teeth, trying not to get angry.

"Marty also told me about your liver," I said quietly.

Mom inhaled a breath. "He wasn't supposed to say anything."

"Well, he did. He said you have six months to live. So are you going to stop drinking now, or what?"

She was quiet for a long moment, so long that I wondered whether she was still on the line.

"If you just called to make me feel bad, then I don't see the point of talking to you," she said.

"I'm not trying to make you feel bad, but I'm trying to make you see how serious this is." I rose from my bed and started pacing. "Mom, you're dying. Your liver isn't going to last much longer. Doesn't that scare you?"

"Doctors are always saying shit like that. I feel fine."

"Marty said that you're jaundiced. Yellow eyes and everything. Come on, be honest here—"

"You always do this. You always act like you know better, but I'm your mother. Stop trying to make me into someone I'm not."

"I want you to fucking live!" I nearly roared the words.

No response.

"I'll talk to you later when you're going to be nice," she said.

I stared at my phone. Then I hurled it across the room, not caring whether the screen shattered.

Why did I keep fucking trying? I thought wildly. *She's never going to change. She's going to die, and there's not a goddamn thing I can do about it.*

I couldn't breathe. I couldn't think. The pain, the anger, the confusion. It all mixed until it felt like jagged glass inside my lungs.

I needed to forget. Not caring about the hypocrisy, I drove to the nearest bar. I needed to numb myself.

Mom thought she was the only one who got to numb her pain? Fuck no. I ordered the largest beer I could and knocked it back, the warm buzz of the alcohol hitting me quickly since I hadn't eaten anything that day.

And then I proceeded to get drunker and drunker because it was the only thing that stopped the endless hurting.

I sat in a dark corner of a dirty dive bar, and nobody recognized me. The last thing I needed was more bad press.

The only smart thing I did before I left was grab a cap to cover my face. And given the pissed-off aura I was putting out, nobody bothered me once I started drinking.

I knew there was irony that I was drinking when Mom couldn't stop drinking. But I couldn't bring myself to care, either.

I drank one beer. Then another. Then liquor, then whiskey. I didn't give a fuck what I drank as long as it didn't stop.

where are u, I texted Grace when I was too drunk to think about what I was doing.

Where are you? she replied.

I laughed darkly. *who knows*

She just texted me a bunch of question marks.

It didn't take her long to ask me if I was drunk. I thought about our role reversals: I was the mess this time.

"Do you need me to drive you home?" she asked when she called me a few minutes later.

It took me a long time to answer. "Uh, no," I slurred. I burped loudly.

"Oh geez, please don't get behind the wheel. Call a taxi or something. Please, Brady. Promise me."

I was annoyed now. "I'm not fucking stupid. I don't drive drunk."

"I know you don't. You've always been careful, which is why I'm worried about you now."

My chest hurt for some reason. Why did Grace even care about me? She shouldn't care about me. I was a piece of shit who didn't deserve her friendship.

"Where are you?" she insisted. "I'm coming to get you."

I told her. She told me to stay put. I laughed, because I'd just done the same thing with her.

When she arrived, she sighed as she sat down next to me. "You look terrible," she said.

My head lolled to the side. "You look great," I shot back.

She looked down. She was wearing a ratty T-shirt and leggings, her hair in a messy bun. She looked like she'd been in bed.

"Okay, come on, let's go." She grabbed me by the arm.

I nearly stumbled and fell flat on my face as I tried to stand. The whole thing made me laugh like an idiot. Grace just sighed and hustled me out to her car.

When she asked for my address, I was surprised that she didn't know it. But why would she? She'd never been to my place before.

A half hour later, she stopped in front of my apartment building. She turned to me, frowning.

"Is this it?" She pointed. "I must've gotten the address wrong."

"No, that's it."

I got out of the car, only to realize that Grace hadn't put it in park. I stumbled, hitting the pavement with a jolt.

Grace stopped the car and got out, hurrying to me. "Jesus! Brady, are you okay?"

"I'm fine." I was fine—probably. I was too drunk to feel much pain. "I'll meet you inside. It's the first apartment on the left."

Grace joined me inside my place a few minutes later. She looked frazzled. For the first time, I felt guilty for bothering her like this.

"I hate parallel parking," she grumbled, sitting down next to me.

That statement made me laugh. "Babe, you live in LA."

"Oh, the irony isn't lost on me."

She kept looking around like she was confused or something.

I knew my apartment wasn't the cleanest, but it was hardly a dump. I'd even gone so far as to get an air fryer recently, and I no longer had my clothes in giant plastic bins.

"This is your apartment?" she said, looking at me closely.

"Yeahhhhhh," I drawled. "Pretty sure it is, at least," I said jokingly.

She frowned. "It's so small."

"Uh. Thank you?"

She looked embarrassed. "I mean, that's not a criticism. Just, you're a famous hockey player. What are you doing living in a tiny apartment?"

She got up and began looking around. My apartment was just a one-bedroom, one-bathroom place. It was old, but it wasn't a dump, at least. The landlord was local and maintained the property.

It also helped that most of my neighbors were older, so they didn't know who I was. Most people on my street didn't know I played for the Blades. The anonymity was nice.

"I don't need a huge place," I said when Grace returned. I shrugged. "I'm never home, anyway."

"It still makes no sense."

I grimaced. I didn't want to tell her the real reason was that I didn't feel like I deserved any better.

I was just some foster kid from the wrong side of the tracks. My mom was a drunk, and my dad was in jail. Who did I think I was, living in a mansion?

"I don't deserve better than this," I said finally.

Grace's eyes widened. "What? What are you saying?"

God, I was still too drunk. I went to the fridge and returned with some sports drinks. I downed one while Grace just stared at hers.

"Thanks for driving me," I said. I cleared my throat. "You don't have to stay."

Hurt flashed across her face. Guilt punched me in the gut. I was fucking everything up.

"Why were you drinking tonight?" she asked.

"My mom is dying."

"Oh, Brady. I'm so sorry."

She touched my arm, and it felt like a brand against my skin. I wanted to shrug off her touch while, at the same time, I wanted to pull her closer.

"She won't stop drinking, and her liver is failing." I shrugged. "And spare me the lecture on me drinking, by the way."

Grace held up her hands. "Considering you just had to drive me home recently, I can't judge."

"You're not the judgmental type, are you? It's something I've always admired about you."

A blush bloomed in her cheeks. It was adorable. I wondered whether the rest of her turned red when she blushed. But I had to push that thought aside or I was going to drive myself insane.

"Thank you," she whispered. She was twisting the cap to the sports drink on and off.

A breeze blew through the open window, making a wind chime sing. Grace turned.

"Is that the chime I gave you?" she said. She got up, setting the drink down. She laughed when she touched the chime. "I got this for you forever ago. I can't believe you still have it."

I remembered exactly when she'd gotten me that. It'd been my first birthday at her parents' place, and she'd told me that the chime would bring me good luck. Ben had teased her about it. Grace had gotten so embarrassed that she'd run up to her room to hide.

Their mom had been pissed at Ben, and he'd gotten chewed out. As for me, I hadn't said anything. I'd been too stunned that this girl had cared enough to get me a gift like that to begin with.

"You gave it to me," I said as if that explained everything.

Grace smiled. "I thought you hated it. I never saw you hang it up, so I thought you'd thrown it out."

"I never would've thrown it away."

Grace raised her eyebrows at my intense tone.

God, I was a fucking mess tonight. It didn't help that Grace's leggings left little to the imagination or that her messy hair made me wonder what she looked like after having sex.

She doesn't know, does she? Because she's still a virgin.

She returned to the couch and touched my knee. "I love that you still have it."

I didn't want to talk about the reasons I still had that wind chime. I didn't want to talk about my mom, either.

So I leaned forward and tried to kiss Grace.

But being drunk, I wasn't smooth about it. Grace ducked before my lips touched hers.

"What are you—" she stammered. She got up; I fell over onto my face on the couch.

"Grace," I said. "I'm sorry."

She was wringing her hands, and she wouldn't look at me. "You should go to bed," she was saying.

I rolled over until I was lying on the couch. Grace grabbed a pillow for my head and then tucked a blanket around me.

"Good night," she said hurriedly.

I grabbed her hand. "Thank you, again."

She just shook her head and nearly ran out the door.

Chapter 10

Grace

It was the first year none of us cried going to Ben's grave.

I expected Mom to cry, but she was dry-eyed. She even laughed a little. Maybe it helped that Dad couldn't attend our annual memorial because of work.

"I know your dad is upset he couldn't come today," Mom remarked as she set flowers in front of the gravestone.

"I could tell," I said.

Dad had been grumbling all morning before he left for work. He hadn't said outright that he was upset, but everybody knew when he was pissed. He was never subtle about it.

Ben had died six years ago now in a car accident. My older brother, who had seemed all-powerful when we'd been kids, had been felled by something that seemed almost mundane.

Ben probably hated that he'd died in a car accident. He would've preferred something more interesting, like dying while skydiving. Or heroic, like running into a burning building to save a bunch of kids.

"It's always surprised me that Dad didn't quit coaching hockey after Ben died," I said.

Mom blinked. "Your dad? Quit hockey? No way. It was all he had, especially after Ben died."

I kneeled and touched the flowers that Mom had gotten for today. "Ben and hockey were all Dad cared about," I said.

"What? Your dad loves you just as much as he loved Ben." Mom looked stricken.

I shook my head. "I mean, I know that. But he and Ben had that special bond. I always knew it was something we'd never have because I didn't care about hockey."

Mom sighed. "I think your dad threw himself into coaching because it was easier than letting himself feel things. I was just grateful it wasn't something worse, like drugs or alcohol."

I winced inwardly because I thought of poor Brady and his mom. I hadn't talked to him since I'd taken him back to his apartment.

What did a girl say to a guy who'd tried to drunkenly kiss her? Nothing came to mind. Worse, I was still embarrassed about him saving me that night I'd gotten drunk.

We were quite a pair, I could say that.

"Come on. Let's get some ice cream," said Mom, pulling me away from thoughts of Brady.

We made sure to stop at the park where my parents had erected a statue of Ben, commemorating his hockey career that had been cut too short. It'd been at this same park where he'd first started playing field hockey, although he'd quickly switched to ice hockey. My parents had tried putting the statue at the rink where Ben had practiced, but apparently the rink wasn't interested.

We walked to the ice-cream parlor where we'd often get ice cream as a family. The owners recognized us and knew that we came only after visiting Ben's grave.

The owner served us both rocky road, Ben's favorite, and told us it was on the house. Mom, of course, had to do her usual song and dance when she tried to pay, but the owner always insisted.

"I wonder how much longer he'll keep giving us free ice cream," I said as we sat down outside. It was a gorgeous, sunny day, as per usual in LA.

"I feel guilty that he keeps giving it to us for free," Mom remarked, frowning.

Considering the constant line at the place, they weren't hurting for paying customers.

"Hey, take the Dead Son Pass for as long as you can," I joked.

Mom clucked her tongue. "Since when are you so morbid?"

That first year after Ben's death, none of us could joke around. We'd been too oppressed by grief. Everything reminded us of Ben. We'd see a kid eating ice cream, and my mind would go to the times Ben would take me for ice cream when we'd been kids.

I didn't know how Dad had kept going to work for a hockey team. How had he not seen Ben in every player, at every game? I was grateful that I was able to leave for college and get away from my own memories.

"I still can't believe he's gone," Mom said quietly. "It doesn't happen as often now, but sometimes I'll wake up and think, 'I have to wake up Ben.' He was such a sound sleeper. He'd sleep through multiple alarms, remember?" She smiled sadly. "But then I remember that I don't have to worry about that anymore."

I squeezed Mom's hand. "Remember when he slept through the earthquake?"

Mom laughed. "Oh God! He was in the tree house back in the Vegas house, and we thought something had happened to him. Nope, he was snoozing away like a five-point-three earthquake hadn't just happened."

I grinned. "Did I ever tell you about the time I shaved his eyebrows in his sleep?"

"What? That was you? I thought it was his friend Dylan!"

"It was Brady's idea, actually. But I was mad at Ben for ignoring me when he had his friends over, so I was the one to do the deed. But I was such a good girl nobody believed Ben when he said it'd been me."

Mom lightly smacked my arm. "Grace Elizabeth! Shame on you."

I just laughed.

We finished our ice cream in companionable silence, remembering the good times with Ben. I wondered what he'd be doing now, at twenty-six. Would he have still been playing hockey? Or would he have finished college and gone on to do something else?

He'd always said he'd been interested in going to law school. Would he have become some high-powered attorney? He would've been good at it, I knew that.

"You and Brady have been spending a lot of time together lately," Mom said.

I nearly jumped out of my skin. "What?" I knew I was stammering.

Mom gave me The Look. "I saw you on the security camera, coming home with him. Well, he was *carrying* you inside. Care to explain that?"

I gaped at her. "I thought the cameras were broken."

Now Mom had the grace to look embarrassed. "They were, until recently. I thought Dad had told you he was getting them fixed?"

I groaned. "Oh God. Does Dad know?"

"No, and I wasn't planning on telling him." She raised an eyebrow. "Unless there is something I should tell him about."

"Do you still have the video?"

"No, I deleted it. Because I knew your dad would flip out."

I sighed, relieved. The last thing I needed was Dad freaking out and going after Brady.

"I got drunk that night I broke up with Will. It was stupid. Brady was nice enough to take me home. That's it," I said in a rush.

"You were so drunk that Brady had to carry you inside?"

I blushed. "Um, kind of. I mean, I'd fallen, so Brady was worried about my knee. He was just being chivalrous."

Mom made a noncommittal noise. "Is there anything going on between you two? Because your dad has been watching Brady, and he seems to pay a lot of attention to you."

I wanted to melt into the bench. I didn't even know where to begin. But I also was tired of keeping all these feelings to myself.

"I had a crush on Brady." I sighed. "No, I still have a crush on him. But that's it. He's never been interested in me like that. We're just friends."

"It takes a very nice friend to pick you up at a bar and carry you inside your house," Mom pointed out.

I frowned. "What do you mean?"

"Just that that doesn't seem like something a friend would do. At least, not a guy friend. He's very protective of you."

"I know. He's like a brother to me." Even as I said the words, I winced. The last thing I felt for Brady was something sisterly.

"Well, you're a smart woman," said Mom, "and I know you won't do anything stupid. Although getting drunk alone isn't very smart. You could've been hurt."

"I know. It won't happen again. The hangover the next morning was terrible."

Mom was silent a long moment. "I keep hearing about Brady getting into fights. He doesn't seem like he's in a good place right now."

"I mean, his mom is still drinking," I said, not wanting to go into too much detail about Brady's mom. "That'd mess anyone up."

"Of course. But something changed in the past few years . . ." Mom sighed. "Then again, we've all changed since Ben died. I know it affected Brady as much as it affected all of us."

Brady had looked up to Ben. Ben had taught Brady all about hockey, and the two of them had spent a ton of time together at the rink. But when Ben had died, Brady had basically acted like Ben had never existed. He'd refused to even mention Ben's name.

I'd never understood it. It'd seemed . . . cold. Like Brady hadn't really cared much about his friend. It was also around that time when Brady had stopped coming by my parents' place.

"Brady has never talked to me about Ben," I said.

"Really?"

"You sound surprised."

Mom frowned. "He was always closed off, but you and he were close. I thought maybe he would've talked to you out of all of us."

"No. At the end of the day, I think Brady has always kept to himself. I think sometimes he acts like he doesn't need anybody but himself."

"When we first agreed to foster Brady, I wasn't really excited about it. He was much older than the other kids we'd taken in. He'd also had some incidents when he'd been aggressive. But your dad was convinced we could make a difference."

"I didn't know that," I said.

"I was also worried about you. You were so young, and we didn't know what Brady was really like besides what his social worker told us. And sometimes DFS fudges things about kids when they're more complicated cases."

"But you changed your mind."

"More like your dad was going to do what he wanted to do." Mom smiled wryly. "I told him that if Brady acted up or, worse, was aggressive with you or your brother, he was out of my house. Fortunately, he never gave us any trouble beyond skipping school sometimes and a bad grade here and there."

I wondered whether Brady had known that Mom was watching him and waiting for a reason to send him away. I hoped not. That would've just fueled his belief that nobody had wanted him.

"I was surprised when you two started getting close," said Mom. "And then it became pretty obvious you had a crush on him."

"Oh my God, Mom—"

"It was so cute. I could always tell when you wanted to get Brady's attention. You'd wear your cutest outfit and do your hair and makeup, but poor Brady didn't know what to do with you. I was worried, at first, but I quickly realized that Brady never saw you like that."

Her gaze narrowed. "At least, not until recently."

I looked away. "You don't have to worry about us. We're just friends like I said."

"You would tell me if that changed, wouldn't you?"

I didn't answer because I didn't know. Or because I knew Mom would never be okay with us being in a relationship.

Is she still looking for a reason to get rid of him? Now, I can't help but wonder.

"Ben always made fun of me whenever I tried to flirt with Brady," I said.

"I think your brother didn't know what to do with you, seeing you like that. He was very protective of you. I know he still would be if he were here."

Would Ben tell me that Brady wasn't the guy for me, even now? I didn't know. I liked to think Ben would've been more pragmatic than our parents, but maybe not. Maybe he would've told me to stay away from Brady.

Mom patted my leg. "Let's head home. I'm getting cold."

On the ride back, I couldn't help but realize that we'd talked about Brady as much as we'd talked about Ben on Ben's remembrance day. It only drove home the point that Ben's life had been cut short. All there was to talk about were memories. No discussion of what Ben would do after he graduated from college, or about his career, or whether the latest girl was the one he'd marry.

But with Brady, there were endless possibilities ahead for him. He was still alive, getting older, and making choices—good or bad.

Hey, I'm sorry about the other night, Brady texted after I'd gotten home that evening.

It's fine, I replied.

I shouldn't have tried to kiss you. Sorry.

Now, I didn't know how to feel. Did he regret trying to kiss me in general? Or just that he'd been drunk?

I was dying to ask, but I was too chicken to do it. Instead, I just told him that maybe we should meet in person soon to talk things over.

Brady called me a few seconds later. "I can't meet for a bit," he said by way of greeting.

"It doesn't have to be right this second."

"No, I mean, I'm going to Vegas." Then he sighed. "Shit, I didn't call you just to tell you this. I wanted to say that I know what day it is. I'm sure you have more important things right now."

My initial hurt at his texts abated. Brady was one of the few people who'd acknowledged Ben's death today. Even extended family tended to shy away from mentioning Ben. It drove me crazy, while Mom and Dad said that everyone meant well. They just didn't know what to say.

"Thank you," I said quietly. Now I wondered if I was going to, in fact, cry today. "I miss him a lot."

"I know you do."

I told him about how Mom and I went to see Ben's grave and then had ice cream. I tried to start a conversation about Ben and any memories Brady might have, but Brady changed the subject quickly.

"I do want to see you," he said, "but I'm going to Vegas to see my mom. I told you that she's sick."

"You said she's dying."

He sighed. "Did I? Fuck. I forgot. She's in the ICU, and shit's not looking good."

"I'm so sorry." And I meant it.

"You know, out of everyone who's said that to me, you're probably the one person who I believe means it." He let out a harsh laugh. "I'm expecting a call from my mom's doctor, so I have to go. But I'll text you when I get back in town."

I knew Brady had a lot of complicated feelings about his mom. Of course he did. But if his mom did die, how would he cope? Would he just push us further away like he had when Ben had died?

"Oh, Brady," I whispered to myself.

What made things worse was that my selfish, silly brain just wanted to know whether he still wanted to kiss me.

What would it be like if he kissed me? Would it be slow and gentle? Or would he kiss me until I couldn't remember my own name?

I buried my face in my pillow. I was such a mess of emotions right then. Sadness but excitement because Brady had wanted to kiss me.

So what if he'd been drunk? He'd wanted me. I'd never thought he would.

"It doesn't matter," I said to myself. "You know it doesn't matter."

I could tell myself that until I was blue in the face. But my heart still filled with hope.

What if I'd been wrong? What if Brady could fall for a girl like me after all?

Chapter 11

Brady

I shouldn't have been surprised to see Grace outside my door, waiting for me the following morning.

But I was. Because why would she get up so early just to see me off?

"I'm coming with you," she said without preamble.

She already had two coffee cups in her hands, and she handed me one. It was an Americano with a shot of cream—my usual order.

"No, you're not," I replied.

She just smiled that smile that went straight to my cock. It was a smile that said, *You can never say no to me.*

"You need moral support. Besides, it's a long drive to Las Vegas. I've done it a billion times, so I would know. And you and I both know you're shit at driving at night, especially if you're wanting to come home right after," she said.

"I wasn't planning on driving at night," I said, even though it was a lie.

My astigmatism made it harder to drive at night, but it wasn't impossible. I did it often. It'd really only been tricky when I'd first started driving as a teenager.

"Well, I know the best rest stops," Grace continued. She then reached out to touch my arm. "Come on. I know you want the company."

I did. The thought of going to see Mom in the hospital, to see her dying, to do that by myself . . . I hadn't wanted to think about it. But now, a wave of relief washed over me.

When I still hesitated, though, her eyes narrowed. That look couldn't mean anything good.

"My mom saw you carrying me inside their house on the security cams," she said.

She didn't need to elaborate. "Did your dad see it?" I asked.

Grace shook her head. "No, but I'm not above using that to get you to say yes to me coming with me."

Now I just laughed. "Dammit, Grace, you're insane. I also am too terrified of you to call your bluff. But if you come, no back-seat driving, okay?"

Grace grinned. "Deal. But I get to choose the music."

Luckily for us both, Grace had good taste. She started us off with seventies folk like the Mamas & the Papas and Fleetwood Mac. Neither of us was awake enough to talk much until after we'd finished our coffees, which was fine by me.

As we drove out of Los Angeles, I couldn't help but wonder what the fuck I'd been thinking, letting her come with me. If Coach Dallas found out we'd gone on an impromptu road trip together, he'd have my head.

"How's your mom?" Grace asked once we got out of the city, the Mojave Desert turning the landscape stark and bright.

I fumbled around for my sunglasses. Grace handed them to me with a raised eyebrow.

"Thanks," I said.

"Your mom?"

I shot her a glare. "You're annoying. You know that, right?"

She just smiled. "I know I am, but what are you?" She poked me in the arm. "Come on, Mr. Grumbly, tell me all your secrets."

I nearly choked. God Almighty, the last thing I was going to do was tell Grace my deepest, darkest secrets. She'd hate me for all eternity if I did.

"She's sick," I said, my tone flat. "I told you that."

"You said she's dying. Can she get a liver transplant?"

I snorted. "You have to stop drinking to get somebody's nice, shiny organ. And my mom isn't about to give up her favorite thing in the world."

Grace's expression turned somber. "That's awful. I can't imagine being so addicted to something that you'd choose death."

"Well, my mom isn't exactly thinking straight. She's convinced the doctors are wrong and she'll get better. Or she won't die, at least."

I stared out at the bright-blue sky of the horizon, not a cloud in sight. "And she's not wrong," I said slowly. "She has survived against all odds. Hell, I remember her doctor telling her ten years ago she had months to live if she didn't stop drinking. Yet she continues. It's amazing what shit you can put your body through."

"I wonder if she'd live much longer, even with a transplant," Grace said quietly.

"The rest of her body is a wreck, too. Pancreas, kidneys, stomach. She throws up blood all the time from stomach ulcers."

I realized I was probably horrifying Grace. I didn't need to unload all this onto her.

"I wish I could say something beyond 'I'm sorry,'" Grace said. She touched my arm and squeezed it. "But I hope you know that it's not your fault. Your mom makes her own choices."

I knew that. I knew that, yet . . . that small voice inside me still whispered that if I'd just tried a little harder, I could've saved her.

I shook myself. "This is getting fucking depressing. I need something to distract me."

Grace didn't argue. Her eyes brightened as she suggested the game Never Have I Ever, only because she knew she'd win because she was such a good girl.

"Never have I ever had a threesome," Grace said, holding up her hands and starting the game off with a bang. She looked over at me.

I sighed and put down a finger.

Her jaw dropped. "You slut! Brady Carmichael. How many times?"

I glanced at her. "I'm not telling you that. And you're a cheater, virgin."

Grace just giggled.

Now, it was my turn. "Never have I ever . . ." I thought a moment. "Eaten sushi."

"What? You live in LA! And that's so boring."

I shrugged. "It never appealed to me. Besides, I knew you loved it." I grinned.

"I need to take you to eat sushi ASAP. You're missing out." But Grace still put down a finger, her nose wrinkled.

We were tied by the time the game got near the end.

Grace didn't look at me when she said, "Never have I ever had drunk sex after Brady Carmichael took me home when I was smashed."

I froze. I should've known this was coming. It'd been my own damn fault, agreeing to this silly game.

"You were drunk," I said, my voice rough. "I wasn't going to take advantage of you."

"So you did want to sleep with me?" She sounded hopeful.

I groaned. "Grace . . ."

"I wanted you to kiss me." Her gaze was direct now, her cheeks flushed.

"Which time?"

"Either time. Both times. But you didn't. Why not? Are you just not attracted to me?"

I had to concentrate on the road. I couldn't stare at Grace, trying to understand what was going on in her innocent yet daring mind.

"Of course I'm attracted to you," I said, irritated. "How could you think otherwise?"

"Um, the not-wanting-to-kiss-me thing?"

"I do want to kiss you." I wanted to drive into the nearest ditch rather than have this conversation, but it seemed like I didn't have a choice. "I want to do way fucking more than kiss you. But it doesn't matter. Nothing can happen between us."

"But why? Brady, I've had a crush on you since we were kids."

I knew she'd liked me when we were kids, but I couldn't believe she hadn't gotten over it yet. I glanced at her, and I nearly drove us off the road.

She looked like a woman who desperately needed kissing. And fuck me, I wanted to be that man more than I wanted anything else.

"Just because we want each other doesn't mean we'd be good together," I said finally.

"And how do you know that? That we'll be bad for each other? Isn't that what you find out after dating for a while?"

She had a point. And like the weak man I was, I wanted to cave. But I reminded myself that if Grace knew the truth about me, she'd agree.

"You deserve better than a guy like me. And I'm not going to change my mind either. I'm sorry I've led you on lately. I'll do better."

Grace was silent. I watched out of the corner of my eye as she wiped away a tear.

God, I felt like the lowest of the low. I was scum, making this gorgeous woman cry.

But I didn't deserve her tears. I didn't deserve her desire, and I definitely didn't deserve her love, either.

I held on to the steering wheel so tightly that my fingers started cramping. I was glad when traffic started getting worse, and I was forced to pay attention to driving.

"I'm sorry," I said after we'd sat in silence for a while.

"I still don't get why you're sorry, but thanks, I guess." Grace shrugged. "If you don't want me, whatever the reason, I'm not going to force you. I respect your decision, even if I don't understand it."

So there it was. Anything that had been brewing between us was at an end.

I should be happy, but I could feel only despair.

"Is this where you tell me you'll always be my friend?" Grace asked, her tone sardonic.

I let out a startled laugh. "Sure, if you want."

"I don't know. Let me think about it."

We arrived in Las Vegas in the early afternoon. After getting some lunch, we headed to the hospital. Although I told Grace she didn't have to come with me to the hospital, she insisted.

"Unless you'd rather go alone," she said. "I realize I'm being kind of bossy when it's your mom we're talking about."

"You, bossy? Never." I grinned, then turned serious. "It's okay if you come. Just . . . keep your expectations low."

Mom was out of it when we arrived. Then again, it wasn't much different from how she usually was. But this time, it wasn't booze making her loopy. She was on such strong painkillers that it took her a second to recognize me.

"Baby," she crooned. She reached out a hand to touch my cheek.

I nearly flinched from her touch. She looked skeletal, and on top of that, she was so yellow from the jaundice that it was shocking. Her skin, the whites of her eyes. A sickly yellow color that I didn't think was possible in a human being.

"Is that the nurse?" she asked me, pointing at Grace.

"She's just a friend, Mom."

"It's nice to meet you." Grace held out a hand, but Mom didn't notice it. She was too busy staring up at me.

"My baby boy, I missed you so much. I didn't think you'd come. You never come to see me, your little old mom. I've waited so long to see you . . ."

I hated myself at that moment. "I'm sorry," I said.

Mom just smiled, but she was missing so many teeth that it made her look like she was ninety, not in her fifties.

"Could you do something for me?" Mom asked.

"Sure, I can."

She tried to whisper, but it came out more like a loud rasp. "Can you get me a bottle of something to take the edge off? I'm hurting something terrible."

I stilled. Grace looked away. Embarrassment flooded me.

"You're in the hospital," I said through gritted teeth.

"They're total Nazis here." Mom scowled. "They won't give me anything. You know alcohol withdrawal can kill you, right? But do they care? No, of course not."

I sighed. I'd spoken with Mom's doctor, and I knew that she was being weaned off alcohol slowly and was under medical supervision with her detox. But Mom didn't care. She just wanted to drink, as always.

Why had I ever thought she'd change? She would go to her grave clutching a bottle of vodka or a can of beer. It was the only constant she had in her life.

"The doctor says your vitals are looking better today," I said, trying to change the subject. "You might be able to leave sooner than they thought."

"They always say that, but then they keep you just to get all your money." Her gaze turned to Grace now. "These places just want money. And then when you die here, they sell your body parts for extra cash."

"Mom, they do not." I wanted to point out that her body parts and organs were pretty useless, anyway.

"Who do they sell them to?" Grace asked.

She didn't sound sarcastic, just mildly curious.

Mom's eyes widened. "To the Illuminati. Look them up. They're everywhere." Mom glanced at the ceiling and then the floor. "Sometimes I can see them from the corner of my eye."

Mom had always been out of it, but this was new. Was it the painkillers? Or just further deterioration from all the drinking?

"Well, Brady is good at keeping people safe," Grace said, her tone serious. "So he'll help you. Don't worry."

Mom's gaze turned back to me. "He's a good boy who loves his momma. And so talented. He gets that from my side of the family. Your dad and his family were useless pieces of shit, you know."

Mom then went down a long tangent about my dad, and my dad's parents, and then somehow we returned to the Illuminati, and aliens, and by the time Grace and I left, I felt a little drunk.

"Sorry about all that," I said to Grace as we got into my car.

She looked surprised. "Why are you apologizing? Like I said, your mom makes her own choices. Besides, I know she's sick. Sick people don't always say the most logical things."

I almost wished Grace would be judgmental. Then I could tell her to go to hell and end this years-long obsession with her.

Instead, she had to be empathetic, thoughtful, and selfless. *The universe loves its cruel jokes,* I thought morosely.

Dinner was an awkward affair. I was brooding over Mom, and Grace seemed like she didn't know what to say. I was glad when it was time to check in to our hotel rooms.

Separate hotel rooms, of course. I didn't trust myself

to behave if we shared a room or, God forbid, shared a bed for the night.

We could've made the drive back to LA, but we were exhausted. So I got us hotel rooms for the night, and we'd leave early in the morning.

I was getting ready for bed when I realized I didn't have toothpaste. I'd packed my toothbrush, of course.

I tapped on the adjoining door to Grace's room. "Grace? You awake?"

I heard her voice, then some rummaging, before she opened the door. She was flushed and wearing only a large T-shirt and booty shorts.

She was also out of breath like she'd been running. "You okay?" I asked.

That just made her blush harder. "Uh. Yeah. Sure. You okay?"

I inhaled, only to catch a scent I knew all too well. My body tightened.

Christ, had she been touching herself? With just a tiny little door between us?

I felt my entire body alight at the thought. We stared at each other, and I watched as her breathing increased along with my own.

Had she been close to coming when I knocked on the door? Or had she already come once and was going for her second or third?

I wondered how she liked to fuck herself. Did she prefer to concentrate on her clit, or did she like a combo of fingers and clit rubbing? The thought of touching her pussy, licking it, watching her body arch as her orgasm built . . .

Fuck, I was going to lose my goddamn mind.

"Toothpaste," I rasped finally.

It took her a second to register what I'd said. "Uh. Yeah, I have some."

She went to get the tube. When she handed it to me, though, I grabbed her by the wrist and pulled her hand toward me.

I inhaled. Her eyes widened.

I'd been right. I knew that smell anywhere. I let her hand go reluctantly.

"Lock the door on your side," I commanded. "Don't let me in, no matter what I say."

She blinked. Then she nodded and said good night before doing as I'd asked.

I collapsed onto my own bed and groaned. There was no fucking way I was going to get any sleep tonight.

Chapter 12

Grace

When I'd agreed to intern for the Blades PR and mar-keting department, I hadn't realized that I'd end up having to listen to why Brady Carmichael was terrible for the brand.

"How do we rein this guy in?" Julia, my boss and the PR manager, asked. She swiveled her laptop around to show us her social media feed. "Or better yet, how do we spin this to our advantage?"

In an unfortunate twist, the internet had turned Brady's fight with Riley into a meme that had spread like wildfire. I'd seen the memes splashed across the internet. Some were rather funny, but I couldn't admit that out loud.

What was worse, though, was that *The Fight* wasn't about to disappear anytime soon. It'd also fueled Brady's reputation as an asshole who didn't care about rules.

Which, normally, wouldn't be a negative. But there was a narrative going around that Brady was unhinged and had punched Riley just because he could.

Every day, I wanted to tell the world that Brady had

been defending me. But I also knew Brady wouldn't thank me for speaking up.

Not that I've even talked to Brady since Vegas. He was avoiding me. Why, I didn't know.

So much for his promises about not playing hot and cold anymore.

"Do we know why Brady punched Riley?" Garrett, my fellow PR intern, asked.

Julia shook her head. "No, but at this point, I'm not sure it'd matter. The narrative that Brady was the aggressor is out there. It's harder to undo something than get ahead of the narrative. Which I blame myself for."

"You had a bunch of other stuff going on then," Sara, Julia's assistant, pointed out sagely.

"So? That's not an excuse."

It hadn't helped that Julia had so many other projects, not to mention that the two other PR folks had been out on vacation. So it'd just been me and Garrett. As interns, we just followed directions.

And Julia had told us to bury the story instead of trying to fight it.

"We need to push new stories about Brady," said Julia, sighing. "What charities is he involved in? Make-A-Wish? The ASPCA? We need photo ops, interviews, whatever it takes. We need to show the world that he's a decent guy, even if it's a lie."

I bristled at that assertion. Brady was decent. He was kind and thoughtful, and although he could be impulsive, he meant well.

But I had to bite my tongue because I knew I'd reveal too much if I started defending Brady out of the blue. The last thing I needed was for my coworkers to think there was a conflict of interest with me being an intern.

"There's a new dance trend that we could have the guys do," offered Garrett. He pulled out his phone and began showing us examples.

Julia looked over at me. "Do you have anything, Grace?"

I knew that Julia wasn't a huge fan of allowing the coach's daughter to be an intern here. Since I'd joined the team, even temporarily, Julia hadn't given me much in the way of assignments. The few that I had done had been my idea to show that I was serious about this job.

But now, put on the spot, my brain stuttered to a halt.

"Uh, let me brainstorm," I said.

Julia looked annoyed. "Nothing? Okay, then."

Right then, I remembered a new trend I'd seen online just this morning.

"It's basically famous people doing those interviews with puppies or kittens. We could do that with Brady and maybe another teammate. Give them a bunch of cute baby animals that they can play with on camera," I said.

Julia thought for a moment. "Hmm, that might work. But we'd also have to find somebody to get us puppies."

"Or kittens," I added.

"Contact somebody at the humane society," Julia said to Garrett. "And we'll go from there."

Garrett shot me a wry look. Julia loved to pile on tasks for Garrett while ignoring me. At least this time, she seemed to like my idea.

After that, Julia created a master plan and gave us our individual tasks, even including me in some.

Fortunately—or unfortunately—I wasn't given anything that involved Brady.

As we got up to leave, Garrett leaned down to whisper in my ear, "I need to talk to you."

I blinked in surprise but nodded. We found an empty office. When Garrett kept looking around like he was afraid someone was listening, I felt a frisson of unease.

"I got a text today from a source about Brady," said Garrett. "Apparently he's going to the same sex club as Mac was caught going to."

"What? And how . . . ?"

Garrett grinned. "I have my ways."

"Have you told Julia yet?"

"No. I'm not sure I will. She'll just freak out." Garrett shrugged. "I appreciated that Mac came out and said in that interview with his girlfriend that it wasn't anybody's business what he did in his bedroom. So if Brady wants to get freaky on his downtime, who cares?"

I sat down heavily. "The public will care."

And I had to admit, *I* cared. The thought of Brady enjoying himself with other women like that made my stomach hurt. Mostly because I wished he would enjoy himself with me.

"Maybe, maybe not. But my source just had a sighting of Brady. No photo or video. So it might not have been him," said Garrett.

I sighed. "Why are you telling me all this?"

"Because you and Brady are friends, right?"

I hadn't realized anyone knew anything about us. "He's kind of part of my family, I guess you could say."

"So I thought you might want to know. Use the information as you will."

"And what if I decide to blast it all over the internet?"

Garrett snorted. "Yeah, right. You and I both know you won't."

I didn't know whether to be annoyed or amused. Garrett and I weren't exactly friends, but we were friendly. I hadn't realized he'd pegged me so easily.

After that conversation, though, I knew I needed to warn Brady. He needed to be careful. The world had its eye on him, and one more fuckup could ruin his career.

I texted Garrett before I could think about what I was doing. *Where's this club anyway?*

Garrett replied quickly with the address. *Dunno how you get in tho. Apparently you need a password.*

I wondered how Garrett's source had gotten in. The source must be a club member. I could only guess that this person didn't want to give out a password that could be linked back to them.

With the address in hand, I went to a nearby lingerie store to find something to wear. I'd heard enough about Mac's exploits to know that this club wasn't one where you just went inside wearing jeans and a T-shirt. I got changed before I left the store. I'm glad that I'd worn my trench coat to work today since it was always freezing in the air conditioning.

I picked out a bra and panty set that was red and lacy, something I'd never worn before. *What the hell am I doing?*

I was doing research. That was all. There was no other reason that I was trying to learn why Brady wanted to spend his time at a sex club instead of with me.

I drove to the address, but when I got there, I wondered whether I'd gotten the address wrong. On the corner was a nondescript office building that seemed to house a marketing company and not much else.

I parked my car and frowned. I sat and watched, pondering my next move, when I saw a few people go to an unmarked door and knock.

A large man answered. And then the couple were ushered inside, the door shutting quickly behind them.

I knew I couldn't hesitate. I went near the unmarked door and hid behind a dumpster, waiting for someone else to arrive.

I was about to give up when a lone man arrived.

"Password?" the door guy asked after the single guy knocked.

"Pineapple," the man said.

I waited until the lone guy went inside. Then, with my heart racing, I decided to try my luck.

When the door guy answered my knock, I didn't even wait for him to ask me for a password.

"Pineapple!" I squeaked.

The door guy narrowed his eyes at me. Then, to my utter astonishment, he let me inside.

I couldn't believe it. As another man escorted me down a long hallway, I half expected someone to jump from the shadows and demand why I was there.

And then I was inside the club: the Scarlet Rope.

The difference between the hallway and the club itself was stark. The club was dimly lit, but as luxurious as the rest of the building was nondescript. The foyer had a chandelier straight out of a fairy tale. There were velvet settees and couches scattered about.

And there were all kinds of people, some dressed in next to nothing, while others were in suits or slinky gowns. Many patrons wore masks. When I came inside still wearing my trench coat, I felt strangely exposed.

"Your coat, madam," a man said to me.

I blinked. Then, with shaking hands, I handed him my coat, clad only in the red lingerie I'd just purchased.

Nobody seemed concerned about my near nudity. I caught a few people—men and women both—shooting me appreciative glances, but that was it.

I was grateful for how warm the club was. It'd have to be, given how scantily dressed everyone was.

I took a deep breath. I'd come this far. I couldn't lose my nerve now.

I considered getting a drink but then thought better of it. I wanted to keep my wits about me. I had no idea what really went down in this place and needed to be careful.

"I've never seen you around before," a woman remarked.

She was wearing a thong and nothing else. Her breasts were large, the areolas sparkling in the low light. I realized that she'd put glitter all over her torso.

"Um, it's my first night," I stammered.

The woman smiled, her teeth flashing. "Oh, I can tell a virgin when I see one."

I flushed. She could tell that just by looking at me? But then I realized she just meant I was a virgin for coming to the club.

"A word of advice," the woman said. "Be choosy. You don't have to say yes to the first person who talks to you. I didn't let anyone touch me during my first three visits. Scope things out. Take your time. There's no rush."

I thanked her for her advice, not wanting to admit that I had zero intention of letting anybody touch me.

I didn't even know where I'd start, for one. How did I just go up to a person and ask them to have sex with me? The mere thought almost made me laugh out loud.

I was a good girl. I didn't have sex with strangers. Hell, I didn't have sex at all! I was still a virgin at the ripe age of twenty-two. I hadn't even wanted to sleep with Will, my ex-boyfriend.

You know why you've been saving yourself. But I pushed that thought aside. Brady had already told me in no uncertain terms that nothing could ever happen between us.

I was soon arrested by everything happening around me. The Scarlet Rope was unlike anything I could've imagined. I thought it was maybe some sleazy basement dungeon, but it was . . . classy.

The nudity, the sex, the air of mystery and desire. It all gathered together to create this aura that I found fascinating, even if I wasn't brave enough to embrace it for myself.

As I passed through one of the main hallways, I was able to watch some of the scenes that anyone in the club could also view. The scenes ranged from straightforward, penis-in-vagina sex to BDSM to orgies to roleplay.

One scene had six participants, three men and three women. The women seemed to be the Dommes in this scenario. They each were equipped with whips that they used liberally on their subs. The men were on their knees, begging for more, the dominatrices giving their subs catlike smiles.

One Domme yanked on her sub's hair so hard that it wrenched his head back.

I couldn't quite make out what anyone was saying, but it didn't really matter. You could see what they wanted on their faces and the way they moved their bodies.

Another Domme pushed her sub forward into her pussy. He began lapping at her as her head went back in ecstasy.

I blushed to the roots of my hair. I was probably as red as the lingerie I'd impulsively bought.

I kept wandering. The next scene was two men. One man was bent over the arm of a plush couch, while his partner pounded into him. The sounds of the slaps of flesh against flesh made the hair on the back of my neck stand.

It was mesmerizing. I'd never seen people so un-abashed in their sexuality. It made me wonder how they could become so open about something I was still trying to understand about myself.

I also wondered whether Brady was the type to be a part of these scenes. Did he like when others watched him? Or did he prefer his exploits to remain private?

The green-eyed snake of jealousy bit into my heart. I hated the thought of Brady being with other women even though he wasn't mine. I had no right to expect him to ab-stain.

But it hurt all the same. Because those women got a side of him he'd told me I would never, ever see.

I kept walking. A few men complimented my lingerie, one even going so far as to suggest we find somewhere pri-vate. I stumbled through the interaction, but the man was kind when I said no.

He handed me a card and said, "If you change your mind." He winked and kept walking.

I stared at the card, tried to put it in my purse, and then realized I didn't have it with me. And I didn't exactly have any pockets, either. I stuffed it into my bra as a last resort.

When I got to a room with a masked man whipping a woman, I was immediately enthralled. It helped that the man was ripped. From his shoulders to his stomach to his legs, he clearly worked out.

He also seemed to know what he was doing. The woman, who was face down on the bed, wiggled and moaned with each lash of the whip.

He reminds me of Brady, I thought to myself.

Looking at him more closely, I realized it *was* Brady. I'd recognize him anywhere. Even wearing a mask, I knew it was him.

I couldn't move. I didn't know how to feel about the scene before me. I was enthralled, sure, but I was also jealous. Hurt. Amazed. Confused.

Brady kept whipping the woman, harder and harder, until red welts rose on her back. I swallowed hard. I had no idea he enjoyed that kind of sex.

Brady walked around the woman and flipped her over before tying her up. He said something to her and then went toward where I was standing.

I almost bolted. But he couldn't see through the two-way mirror, right?

But when his gaze landed on me, he stopped in his tracks. We stared at each other for the longest moment of my life.

"Grace?" he mouthed.

So much for two-way mirrors, I thought before Brady stalked from the room.

Chapter 13

Brady

When I grabbed Grace's arm, I half expected her to disappear like a ghost. But no, she was as real as I was.

And wearing basically nothing.

"What the fuck are you doing here?" I demanded.

Grace had the gall to scowl at me. "I have just as much a right to be here as you do."

She did, and I fucking hated it. Had she been looking for some guy to sleep with? To give her virginity to?

Christ, the thought of another man—or woman—touching her sent me into a jealous, raging tailspin.

It didn't help that I'd never seen her dressed like this. Her lingerie left very little to the imagination. The lace barely covered her nipples, for God's sake.

Underneath her usually conservative clothes was a banging body: curvy and lithe. Her breasts were small but pert. I wondered how they'd feel in my hands.

Worst of all was the pair of panties that were almost a thong on her. Her tight little ass was just right there for everyone to admire.

I wanted to throw a blanket over her and run out the door. Nobody should be able to see Grace like this.

Nobody but you? my traitorous brain asked.

"What are you doing here?" I asked again, my jaw clenched.

"I could ask you the same question."

I knew that we were drawing a nice little audience, but I didn't give a fuck. Most of all, I wanted to understand why Grace was here at all.

I grabbed her arm again, but she pushed me away. A guy in a blue mask stepped up.

"Is there a problem here?" he asked Grace.

I gritted my teeth, forcing myself not to deck the guy for interfering.

Grace raised her chin. "Everything's fine. My friend here was just going to buy me a drink." Her gaze slid to mine. "Weren't you?"

I scowled but finally nodded. The last thing I needed was to get thrown out of the club for fighting.

Grace shot the blue-mask guy a smile that only pissed me off more. I needed to calm down.

Grace was an adult. If she wanted to enjoy herself at the Scarlet Rope, what right did I have to stop her?

When we reached the bar and had ordered drinks, I led Grace to a semiprivate booth in the corner. We sat down and stared at each other, waiting for the other to say something.

Then Grace burst out laughing. "You look like you're about to have a stroke. Or that you're just super constipated."

I wasn't going to laugh. This was a serious matter. But hearing Grace's laughter melted away my anger, damn her.

"I think I'd prefer a stroke," I said wryly. "At least then you'd feel sorry for me."

She grinned. "I'd never feel sorry for a big, strong man like you. You don't need my pity."

"No, but I do need you to explain why you're here."

When she just pouted, I sighed. Christ, I was putty in her hands, wasn't I?

"Mac invited me," I said. "He told me this was a good way to distract myself."

"And did it work?"

"Kind of."

"You seemed very . . . interested in what you were doing back there."

Although it was dim, I could see a blush creeping up Grace's cheeks. How much had she seen? Had she watched me whip Shayla?

And if she had, had she enjoyed watching it?

"I mean, you can sleep with whoever you want," Grace was saying.

"I haven't slept with anyone from here."

Grace blinked. "Seriously?"

I felt embarrassed for some reason. So much for my playboy reputation. "I just came here to . . ." *Whip a woman who looked like you to make myself feel better?*

Yeah, like I could say that to Grace.

"I want to experiment some with BDSM. Mac loves it. I wondered if I would," I said.

"Did you? Like it?"

"Some of it, but I don't think super-kinky shit will ever be my bag."

"Huh. There's a limit to Brady's interest in sex. I'm shocked."

I glowered at Grace. "What, did you think I had a basement full of whips and chains?"

"Well, seeing your apartment, you clearly don't have a basement."

I laughed. Then I forced myself to be serious again. "Why did you come here? Because we both know you aren't kinky either."

"I mean, how would I know since I've never had sex?" At my look, Grace sighed. "Okay, fine. I was looking for you. Somebody told me that you'd been seen here, and I wanted to see it for myself."

She'd come here for me? "Why would you want to confirm that for yourself?"

"I guess I wanted to understand you better. Besides, 'curiosity killed the cat' and all that."

I groaned. "Grace, you can't take risks like this—"

"What, and you can?"

I didn't have an answer to that. But in my mind, yes, Grace shouldn't take risks like I would.

She was different. She was innocent. What if someone had taken advantage of her? Just because this place had rules didn't mean bad shit never happened.

"What do you want with a *sex club*?" I waved a hand. "You're a virgin."

Grace made a face. "And whose fault is that? You're the one who keeps saying no. Maybe I wanted to find somebody who'd take me up on that offer."

I gaped at her. Was she serious? I couldn't tell. Or was she just doing this to get under my skin?

"Promise me you won't come here again," I said.

"You don't get to tell me what to do."

"I do when I know you don't know what you're getting yourself into. And if anything happened to you and your dad found out I didn't stop you, he'd kill me himself."

That seemed to make her pause. "I'm not a child," she said.

No, she wasn't. She was a woman with an amazing

body and endless sex appeal. She was a woman who made men turn their heads for a second look.

She was a woman, and if she wanted to have orgies for all to see here, what right did I have to stop her?

"I just want you to be safe," I said, knowing I was losing this battle.

"That's fine. But again, if I want to have fun, I'm going to have fun."

My fists were clenched under the table. I took a long drink of my beer, needing the alcohol to cool my thoughts.

"I don't want to see you here again," I growled.

Grace laughed. Laughed! "Sure. You'll never see me here again."

"I don't get why you're laughing about this. It's not funny to me."

Now she looked a little ashamed. She took my hand and squeezed it. "I know you're just trying to protect me. I get it. But that's not your job. You're not my big brother or my dad."

I stilled. Although I knew she was trying to console me, I couldn't help but feel hurt by her words.

Not that I wanted her to see me as a brother. But I also hated that she didn't see me as important a person as Ben had been. Or that my concern didn't weigh on her like her dad's would.

"I don't think coming to a place like this just because you're curious is a good idea," I said.

Grace frowned. "Um, isn't that why you came? Curiosity?"

"I knew I'd probably—do stuff," I said weakly.

"Mmm, 'do stuff.' What kind of stuff? Although I already got a good preview. Whips and all. What else have you tried? Chains? Hanging girls from the ceiling? Butt stuff?"

I barely restrained myself from covering her mouth. "Can you not?" I hissed.

She giggled. "We're in a sex club. It's okay to talk about sex."

"And that's something you know nothing about."

"And once again, whose fault is that?"

I growled under my breath. "It's not my fault, and you know it. You could sleep with whatever guy you want. What about Will? He wanted to fuck you."

"You want me to sleep with other guys?" Grace looked hurt and confused.

I raked my hands through my hair. "No. But I'm not going to do it either. I've already told you this."

"Yet you and I both know you want me, and I want you. We're adults. We aren't in relationships already. What's the hang-up? Or have you suddenly taken a vow of celibacy, minus the whole whipping thing?"

I didn't know how to answer that. How did I convince Grace she should stay away from me, the club, and everything that could hurt her?

"Promise me that you won't keep coming here. You could end up getting hurt," I said.

"You're being dramatic."

"Am I? You don't know what the guys in here are thinking, seeing you. They see a woman who's open to kinky shit. What if you get persuaded to do things you don't want to do? Or you end up seduced and dumped? Or even physically hurt? People don't fuck around here. This isn't Disneyland."

Grace folded her arms, but I could tell my words were having an effect.

"You must think I'm stupid. Or just overly naive," she said finally.

"You are naive. That's not a bad thing, either. You're lucky that you're innocent about a lot of things."

Grace was silent for a long moment. Then she sighed.

"I can't promise you anything other than I know I'll be careful. So trust me on that, okay?"

It wasn't that I didn't trust Grace. I just didn't trust everyone around her. Right then, it took every ounce of self-control not to throw her over my shoulder and take her home, her protests be damned.

Mac nearly dropped the beer he was drinking. "Grace was at the club? Grace Dallas?"

I nodded. "Yeah, she snuck in. She almost gave me a fucking heart attack when I saw her."

Mac gaped at me. "Holy shit. What did you say?"

It'd been two days since that eventful night at the Scarlet Rope. Grace had bounded away after our little talk, and despite my best efforts, she'd disappeared into the club. I'd texted her after I'd left, but she'd assured me she was fine.

I'd needed to talk to Mac about this situation. He'd invited me over to his place for some barbecue and beers. Mac's fiancée, Elodie, was at the grocery store picking up a few things.

"Was this my fault?" I asked.

"Your fault? How?"

"I led her down this path. I mean, she went to the club to look for me."

"Grace is an adult who makes her own choices. If she wanted to go exploring, that's on her."

I knew that. Everyone kept saying that, but it didn't make me feel any better.

It just made me feel powerless. It made the gulf widening between us even bigger. Because when we'd been younger, at least I could tell myself I'd been protecting her by sticking close.

Now, though, she didn't need me to act like a big brother. It seemed Grace Dallas could handle herself.

"You know if Coach finds out about this, he'll still blame me," I said darkly.

"Because Coach also can't see that his daughter is grown. But once again, that's not your fault. It's also not your job to make sure the Dallas family is happy."

I was about to tell Mac how wrong he was when Elodie came home. Mac got up to help her with the groceries, and then they were kissing and being disgustingly happy right in front of me.

"Look what I got you." Elodie pulled out a bag of sour-cream-and-onion chips.

Mac's eyes lit up. "Baby! My favorite." He immediately opened the bag and tossed a few chips into his mouth.

I rolled my eyes. "You guys are pure cheese."

Neither Mac nor Elodie was offended. They just laughed.

"Believe me, man, the day your lady brings home your favorite bag of chips, you'll be as happy as I am," Mac quipped.

"We are having a barbecue, after all," said Elodie. "Chips kinda come with the territory."

We helped Elodie prepare a few of the sides for the barbecue. I was mixing a bowl of coleslaw when Mac said, "Brady was telling me he saw Grace Dallas at the club a few days ago."

Elodie's eyes bugged out. "What? Grace? Are you sure it was her?"

"Unless I was hallucinating, yeah, it was her," I groused.

"What in the world . . ." Then she poked Mac hard in the chest. He protested loudly as she said, "This is your fault!"

"My fault? I didn't give Grace a password!"

"You told Brady, and everybody knows Grace is obsessed with Bra—" Elodie made a face and immediately stopped talking.

I froze. "Keep going," I said.

Mac shot me a look. "Elodie just meant that Grace seems to follow you around a lot. That's all."

Elodie snorted.

"So? What are your thoughts on this whole thing?" I asked Elodie.

Elodie shrugged. "Grace is exploring her sexuality? Sounds like a great idea to me. Sure, the club is overwhelming at first, but it also has a lot of guardrails to keep things from going crazy."

"Grace doesn't know what she's getting herself into. Besides, she told me she only went to see what I was doing there." I said the words in triumph.

Elodie glanced over at Mac. "Well, if that's the case, then maybe not. Maybe she is just obsessed with you," said Elodie.

"She can't be obsessed with me because nothing can happen between us," I said.

"So you *want* something to happen?" Elodie raised an eyebrow.

Mac just shrugged and kept stirring his bowl of salad. I sighed. "Maybe," I admitted. "Yes. Okay? I'm attracted to Grace. But that's as far as it can go."

"I mean, you're both adults. You're both single, as far as I know," said Elodie. "So why can't you guys be together? Are you promised to some long-lost betrothed?"

Mac shook his head. "More like Grace is being locked in a tower by her dad."

Elodie pointed a large serving fork at me. "Well, whatever is happening, you need to figure your shit out. If you have feelings for Grace, don't be a big baby and keep them to yourself. I know you guys think having no feelings is manly, but it's dumb."

I held up my hands. "Geez, Elodie, you're scary."

Elodie made shooing motions to get us out of her kitchen. Mac gave her a big smacking kiss and a nice tap on the ass before we returned to the living room.

"She's right, you know," said Mac as we sat back down.

I groaned. "God, not you, too."

"You've been hung up on Grace for ages. I know you're convinced nothing can happen, but what if you could be honest with Grace? Tell her how you feel?"

I glowered at Mac. "Now you're turning this into some Lifetime movie."

"So you're going to kidnap Grace and lock her in your cabin?" Mac laughed. "Sorry, Elodie loves Lifetime movies. At any rate, maybe all you can do is hope that Grace stays home and doesn't go to the club a second time."

A man could dream. But knowing Grace, she'd go a second time just to show me that she could do what she wanted, consequences be damned. I should never have tried to order her around.

Maybe I should've acted like seeing her there was no big deal. But I'd nearly lost my mind when I'd first spotted her through that glass. And then all those guys, looking at her, trying to get her attention, coming over to possibly touch her . . .

"Grace isn't the type to be into a sex club," I said.

"Elodie would've said the same thing, but she came around to the idea quickly. We've had a lot of fun since. Although, to be fair, we haven't been to the club in a while. We keep ourselves busy at home." Mac shot me a grin.

"You two are insufferable."

Mac didn't disagree. He just smiled, his thoughts far away now.

Even if my friends were right, I couldn't give in to temptation. There was too much at stake. Because I could live with keeping Grace at arm's length.

I could live with just being her friend. I couldn't live with the thought of her despising me, though.

Maybe she'll come back again. And I'll be ready for her this time.

Chapter 14

Brady
Eight Years Ago

I looked at my watch. I had fifteen minutes before it was officially the afternoon.

Fifteen minutes until I needed to tutor Grace in math. But when I'd agreed to tutor her, I hadn't specified a time.

So maybe I had an hour. Maybe even three. What did "afternoon" mean, anyway? When did afternoon end and evening begin?

Or I could suck it up, tutor her for a half hour, and go back to my room. Nobody had said I needed to tutor her for very long.

I could do this. I could tutor her. It wasn't a big deal. I'd done it before, right?

But that had been *before*. Before I'd started seeing Grace as a girl instead of as a sister.

When I'd first been welcomed into the Dallases' home, Grace had been an annoying little sister who liked to follow me and Ben around.

That type of thing I was used to. I'd been in enough foster homes with other kids, a lot of them younger than me. In my last home, their daughter had been a toddler. My foster parents would often have me babysit—for free, of course.

But Grace had started looking more like a woman lately. The first time I'd noticed, it'd taken every bit of ingenuity to get upstairs without anyone noticing my boner. It'd been humiliating.

Grace had come downstairs wearing tiny soccer shorts and a tank top. She also hadn't been wearing a bra. And in the past few months, she'd been developing quickly.

She sat down next to me in the living room, and my gaze zeroed in on her nipples poking through her shirt.

"Why are you looking at me like that?" She gave me a confused smile.

I could feel Ben glaring at me. I grabbed a nearby pillow to cover my crotch.

"I'm not looking at you," I replied, defensive.

"Yeah, you were," said Grace.

"Why would I look at you? You're just a baby. I don't care about babies."

Grace looked hurt. She got up and went to a chair opposite, her expression like I'd kicked her.

"You're a jerk, Brady," she said as she wiped her nose.

My boner had gotten worse when she'd gotten up. She was so . . . bouncy. How had I never noticed that before?

I waited a few more minutes and dashed upstairs to my room, locking the door behind me.

Then there was another instance when we'd all gone to the local swimming pool. Grace had worn a two-piece for the first time, at least that I'd been aware of.

"Dad know you're wearing that?" Ben had asked his sister.

Grace raised her chin. "No, and who's going to tell him? You?"

"Uh, I might."

"Then I'll tell him I saw you making out with Carrie last Sunday. And you had your door closed when you know you're supposed to keep it cracked."

Ben glowered. "You little shit."

Grace just stuck out her tongue and jumped into the pool.

Ben turned to me. "You're so lucky you don't have a sister. They're the worst."

I barely heard him. I was focused on Grace standing near the shallow end, water sluicing down her body, her bikini barely covering her—

And then, last weekend, Grace's parents had been out of the house to attend one of Ben's hockey games. It meant that Grace and I were alone. Usually, that wouldn't have been a big deal, at least before I'd started noticing her. I usually did my thing, and she did hers.

A lot of the time I was playing hockey anyway. Hockey was also a good way to avoid being around Grace. I didn't need to keep feeling these weird feelings anytime she came around.

But today? Today, it'd been too hot to go outside, so I'd been stuck inside without much to do, so I'd been going between watching TV and messing around online to pass the time.

It was near dinnertime when I called up the stairs to Grace. "Do you want me to order pizza?" I yelled.

After a few seconds, Grace yelled back, "Okay!"

Mr. and Mrs. Dallas often left us some cash to get food when they were gone. The first time they'd done it, I'd been shocked that they'd trust their kids with money like that.

None of my previous foster parents would've let me get within ten feet of their money. More than one kept their wallets, purses, and other valuables in safes or behind locked doors.

I hadn't blamed them. Too many kids like me were prone to steal. Hell, I'd stolen shit when I'd had no other choice. When you're hungry, you'll do whatever it takes to fill your empty belly.

"This is for food," Mr. Dallas had said as he placed a crisp twenty on the kitchen table. "And I know how much a pizza costs, too."

Grace had just rolled her eyes at her dad. I'd been too astonished to say anything at all.

But I'd gotten used to this setup now. It wasn't strange for me to call the pizza place, or to make sure I was around to answer the door when it arrived. I paid the pizza guy, a kid I recognized from my high school, and then called up to Grace a second time.

I was getting plates and cups when Grace walked into the kitchen. I nearly dropped what I was holding when I saw her.

At fourteen, Grace had started looking less like a kid and more like a young woman. Even though I'd hated noticing such a thing about her, I'd noticed.

But Grace usually wore pretty boring clothes. She wasn't the type of girl to doll herself up.

Until tonight. Wearing shorts that should be criminal along with a tube top, she looked like my worst nightmare.

Because it reminded me that she was trouble incarnate.

I stared at her, and I watched as a blush grew on her cheeks. She wouldn't meet my gaze as she took the plates from my hands.

"I'm starving," she said, as casual as you please.

When she turned around, I couldn't help but notice her butt was almost hanging out of her shorts. There was no way in hell her parents would be okay with this outfit.

I decided to act like I hadn't noticed her new skimpy clothes. I grabbed a soda and went to the living room.

Grace followed me, damn her.

"I'm gonna watch *The Terminator*," I said, only because I knew she hated action movies.

"Okay." Then she sat down next to me on the couch. So close that our legs were almost brushing.

"Do you want to watch *The Terminator*?" I asked, annoyed now.

Grace shrugged. "I've never seen it. So why not?"

I groaned inwardly. I turned on the movie, ignoring Grace, but she didn't seem deterred.

In fact, I nearly jumped out of my skin when her hand touched my leg.

My body reacted, even though I hated myself for it. I could smell her body wash on her skin and feel her warmth. I wondered what she would do if I kissed her.

I got up and sat on the large recliner in the corner. Grace's expression fell.

"It's too hot," I said weakly.

It took another few minutes before Grace got up and went back to her room with tears in her eyes.

Since that whole thing had happened, I'd been avoiding Grace. When she'd reminded me earlier this morning about tutoring her, I'd tried to get out of it. But her mom had overheard and had thanked me for helping Grace.

I stared at my watch. Maybe Grace would forget about the tutoring. Or maybe she'd catch the hint that I wanted nothing to do with her.

Yeah, fucking right. You can't stop thinking about her.

I needed to do something drastic to get Grace away from me. Ignoring her wasn't working, clearly.

An hour later, I opened the front door and let Samantha inside. Samantha was in my grade, and one of the prettiest girls in our high school. She also loved to wear tight, revealing clothing, and today she was showing off her cleavage.

"Thanks for inviting me over," Samantha said, trying to seem coy.

I heard footsteps behind me. I knew it was Grace.

I took Samantha by the arm and led her upstairs, passing by Grace without a word. But I could feel Grace's gaze on me like a laser beam. I could feel how pissed she was at me.

Right before we reached the top of the stairs, Grace called out, "What about tutoring me?"

Samantha giggled. She looked over the railing down at Grace. "Seriously? It's Saturday."

I also looked over the railing. "Yeah, it's Saturday," I drawled. "Go play with your dolls or something."

That made Samantha laugh again. Grace's expression turned indignant as Samantha and I kept walking upstairs.

Good, get pissed at me, I thought. *I'm not good enough for you. Just leave me alone and find somebody better.*

I knew I was playing a dangerous game here. I also knew that Mr. and Mrs. Dallas would be pissed at me for bringing a girl over without their permission.

Even then, I didn't care. All I cared about was getting Grace to stop whatever this was.

It was better for her in the long run anyway.

It was a close call getting Samantha out of the house before Mr. and Mrs. Dallas returned. When I heard their SUV pull up in the driveway, Samantha and I were making out in my bed.

I stilled, listening. Samantha tried kissing me again, but I made her stop. She pouted.

"What is it?" she asked.

"Shit. You need to leave."

I jumped out of bed and went to the window. Although we were on the second floor, there was a trellis that I'd used before to get in and out of the house undetected.

"What? You're kicking me out?" Samantha sounded outraged.

"I'm not supposed to have girls over."

"You said it was okay!"

I grimaced. "I lied. Now get going unless you want to get us both into trouble."

Samantha had gotten suspended from school more than once this year, so I knew she didn't want to get in trouble again. She made a face and started to descend from the window.

"Go around the back when I tell you," I hissed at her.

I couldn't see her expression, but I would have bet anything she was rolling her eyes at me.

I heard the front door open and close. I signaled to Samantha to run. To my relief, she didn't protest.

I waited, listening. Then I let out a sigh of relief when it seemed like I'd gotten out of this scot-free.

Well, except for Grace. She knew about Samantha, and she knew it wasn't allowed. I scowled. Would she rat me out?

I didn't have time to tell her to keep her mouth shut before Mr. and Mrs. Dallas were coming upstairs.

I waited in anticipation for Grace to say something, but before I knew it, her parents were shutting their bedroom door to go to sleep.

I lay in bed and tried to sleep. Guilt gnawed at me. Samantha and I hadn't really done anything, but even then, I hated the thought of disappointing Mr. and Mrs. Dallas.

They were the first family who seemed like they gave a shit about me. Which meant that I gave a shit about them.

Who says they'll keep caring about you once you turn eighteen?

It was a sobering reminder of how often foster kids were kicked out and forgotten once they reached eighteen. I needed to remember that the Dallases weren't my family, not really.

I must've fallen asleep because the next moment I heard footsteps. I sat upright in bed, my heart pounding, only to see Grace standing over me.

"Jesus Christ," I growled, "you scared me."

The full moon through my window was enough illumination to see Grace grin. "Serves you right," she shot back.

I waited for her to explain why she was in my room. It was then I realized I was wearing only my boxers and nothing else. I grabbed a pillow and covered my crotch, embarrassed.

"What are you doing in here?" I hissed.

To my surprise—and dismay—Grace sat down on my bed. "Who was the girl?"

I groaned. "Grace, what the hell—"

"Tell me, or I'm going to go wake up my parents and tell them what you did."

"Tattletale."

Grace crossed her arms, waiting. "Is she your girl-friend?"

Samantha? Hell no. "She's just a friend." I sounded defensive now.

"Did you have sex with her?"

I nearly choked on my own saliva. I coughed into my fist, hoping I wasn't so loud as to wake anybody else up.

I was shaking my head and saying, "What is wrong with you?"

"Hey, I just wanted to know the details." Grace smoothed a hand over my comforter. "Well, did you?"

"No. Jesus."

She seemed mollified by my answer, at least. But she didn't seem in a rush to leave either.

She was picking at a string on my comforter when she said, "You said before that I could come to you if I had a problem. Right?"

I was wary as I replied, "Sure."

She took a deep breath like she was preparing herself. "What's sex like?" she finally blurted.

I gaped at her. And then my body reacted because my brain was instantly filled with images of kissing Grace, touching Grace, taking Grace's clothes off—

"I'm not answering that question," I growled.

She looked surprised. "Why not? I want to know if it's as good as everyone says it is. At least what boys say. Girls don't seem like they like it as much. Why is that?"

I'd had sex before, but not as much as Grace had imagined. Not a lot of girls wanted to sleep with a foster kid like me, especially in this town full of rich kids.

Grace was fourteen, though. Too young to think about having sex.

You were having sex at fourteen, I reminded myself.

"I'm not talking to you about sex," I said.

"I can't go to anyone else in my family. My parents would freak out, and Ben is my brother—"

"I'm your brother."

That made Grace look away. "Not really," she mumbled.

I didn't know how to respond to that. Then, as if from a dream, Grace touched my leg like she had on the couch.

I realized she was doing this to get my attention. Was she just fucking with me? Or did she really like me?

"You need to leave," I said, my tone harsh. "And don't come at me with that *you're going to tell on me.* Do it if you want. I've gotten in trouble before, and I can deal if it happens again."

Grace was silent. "Why don't you like me anymore?" Her voice was small now.

I hated myself at that moment. But even at sixteen, I knew that Grace wasn't the girl for me.

"Nothing will ever happen between us," I said. "So get over it already."

Her shoulders sagged. I pulled at the thread she'd been playing with until it snapped.

"You're a jerk." Then she left—finally.

I locked my door a moment later. But I couldn't get back into bed. Not when it reminded me that Grace had been sitting next to me only minutes before.

Grace was young for her age. She'd get over me eventually. She only had a crush on me because I was close by.

She probably thought I was some charity case she needed to make over. And who the fuck needed that? I didn't need Grace. I didn't need the Dallases, either.

I'd taken care of myself since I was a kid. I needed to remind myself that they could kick me out and hand me over to another family whenever they wanted. There was no guarantee I'd still be here when I turned eighteen.

The only person you can rely on is yourself.

Chapter 15

Grace
Present Day

I couldn't stop thinking about the Scarlet Rope. More specifically, I couldn't stop thinking about Brady enjoying himself there. Because that meant there was a part of him I didn't know about, a part of him that I was now desperate to understand.

It was a Saturday evening, a week after the first time I'd gone to the club. My parents were at dinner tonight, so there wouldn't be any awkward explanations if I left for a few hours.

And I really, really wanted to understand why Brady had decided to join the club. He'd said he wasn't into BDSM like Mac was, but I'd seen Brady with a whip in his hand. Had he just not wanted to be honest with me? Was he embarrassed about this newfound fetish?

I didn't let myself think too hard. I got in my car and drove over to the club, arriving a little after 6:00 p.m. I hoped that it was early enough that there wouldn't be a lot of people inside yet.

I also hadn't worn anything scandalous this round. Would they even let me inside, wearing just jeans and a boring black blouse?

The man at the door gave me a look that told me that I wasn't in the right place at all. "A&B Marketing is on the second floor," he said, turning away.

"I'm not here for a meeting," I stammered. "Um, I have a password."

The bouncer looked me up and down. "Well?"

"Pineapple."

He just gave me an annoyed look. "Incorrect. Have a nice evening, ma'am."

"No, no, wait!" I stopped myself from grabbing the guy's arm. "I know Brady Carmichael. And Mac Mackenzie. The Blades hockey players."

The man rolled his eyes. Seeing I was serious, he said, "Prove it."

I fumbled for my phone, glad I'd taken a selfie with Brady a few weeks ago to send to Kelly. I showed it to the bouncer, then showed him a few of Brady's texts to me. I also showed him that I knew the Blades coach, although I didn't feel inclined to mention the coach was also my dad.

"Do you believe me now?" I asked, a little frustrated.

The bouncer gave me one last look and then let me inside. "Ask for Serena," he said as I walked past him.

I let out the breath I'd been holding as I made my way to the club's entrance. The bouncer must've messaged someone inside because before I knew it, I was being ushered into a back office and told that Serena would arrive shortly.

I had no idea who this Serena person was. Was she the owner? Or was she going to call the cops on me and have me thrown out?

When a gorgeous woman entered the office wearing a pencil skirt and blazer, I was extra confused.

She looks like an accountant. Albeit a sexy one.

"Ms. Dallas," Serena said, her voice smooth as honey. She held out her hand. "Lovely to meet you."

"You know my name?"

Serena sat down across from me and opened her laptop. "We make it a point to know who everyone is that comes through our doors. Now, I hear that you know a few of our esteemed patrons. Although we appreciate referrals and new membership trials, please know that to enjoy everything we have to offer, you'll have to eventually join and pay a membership fee."

"Oh. That makes sense."

Serena typed something and then glanced at me. "What brought you to our club? Anything in particular?"

I felt a little like I was at a store and being asked if I needed help picking out curtains. "Uh, I'm not sure. I'm just exploring my options."

"Of course." Serena typed for a moment. "At the Scarlet Rope, we pride ourselves on offering a variety of kinks and fetishes for our members to enjoy. Truly nothing is off-limits, as long as everyone consents beforehand."

Her expression turned serious. "We have a zero-tolerance policy here. Anyone caught harassing or disregarding another member's boundaries will be placed on probation and thoroughly investigated. If the member is found to be in violation, they will be removed and banned from the club entirely."

I was impressed—and intimidated.

Serena brought out some paperwork and explained more about how the club worked and how much it would be to join. It also involved signing an NDA that she assured me was backed up by some pretty powerful attorneys.

"You guys don't mess around," I said jokingly.

Serena's smile was catlike. "Indeed."

After some more discussion, I decided to sign up for a thirty-day membership at a discounted rate. Serena assured me that if I decided the club wasn't the right fit for me, there would be no hard feelings.

In all honesty, I wasn't even sure I really wanted to enjoy the club as a real patron. I just wanted to understand why Brady liked this place.

After I signed what felt like a hundred documents, Serena shook my hand again and said, "Welcome to the Scarlet Rope. We're so happy you've joined us."

"Although you can wear whatever you like," Serena had said as I was about to leave, "we usually recommend something other than jeans."

She'd winked at me, even as I'd blushed at the gentle criticism. I drove straight to a sex shop nearby. I wondered how many club patrons also went here, but after signing that ironclad NDA, I knew I had to keep my mouth shut.

I'd never been to a sex shop before. After going inside, I nearly started giggling like an idiot at the wide array of dildos on one wall.

Some dildos looked just like penises in a variety of skin tones. Some dildos were more colorful. I picked up a sparkly purple one that seemed absurdly large.

How did anyone get that inside them? I wondered.

"Do you need help looking for anything?" the store

clerk asked. She had pink hair, a bunch of piercings, and arms covered in tattoos.

I placed the purple dildo back. "Uh, just some lingerie. I think."

The clerk showed me to their clothing section. I was impressed at the sheer variety: not just lingerie, but all kinds of costumes. Sexy maids, sexy nurses, sexy teachers, sexy scientists, and even sexy clowns.

I went through the racks, wondering what Brady would like. I ended up picking out a skimpy leather dress, lacy black panties, and some stilettos with spikes on the heels.

If I wanted to join a sex club, I needed to look the part.

But with my purchases in hand, I didn't want to go home. The last thing I needed was my parents asking me questions.

I called Kelly. She'd been so busy with grad school that we hadn't seen each other in weeks. I also hadn't told her about all my recent exploits.

Fortunately, Kelly was free and told me to come straight to her place for some wine and a nice long chat.

When I brought my purchases inside, Kelly pulled them out of the bags and gaped at me. "Girl, what the hell?"

I just laughed. "I have so much to tell you."

I then told her all about Brady, the Scarlet Rope, and everything in between. Kelly was so focused on me that she didn't even drink her glass of wine. When I'd finished, Kelly was shaking her head.

"Holy shit, woman," she kept saying. "This does not sound like the Grace I know."

"The Grace you know was boring," I groused.

Kelly chuckled. "Maybe. And I'm not criticizing you either. I'm just impressed." Kelly picked up her glass of wine and proceeded to drink it in a few quick gulps. "Want another glass? Because I need one."

After a little more wine, we were both tipsy and laughing like lunatics. Kelly and I had met back in high school and had stayed in touch through college. She'd always been way more adventurous than me.

As teens, Kelly had been the one getting caught smoking and drinking. When she'd gotten suspended for spray-painting the side of our high school, I'd nearly had a heart attack. Kelly had been unfazed.

"I get to stay home from school? Awesome," she'd *said with her usual grin.*

Fortunately, she'd given up her criminal ways when she'd gone to college. When she'd decided to get a master's in psychology right after undergrad, I'd been shocked. That decision had seemed so . . . grown up.

But this Kelly, laughing and making inappropriate jokes? This was the Kelly I recognized.

"You need to try this on!" Kelly said, holding up the dress I'd bought.

"I already did at the store."

"So! I want to see it." Kelly shooed me into her bedroom and told me not to come out until I'd put the outfit on.

I did as she said, coming out and giving a little twirl.

"Are you wearing granny panties?" Kelly demanded.

"I never wear new underwear without washing it first," I replied primly.

"What a Grace thing to say."

At that, I suddenly felt self-conscious. "Is it too much? Do I look stupid?"

"What? No way! You look hot as fuck. If I were gay, I'd hit on you."

"Thank you. I think."

Kelly's eyes widened. "Do you think you can get me an invite? I've never been to a sex club."

"Maybe? I can ask."

Kelly was giddy at the thought. Strangely enough, I wasn't entirely sure I wanted Kelly to join.

The Scarlet Rope was my thing. Did I really want to share this new adventure with my best friend?

I knew I was being selfish. But Kelly was also the type to do something just because it would make a hilarious story later. The club wasn't a joke to me.

The club was a place where I could get to know the man I'd been obsessed with for the past ten years. A place where I might be able to unlock why he was so insistent that we could never be together, no matter how attracted we were to each other.

The next time I entered the Scarlet Rope, I was a member. Wearing the outfit I'd bought at the sex store along with a mask Kelly had given me, I felt confident.

Sexy. Alluring. And not at all the shy virgin I was used to feeling like.

I could feel gazes on me—both male and female—and instead of feeling awkward, I felt empowered.

Was this why Brady liked coming here? I'd been so focused on what Brady liked that I hadn't considered what I liked.

Maybe I'd discover some things about myself that I'd never expected to find.

But I also knew I needed to be careful walking in these stilettos. I nearly face-planted when I started walking toward the long hallway. I caught myself in the nick of time, laughing it off when a man and a woman stopped to help me.

"I didn't see that bump in the rug," I said, waving a hand.

The woman cocked her head to the side. "A bump?" She looked down at the floor and frowned. "I don't see anything."

I didn't stay to explain. The last thing I needed was to gain a reputation as a total klutz instead of the sexy, mysterious woman I wanted to portray.

I was soon distracted by all the scenes. I passed by a large orgy, and then I saw a man tied up and hanging from the ceiling as another man sucked him off.

I stopped in front of a threesome with one woman and two men. I watched as both men fucked the woman: one man under her, one man on top of her.

The woman was moaning and writhing as two huge dicks pounded into her. A flush rose on my cheeks as I watched.

I'd never even considered doing something like that. It was hard to believe people enjoyed threesomes like this outside of staged porn.

The two men kept fucking the woman until she started shaking. The man on top had to pull out when the woman came so hard that she squirted.

"Oh my God!" the woman kept saying over and over again. She started coming again only moments later. Her entire body was flushed. The man underneath her pulled her hair back and sucked on the side of her neck as his hips moved faster and faster.

Standing there, watching this, I felt like I was feverish. I pressed a hand to my cheek. When a man next to me caught my eye, he shot me a devilish smile that, to my surprise, went straight to my pussy.

Christ, I'd had no idea I could be so horny. And, of course, the thought of sex inevitably made me think about sleeping with Brady, and I had to tear my gaze away from the threesome scene to catch my breath.

My heart was pounding so hard that I felt a little dizzy. I found a quiet, dark corner to take a few deep breaths. I felt overwhelmed, confused, and, most of all, extremely turned on.

I went to the bathroom to press a cold paper towel against my forehead. After washing my hands, I returned outside, telling myself that I should definitely get a drink before things got too out of hand.

As I passed by what felt like hundreds of people, I wondered how everyone could seem so cool and collected. Or had they been here so many times that they weren't discombobulated by what they saw?

I went to the bar and ordered a vodka cranberry, my latest obsession, along with an ice water for good measure.

After drinking the water down so fast I gave myself a brain freeze, I started sipping my cocktail, and a man sat down next to me.

He was dressed in black pants and a white shirt, the collar open. He looked like he'd come straight from his office and had just taken off his tie before he'd arrived.

He also didn't wear a mask. He was handsome, his jaw chiseled, his dark hair curling a bit. When he smiled at me, I couldn't help but smile back.

"I've never seen you here before," he said smoothly. He glanced at my drink. "Would you like another drink once you finish that one?"

"Maybe. We'll see what happens."

His eyes flashed at my flirtatious tone. He leaned closer to me, and I could smell his cologne, a woodsy scent.

"I'm into pain," he said, nearly making me choke on my drink in surprise. "Do you have a favorite kink?"

"Um. I'm not sure. I'm still discovering what I like." After a pause, I asked, "You like giving pain? Receiving?"

"Giving. Definitely giving."

I cocked my head to the side. "I'm curious. How did you figure that out? Was it something you were always interested in, or did it surprise you when you decided it was your kink of choice?"

The man chuckled. "Is this an interview?"

I flushed. "Sorry. I'm just insanely curious."

"Oh, I don't mind. I think it's adorable." His smile was warm, with an edge to it that made me want to shiver.

"I've always liked being in control," he said. "But it was an ex that introduced me to BDSM. She was into it, and then one day, she told me we should try it. That was when I realized that I liked giving pain and hated receiving it."

"Do you ever feel like you've gone too far? Or like you've tried one thing, and now you have to level up?"

His expression was thoughtful. "When I was younger and wilder, yes. But I've learned to appreciate that it's not about leveling up. It's about everyone receiving pleasure and fulfillment through pain. And that takes a lot of practice and self-control to master."

He continued, "Would you be interested in a demonstration? We'd start slowly since you're new at this. Perhaps we could see if you like the Saint Andrew's cross."

I was about to ask him what that was when my companion was suddenly pulled backward in his chair. A forearm was pressed against his throat.

And then Brady's voice said, "Put one fucking finger on her, and you'll wish you'd never been born."

Chapter 16

Brady

"**B**rady!" Grace jumped out of her chair and grabbed my arm. "Stop! He didn't even do anything!"

It didn't matter. This stranger had talked about hurting Grace. *My Grace.*

Grace's voice was all that kept me from doing worse. I finally let go, the guy coughing and sputtering.

"What the fuck, dude?" he kept saying. "Who the fuck are you?"

I grabbed Grace and hauled her into a back closet that was blessedly unlocked. It was either that or dragging her out to my car.

"What has gotten into you?" Grace demanded.

I barely registered her words because even in the dim light of the closet, I could see she was wearing a leather dress and spiky heels. And this dress hardly even covered her luscious ass.

"I told you not to come here again," I growled.

Grace crossed her arms. "So? You aren't my keeper. I can go where I want."

"That's not the deal we made."

"Deal? You giving me commands just to be overbearing is not a deal. That's just you being a . . ."

I smirked. "What?"

"Asshole," she finally spat out. "You're being an asshole, and it's pissing me off."

I had to admit, Angry Grace was extra gorgeous. But I also had the presence of mind to know that if I said as much, she'd probably stab me in the eye with one of her heels.

"And anyway," she was saying, "if you'd just answered my questions, I wouldn't have had to come here to do my own research. So, really, this is all your fault."

"I told you to stay away from here!"

Grace rolled her eyes. "Yeah, and look what happened. Did you really think I'd just nod and go home? Come on. You're smarter than that."

I growled low in my throat. I'd never met a more frustrating, stubborn, sexy, alluring woman in my entire fucking life.

I also realized what exactly she was saying. *Doing her own research.* I swallowed, feeling ill.

"Were you seriously thinking about letting that guy touch you?" I asked.

Grace shrugged. "I was considering it. Because at least I'd understand why you liked that kind of stuff."

I gaped at her. I didn't know whether to be horrified or flattered.

"Jesus Christ," I groaned.

"But in all honesty, I was just asking the guy some questions. What's wrong with information? And anyway, I decided to do the limited trial membership to see what this place was all about."

Information? Yeah, fucking right. Grace was easy prey in a place like this. She was innocent and curious. It wouldn't take much for some guy to seduce her. Did she even realize how much danger she was in?

"You signed up? Christ Jesus above, Grace. Your dad would kill me if he found out," I said.

Grace made a face. "My dad has nothing to do with this. Gross. I'm an adult, in case you didn't notice. What I do on my own time is nobody's business but mine."

I sighed. She didn't get it. It didn't matter what she thought. What mattered was that my influence had created her interest in this place. And so Coach Dallas would have every reason to take me out back and shoot me.

"What can I do to stop you from coming around here?" I asked.

"Show me what you like."

"I'm not going to show you anything." At her frustrated expression, I conceded, "I'll tell you about it. How about that? You said you just wanted information, right?"

Grace considered my offer and then thrust out her hand like we were in a fucking board meeting. "Spill your guts, Carmichael."

I guffawed. Then I realized that standing in a supply closet was a terrible place to have this conversation. I found Grace and me a table in the corner of the bar.

I considered booking a private room. But I knew that would test my self-control, which was hanging by a thread already.

At least here, enough people were around to keep me from throwing Grace over my shoulder like a caveman.

It's a sex club, my brain reminded me. *Nobody would bat an eyelash if you did throw her over your shoulder.*

Grace took off her mask and folded her hands. I half

expected her to pull out a notebook and start jotting down things.

"What do you want to know?" I asked.

Grace tapped her chin. "Well, I guess I'll ask the same questions I asked the guy you nearly strangled." She smiled, her expression sardonic. "Do you like to give or receive pain?"

"Give."

"How did you figure that out?"

"I've never been the type of guy to submit."

She snorted. "Well, that goes without saying. But inflicting pain on somebody—that's a whole different thing."

I considered her question for a long moment. "Mac told me this place was a good idea to let off some steam. I was curious, but I wasn't sure if it was something I'd be into. Then I met a woman—"

I bit my tongue. Did Grace really want to hear about Shayla?

But Grace didn't seem judgmental, only curious.

"You met a woman," Grace prompted.

"And she showed me how to whip her."

"So you liked it."

I nodded. "Something about being in control like that was intoxicating. I could do whatever I wanted to Shayla. It was . . . freeing."

"But you guys had a safe word, right?"

I raised my eyebrows, surprised. "You've done your research, then."

"I might be a virgin, but I'm not a nun. I know things." Grace sniffed.

I had to restrain a laugh. As far as I was concerned, Grace *was* a nun. Or, at least, that was how I needed to think of her.

"I also realized that I felt better after being dominant like that," I admitted. "I have a lot of anger. It's probably why I like hockey."

"Ah," Grace replied.

Did that scare her? That I was angry? That I needed to take that anger out on someone else, however willing that other party was?

"You haven't had a lot of control in your life. It makes sense that this is a way to take that back," Grace said.

"I really didn't intend for this to become a therapy session."

"Nothing wrong with a little therapy. Besides, you've had a lot going on lately, especially with your mom. Do you think that's why you needed to try this place out?"

"I guess so."

I wasn't about to admit it was more because I couldn't touch Grace, so Shayla had been a convenient stand-in.

"Tell me what you guys did," Grace said.

"What? Me and Shayla?"

"Yeah."

I hesitated, but if Grace wanted the truth, then who was I to stop her? Like she'd insisted, she wasn't a child. And she wasn't stupid, either.

"I started with a flogger," I began. "It's a whip with a leather strap on the end of it. It doesn't look like much, but it can inflict different levels of pain, depending on where you use it."

Grace inhaled and gestured for me to continue.

"Shayla showed me where she liked to be hit. Her ass, but most especially the skin between her thighs and ass. She'd moan every time I'd whip her there. She also liked it across her entire back. At first, I didn't hit her very hard. I was afraid of hurting her." I chuckled.

I could tell that Grace was breathing hard. Was she scared? Or worse, turned on?

I felt my own body react to my story. Hell, I was half hard anytime I was near Grace. She had a constant effect on me.

"Watching her skin bloom red," I continued, "was nothing like I'd ever experienced. She writhed and made these little moans every time I hit her harder. She was even begging me to fuck her, but I didn't. This wasn't about sex. Not really."

Grace licked her lips. "It wasn't?"

"It was hot as fuck, but no, I didn't want to fuck her. I just wanted to experiment with BDSM. And I discovered that I liked it more than I thought I would."

We stared at each other for a long moment. Grace had leaned so close to me that I could close the distance and kiss her. It didn't help that she was breathing hard, her breasts pushing against the tight leather of her dress.

"I'll stop coming here on one condition," she said quickly.

"What's that?"

"That you show me exactly how you whipped Shayla."

"*Fuck no,*" I snarled.

Grace just shook her head. "That's my deal. Take it or leave it."

I wanted to shake her. I wanted to take her to the back and show her why she shouldn't poke the bear. Most of all, I wanted to hear her scream my name as she came.

I was almost vibrating with desire—and anger.

"You don't get to force my hand like this," I growled.

"I thought you wanted to make a deal. This is it."

She'd backed me into a corner, damn her. Well, then I should call her bluff. We'd see how long she lasted before using her safe word.

"Pick a safe word," I said.

Grace perked up. "You're going to do it? Really?"

"Against my better judgment? Yeah. But we'll see how long you can take it."

For the first time, Grace looked a little frightened. Good. Maybe she'd realize she shouldn't fuck around with guys like me.

But she didn't back down, God bless her. She just thought a long moment before saying, "Galoshes."

"That's your safe word? Really?"

"I mean, isn't it supposed to be random?" Now she seemed unsure.

I shook my head, chuckling. "Sure, *galoshes* it is." I got up and took her by the hand. "You can say no still. You don't have to do this."

She just raised her chin and said, "Let's go."

This was insane. What the fuck was I doing?

But I had no choice. If this was how I was going to get Grace to stop coming to the club, I had to do this.

Like you aren't desperate to do this to her.

I got us a private room and shut the door, locking it behind me.

"Only to keep other people out," I said.

Grace looked nervous, but she didn't seem afraid either. "I know. I trust you."

You shouldn't, I wanted to say. I wanted to shout at her to get far, far away from me.

But apparently, I was a weak man because I didn't have the strength to send her away.

Grace accoutrements began looking around the room. There was a bed covered in silk sheets. Along the wall were all kinds of: whips, chains, floggers, paddles, handcuffs, ropes. On the opposite wall was a Saint Andrew's cross, and dangling from the ceiling were ropes to hang people by their wrists.

There was also an impressive collection of dildos and vibrators. Grace picked one up, a giant blue cock.

"This looks like a Smurf penis," she remarked.

I laughed. "What Smurfs were you watching?"

She picked up one that was a more human color. She held it up near my crotch. "How does it compare to the real thing?"

I groaned. I took the silicone cock from her and set it back down.

"I wonder how they keep all these things clean," Grace was musing. "They'd have to sterilize everything. I wonder who's in charge of that—"

I pressed a hand to her mouth. "Good lord, woman. You're killing me."

She licked my palm, and it made my eyes nearly roll back inside my head.

"Go there," I commanded, pointing at a spot near a settee and chairs. "And don't move unless I tell you to."

"Yes, sir," she murmured.

I shuddered. She did as I said, kneeling and waiting for my command.

I went to the wall of whips, and my brain was a complete mess. But I soon realized I didn't want to use anything but my hand on Grace tonight.

"We're going to start slowly," I said, approaching her. I sat down on the settee and motioned for her to stand. "Drape yourself over my legs."

Grace licked her lips. She did as I said. Soon she was lying across my legs, her ass within easy reach.

I smoothed a hand down her spine. "Doing okay?" I asked.

She nodded.

"What's the safe word?"

"Galoshes."

"Good girl." I gently pushed her leather dress up her hips. When I discovered she was wearing a black thong, I had to grit my teeth at the surge of desire that exploded inside me.

Her ass was pale and round, and I could imagine it red from my hand. I rubbed one side, then the other, getting her used to my touch.

"I'm going to spank you," I said slowly, "because you've been a naughty girl tonight. You've pushed me to my limits. You need to learn to behave."

When she said nothing, I spanked her. She yelped.

"Answer me when I talk to you," I said.

She glanced back at me. "Yes, sir."

"Good girl." I rubbed where I'd hit her. Red was already blooming on her pale skin.

I started spanking her now. I rotated from one side of her ass to the other. I kept things light at first, more of a light slap than anything. But as Grace started moaning and bucking, I increased the force of my hits.

"You," I said between slaps, "are a"—*slap*—"bad girl"—*slap*. "You do not disobey again. Do not come to the club unless I allow you to."

Her ass was a bright crimson now. I could make out the shape of my handprints on her skin. It was so arousing that my cock was about to burst from my goddamn pants.

"Yes, sir," Grace was saying, panting hard.

I brushed my hand down her back, soothing her. I kept rubbing her back until her breathing slowed. Then I gently turned her over and pulled her into my arms.

"Oh my God," Grace whispered. She still shook a little. "I had no idea."

I had to admit that I felt similarly. This was not fun experimentation with Shayla.

I'd unlocked something not only within myself but also within Grace. How had I ever thought Grace would back down? She'd taken the spanking like a champion.

"You were amazing," I said into her hair.

"I wasn't sure I'd go through with it," she admitted. "But then it turned into something that I didn't expect."

"Something you enjoyed?"

"Yeah." She looked into my eyes. "Is that weird?"

"Not at all."

I then had her lie face down. I went to get a salve that Shayla had told me to use after sessions. I returned and began to spread it on Grace's ass.

She shivered a little. "That's cold!"

"It has menthol and arnica in it. It'll help if you bruise."

As I rubbed the salve into her skin, guilt hit me for the first time. I'd spanked Grace Dallas so hard that she had handprints on her ass. What kind of a freak was I?

But even as I expected Grace to run flying in the other direction, she didn't. She just let me cuddle her until we were both ready to leave.

"You won't come here again, yes?" I said quietly. "That was our deal."

When she said yes, I almost believed she was telling the truth.

Chapter 17

Brady

A week later, I was on a flight with the Blades for an away game in New York City. I'd thought it'd give me a break from thinking about Grace, but to my horror, she and the rest of the marketing and PR team were on the flight.

"Apparently, they're attending some fancy gala with a few of the guys the night after the game," Mac told me with a shrug.

I'd been tormented by memories of spanking Grace that night at the club. I'd told myself it couldn't happen again. I'd done my best to avoid her.

But apparently, fate was a fickle bitch and wanted to make me miserable.

The only good thing was that Grace, Julia, and the rest of the team were seated in the back of the plane while the team was up front. Although it was a six-hour flight to New York, there was a good chance I wouldn't even see Grace the entire flight.

"Something to drink?" the flight attendant asked Mac and me, who were seated together.

I nearly groaned aloud when I saw who the flight attendant was. Tatiana was a gorgeous, curvy brunette whom I'd definitely hooked up with a few times during some long layovers.

Tatiana leaned into me, only inches away, her lips a deep red. She smelled like roses.

"Coke for me," said Mac. When I didn't say anything, he elbowed me. "Brady?"

"Ginger ale," I said, though I didn't even like the stuff.

Tatiana made a whole show of pouring our drinks, going as slowly as possible. Or maybe it was just because I hoped she wouldn't flirt with me this time. The last thing I needed was Grace seeing Tatiana trying to get into my pants.

"It's been a while," said Tatiana as she handed me my ginger ale. "How've you been?"

I could feel Mac's amused gaze on me. "Busy," I grunted.

"Me too. I've flown to London, Dubai, and Tokyo, all in the past month. But I don't mind living out of a suitcase. I'm sure you boys are used to that kind of life, too," she replied.

"We do spend a lot of time in hotels," said Mac when I remained silent.

"Oh, I bet you do." Tatiana gave me a wink. She then leaned over me, her breasts nearly in my face as she adjusted my headrest.

"Just making sure you're comfortable," she said.

"Appreciate it," I muttered.

Finally, she continued onward down the aisle. After a moment, Mac burst out in laughter.

"What are you laughing about?" I asked, irritated.

"Dude, your face. You looked like you were going to have a stroke. Did you sleep with her?"

"Yeah, a few times."

"And you don't want Grace to see her rubbing all over you."

I glared. "Christ, keep your voice down."

"Nobody can hear us. Besides, Coach is down near the PR team." Mac leaned closer and said in a lower voice, "But what's up with you? You've said all of two words since we got to the airport."

I hadn't planned on telling Mac about spanking Grace, but I realized I needed to tell somebody who understood. In hushed tones, I gave him a quick rundown, trying to gauge his reaction.

When I'd finished, Mac let out a whistle. "Shit. And with Grace Dallas? Seriously? I can't believe she was up for it. It took me forever to convince Elodie to try things out, and she wasn't a virgin."

"Grace is still a virgin," I growled.

Mac blinked a few times. "You sound very . . . possessive about that."

"Yeah? Well, it fucking sucks. I wished I didn't care. But I've been avoiding her for the past week. I don't even know how to look at her now."

Mac clapped me on the shoulder. "I can't believe this is finally happening. Brady Carmichael, undone by a woman. I never thought I'd live to see the day."

"Don't sound so smug, asshole."

Mac just grinned. "My advice? Don't avoid her. Because if she's anything like Elodie, she won't be easy to shake off."

I didn't respond even though I knew Mac was right.

Grace was relentless. Stubborn, reckless, hotheaded . . . and so sexy it made me want to throw myself off the nearest bridge.

I put in my earbuds and tried to sleep. But to my dismay, one of the songs playing while I'd spanked Grace came on. It wasn't even one of my favorite songs, so there was no reason the algorithm should've played it.

But, of course, hearing the song made me remember that night. All the noises Grace had made, how red her skin had turned, how excited she'd gotten. I'd wondered how I hadn't fucked her right then and there.

My cock hardened despite my best efforts. God, the last thing I needed was a hard-on during this goddamn flight.

Fortunately, the lights had dimmed in the cabin since this was an evening flight. I got out of my seat and headed to the bathroom before my erection got worse.

I shut the door and leaned over the sink, breathing heavily. I then rinsed my face and neck with cold water. After some more deep breaths and thoughts of the least sexy things ever, my cock decided to behave itself.

Maybe I should ask Tatiana to get me some ice to put down my pants, I thought wryly. Then again, Tatiana might just offer to help me herself.

I opened the door to the bathroom, only to find myself being pushed back inside and the lock clicking.

I gaped at Grace. "What the fuck?"

She grinned. "Finally. I've been waiting for you to go to the bathroom."

My erection returned within moments because Grace had her breasts pressed against me. *Damn her.* I groaned under my breath. Why did this woman not leave me in peace for just one night?

"Grace, what the hell are you doing?" I asked.

"I just wanted to tell you that I can't stop thinking about the other night."

I groaned. This woman was sent to earth just to torment me, wasn't she?

"That can never happen again," I growled.

Grace seemed undeterred. "You keep saying things, but that doesn't mean they're true." She pressed a hand to my chest. "I can feel your heart pounding. I know you're excited."

"My body's response is one thing. My brain's response is another. And my brain is saying, 'danger, danger.'"

"Since when did you care about something being dangerous?" She smirked up at me. "Come find me when you want to have some fun again."

It took a moment to get myself under control after she slipped out. I also couldn't believe Grace Dallas had come on to me like that.

Where had she gotten this newfound confidence? And how the fuck was I going to say no to her now?

When I left the bathroom, I ran into Dave, who dressed up as the Blades mascot.

"The coach's daughter? Seriously?" Dave asked. "Do you want to get traded to Canada?"

I shot him a dirty look. "Keep your mouth shut if you value your life."

Dave put up his hands. "Don't get testy with me, dude. But be careful."

I didn't need his warning. I knew exactly how fucked up this situation was.

The worst part? I was to the point that I didn't even care.

There must've been some kind of magic in the air because having Grace in the stands meant I had one of the best games of my career.

The Hurricanes were a tough team, and Coach made everybody on edge, telling us that we couldn't afford to lose this match.

"Don't disappoint me, boys," he'd said as we'd gotten onto the ice.

As I'd gotten into position, I'd spotted Grace in the stands. She waved wildly at me and then turned around to show that she was wearing my number.

Apparently, that was the good luck charm I needed. I scored three goals, one after the other, until we'd gotten a solid lead that the Hurricanes couldn't push past. By the time the game was over, the entire team was already celebrating.

The crowd erupted when I scored that last goal, defeating the Hurricanes like we'd never done before. Mac and my teammates nearly smashed into me as we all collided into a group of ecstatic, sweaty idiots.

But I had eyes only for Grace. I didn't take my gaze off her as we left the ice.

Everybody celebrated late into the night. It was close to 3:00 a.m. when I staggered to my hotel room, drunk as a skunk and happier than I'd been in a long time.

Grace had been at the after-party for a little bit, and she'd disappeared on me before midnight. I didn't even know what room she was in.

I collapsed onto my bed, the world spinning as I laughed. Christ, I hadn't had a game like this in way too fucking long.

A knock roused me from my drunken stupor. I opened the door to find Grace herself, like an angel come down from heaven, standing at my door.

"You," I said, narrowing my eyes. "Where did you go?"

"I had a headache, so I went to my room."

"Oh. I'm sorry."

She smiled. "Don't be. I feel much better now. And I was waiting for you to get back to the hotel."

I glanced around. "How did you know which room I was in?"

"I have my ways, Carmichael." She leaned toward me, and I could feel her breath against my chin. "I brought something with me. A brand-new paddle you could use on me. It needs to be broken in, you know."

I stared down at her, my heart pounding fast. My body instantly reacted to her words.

"Fuck, Grace," I snarled.

"Or you could just spank me again." She fluttered her eyelashes. "I know how much you love making me squirm."

"Get out of here before I do something we'll both regret."

She just smiled and flounced away. I watched her leave, wishing I didn't have to be so noble.

I shut the door and then locked it with the chain for good measure. I didn't trust Grace not to find a way to sneak into my room. I glanced out the windows. I was on the tenth floor. Surely she couldn't climb into my room through a window?

I shook my head. Christ, I was drunk.

I went to take a shower, the hot water clearing my head a little. But it didn't help dissipate the thoughts of bending Grace over my knee and paddling her perky little ass.

I took hold of my cock and started stroking it as I imagined the lurid scene. I'd paddle her until she was dripping wet, her legs kicking with every hit, every slap. How quickly would her ass turn red? I'd bet money it wouldn't take much.

I quickened my pace as I squeezed my cock. I gritted my teeth as I imagined delving between Grace's thighs to find her pussy wet. Wet and juicy, just for me. She'd probably try to get me to rub her clit, but I'd want to torment her first.

Just like she'd been tormenting me.

I'd dance around her tight opening, my fingers just glancing her swollen clit, making her beg and cry out. She'd probably writhe so much I'd have to hold her down.

And then I'd spank her until she understood how she drove me crazy, how much I hated the power she had over me. I'd make her pay for making me want her so much that I'd jeopardize my career.

I'd paddle her one last time as she begged for mercy.

I came with a shout, my cum shooting all over the shower wall. I came until I felt like I'd emptied my balls.

Fuck, I'd needed that. But even as I dried off and got into bed, I still felt unsatisfied.

I knew I'd never be fully satisfied until I finished in Grace's tight virgin pussy.

Coach had informed us that the entire team was expected to attend the gala the following night. Fortunately, one of the sponsors was a fashion house that had tuxes for all the players to wear.

The gala was going to be at a huge, fancy hotel in Manhattan. My only hope was the booze would be flowing freely.

I wasn't excited to attend, but the second I saw Grace, I changed my mind.

Wearing a slinky black dress with a plunging back, Grace looked sexier than I'd ever seen her. Her hair was in a loose bun, tendrils framing her face. She wore only small diamonds in her ears.

She didn't need jewelry. Her face, her silky, pale skin, the way she moved—all of those were miles beyond what any diamonds could do.

She was also wearing stilettos. Her shoes reminded me of the leather outfit she'd last worn to the Scarlet Rope.

"You look gorgeous," I said, taking her hand and escorting her into the ballroom.

She blushed. "So do you. You definitely clean up nicely."

"I never thought you'd wear a dress like that."

Grace blinked. "Like what?"

I gestured vaguely. "Sexy. Low cut. The Grace I know would wear something that covered up."

I realized that I sounded like I was scolding her. And maybe I was. I could tell how much her appearance made men turn their heads.

Jealousy gnawed at my gut. I hated the thought of any man making eyes at this woman. At *my* woman.

"You don't like my dress?" Grace questioned, frowning.

"No." I turned toward her, stopping us in the middle of the crowd. "I just don't like other men looking at you."

Her eyes brightened. "Oh, so you're jealous? How lovely."

I swore under my breath, but she just laughed.

Once again, I marveled at where this newfound confidence of Grace had appeared. What had I unleashed by giving in to her demands?

"I'm not wearing any panties," Grace whispered.

I barely stopped myself from groaning aloud. "Not here."

"Why not? Nobody can hear me."

"Because I don't need you to tempt me right now."

She just kissed my ear and said, "Then I'll come back later to see if you've changed your mind."

Despite my best efforts to avoid Grace this evening, she was determined to drive me insane. She kept coming up to me and saying dirty nothings in my ear. Reminding me of when I'd spanked her. Telling me about the paddle she'd brought with her. Describing how easy it would be to reach under her dress to stroke her thighs.

Every time I told her enough was enough, she'd just giggle and flutter away. And I didn't even mean it, anyway.

I loved that she was flirting with me. I love that she felt comfortable playing with me. It was an entirely new dynamic to our relationship that I never realized I'd wanted.

But as the evening wore on, my self-control was splintering. I ran into Mac, who took one look at me and laughed.

"Jesus, what's wrong with you?" he asked.

I gestured toward where Grace stood and talked to some of her PR friends. "That woman is trying to kill me."

"Oh, man. You're in deep, aren't you?"

"I'm sticking with you for the rest of tonight."

Mac patted my arm, grinning. "I'll keep you safe from the scary lady."

I glared at my friend, but he didn't care. He was just enjoying this whole thing way too much.

It was near the end of the event when I stepped outside to get some fresh air. The ballroom had gotten way too packed with people. I inhaled deeply, feeling my shoulders relax a little.

It was a full moon tonight. I remembered when Grace was younger and would always drag me outside to show me the moon, especially if it was full.

It's just the moon, I'd said.

But look at it! It's beautiful.

I hadn't understood why she'd cared back then. Now I wondered whether she'd done it just to have a reason to talk to me.

"Beautiful night, isn't it?" Grace said behind me.

"Did you see the moon?" I asked.

I could feel her smiling. She came to stand next to me. "Mmm, it's gorgeous."

Now, my gaze was on her face. "Yeah. It is."

She just kept smiling. I realized that we were alone—and how dangerous that was for my self-control.

Grace turned and wrapped my arm around her waist. "I lied earlier, you know," she said.

"Oh really?"

She opened her purse. To my dismay, she pulled out the paddle she'd been talking about.

"I didn't leave this in my room. I brought it with me."

I stared at it. I stared at her. And then, like glass shattering, my self-control finally broke.

I grabbed the paddle and, after stuffing it back into her purse, hauled Grace into my arms.

"You want to keep poking the bear?" I growled. "Then you're going to get eaten."

She didn't even have time to speak before I kissed her. I kissed her hard, kissed her so she would know how much she was driving me insane. Our tongues tangled, our moans entwining, my hands running down her bare back.

I rubbed my groan against her. I wanted her to know what she did to me.

I pushed until she was pressed against the nearest wall. I imprisoned her in my arms. She wasn't going to get away from me now.

She tasted like wine and strawberries. I dug my fingers into her hair. I wanted to muss her up, to make sure that everyone knew what we'd been doing when she went back inside.

"Brady," she whispered, her eyes glassy.

I silenced her with another kiss. I didn't even hear footsteps until it was too late.

Chapter 18

Grace

I felt like a live wire when I returned to my room that night. After some embarrassed server had caught Brady and me, Brady had immediately returned inside.

I'd had to stand out there by myself, trying to catch my breath.

Now I was back in my room, and I hadn't calmed down. Not by a mile.

Brady Carmichael had kissed me. Finally! He'd finally kissed me.

I knew it was strange that I felt more triumphant about this than when he'd spanked me. But he'd kissed me like he not only wanted me, but needed me. That he couldn't fight his feelings for me anymore.

You're reading way too much into this, I warned myself.

But I didn't care. I did a giddy little spin around my room. When I caught my reflection in the bathroom mirror, I almost didn't recognize the woman looking at me.

This wasn't shy, virginal Grace Dallas. The woman looking back at me knew how to drive men crazy. She knew how alluring her own sexuality was.

I smiled. Then I laughed, feeling like I was on top of the world. But even as I danced in my tall stilettos, reality beckoned.

My feet were killing me, and I'd barely eaten anything all evening. I'd been too afraid of getting something on the couture gown that I'd been allowed to borrow from a famous designer.

I took off my dress, making sure to hang it up, and sighed with relief when I took off my shoes. I flexed my toes.

I knew I looked hot in heels, but damn, why did they have to hurt so much?

I started running a bath. I needed to relax. I knew I wouldn't sleep a wink if I didn't make myself chill out.

I found some bubble bath and soon sank into the hot water. I made a happy noise of contentment.

I let my thoughts wander, but despite my best efforts, I couldn't stop thinking about Brady. The way he'd pulled me into his arms. How strong he'd felt. How he'd kissed me until my brain had turned to mush.

When we'd been interrupted, I'd almost wanted Brady to keep on kissing me no matter who was watching us. But Brady had sworn under his breath and stalked away like he'd been doused in ice water.

Hadn't Brady told me he wouldn't keep doing the hot-and-cold act with me? I snorted. So much for that promise.

As I soaked in the tub, my thoughts returned to the night at the club when Brady had spanked me. I'd been nervous when he'd taken me into that room. I'd almost been tempted to call his bluff and go home.

But when he'd bent over my knee, pulling my dress up to my hips, exposing me to his gaze and his touch . . . it'd felt like I'd fallen into a whirlpool of sensation.

Then he'd begun spanking me. It'd hurt, but there'd been something so pleasurable about the experience, too. Every smack had ratcheted up my desire for him.

The worst part had been that he hadn't touched my pussy. I'd been vibrating with need when he'd stopped. I'd half expected to come right then and there since I'd been so turned on.

I reached through the water to stroke a finger through my folds. I was wet just at remembering how Brady had spanked me. I sighed.

I imagined that next time, he'd paddle me. He'd start slowly, teasing me with light smacks, scolding me when I moved too much.

As I imagined this scenario, I circled my clit, feeling it harden under my fingers. I thrust a finger inside my tight sheath. I added a second because I knew Brady's fingers were thicker than mine.

What would it feel like to have him finger me like this? Would his eyes grow dark as he felt how wet I was?

I threw my head back as I finger-fucked myself. I rubbed my clit with my other hand. All the while, I could feel Brady's hand connecting against my ass.

Over and over again, spanking me, telling me how I was a bad girl who'd better stop testing his patience.

Do you want me to fuck you for real? he'd growl. He'd delve between the seam of my legs to find my wet pussy. *How badly do you want me to fuck you, baby?*

I groaned aloud as I increased the speed of my own hands. I arched upward, not caring that I was probably getting water all over the bathroom floor. I imagined that it was Brady touching me as I rubbed my clit, that it was Brady hooking his fingers inside my pussy to hit my G-spot, that it was Brady telling me to come right then and there—

And then I heard a knock on my door. I paused, uncertain. Then another more forceful knock.

"Grace, it's Brady."

I nearly launched myself out of the tub like a crazy woman. I grabbed a robe and put it on as fast as I could.

"Coming!" I yelled. I realized the double entendre and had to stifle a hysterical laugh.

I threw open the door so fast that I surprised Brady.

"Grace?" He looked me over. "Sorry, were you in the shower?"

"Bath."

As if sensing something was off, Brady narrowed his eyes.

"You were masturbating again," he growled.

I blushed. I realized that one of my hands was near the doorframe, which wasn't far from his nose, which meant—

I pulled my hand back. "Did you need something?" I asked primly.

Brady just pushed past me into my room. He started pacing like a caged lion.

"I can't keep doing this," he burst out. He shot me a look of desperation. "You can't keep doing this to me."

"I'm confused."

"This." He gestured vaguely. "Jerking off. All of it."

I folded my arms across my chest. "Um, you interrupted *me*. What I do in my own hotel room is my business."

Brady wasn't even listening to me. He was just pacing and raking his hands through his hair. He really did seem like he was at the end of his rope.

"Besides, you got me all hot and bothered by kissing me," I pointed out.

"That's the thing. We can't keep doing this."

Not this again. "Brady, I already know what you're going to say. 'I'm not right for you, this can't happen, it's wrong, I'm actually a prince in disguise and I'm betrothed to another woman.' Blah, blah, blah."

That little speech made Brady stop pacing, at least. His lips twitched. "A prince in disguise? What Hallmark movie is this?"

"An annoying one." I sat on the edge of my bed with a huff.

Brady eventually sat next to me. "No, I wasn't going to say all of that. Not this time. After our kiss downstairs, I had a good, long think in my room."

I raised an eyebrow. "And did you come to some new conclusion?"

"You're sassy tonight." He flicked my arm. "But yeah, I did. I want us to date."

"What?"

"I want to take you out on real dates. No more of this sneaking around and shit. You deserve better than that." He looked away. "And I don't think the club is the best place to get to know each other either."

My shoulders fell. "But I really enjoyed our . . . encounter there."

"I know you did. I did, too. But the club isn't reality. It's manufactured. It's all a fantasy." His gaze was serious as he looked at me. "I want to experience more than that with you. I want to experience reality with you."

I didn't know what to say. I reached out to touch him, but he pulled away from me.

He let out a bitter laugh. "I'm about to pounce on you, so maybe don't touch me."

"Would that be such a bad thing?"

"I'm trying to be chivalrous here. We haven't even gone on a date yet."

He rose from the bed. "Good night, Grace," he said before shutting the door behind him.

I was mystified. I was elated. I was annoyed.

But right at that moment, I was still horny as hell. Brady had interrupted me before I'd come, damn him. I lay down and opened my robe.

I wondered if Brady was going to jerk off in his room. I could just imagine him pulling his cock out, already half hard. It wouldn't take long for him to be fully erect.

How big was he? I had a feeling that he'd be huge. Thick and veiny and pulsing with desire. In my vision of him stroking himself, there was a bead of precum at the tip that slowly dripped down the side.

Would he be thinking about me? I hoped so. I rubbed my clit as I thought about him increasing the speed of his strokes. His fist would tighten, a grimace on his face, his toes curling as he felt his own orgasm building inside him.

I thought of him shouting as he came, semen spurting from the tip. I imagined it hitting my tongue the exact moment my own orgasm slammed into me. I came with a scream I bit back just in time, all too aware that the walls in this place were probably thin. The waves hit me, seemingly endless, my body completely out of my own control.

I felt like my bones had melted. I tossed the robe aside and climbed under the covers. Yawning, I fell asleep within moments, my dreams filled with Brady.

The following Saturday after we'd all flown back to LA, I went to dinner with my mom. When she'd suggested inviting Dad as well, I'd told her that I needed some motherly advice.

"You mean you don't want your dad flipping his lid," Mom had said.

We'd gotten Mexican at one of our favorite places and had gone to a nearby beach to walk around. It was a warm evening, and plenty of people were out and about on the beach.

"So what's up?" Mom asked me as we sat down on a bench.

I wiped my suddenly sweating palms on my jeans. "Um, it's about Brady."

"I figured."

"He wants us to date."

That made Mom's eyebrows go up. "Reallllly?" she drawled. "Now, I hadn't expected that."

"He says he wants to see if we could be good for each other. But I'm not so sure. Would Dad freak out if we started dating?"

Mom was silent for a moment, then she sighed. "I hate to say it, honey, but I don't think your father would approve of you dating Brady. I mean, you know his reputation. Since when has he even been in a serious relationship? Did he say he'd be monogamous?"

"I think so." But now I wondered whether I should've asked Brady to be crystal clear.

"Brady isn't a bad guy, but he's not the right guy for you. You two are from completely different worlds. Brady grew up on the wrong side of the tracks, if you catch my drift."

Now, I was offended on Brady's behalf. "I never thought you'd be judgmental like that."

"I don't judge Brady for his past, but he has a lot of baggage, too. I would bet you a million dollars one of the reasons he sleeps around is because of something lacking inside him. Do you want to just be another notch on his bedpost?"

I felt a little sick to my stomach. When I'd decided to ask Mom her opinion on Brady and me dating, I had the stupid hope that she'd tell me to go for it.

Mom took my hand and squeezed it. "I'm sorry. I know it's not what you want to hear. I just want to protect you. You need a stable man. And you know these athletes. They burn themselves out completely. They burn bright for a few years, and then . . ." Mom shrugged.

"Brady might want to change." My voice sounded small.

"Maybe he will." I could hear Mom's skepticism in her voice. "But there's also the issue of your dad. He'll never be okay with you dating a hockey player. He knows those guys too well."

Mom's expression was serious now. "And I'd worry that you dating Brady might hurt his career. He might be accused of nepotism, or that he's dating his coach's daughter for special favors."

"What? That's crazy! Everybody knows Brady isn't like that."

"My dear, when it comes to money and fame, people will do a lot of things. Even people like Brady."

I hated that I was listening to this. I hated that I felt a bit of doubt bloom inside me.

What if Brady was allowing this because he'd realized that he could get special treatment if he got me to date him?

"You said yourself that Dad would freak out," I asserted. "So there's no way Brady would think he'd get anything out of dating me. He'd probably hurt his career more than he'd help it."

"You're probably right. And is that something you want to feel guilty about? What if your dad gets Brady traded to another team?"

I hadn't considered that. Would Dad do something like that?

I winced inwardly. If Dad truly thought it was in my best interest to send Brady to Siberia, he'd do it. I knew my dad well enough to believe he was capable of that.

"I also just don't see Brady as my son-in-law," Mom remarked.

"We're just talking about dating, not getting married."

"Sweetheart, you and I both know that you aren't the type to date casually. Brady is. And I'll be honest, for that reason, I'd have a hard time trusting him." She patted my leg. "I know you wanted to hear me say something else, but I have to be honest here."

"I know."

I understood where Mom was coming from, even if I didn't totally agree with her. But her words made me pause, because what if I was heading straight into disaster? Was I letting this crush of mine block out the truth about Brady?

Brady isn't a bad guy, I reminded myself. In fact, he was the opposite. Hadn't he tried his hardest to stay away from me, but I wouldn't let him? He'd always been protective of me as well.

And now he wanted to date me. If he didn't care about me, why even bring that suggestion up?

I had a feeling that my parents simply misunderstood Brady. Just like the world would misunderstand if they found out that he'd been going to a sex club.

God, I couldn't imagine the uproar if Dad found out about Brady and me going to the Scarlet Rope. He wouldn't just banish Brady; he'd murder him.

Despite all my misgivings, I was still excited to go on actual dates with Brady. And, really, what could a date or two hurt? Maybe we'd realize we actually had nothing in common besides animal lust.

Sorry, Mom, I thought to myself after we'd returned home. *But I can't listen to you this time.*

Chapter 19

Grace

I looked myself up and down in the mirror, frowning. "What about this one?"

Kelly lounged on her bed as I tried on outfits for my first date with Brady. Kelly just shook her head and waved a hand. "Next."

I rolled my eyes but did as she commanded. Kelly knew better about picking good date outfits than I did.

I stripped out of the yellow sundress and put on a tight little magenta number.

Kelly sat up, her eyes wide. "Holy shit! Woman, that is your dress for sure."

The dress was so tight that I felt like I was naked. "How do you wear any underwear with this?"

"That's the thing. You don't." Kelly got up and pinched my ass, making me yelp. "Brady will definitely appreciate that little detail."

"I have to wear a bra—"

"Nah, you're good. You have little boobies." Kelly squeezed her chest. "You don't have monsters like me.

Have you ever tried to find cute bras in a 38G? Yeah, they don't exist."

I'd always envied Kelly her figure. She was curvaceous, a perfect hourglass, and yes, she had big breasts to boot.

My breasts were small. When I'd been younger, I'd been self-conscious enough that I'd wear padded bras. Once, as a teenager, Mom had caught me stuffing my bra with tissues, and she'd gently told me she'd buy me a padded bra instead.

"I wish I had bigger boobs." I sighed. "What if Brady likes big breasts?"

Kelly turned me around to face her. "Let me tell you a universal truth: straight guys love boobs. It doesn't matter the size, shape, or color. They love them all. Sure, some guys *really* like big titties like mine, but no guy is going to see boobs and think, 'never mind.'"

I grinned. "You're ridiculous."

"And I'm right. You know I am. Besides, Brady is already into you. Which means he likes what he's seen. And didn't he see you in lingerie twice now?"

"Yeah, but it was dark in the club." I blushed as I remembered the night I'd gotten drunk. "Okay, and there might've been another time, but I don't think he really saw much."

"What? Another time? You're killing me, babe. But remember, you're hot as fuck. Own it, okay?"

I glanced in the mirror again. I *did* look hot. I needed to own that.

I wasn't going to act like the shy virgin anymore. I wanted to be sexy and confident. I wanted to be a woman who Brady couldn't get out of his mind.

Kelly helped me with my hair and makeup, chattering about her grad program and how she wanted to murder one of her classmates for constantly talking over her.

"If I ever see that guy in a dark alley," she vowed, "I'm gonna beat his ass."

"Maybe he likes you."

Kelly's eyes bugged out. "Christ, don't say that. He's the worst. He mansplains constantly. He tried to tell me that I didn't know how periods worked. Periods, Grace!"

"Why were you talking about periods?"

Kelly waved a hand. "It doesn't matter. Just know this guy is the worst."

I still had an hour before Brady arrived to take me on our date. My stomach was filled with butterflies. What was even stranger was that I was more nervous about this than I was about going to the Scarlet Rope.

The club felt like a fantasyland where you could lose yourself for a bit with zero consequences. But a date, a real-life, honest-to-goodness date?

That was different. That meant that Brady wanted more than just a few spanking sessions to blow off some steam. That meant he *cared*.

"So do you have protection?" Kelly asked.

"Uh." My brain stalled. "I'm on birth control."

"You are? Why?"

"I got on it in college for acne." I shrugged.

"Well, that's convenient. Okay, but you'll still need condoms. Brady's stuck his dick in a lot of ladies."

I felt embarrassed that I hadn't even thought about condoms. Clearly, I was still acting like a virgin and not like a woman who was planning on getting laid.

"Won't Brady have condoms?" I asked.

"He might, and if he's smart, he should. But do you know how many times I've been with guys who suddenly either don't fit into any brands or are magically all out that night?" Kelly sighed. "Men are scum. Why do we date them?"

My lips twitched. "Maybe you should set the bar higher for yourself."

Kelly had wandered into her bathroom and then returned with a whole collection of condoms. "Here. I have all kinds of sizes. These purple ones are flavored."

I took her offering of condoms, nonplussed. "How much sex do you think we're going to have?"

"You're right. Give me back all but three of those and buy your own next time."

We had a faux tussle with me ending up with ten condoms. Kelly opened one of the flavored ones and licked it. She made a face. "Yeah, that's not good."

I gave it a lick and had to agree. It tasted like something, but it wasn't grape.

"My first time was terrible," Kelly said as she tried to blow up the purple condom. "It lasted like three minutes. I asked the guy if he was in. At least he was too small for it to hurt."

I'd imagined my first time on many occasions. And, of course, Brady was almost always the guy who took my virginity.

"I'm worried I'll be too awkward to be good at it," I admitted.

"You probably will be, but that's okay. Just like blowing up a condom"—Kelly grinned as she tried to tie off the air-filled condom—"you get better with practice. And it helps if your partner knows what he's doing, which Brady does. I'm sure you'll have an amazing time. I bet you even have an orgasm, you little shit."

I blushed, hoping Kelly was right. But at the same time, I didn't expect that Brady and I would have sex tonight.

What if he does want to sleep with me? The thought made me shiver with anticipation.

When the doorbell rang, I nearly ran to answer it. Brady wore a button-up shirt and slacks with his hair slicked back. His collar was open, and I had the sudden urge to taste that spot at the base of his throat.

He also held a bouquet. "Wow," he said, his eyes widening. "You look fucking amazing."

"Thank you. So do you."

He handed me the flowers, a cluster of red roses. "I realize now that since this is your friend's place, you can't leave the flowers here."

"I don't mind taking them with us. Do you want to come inside?"

"No, I don't want to break any rules before we even start."

I was about to ask him what he meant when Kelly came up behind me. Then she reached out a hand to Brady. "Kelly Wright, nice to meet you. I'm a huge fan."

Brady returned the handshake. "Love to hear it. Nice to meet you, Kelly."

Kelly shot me a mischievous grin. "Okay, well, you two have fun. You put those items I gave you in your purse?"

Brady asked, "Items?"

I blushed scarlet. "Uh, yeah. See you later, Kelly."

Brady took me out to one of the new sushi spots that had recently opened near the Grove. After Brady had handed his keys to the valet attendant, we were escorted to a Japanese-style room with sliding doors, a low table, and bamboo mats.

We sat down and gave our drink orders to our server. Brady said, "I might not have thought this plan through."

"What? Why not?"

He winced and then repositioned his legs. "Sitting like this is uncomfortable as hell."

I laughed. "I'm okay."

It took a few different tries, but Brady finally found a sitting position that worked for him, grumbling the entire time.

"I can't believe you're taking me out for sushi," I said. "Are you sure you're okay with this?"

"You said I had to try it someday. Besides, if it makes you happy, I'm happy."

His comment made my heart squeeze.

Once we'd been served platters of beautiful, colorful sushi, sashimi, and nigiri, the two of us were too preoccupied with eating to talk much. And I had to admit, I was thankful for it.

I was nervous still. I didn't know how to act like Brady's date. For so long, I'd been his foster sister, and he'd been the guy who'd refused my advances.

Then suddenly he was attracted to me, and now he was acting like . . . a boyfriend?

It was all so strange that my brain couldn't wrap my head around everything happening.

After that, we were focused on our food. To my delight, Brady ended up admitting that the sushi was amazing. He ate everything like a champ. It got to the point that we were almost brawling for the last slice of ahi tuna, which made us both laugh like idiots.

"So I wanted to talk to you about something," Brady said after we'd finished our entree. He pulled out a piece of paper from his back pocket, along with a pen. "I wanted to set some ground rules."

"Rules? For what?"

"Dating." I could see that Brady had already written down some things. "For instance, no more being indoors together alone. That only leads to—"

"Fun things?" I interjected.

Brady glowered at me. "Second," he continued, "no more showing up at my hotel room or sneaking into places to see me, or showing up near the locker rooms. Third, our first kiss can only last one minute. Our second, two minutes. Third, three. You catch my drift?"

He looked so serious that it took every ounce of self-control not to giggle. "I understand what you're saying, but this seems a little extreme."

"Extreme? No, I think this is the first smart thing I've done when it comes to you. Do you have any suggestions?"

I shook my head. Brady grunted and wrote down a few more things and then offered me the list.

I took it, read through it, and then promptly tore it into pieces.

"I agree to none of this," I proclaimed, rather amused at Brady's shocked expression. "Well, except sneaking into places to see you. I don't want to get caught, especially by my dad. At least not yet."

"I'm still going to have rules for us," Brady said, crossing his arms over his chest. "We need to go slowly."

"Brady, we've been doing foreplay for like a decade now. How much slower do you want to go?"

That made his lips twitch. "Slow, Grace. Just trust me."

"So you're saying I'll be eighty-five before we have sex. Awesome."

"Slow, Grace." Brady leaned forward, his gaze intent. "Being patient will pay off for us both. Besides, I never said we'd be sleeping together."

So much for all the condoms Kelly had given me. "Mmm, sure. Keep telling yourself that."

Brady didn't get a chance to respond before our server returned with our dessert, matcha ice cream and cherry-flavored mochi.

"How are your legs?" I asked Brady while we waited for the valet to bring Brady's car around.

He winced. "So much for being an athlete."

"Maybe you're just getting old."

"Behave yourself or I will take you over my knee again," he said in a low voice near my ear.

I shivered. I could only hope he would. At my excited expression, he just sighed.

"You're going to kill me, aren't you?" he said, almost to himself.

"Oh, absolutely."

"Are we going back to your place?" I asked as Brady began driving.

"No."

"A hotel?"

"No, Grace."

"Okay, well, if it's a motel, then I might still say yes, but you could spring for something nicer, you know. Seems kinda cheap of you."

Brady rolled his eyes. "I'm taking you skating. At a rink. No hotel, motel, or Holiday Inn."

I was disappointed, but I didn't protest further. At least Brady wanted to spend time with me. And whenever he gazed at me, I could see the heat in his eyes.

He wanted me. If we did go to his place, I knew he wouldn't have the self-restraint to keep refusing me.

"You never would go skating with me, would you?" Brady remarked after we'd gone inside the rink.

To my surprise, he had keys to the place from the owner himself. Which meant that we'd have the entire rink to ourselves.

"How exactly did you manage to get the owner to let you have keys to this place?" I asked, incredulous.

Brady grinned. "His daughter is a huge Blades fan."

"Of course she is."

Brady, though, seemed intent on getting me onto the ice. Ironically, I'd never really learned how to ice-skate, despite the fact that Ben played hockey.

"Do you want figure-skating skates or hockey?" Brady asked me as he went behind the desk to get skates for us.

"Um, your choice."

"Hockey skates it is."

When we finally got onto the ice, it took all of ten seconds before I fell on my butt. The first time, Brady caught me before I fell too hard. The second and third times, I nearly pulled Brady down with me.

"How do you not know how to skate?" he asked.

I shrugged. "I never got around to it."

Brady showed me how to skate, where to put my weight, and how to stop. He also told me that it was mostly about confidence. If you were overly worried about falling, you would.

"When you learned how to ride a bike, you probably were afraid of falling over, right?" asked Brady as he held my arm for a slow skate around the rink.

"I threw a fit when my dad took away my training wheels," I said with a laugh.

"But when you finally felt like you could ride your bike without worrying about falling, you didn't."

"So I should just not worry? Wow, great advice," I said.

Right then, Brady let me go. I nearly fell but managed to keep my balance this time. I kept skating, slowly gaining confidence with every second that passed without wiping out.

By the end, I felt more confident that I could learn how to skate. But even as I gained confidence, I had a hard time enjoying the ice.

Skating brought back a lot of memories I would've rather forgotten.

When I told Brady I needed a break, we sat down on a bench right outside the rink. Brady handed me a bottle of water.

"You seem like you're far away," he said.

"Oh. Sorry."

"Don't apologize. I just want to know why. At least, if you want to tell me."

This was maybe one of the first times I'd seen Brady unsure. It was also unusual to ask about my feelings like this. I was the one usually trying to get him to open up.

"There's a reason I never learned how to skate," I said quietly. I traced a line on my jeans, feeling suddenly vulnerable. "Ben was supposed to teach me. I'd been begging him for years, but he'd always told me he was too busy. The day he agreed to teach me, well . . ."

I could feel Brady stiffen beside me. "Oh, Jesus."

"Weird, right? The day my brother dies was the day he was supposed to teach me about his favorite sport."

I shrugged. "I took it as a sign that I wasn't meant to skate. Or maybe I just didn't want to. It didn't seem like a fun thing after that. It seemed cursed."

Brady was silent for a long moment. I glanced over at him, and I could tell he was tense. Was he thinking about Ben? Or had I upset him by telling him all this?

"I'm sorry. I should've asked you if you wanted to skate," Brady said finally.

"Oh, no." I touched his arm, and his gaze flew to where my fingers rested on his skin. "Don't apologize. This was fun. I wished I'd done this years earlier. It felt kind of therapeutic."

I could feel the tension in Brady's body slowly dissipate. He blew out a breath.

"I should take you home," he said before helping me up.

Brady was quiet on the drive back to my house. I had all kinds of thoughts running through my brain. Was Brady thinking about Ben? Or had his brain returned to the earlier subject of our date?

I doubt he's going to make a move on you when your parents are home, I thought to myself.

I really needed to get my own place if I wanted to get rid of this pesky virginity of mine.

I also needed to be brave. I couldn't wait around for Brady to make the first move. Based on his ridiculous "rules," he probably thought he wasn't allowed to touch me until ten years into our marriage.

"Park down here," I said.

"Wait, isn't your house a few blocks from here?"

"Exactly. I don't want my parents to see us on their security cam."

Brady did as I said and turned off the car. "Why do I feel like I'm doing something illegal?"

"Why, are you planning on burglarizing somebody's house after I go home?" I joked.

Brady didn't laugh. I could tell he was tense again.

Before I could lose my nerve, I took off my seat belt and climbed over the front console, sitting in Brady's lap.

With the steering wheel pressing into my back, we had only a few inches of space between our bodies. Brady's eyes narrowed.

"What are you doing?" he growled.

"Making a move." I pulled his head in for a kiss.

He seemed surprised at first, but it took only a milli-second before he groaned and deepened the kiss. Our lips and tongues moved in a rhythm that seemed to beat in the pit of my stomach.

Brady dug his fingers into my waist as the kiss intensi-fied. I raked my fingers through his hair, loving the way he responded to my touch. He shivered when I scratched my nails on the nape of his neck.

"You're playing with fire," he rasped.

I could feel his erection pressing against my pussy. It only made me want him more. I wanted to feel how hard he was in my hands, feel him pulse against my fingers—

"I need to touch you," I whispered.

Brady shook his head. "We can't."

I rubbed against him, making him grit his teeth. "Please," I mewled.

Brady kissed me hard one last time and then said, "I'll take you home."

I could tell he wasn't going to change his mind. I sighed and awkwardly returned to the passenger seat. I blushed when I realized that my dress had been pulled so high that Brady probably saw that I wasn't wearing any panties.

The three blocks to my parents' seemed like three thousand miles. It didn't help that I was so horny I felt like I was going to burst. I could see Brady's erection pressing against his pants. Weren't blue balls painful? I didn't understand how he could say no when his body was clearly desperate to say yes.

"Have a good night, Grace," said Brady. He wouldn't even look at me now.

"Oh, I will. With my vibrator." I blew him a kiss as I got out of the car.

I heard Brady groan and say, "Damn, you're evil," making me laugh like a crazy woman.

Chapter 20

Brady
Seven Years Ago

"Can you pick me up?" Grace asked.

Grace had called me in the middle of trying to finish a paper for my English class. I'd been so surprised that she'd called me that I'd picked up after the first ring.

"Can't Ben get you? I'm writing a paper," I said.

"I can't get ahold of him. And I can't call my parents."

"What about your friend? Didn't she drive you?"

I knew Grace's friend Meredith was sixteen and already had her license. Meredith often came to the house to pick up Grace; she'd also flirt with me even though I knew she had a boyfriend.

"Meredith had to go home because she got sick." Grace paused. "And the other kids brought beer with them. I think they're drunk. So I don't want to ride with them."

I sighed. Well, I already knew I'd be pulling an all-nighter on this stupid essay on *The Scarlet Letter*. "Okay, fine. I'll come get you. And do not get in the car with any of those other people."

I hated drunk drivers. Mom had driven drunk more times than I could remember and had gotten plenty of DUIs. Every time I heard about her getting arrested for drinking and driving, I almost wished she would've gotten somebody else hurt. Then maybe she'd get a wake-up call to fix her life.

Now that I was seventeen, though, I hadn't had much contact with Mom. It wasn't worth the drama. When I'd been younger, I'd hoped that she'd get her life together so I could go back home.

Every year, from ages six to ten, I'd wish on my birthday that Mom would stop drinking.

By age eleven, when she'd left her millionth rehab after only three days after I'd begged her to go, I'd realized that she was never going to change.

Then, when I'd gotten older and had started earning money at part-time jobs, she'd hit me up for cash. Sometimes she'd managed to guilt-trip me into giving her a twenty here and there. Usually, that was when she was homeless and starving.

I'd driven to the outskirts of the city to find her when I'd only had my learner's permit. But I couldn't tell Mr. and Mrs. Dallas what I was doing.

I found Mom outside an abandoned house with a bunch of other homeless people. A few were shooting up heroin right out in the open.

"Baby!" Mom's eyes lit up when she saw me. "You made it. Let me introduce you to my friends."

Even at fifteen, I knew these people were no friends. I avoided their gazes and took my mom aside.

"I only have forty bucks," I said as I handed her the cash I'd saved up from my part-time job as a server.

Mom's face fell. "Only forty? Baby, I have bills. You sure you can't spare any more?"

I could feel one guy leering at me, and it creeped me the fuck out. "I don't have any more," I protested.

Mom's expression shuttered. She took the cash and stuffed it into her pocket. "Whatever. I know that family you live with. They're rich. You could ask them for money anytime."

"I can't ask them!"

"Then steal it. You think they'd notice when they're rolling in it? I'm out here, homeless, and you're acting like you're too good to help me."

I shook my head. I couldn't believe this. Anger made me snarl, "Go fuck yourself. I'm done."

After that incident, I'd pretty much stopped talking to my mom. When she'd call the Dallases, I'd tell them to tell her that I was busy. Mrs. Dallas had tried to ask me what'd changed, but I'd clammed up.

What was worse was that sometimes I'd consider what she'd said. The Dallases had plenty of money, while Mom was out on the streets. If I could steal enough to get her into a legit rehab center, maybe, just maybe . . .

But then I'd shove the thoughts aside, disgusted with myself. The Dallases didn't need to deal with my mom's insanity. And I was done with dealing with it, too.

So, yeah, I didn't have much patience for kids my age drinking and driving. Getting drunk? Sure, whatever. I'd done it, and I'd do it again.

But driving and potentially killing yourself or others? That was bullshit. It also meant you didn't have control of yourself, just like how Mom had never been in control of herself.

Which meant that if Grace needed me to pick her up when I had a paper to write, I'd do it. If I could do anything to keep her safe, I'd do it, no questions asked.

Because she's like a little sister to you? Or because you want her to be something more than that?

It took twenty minutes for me to get to the theater. When I arrived, though, I didn't see Grace outside. I circled the parking lot twice before I finally parked to go find Grace myself.

Had she given up on me coming to get her? The thought of her getting in the car with a drunk driver made me want to punch something. I went inside the theater, but I didn't see Grace anywhere.

I was about to call her when I saw two people near a dimly lit wall outside. The couple then moved a few inches, enough that they were now somewhat illuminated by a streetlamp.

That was when I realized it was Grace and some boy I'd seen around our high school. And, to my shock, they were kissing.

I was glued to the spot. Every emotion under the sun ran through me—surprise, envy, annoyance. What the hell was she thinking, making out with some kid right outside the movie theater?

The two clearly didn't give a shit if they had an audience. I crossed my arms, watching the free show, irritated with myself when I grew hard.

Grace was running her fingers through the kid's hair. I could tell she was into kissing this nerd, whoever the fuck he was.

I wondered what it would be like if Grace kissed me like that. If she ran her fingers through my hair, arched against me, her body rubbing against mine—

I swore under my breath. I stalked back to my car and called Grace's phone. I could still see her from where I'd parked. I could also tell that she was ignoring my phone call.

Finally, I saw her pick up. "Yeah?" she answered, sounding breathless.

"I'm here, near the entrance. I'm parked next to a big red truck."

I snorted when I saw her looking around for me. Was she worried that I'd seen her making out with that boy?

Thinking about Grace like this was strange. She'd always seemed like too much of a Goody Two-shoes to pull a stunt like this. Then again, I'd noticed she'd been hanging around a shitty crowd lately.

It hadn't helped that Grace's friend Meredith seemed to be the instigator. Meredith had started dating Tom Garrison, who was notorious for smoking weed out in the parking lot, skipping class, and getting suspended for vandalism. And as far as I knew, Meredith had started joining her fuckboy boyfriend in his bullshit.

Grace finally found my car and climbed inside. Her cheeks were red, and I had to bite back a sarcastic remark when I saw how messed up her hair was.

"Sorry, were you waiting long?" she asked. She yanked on the seat belt too hard, making it catch. She did that a few more times before she finally managed to put it on.

"You good?" I drawled.

"Fine." Grace was running her fingers through her hair now. "Do you have a comb, by chance?"

"No." Then I turned on the radio for the rest of the ride home.

Grace seemed like her thoughts were far away, which was fine with me. I wasn't about to ask her about that boy she was kissing. It was none of my fucking business, anyway.

It didn't matter that she'd grown into a beautiful young woman lately, or that I had dreams about her that I could never, ever tell anyone about. Or that whenever I passed by her in school, I had to act like we were strangers.

Because I knew being just her friend would never work. I had to be cold. I had to act like she was just an annoyance, a younger sister who got on my nerves.

You need to get yourself the fuck together, I thought. *You can't keep thinking about Grace like this.*

I also knew that her parents and Ben would never, ever let us be together. Her dad would strangle me, and then Ben would join him.

Once Ben had caught me staring at Grace when she came downstairs wearing a tiny sundress. He'd taken me aside later and said if he saw me eye-fucking his sister again, he'd break my spine.

I hadn't even been pissed at Ben's threat. I was nothing. I was the foster kid with fucked-up parents who were too addicted to drugs and alcohol to live decent lives.

I wasn't the type of guy Grace deserved.

"Are you okay?" Grace asked me after we got off the interstate. "You seem mad."

I turned down the radio. "I'm not mad."

"You sure? I'm sorry I made you come get me."

"I mean, I'm annoyed because I have to finish a paper, and you should've made sure you had a ride home."

Grace winced. "Meredith was supposed to take me home."

"Didn't Meredith flake on you not long ago? Left you downtown to go meet up with her boyfriend?"

"She asked me if that was okay, you know."

I snorted. "Sure, okay."

"Why don't you like Meredith?"

"I don't give a shit about Meredith."

I knew I was being an asshole, but I'd rather Grace think that I was a dick than realize I was annoyed that I'd seen her kissing another guy.

Grace huffed. "Now I know that you're mad."

"Think whatever you want."

We said nothing when we arrived home. Grace immediately went upstairs to her room, stomping the entire way. When I heard her slam her bedroom door, I shook my head.

Hate me all you want. It's better this way.

Grace had had a crush on me for ages. It was good that she was moving on. If she dated other guys, she'd forget about me.

I returned to my room and tried to focus on writing my paper, but my mind wouldn't stop thinking about what I'd seen at the theater.

When had Grace started dating? Was this her first boyfriend? I'd never heard about her dating somebody else.

And how had she learned to kiss like that? Had that guy taught her?

I was gripping my pen so hard I almost snapped it in two. I groaned, rubbing my face.

My dick was hard again, thinking about Grace kissing that guy. Christ, what the fuck was wrong with me? And would I ever get rid of this attraction to a girl I could never have?

Chapter 21

Grace
Present Day

"Have you guys ever been here?" Elodie asked as we all sat down at a booth. "The chicken and waffles are divine."

"I've been here once," said Brady, "but it was a long time ago."

"Didn't you come here after you'd hooked up with that Russian model?" Mac said, grinning.

Elodie elbowed her fiancé, and he winced. "Grace, don't listen to him," she said.

I shrugged. "I know Brady has been a man whore. It's okay."

Mac laughed, especially when Brady looked embarrassed.

"I haven't slept with that many women," Brady groused, staring at the menu now.

"Oh, come on, you and I both know you've been even more prolific than me." Mac then remembered I was still there. "Uh, but that's all in the past. Completely forgotten."

Elodie rolled her eyes. "Men are idiots," she said to me.

"You don't have to tell me," I replied.

Brady had suggested that we go on a double date with Mac and Elodie. Part of me had been excited, while the other part of me knew this was just another ploy to keep Brady from touching me.

He couldn't pull me into some dark alley to feel me up if his best friends were around. It was like having chaperones, except they weren't your overly strict aunt Linda who liked to remind you to save room for Jesus.

Elodie had suggested her favorite diner, to which we'd all readily agreed.

After we'd ordered, Elodie said to me, "How's it going with you two so far?"

Brady and I exchanged glances. "Good. I think?" I replied.

Brady frowned. "You think?"

"I mean, this is only our second date."

"What did you do for your first date?" Mac asked.

"We got sushi, and Brady complained about sitting on the floor," I said.

Brady snorted. "You try sitting at those low tables and see how you feel."

Right then, a few women came up to our booth, their expressions agog. They were clearly Blades fans, and they had their phones ready.

"Can we get a selfie?" they asked Mac and Brady.

"Not right now," said Elodie, firmly but gently. "The guys aren't working tonight."

The girls looked annoyed, but they didn't push their luck. They finally went back to their seats, but not without whispering in each other's ears.

"You know they're probably going to post on social media that you're a jerk," said Mac.

Elodie shrugged. "Whatever. You don't always have to say yes to fans. You're out to dinner right now."

"Elodie was still polite to them," I said.

"Oh, I know," said Mac, sighing, "but I know what happens when you piss people off. Sometimes it's easier to just say yes and avoid the bad press."

"Since when did you care about bad press?" Elodie asked, frowning.

Mac's expression turned serious. "When I started dating you, babe. People can say whatever they want, but when they say shit about you . . ." He grimaced. "It fucking sucks."

"Hey, whatever. It's okay to say no," said Elodie. Her gaze turned toward me. "But I will say, dating a famous person has a lot of baggage that comes with it. It doesn't help when fans get offended when their favorite celebrity starts dating somebody."

I bit my lip. Since Brady and I weren't officially dating, I hadn't had anybody talking about me online. Nobody even knew that I existed.

"I won't let people fuck with you," Brady said to me. He squeezed my hand under the table.

"You can't really control that, unfortunately," said Elodie.

"But you can always change the narrative. You just have to stay on top of it. If something blows up, get it under control as soon as possible," said Mac.

I couldn't help but think about Brady going to the Scarlet Rope. He'd said he didn't care if people found out, but was that true? And what if fans found out we'd been there together?

I realized I hadn't been as careful as I should be. I felt a little sick to my stomach.

"And women are always throwing themselves at these guys," Elodie was saying as she rolled her eyes. "It's insane. I'll be standing right there, and women will try to get you to go home with them."

Mac looked embarrassed. "I never say yes."

"I'm not worried about you. But it's just so brazen." Elodie shook her head. She said to me, "Anyway, I don't know if this is helping you feel good about dating Brady. But you should know the downsides, too."

"I think I'm more worried about how people will react when they find out I'm the coach's daughter," I admitted.

Mac and Elodie glanced at each other.

"How are you going to deal with that, exactly?" Mac asked.

Brady answered for me. "One day at a time," he said firmly. "And we don't owe anybody an explanation."

"Maybe, but you might think about how you'll frame the story. Turn it into a star-crossed lovers romance that people will think is romantic instead of, you know, nepotistic," said Elodie.

"I was already on the team," said Brady, frowning. "How is this nepotism?"

"My man, people will find a reason," said Mac, shaking his head. "Believe me."

"Well, whatever does happen, you guys were already friends, so that helps a lot. Mac and I have already gone through a bunch of shit, but we got through it because our relationship was worth fighting for," said Elodie.

Mac looked down at his fiancée, love pouring out of his expression. It was so intense that I almost looked away.

I wondered if Brady would ever look at me like that. Sure, he wanted me, but would he ever *love* me? And not just as a guy who'd been around my family for years and cared about us all in a general sense.

Our food arrived right then, diverting my attention. We all focused on our food. And I had to admit, it was amazing. I hadn't had fried chicken like this in ages.

When I moaned and licked my fingers, Brady gave me a heated look. I just licked my fingers a second time to remind him of what he could be enjoying tonight if he wanted.

"Stop it," Brady growled under his breath.

I grinned. "Make me."

"Hey, you two, get a room," joked Mac.

"Please tell that to Brady, because he won't get us one," I complained.

Elodie raised her eyebrows. "Wait, are you saying—"

"We're not talking about this," interjected Brady. He gave me a warning look. "Besides, I'm trying to be a gentleman. Is that such a bad thing?"

"I thought you just said you weren't talking about this," I pointed out.

Mac laughed. "Oh, man, you're in for it, Brady."

"You want to be a gentleman, but that doesn't mean you have to deny yourself or me," I added, speaking to Brady.

"I want to protect you." Brady looked frustrated.

"I wish you wouldn't, then," I said quietly.

Mac quickly changed the subject to discussing the Blades upcoming match. Elodie and I listened and sometimes rolled our eyes at each other when the guys got heated about a teammate or ref they hated.

"That asshole in Vancouver always gives me penalties," Mac complained, "even when I haven't done a goddamn thing. I didn't even touch Murphy that last game. And I fucking wanted to."

"I know, I know," said Brady, shaking his head. "Aren't Canadians supposed to be nice? Because that guy is an asshole. He loves to put you in the box."

"Maybe he has a penalty box kink," Elodie said, tapping her chin.

I laughed. "Don't give these guys any ideas."

The dinner ended with us hugging and saying goodbye while promising to do this again. When Elodie hugged me, she whispered in my ear, "Brady is a good guy. I know he'll do right by you."

But as I drove Brady to his place—he'd needed me to drive tonight since his car was in the shop until tomorrow—I wondered at Elodie's words.

Not that I didn't believe Brady wasn't a good guy. He was. I already knew that. But I didn't know if he would do right by me.

How could he, when he refused to touch me no matter how much I begged? Sometimes I felt like a china doll he was afraid to break.

It also didn't help that Brady looked extra hot tonight. He'd worn a fitted tee and jeans, nothing fancy, but the T-shirt showed off his physique. He also sported a five-o'clock shadow that I wanted to run my palms along.

God, I was desperate for this man. I could feel myself getting wet just imagining him touching me.

Would he at least kiss me tonight? He'd said he would when he'd made up those silly rules. Two minutes for the kiss on date number two.

After I'd parked in front of Brady's apartment, I got out of the car to follow him inside.

"Babe, I told you to go home," Brady protested.

I steeled myself. "I'm not going home. Not yet."

He looked frustrated. Raking his fingers through his hair, he sighed. "This is a terrible idea."

"You didn't even kiss me." Now, I sounded petulant, but I didn't care.

His eyes darkened. "This is just about a kiss?" He pulled me into his arms, pressing my body against him. "Because I was always going to kiss you good night."

Before he could kiss me, though, I extricated myself from his grasp. "Not out here. Inside."

He swore. I ignored him. When we got to his door, he tried one last time to tell me to go home, but I refused.

"You were put on this earth to drive me insane, weren't you?" Brady asked, almost to himself.

I felt giddy with excitement, but also nervousness. I'd had an idea of what I wanted to do tonight, but I wasn't sure I would work up the nerve.

I'd given one other guy a blow job before. It had been . . . lackluster, to say the least. I hadn't known what I was doing, and he hadn't provided much in the way of instruction. When I'd struggled to finish him off, he'd sighed and had said I could stop.

But I wanted to try with Brady. Brady would make sure we both had an amazing time. And I wanted to show him that I could give him pleasure just like he'd given me with the spankings and the kisses.

"I want to blow you," I blurted.

Brady froze in his tracks. "What?"

"You heard me." I stood up straighter. "Where do you want to do it? In your bedroom?"

Brady was still gaping at me. "Christ, Grace, where did this come from?"

I decided that if this was going to happen, it would be right here. I dropped to my knees and began to unbuckle his belt, looking up at him the entire time.

His pupils widened as I undid his belt and slowly unzipped his fly. I rubbed my other hand over his erection, which I could feel growing against my palm.

His breathing increased. "Grace," he growled.

"Tell me to stop," I said, "and I will."

I waited. He seemed to be fighting an internal battle. But he just nodded, his expression telling me that he'd die if I stopped.

My own heart was pounding with anticipation. I'd wanted to see Brady's cock for so long. Not just see it, but lick it, taste it, watch it grow and throb as he finally came all over my face.

I rubbed him a little longer through his jeans. My eyes widened when I realized how large he was getting. But I couldn't stop the gasp when I finally saw his size with my own eyes.

"Lord Almighty," I whispered. How the hell would I ever get this inside me? He'd split me in two.

"It'll fit," he rasped. "Believe me."

I shook my head, even as I wanted to believe him. Then again, he'd know better than I ever would.

I sat back on my heels, gazing at him, loving the tension thrumming through him as I made him wait for my touch. His cock was hard, veins pulsing on the sides, the tip already excreting precum.

I took hold of his cock and lick the tip of it. He tasted salty. I hummed in my throat as I began to stroke him with my hand while I swirled my tongue around the tip.

I couldn't tell whether Brady was really enjoying this, though. He was just gazing down at me with those eyes that seemed to burn through me.

"How is it?" I asked, suddenly feeling shy.

He caressed my cheek before taking my hand and squeezing it. "Harder when you stroke me. Yes, like that. You won't hurt me. And when you do that, try to take me into your mouth."

I did as he asked. He groaned when I slowly took his length into my mouth until the tip was touching the back of my throat. I forced myself to stay still, not giving in to my gag reflex.

I sucked him until he started groaning and digging his fingers into my hair. I let him go with a pop as I sucked in air.

"Jesus, you're a natural," he said, his cheeks flushed. "I'm going to finish soon if you're not careful."

"Isn't that the goal?"

"Not always." He wiped saliva from my chin. "I never thought I'd see you on your knees for me. It's sexy as fuck."

I squeezed the base of his cock and began fucking him with my mouth. I loved the way he swore and moaned. The last—and only—guy I'd given a blow job to had been dead silent.

Brady, though, wasn't shy. He moved his hips in time with my mouth, until he was hitting so far inside my throat I didn't know how I was managing it.

"Grace, I'm coming," he gritted out. "If you need to stop now—"

I kept going. I sucked him so hard that he shouted. Then I felt him shoot into my mouth. He came with seemingly endless pulses. I swallowed his cum, looking up at him as I did so.

He was shaking his head at me. "Dammit, Grace." He lifted me up and kissed me so hard that it almost felt like he was angry with me.

Or maybe he was just angry with himself.

"Fuck it. We already broke the rules tonight. I'm not going to let you go home without my mouth on you," he said.

He carried me to his bedroom and laid me on his bed. He stripped off my jeans and panties with alarming speed. If I weren't so desperate for him, I might've been afraid.

He parted my thighs and gazed at my pussy for so long that I squirmed. "What are you staring at?" I asked.

"You're beautiful." He parted my pussy lips and groaned. "You're dripping already. Did sucking my cock turn you on, baby?"

I nodded. He sighed and then leaned down to lick me from taint to clit.

I squealed. I'd never had a guy go down on me before. I'd imagined it, dreamed about it, wondered what it would be like, but nothing could compare with the real thing.

Brady buried his face in my pussy and went to work. He licked and sucked at my clit as he pushed a finger inside me. I writhed, the pleasure nearly unbearable.

"Oh God, I'm going to come too fast," I complained.

Brady's eyes crinkled. "Is that a bad thing?"

I didn't get a chance to answer. He just kept licking and sucking until I couldn't breathe. When he hooked his finger upward inside me, my eyes flew open at the burst of pleasure.

"Oh my God," I moaned. I was humping his face to the point that he had to use his arm to keep my hips on the bed.

"Come all over my face," he commanded. He increased the pressure of his fingers against my G-spot. "Come for me, Grace."

I didn't have to be told twice. I came with a scream as my body was wracked by the intensity of my orgasm.

Brady growled, holding me down harder as he kept my orgasm going for as long as he could.

I was panting when Brady took me into his arms. I vaguely heard the sound of a phone ringing.

"Ignore it," Brady said.

But his phone kept ringing, and ringing, and then it started ringing again. Brady swore and pulled his phone from his pocket, answering the call with a gruff, "What is it?"

He was silent for a long moment. I sat up, concerned, watching a variety of expressions move across his face.

After he hung up, he said, "It's my mom. She's dying."

Chapter 22

Brady

When Grace told me she was coming with me to Las Vegas, I didn't have the strength to tell her no. And as we drove to the hospital, I couldn't help but be thankful that she was with me.

Mom's nurse said she had only days left. When I'd called the nurse after we'd gotten into town, the nurse had told me that Mom was hanging on.

"I think she's waiting for you to say goodbye," the nurse had said, her voice kind.

I didn't want to think about that. I didn't want to believe that this was truly the end.

How many times had Mom gotten so sick that the doctors had thought this was it? Too many to count.

Then again, there'd always been the hope that if Mom turned her life around, she would recover. But now that wasn't the case.

It was too late for her to get over the addiction that had destroyed her life.

"Am I a bad person?" I asked Grace. "Because I don't want to go to the hospital at all."

Grace looked surprised. "You're not a bad person. Of course you don't want to see your mom sick."

"Not just sick. Dying." I shook my head. "Is it weird that I can't believe that? She's been dying for years, it feels like. One drink away from her organs failing. One drink from getting cancer, or whatever. I've heard it a billion times."

"You're allowed to feel whatever you feel. There's no rule book for grief."

I glanced at her. How could I have forgotten? She knew what it was like to lose someone she loved. I squeezed her hand, and she squeezed back.

"The craziest thing is that I still believe I should've done more," I admitted. "I had the money. I could've sent her to the best rehabs in the country. I could've paid somebody to make her stay in one. It would've been unethical, but I could've done it. I could've made her get sober."

"You and I both know you can't make somebody sober if they don't want to be," Grace said.

"Maybe I should've had her live with me. I could've looked out for her. Made sure she didn't drink all the time. I've looked after her before when she was in withdrawal. I could've hired nurses, even."

I knew I was sounding like a crazy person. But guilt weighed on me, heavy and oppressive.

Guilt that I hadn't tried harder. Guilt that I hadn't thrown every last penny into getting my mom better. Guilt that I'd failed her in the end.

"It's my fault she's a drunk," I said, sighing.

"Brady, of course that's not true. Your mom has always made her own choices."

I shook my head. "She got pregnant with me when she was sixteen. Her parents kicked her out of the house. She was homeless for a while, and it was bad. Real bad. My dad was a piece of shit and too busy selling drugs to care about me or Mom. She told me once that she'd started drinking because it was the only way to stay warm at night in the desert."

"That was not your fault," Grace said, her tone firm. "You were a baby. And even now, as an adult, you're not to blame."

Although I appreciated Grace's words, I couldn't believe them. Because if I did, it meant that I had to admit that I couldn't control everything that'd happened in my life. That I couldn't have willed Mom to get better.

We arrived at the hospital later that afternoon. The place was a mess, with nobody at the front desk who seemed able to figure out which room Mom was even in.

"You're sure she's checked in to this hospital?" one attendant asked me for a second time.

I gave the name of the nurse I'd spoken to. That nurse's shift had ended, so she was no help.

Finally, after what felt like an eternity, we were given Mom's room and pointed vaguely in the direction of where we should go.

"I should've transferred her to a better facility," I muttered to Grace as we went upstairs to the fifth floor. "Not this fucking hellhole."

When we got to Mom's room, though, I knew in an instant that it was too late to transfer her.

She was a shell of herself, so thin that I could see the bones sticking through her chest. Her eyes were sunken in; her skin was a horrific yellow color. She was on a ventilator, so she was completely sedated.

"Mom? It's Brady," I said, sitting down next to her. I took her hand, which was so bony and thin that my heart ached. "I'm here."

Grace sat down next to me and put a hand on my arm.

Nurses came and went, taking Mom's vitals and answering my questions. One assured me to keep talking to my mom, even if it felt like she couldn't hear me.

I felt ridiculous talking to somebody who was sedated, but I did it anyway. It helped that Grace talked, too. We told Mom all about my latest game, and how much fun we'd had going out on dates together.

The afternoon waned into the evening. We ate some terrible hospital food and returned to Mom's room. When I told Grace she could check in to a hotel for the night, she declined.

"I'm not leaving you," she promised.

I just sighed and helped her make a bed on the hard couch near the window. For me, I stayed sitting in a chair next to Mom's bedside.

I must've dozed off because the next moment, I woke to the sound of alarms and nurses rushing into the room. I stood to get out of their way.

"She's in cardiac arrest," a nurse said.

"Aren't you going to fucking do something?" I yelled, horrified at her inaction.

The nurse gave me a sad look. "Your mom signed a DNR before she was put on a ventilator. There's nothing we can do."

I couldn't believe it. I wanted to argue, to beg, to demand that they resuscitate Mom anyway.

Grace took my hand. Tears were in her eyes, but she didn't say anything.

A physician came into the room. We all watched as Mom's heart finally stopped beating completely. And then the nurses began turning off the ventilator and taking out the breathing tube.

"Time of death, one thirteen," said the head nurse quietly.

I was squeezing Grace's hand so tightly that I was probably hurting her. But she didn't pull away.

It was only her standing next to me that kept me from falling to my knees and screaming in agony.

After that, it was a lot of paperwork, condolences, brochures for funeral homes, and assurances that Mom was no longer suffering. Before Grace and I headed to our hotel, I gave Mom a kiss on the cheek and told her that I loved her.

"How will we check in to our room?" I asked Grace, my brain filled with sludge.

"Don't worry," she told me.

I realized that she'd made sure we would be able to check in no matter the time since the hotel had check-in kiosks. That extra bit of effort made me want to burst into tears.

How had I ever deserved this woman in my life?

Once we finally got into our room, I just sat down on the bed, exhausted but knowing that there was no way I was going to be able to fall asleep again.

Grace sat down next to me.

"There's a game tomorrow," I said suddenly. "I can't go."

"I already let Mac know. He'll tell my dad," Grace replied.

"Okay."

I couldn't look at her. I couldn't move either. I felt her hand reach for mine, but I didn't want to be touched right then.

Touching hurt. Touching reminded me that Mom couldn't feel any kind of touch again. She was cold and lying in the hospital morgue.

"I need to shower," I said abruptly, getting up.

The moment I stood under the hot water, the tears started. I'd almost thought I didn't have any tears to shed for Mom anymore. I'd cried enough about her over the years. As a kid, I'd quickly realized how pointless crying was.

But I couldn't stop. I sobbed until I had to lean over, trying to catch my breath. I'd never felt like this before. Completely overwhelmed with emotion.

It hurt. Why did it have to hurt this much?

"Oh, Brady." And then Grace held me in her arms, letting me cry against her shoulder. She helped me up when I couldn't do it myself.

I cried until my eyes hurt and the water was running cold. It was only when Grace helped me out of the shower and handed me a towel that I realized she was still wearing her clothes.

"You're soaked," I said, my voice hoarse.

She shrugged. She dripped all over the floor, her hair plastered to her head, her mascara running. She looked absolutely gorgeous.

"I'll hang my clothes on the balcony. Now, go get into bed, okay?" she said.

I did as she bade. I didn't have the energy to protest. After getting under the covers, I waited for her to join me.

There'd been no discussion of separate rooms this trip, and I was infinitely grateful for it. Even if I wasn't up for sex, I needed Grace's company to get through this.

I've never felt so weak, I thought. I hated it. But thank God the only person to see me like this was Grace.

I felt Grace climb into bed behind me, putting her arms around me. I pressed her hands to my chest and fell asleep.

I woke up right before dawn. Grace was already awake; I could smell coffee brewing.

"Good morning," she said softly and returned to the bed. "How are you?"

"I feel like shit," I admitted. It was true: my eyes still hurt, my head ached, and I felt like I'd been run over. "Maybe I'm getting sick."

"I think you're just exhausted." Grace pressed a hand to my forehead. "No fever."

"What do I do now?"

Grace sighed and lay back down in the bed. "You do all of the things you have to do. You call the funeral home. You choose cremation or burial, depending on what the person wanted.

"You think about what color coffin they'd want, and then feel weird that you're even thinking about it because they're not really dead. It just can't be true. But you still have to call people to tell them the news. I think that might be the worst part of all, telling people. That makes it seem real."

Her voice trailed off. I took her hand as her gaze caught mine.

"I helped my parents when Ben died," she said. Sadness filled her face. "My mom was too devastated to do any of it. My dad did his best, but he needed help."

"And you stepped in," I said.

Grace shrugged. "So lucky for you, I've done this before. I can help you."

And Grace did just that: she helped me with anything she could. After we'd done all the necessary steps, we received the few personal items Mom had had with her from the hospital's front desk.

"I'm sorry for your loss," the woman said. Then a second later, she was on the phone and yelling at somebody about a billing error code.

I hadn't planned on going to Mom's place, but something drew me there. I told myself it was just to make sure everything was in order, or, worse, she hadn't left some poor dog or cat to starve. Mom had tended to go through pets quickly, although in recent years, she hadn't wanted to spend the money on anything but booze.

When I unlocked her apartment door, I was assailed by a scent of cigarettes and marijuana that nearly made me choke. Grace went to open a window and turn on a fan, but that only made it worse.

"Jesus, Mom," I muttered, looking at the mess.

The place was a hoarder's dream—or nightmare. Every available surface was covered with stuff: from trash to magazines to records to bags of unopened purchases. I went through a few of the plastic bags, finding things that ranged from cooking utensils to stuffed animals to books that clearly had never been read.

"How did she buy all this stuff?" I asked, shaking my head. "I don't get it."

Grace was wiping dust from a photo album. Upon opening it, she discovered there were zero photos inside.

We wandered around the apartment, taking it all in. Despite all the crap, I couldn't help but feel strangely at home. Mom's personality and craziness were in every-thing, from the stuff to the random decor.

Weird posters and paintings that looked like they'd been grabbed out of dumpsters. Ugly lamps that looked older than me and rugs in garish colors. There was no theme to Mom's decor, besides being bright and obvious.

When we went to Mom's bedroom, I felt sick. The room was covered in bottles: wine, beer, liquor. Rows and rows of them covered tables, dressers, her nightstand. When I pulled a drawer from under her bed, it was full of bottles. All empty.

"Wow," said Grace.

"My mother, ladies and gentlemen," I said, bitterness dripping from my voice. I slammed the drawer back under the bed.

"Hey, Brady," said Grace, motioning at me, "look at this."

Grace handed me an album. Half expecting it to be empty like the one in the living room, I was shocked to find it filled. And it was filled with photos and articles about me.

Not only were there recent articles that Mom had taken the time to print, but there were even stories of my wins in junior hockey leagues as a kid. Interspersed throughout were photos of me with her handwriting in notes next to the photos.

My handsome boy 16 yrs old

Brady the hockey star 22 yrs old

Where did my sweet baby go? 3 yrs old

I sat on the edge of Mom's bed and flipped through the pages. I couldn't believe she'd saved all this. I found movie theater stubs from when we'd gone to the movies together; I even found tickets from the few hockey games she'd been able to take me to.

The photos of me petered off after age five, when I'd gone into foster care. But there were still more than I'd expected. She must've been asking for updates about me from my foster families.

"She really loved me," I said, marveling.

"Of course she did. She was your mom."

I shook my head. Seeing this made me feel even guiltier. I should've done better by Mom. I should never have left her to stay sick and die alone.

"Everyone I love only gets hurt around me," I whispered. I looked Grace in the eye. "I don't know if we should be together for that very reason."

"Really?" Grace beamed at me. "Because what I'm hearing sounds a whole lot like you love me."

Chapter 23

Brady

I went for a drive alone after Mom's funeral. Grace had been hesitant to let me be by myself, but I'd insisted.

I needed time to think. Although Grace's presence gave me a lot of comfort, a part of me still needed to be away from her.

Maybe because I felt guilty for involving her in this. What right had I to drag her into my life drama?

Only a few people had been able to attend Mom's funeral. Marty had given me a brief hug, telling me how sorry he was. I met a few of Mom's fellow AA members who'd known her for a long time.

But there weren't any other family members to attend. Mom's parents had died a long time ago, and she'd been estranged from her two siblings since before I'd been born. My dad was God knows where. After he'd gotten out of prison, he'd disappeared. For all I knew, he was dead, too.

Grace had stood next to me throughout the service. She'd greeted the few attendees, chatting with them all, besides helping me arrange everything. She'd been my rock through the entire process.

She'd asked me whether I'd wanted her parents to attend, but I'd declined. I didn't want Coach Dallas's pitying glances or Elise's sympathetic hugs. I knew they'd mean well, but they were just a reminder of the parents I never had.

So now I was driving on the outskirts of Vegas, the desert sun bright and blinding, the afternoon heat cloying. I didn't have a destination in mind. But when I drove up to the Dallases' old house, I couldn't be surprised at myself.

It was a charming two-story house with white shutters and a small porch. It looked much the same as when the Dallases had sold it, except for the landscaping. The new owners had gotten rid of the grass and had planted all kinds of succulents instead. I smiled, thinking of how much pride Coach had put into that damn lawn. He'd flip a lid if he knew these owners had torn up his precious sod.

There was a small park across the street. I went to sit on a bench under a tree, staring at the house I'd loved so much and thinking about the family who'd taken me in when I'd needed them.

The Dallases had shaped me in ways that could never be repaid. They'd supported my hockey career and had always made me feel like one of their family members. Even though Coach would never support me dating his daughter, I didn't resent him for it.

Because he knew I wasn't good enough for his daughter, something that I was also aware of. But my problem was that I couldn't stay away from Grace despite my best efforts.

I thought of what Grace had said last night, that I loved her. And I realized at that moment that I did love her, and I couldn't let her go. I didn't have the strength. Losing Mom made me realize that life was too short to be alone. If we had only a few weeks or months together, it'd be worth it.

I knew I'd disappoint the Dallases if I stayed on this path. That thought almost made me want to change my mind. But what I felt for Grace was stronger than the fear of their disapproval.

I sat on the bench and watched as a family went inside the house. They were a young family with two kids, it seemed. That made me happy. I liked the thought of the house being filled with love and laughter again.

I got up and went to their front door, hesitating for just a second. Then I knocked on their door and waited.

The evening after the funeral, I returned to the hotel to get Grace. When I told her I wanted to show her something, she didn't protest. She just nodded and got into the car.

It didn't take her long to figure out where we were going. When we stopped in front of her old house, she seemed happy and confused.

"Let's go to the tree house," I said.

Her eyes widened. "Uh, I think that would be trespassing."

"Don't worry. The owners told me it would be okay. They're out at a barbecue tonight anyway."

Grace looked skeptical but then told me that if we got arrested, she'd blame me entirely. I smiled for the first time in what felt like an eternity.

I took her hand and guided her to the backyard.

"Oh lord, they got rid of the grass," said Grace, shaking her head. "Don't tell my dad."

I chuckled. "And give him a stroke? No way."

Grace looked around; I could tell her curiosity was piqued. She pointed at a tree near the eastern edge of the backyard. "That's where we buried our first dog, Lola. I tried planting tulips, but they never grew. Probably because tulips don't do so well in the desert," she said.

The house still had the swimming pool, which reminded me of when Grace had taught me to swim. A variety of kids' toys were scattered everywhere, to the point that Grace and I had to be careful not to trip over something in the dim light of twilight.

Grace started climbing up into the tree house before I followed her inside. The tree house was smaller than I remembered. Then again, I hadn't been up here in years.

"Oh, man, look," Grace said. She pointed at one of the beams. "Look, my initials are still here, along with Ben's."

At the mention of Ben's name, my heart sank. I could also tell Grace was far away, thinking about her older brother.

"I was thinking about what you said last night," I said quietly. "About me loving you."

Grace's eyes widened, and I could just make out a blush on her cheeks. "Yeah?"

"I do. I mean, I do love you. I think I have for a long time."

"Oh."

I took her hand and pulled her onto my lap. "Do you . . . feel the same?"

She was breathing hard. I worried I'd pushed her too fast, too soon. But then she started laughing.

"Brady Carmichael, how can you even ask that? I've loved you for years. Isn't it obvious?"

I was nonplussed. "Really?"

"Yeah, really! Honestly." She shook her head. "Men can be so dense."

My heart soared at her words. I wasn't even offended by her insult.

I wrapped my arms around her and kissed her neck. She sighed happily.

"You said you've loved me for years," I said. "Does that mean there's nothing I could do to change that?"

Grace turned to look at me. "What do you mean?"

I knew I was in dangerous territory, but I couldn't seem to stop myself. "How much do you really love me?"

"If you're saying I could stop loving you, no, probably not. But you could definitely do things that'd make me think that love wasn't enough."

I was the one breathing hard now. "Like what?"

"Uh, well, I'd probably break things off with you if you murdered somebody. That's kind of a big one." She held up a finger. "Cheating, definitely. Oh, and just being dishonest in general. I hate lying. How can I trust somebody if you lie to me all the time?"

My stomach twisted. I'd walked into this trap all on my own, I knew. I should never have asked questions to receive answers I didn't want to hear.

You've kept your secrets to keep her from getting hurt, I reminded myself. *That's not the same thing as outright lying.*

I pulled her back into my arms and held her tightly, hoping against hope this wouldn't be the last time I could touch her.

We returned to the hotel a few hours later, exhausted both

physically and emotionally. Grace hopped in the shower while I tried in vain to find something to watch on TV.

But my brain could think only about her being wet and naked in the shower. I closed my eyes, groaning silently.

I couldn't help but imagine Grace soaping up her entire body, the suds slicking down her torso, her nipples peeking out from behind the soap bubbles. Did she ever use the showerhead to masturbate?

Nearly every woman I'd talked to loved using that thing. More than once, I'd enjoyed using it on a lover.

Would Grace use her fingers first? Or would she immediately spray her clit until her body started trembling with her building orgasm?

I was already hard and aching just from my imagination. I turned over, burying my face in a pillow. *This is not the time or the place, you sick freak.*

But right now, I couldn't believe my own words. Life was too tenuous, too fragile. What the fuck was I doing, denying myself the woman I loved, a woman who wanted me as much as I wanted her?

I swallowed. Then, getting up, I opened the bathroom door to find Grace standing in front of the mirror. Steam rose all around her. Her entire body was pink.

Her eyes widened. "Brady," she whispered. But she didn't seem shocked—if anything, she looked pleased.

"I can't fight this anymore," I admitted with a sigh. I wrapped my arms around her from behind. "Tell me you feel the same."

She inhaled sharply. "Do you even have to ask?" Then she turned in my arms and cupped my face.

I closed my eyes. "You have one last chance to say no."

"Then I say yes, and yes, and yes, again," she said resolutely.

I kissed her. I groaned as our mouths met and groaned even louder when she arched against me. My hands ran up and down her back; I squeezed her ass, kneading the firm globes. Our tongues tangled together as I deepened the kiss.

"What's your safe word again?" I rasped.

Her pupils were dilated and her cheeks a bright red. "What?"

"The safe word."

"Uh, galoshes. Right?"

"Right, baby." I kissed her forehead. "I'm going to take good care of you."

"I know. I've never doubted that."

I carried her to the bed and laid her down. I took in her body: her flushed cheeks, her hard nipples, the indent of her waist, and even her red-painted toes.

As she watched, I stripped out of my clothes until I was as naked as she was. I stroked my cock, loving the way she licked her lips in anticipation.

"What are you waiting for?" she asked, reaching for me.

"Patience. I want this to be good for you." I got on the bed and caged her in with my body. "I don't want this to be a three-second pump and dump."

That made her giggle. "If I could do that to the legendary Brady Carmichael, I'd be proud of myself."

I kissed her, forcing myself to go slowly. This was her first time, after all.

I'd been with a virgin only once when I'd been a virgin myself. I'd been just a teenager, and I'd had no idea how to pleasure a woman. My girlfriend had seemed bored throughout the entire thing, even asking me if I'd finished yet.

I knew better now, though. I knew how to bring a woman to the brink of orgasm, over and over again, until she was begging to come.

I began kissing down her neck as I touched her breasts. "Do you play with your nipples when you masturbate?" I asked, curious now.

Grace looked away. "Sometimes," she admitted.

"It's nothing to be embarrassed about."

I began plucking and tweaking her nipples, wanting to see how hard she liked it. Fortunately for me, Grace was vocal about what she did—and didn't—like. When I sucked one nipple into my mouth, she moaned and arched upward.

"I wonder if I could make you come just from this," I mused. I sucked on the other nipple until they were both hard, red berries. "Your tits are gorgeous, baby. I've wanted to do this for ages."

"They're kinda small, though."

I shot her an annoyed look. "Sweetheart, tits are tits. We love them no matter what. Believe me, no guy is disappointed seeing tits like yours. It's been hell on earth when you wear those dresses without a bra on, when I can see your nipples harden through the fabric."

"I didn't think you'd noticed that."

"I notice everything about you."

That made her smile. I moved down her body, kissing every inch of her soft, milky skin. When I found a collection of freckles on her inner thighs, I couldn't help kissing those until she giggled.

"That tickles," she said with a moan.

I kept kissing her until I reached her ankles. I tickled the soles of her feet until she begged for mercy. Then it was easy to part her thighs to find the best prize of all.

She was pink and wet already, dripping for me, and all I wanted to do was bury my face in her pussy. I slicked a finger from her clit to her asshole, which made her moan loudly.

"Someday I'd love to fuck this tight ass," I said, rubbing her asshole. I licked her there and then moved upward to plunge my tongue into her pussy.

"Oh God, Brady," she groaned, gripping my hair.

She was trembling already, and I knew it wouldn't take long to make her come. I gently pressed my thumb against her clit as I fucked her with my tongue. Her juices poured into my mouth; I moaned as her moisture only increased with every stroke.

She was arching and writhing so much that she nearly bucked me off the bed. I mouthed her clit and thrust a finger inside her, feeling her tighten around me like a vise.

"Oh my God, oh my God—" Grace was saying, over and over again. Then she came with a scream that I was sure everyone in the entire hotel heard.

I grinned evilly. I wanted everyone to hear how well I fucked my woman tonight.

Grace was limp and panting by the time I returned with a condom on. She pulled me into her arms as I slowly entered her.

"Fuck," I groaned. "You're so tight, baby."

She winced as I inched farther inside. I kissed her, stopping myself so she could get used to me.

"How does it feel?" I asked. I kissed her jaw.

Grace shook her head. "I feel . . . full."

It took every ounce of my self-control not to thrust to the hilt right then. I was shaking, my entire body on fire, my cock begging for more of her tight pussy.

I started thrusting into her slowly, watching a thousand different expressions flit across her face. And then

I was completely inside her, my balls resting against her taint, so tight and warm that it was a miracle I didn't lose my fucking mind.

"Brady," said Grace. She took my face in her hands and kissed me. "I love you, Brady."

I groaned. I hooked her legs over my arms and pulled out before thrusting hard back into her. She squealed, but when I stopped, she just shook her head and begged me to keep going.

That was all I needed to unleash everything. I pounded into her sweet virgin pussy, lifting her lower body upward to get even deeper inside her.

"Rub your clit as I fuck you," I said. Sweat dripped down my face. "I want to see your pretty fingers play with your pussy."

Grace panted and moaned as she did as I asked. I watched her rub her clit as my cock pounded into her. It was one of the most erotic sights I'd ever seen.

Not just sights—sounds, smells, everything. With every plunge of my cock, her pussy made a squelching sound. I could feel her wetness dripping onto me and getting the bed wet. The scent of her drove me wild, and with every plunge into her, I could smell her only more.

I was close to coming. I could feel my balls drawing up. But I could tell by the tightness of Grace's pussy that she was close to coming a second time. I reached down between us and rubbed her clit for her.

"Come on my cock, baby girl," I crooned. "Show me how much you want me."

Grace's eyes were glassy. She was so far gone that I had a feeling she didn't even know her own name. I kept fucking her, harder and harder, my thumb relentless on her clit.

Then she came with a long, loud scream, even louder than during her first orgasm. Her entire body was wracked with shudders.

As she came, my orgasm hit me. I let out a shout as I came, filling up the condom with cum I wished I could've left inside Grace's sweet pussy.

I rolled off Grace and collapsed, panting and dizzy. My cock was still twitching. I pulled Grace into my arms and held her close.

"Oh, wow," Grace was saying as she began coming off her high. "Holy crap, Brady."

I chuckled, my voice hoarse. "You could say that again."

"Is it always like that?"

I kissed her sweetly. "No, baby, it's not," I said honestly. "I've never had sex that good in my entire life."

Grace looked smug.

Me? I was fucking *terrified*.

What have I unleashed inside us both?

Chapter 24

Grace

I woke up to Brady watching me. Shyness made me blush.

"Was I drooling?" I asked, wiping my mouth.

Brady chuckled. "No. You just looked so beautiful while you slept."

"Oh. Really?" If his expression weren't so serious, I would've thought he was teasing me.

After we'd had sex, we'd both fallen asleep quickly. I'd been surprised at how comfortable I'd been sleeping in the same bed with a man. I'd never done that before.

"During Christmas one year, you fell asleep on the couch after we'd opened presents and eaten," said Brady as he brushed my hair from my face. "I found you like that. I think *White Christmas* was playing on the TV. You looked so peaceful that I watched you for a while."

My eyes widened. "Seriously?"

Now, Brady was the one who looked embarrassed. "Yeah. Crazy, right? Maybe I shouldn't have told you that."

"No, I think it's sweet. But did you like me back then? I thought you only saw me as a younger sister when we were teenagers."

Brady sighed. "You were too young and innocent for me. I was into you, but what could I do about it? Both your dad and your brother would've killed me for making a move on you."

The realization hit me fast. "Is that why you stopped coming around for holidays? Was it because of me?"

"Yeah. I had to put distance between us, even then."

My heart was pounding so hard that I felt dizzy. I couldn't believe it. All this time, I'd been convinced that Brady wasn't interested in me until recently.

But I'd been wrong. He'd just thought he couldn't pursue me. So he'd given me the cold shoulder.

I punched him in the arm, making him yelp.

"What the hell was that for?" he demanded.

"For not telling me the truth for so long. You could've been honest with me and saved us both a lot of heartache. You made an assumption that I'd be too afraid of my dad and brother to date you. How is that fair?"

Brady's expression darkened. "And what exactly are we doing now? Because I don't see you calling your dad up and telling him we slept together."

He had me there. I still hated the thought of upsetting Dad. I'd never been the type of person who was good at confrontation. I always preferred to keep the peace.

"I'll get there, eventually," I muttered. "At least we don't have to deal with Ben."

Brady looked aghast. "Grace—"

"Oh, don't freak out. I loved my brother, and I miss him, but he was a pain in the ass, too. And we both know he had a dark sense of humor."

Slightly mollified, Brady said, "If you say so."

"Grief isn't just being sad all the time. You get angry, too. Why did my brother have to be on that road that day? Why couldn't he have just stayed home for once?"

Brady was quiet. I could tell he looked uncomfortable. Despite the fact that he'd cried in my arms over his mom, he hadn't wanted to talk about her since the funeral.

I couldn't blame him. He was probably still in the denial stage of grieving. It took a second before it sank in that your loved one was not coming back.

I moved so I was in Brady's arms, pressed up against him. We were both still high off of sex from the night before. Just thinking about it made me feel hot.

Brady's eyes darkened. "What are you doing?" he rasped.

"Seeing if we can have some more fun this morning."

He groaned when I began stroking his cock, already half hard. "You're playing with fire."

"Am I supposed to say I'd like to get burned? Because I would. Please and thank you."

Brady rolled his eyes before he kissed me, hard. My lips felt swollen from last night, so our kiss felt even more intense.

I clung to him, desire rising inside me quickly. I'd never thought sex could be like this.

Sure, I'd dreamed about it, hoped for it, but the reality couldn't compare to my fantasies. Because reality meant being able to touch Brady wherever I wanted, to hear him groan and growl, to feel his cock deep inside me.

I shivered.

"We don't have to have sex again," Brady murmured as he kissed my ear. "Especially if you're too sore."

"I'm okay. More than okay." I wrapped my arms around his neck. "Do whatever you want to me, Brady."

That made his eyes darken. "You sure about that?"

I nodded eagerly. With a wicked smile, Brady turned me over onto my stomach so I was lying across his lap, just like that time at the Scarlet Rope.

I was wearing only booty shorts and a tank, so it was short work to strip me bare. Brady massaged the globes of my ass.

"It sounds like my girl needs a spanking," he said in that tone that made me wet. "My sweet little virgin just wants a cock inside her all the time, doesn't she?"

I swallowed. "Yes," I whispered.

Brady spanked me with one sharp slap. I gasped.

"I didn't hear you," he growled.

I looked over my shoulder at him. "Yes, I want your cock inside me," I said.

A flush spread over his nose and cheeks. Then he spanked me again, making us both groan.

"God, I wish I'd brought a paddle with me," he said between slaps. "But this will have to do for today."

I wiggled and writhed as the punishment continued. I was panting, desperate for him to keep going while at the same time wondering how much more I could take.

"I wish you could see how red your ass is," he said. "With my handprints all over it. I want to spank you so hard you can't sit down for days."

I moaned. "Brady . . ."

"Hush. Do you want everyone in the hotel to hear you?"

I blushed, only because I knew they'd probably all heard me last night. I hadn't even thought about that until this moment. Mortified, I buried my face in my arm to muffle my cries.

Brady spanked me until my ass was on fire. Then, before I even knew what was happening, he flipped me over and yanked me to the edge of the bed, parting my thighs and burying his face in my pussy.

"Brady!" I squealed.

His fingers dug into the sensitive flesh of my ass as he licked me. His gaze was intense as he watched my reaction. I felt a flush rising from my chest to my cheeks.

"Your pussy is so sweet," he crooned as his tongue circled around my tight hole. "Sweet virgin pussy made just for me. Isn't that right, baby?"

I nodded. That earned me a slap on the back of my thighs.

"Answer me," he commanded.

"Yes, yes. My pussy is all yours."

"Good. No other man will taste your juices or suck your clit but me."

I threw my head back as I felt my climax building. But right before the wave hit, Brady pulled away, leaving me on the edge and trembling.

"Not yet. I don't want you to come yet." He stripped out of his clothes to reveal his hard cock.

I reached for him and squeezed him at the base. I still couldn't believe I'd taken this last night. Just the thought of being filled with his huge cock made me shudder.

"Take me in your mouth," he commanded.

I licked my lips. "Of course, Master."

It was his turn to shudder. I licked him from base to tip before swallowing as much of his cock as I could. I could taste the salt of his precum on my tongue.

"What a good cock sucker you are." Brady combed his fingers through my hair, his touch gentle now.

I bobbed my head as I took more of his length. When he touched the back of my throat, I forced myself not to gag.

"Fuck, baby. God, you're amazing," said Brady.

I sucked and took him into my throat until I could feel his balls starting to draw up. Even I knew that that meant he was close to coming. Finally, Brady made me stop.

"Shit," he said with a laugh before he kissed me. "You're too good at that. I was about to shoot my load in your throat."

"What about shooting it in my pussy?" I blushed as I said the words.

Brady pressed his forehead to mine. "Not yet, baby. But soon." Then he turned away and barked, "Condom," almost like he was commanding himself instead of me this time.

I sat back down and closed my eyes, listening to him open the foil packet before he returned to the bed.

He then flipped me back over and had me on my hands and knees, making me squeak in surprise, my eyes flying open.

I grabbed a pillow to hold on to right as Brady plunged his cock deep inside me. I screamed into the pillow. He was too big, too deep—it was almost unbearable.

"Fuck," Brady growled as he pounded into me. "I wish you could see how tight your pussy is gripping my cock."

I didn't need to see it. I could feel it. I didn't know how something so large could fit inside me. I gasped and groaned and took this punishment wrapped up in the sweetest pleasure. As Brady fucked me, his pelvis slapped against my sore ass-cheeks, only intensifying the sensations coursing through my body.

"Are you gonna come on my cock like last night?" Brady grabbed my hair and pulled my head back. "I can feel you getting tighter and tighter around me, baby."

He was relentless. My vision blurred as my orgasm reached fever pitch. Then with a scream, I came, my pussy clamping down around Brady's cock.

Brady kept thrusting and thrusting, a battering ram inside me, as I screamed in pleasure. At that point, I didn't care if the entire hotel heard me.

"Fuuuuuuuck." Brady groaned and swore as he thrust one last time and came. I could feel his cock twitching inside me. It was so amazing that it brought on a second orgasm, which made me collapse onto the bed.

Brady gently turned me over and got on top of me, kissing me deeply. I could feel his still-hard cock brushing against my sensitive clit.

"I wonder if I could make you come a third time," he mused.

I groaned. "No more, please. You'll kill me."

But Brady didn't listen to me. He just kept gently stroking his cock through my folds, which were slick with my juices. I panted and moaned. He kissed me as he teased me into another orgasm.

He caught my screech with his mouth as my third climax hit. I couldn't breathe. I wasn't sure I'd survive this one. It was so intense. I could only hold on to Brady and pray that I came back to earth eventually.

"Shh, I've got you," Brady whispered as he rolled onto his side and pulled me into his arms.

I realized I was crying. I buried my face in his shoulder.

"You're safe, baby. I've got you." He kissed my temple and rubbed my back.

Slowly, the tears and my trembles subsided. I gulped in air like I'd been pulled from deep waters.

I wiped my cheeks, feeling embarrassed now. "I don't know what that was about," I said, avoiding Brady's gaze.

"Sometimes sex does that. And that was some fucking amazing sex. Don't be ashamed."

I nodded. I made myself keep taking in deep breaths until I felt calm come over me.

"Better now?" Brady asked, smiling.

"Yeah. Wow. That was . . . something else."

"And that was just your second time." He grinned. "It can only get better from here."

I groaned. "I need a recovery period. Can I get a rain check? For like a month?"

"If you can wait a whole month to have sex again, sure. But you and I both know you don't have the willpower."

I sighed because I knew he was right. Sex with Brady would quickly become its own addiction.

And, really, why shouldn't I enjoy it? Wasn't this something I'd been wanting for years?

I snuggled closely against Brady, loving the sound of his heartbeat against my cheek.

And who's to say how long this will last anyway?

Brady turned on the shower and looked me over. "Are you sore?" he asked, concern in his voice.

"Not really."

He grimaced. "That means yes."

Despite my best efforts, I couldn't get Brady to believe me when I said I wasn't that sore. And even if I was, it didn't mean I hadn't thoroughly enjoyed having sex with him.

It was still strange to think that I was no longer a virgin. I'd waited so long to have sex that now that it'd finally happened, it didn't seem real. After our shower together, I stood in the bathroom alone, gazing at my appearance.

I almost expected that I'd look different now. I *felt* different. I felt like a burden had been lifted from my shoulders, in a way. Because now the unknown was no longer the unknown. Sex wasn't this exciting—but terrifying—prospect.

It was messy, it was awkward, it was pleasurable, it was amazing. It was everything I'd expected and nothing I'd expected.

I smiled when I found a hickey on my breast. I didn't even remember Brady doing that since I'd been so caught up in the entire experience.

Brady, though, kept giving me looks like he wanted to flog himself for causing me pain, even when everything we'd done had been consensual. When I made a face as I sat down to put on my shoes, he looked like he wanted to fling himself out the nearest window.

"We're going to the store," he said as he helped me up. "You're not going to be in pain all day."

My stomach grumbled. "Fine, but not before we get something to eat. I'm starving."

Brady acquiesced, albeit grudgingly. I really wasn't *that* sore. It was a pleasant kind of soreness, like after a hard workout.

We went to a drugstore, where Brady bought a variety of Epsom salts along with some arnica and menthol creams. I had to restrain a laugh at how full his shopping basket was when he caught up with me in the makeup aisle.

"Brady, I'm not dying," I protested. I held up some bandages. "Or bleeding, for that matter."

"I got some things just in case."

I bit my lip as we went to the register. The cashier didn't seem at all fazed by the variety of items: not only the creams and bath salts but also the bandages, antibiotic ointments, and condoms and lube.

"Maybe I should've gotten a vibrator," I joked as we got back into the car to go to lunch. "They had a decent selection for a drugstore."

"The only thing you're getting later is a nice hot bath," replied Brady resolutely.

We went to a local burger joint where the burgers were famous for being huge. A few people recognized Brady, but fortunately, nobody bothered him too much. We got our food and sat down at a corner table. I sighed in delight when I took a sip of my chocolate milkshake.

What was more satisfying than amazing sex followed by greasy food? I couldn't believe it'd taken me this long to experience the two things together.

While we were eating, I got a text from my mom. It was innocuous, asking me how I was doing, but it reminded me that reality was waiting to bite us in the ass.

"We probably need to tell my parents soon," I said after we'd finished our lunch.

Brady sighed. "You're probably right."

"You don't sound excited."

"Neither do you."

I didn't know how to feel. I didn't want to hide our relationship anymore, but I also hated the thought of upsetting my parents. Especially my dad. And what if our relationship affected Brady's career? That thought alone made me feel sick to my stomach.

"Come on," said Brady, "let's get back to the hotel for your bath."

As we left, I felt people watching us as we exited the restaurant. To my dismay, a few paparazzi were waiting outside. They snapped a few photos of us as we got into the car and drove off.

After my bath, I was more relaxed, but then my phone rang.

"Grace Dallas," my dad roared the moment I answered. "Why the hell were you just seen in Vegas buying condoms with Brady fucking Carmichael?"

Chapter 25

Brady

"Carmichael!" Coach barked after we'd finished practice. "My office. Now."

Mac shot me a look and raised his eyebrows. After returning to LA from Vegas, I hadn't had a chance to update Mac on everything that'd happened. But Mac—and everybody else—had seen the pap photos of Grace and me.

Coach had been surprisingly neutral toward me throughout practice, which had been even scarier than if he'd ridden my ass. It meant that he'd had enough time to turn his rage into something colder and more menacing.

"Sit," Coach said.

I sat, only because I wasn't sure what Coach would do to me if I didn't.

He crossed his arms. Then he said, "I'm sorry to hear about your mom. Condolences."

I felt like I'd just been given whiplash. I swallowed, a lump rising in my throat. "Thank you," I croaked.

"I know you and your mom had a complicated relationship." Coach cleared his throat. "Just, if you need anything, you know you can come to me or to Elise."

I stared at him. Now I was completely confused. Was this not what I'd assumed this would be about?

"Uh, thank you," I repeated.

Coach nodded and uncrossed his arms.

"Now," he began, his expression turning ominous, "what the hell were you doing with my daughter in Vegas? Because it looked like you two were dating. Holding hands, buying condoms—" He grimaced. "Christ, what the hell were you thinking?"

I had to bite back a dark smile. This was more what I'd been expecting, and I had to admit, something was comforting in its familiarity.

I didn't want to think about Mom, or my complicated grief about her passing. I'd rather Coach yell at me so I could yell right back.

I cocked my head to the side. "Do you want to hear the truth, or do you just want to yell at me?"

Coach narrowed his eyes. "You seriously getting sarcastic with me right now? Because you are on major thin ice here."

"Well, your daughter is an adult. Which means she makes her own decisions about who she dates."

"Stop fucking tap-dancing around the question. Are you dating my daughter? Yes or no? It's a simple answer."

I waited a beat, letting the suspense draw out. I wondered what would happen if I lied even though everybody and their dog had seen those photos of us together.

Then I replied, "Yes, I am."

Coach swore. He started pacing, like I'd just told him I had an incurable disease.

I had to admit, his visible disappointment was a punch to the gut. I'd known he wouldn't react positively, but it still hurt.

Because it would mean that he agreed that I wasn't good enough for his daughter. It meant that, in the end, I was still some punk foster kid who'd never be a real part of their family.

Coach sighed and sat down heavily. "I hate this, Brady. I really do. You're a decent kid. I've always thought so. But you're not the right guy for my daughter. I thought you knew that."

I flinched at his words. Had I really been hoping for a fucking miracle? That Coach would welcome me with open arms into the family?

You're fucking delusional, I thought. *You already knew how this would go down. It's your own fault for hoping for something that could never happen.*

"My daughter is innocent. She's a good girl. She's not the type of girl you like. You and I both know you have a . . . certain type, shall we say," said Coach.

"Maybe I've changed."

That made Coach bark out a laugh. "Seriously? Come on. I saw you on the plane with that flight attendant. *She's* the type of woman you're after. Which means you must be pursuing my daughter because you're bored."

I gritted my teeth. "You have no idea what you're talking about."

"Come on. Don't fuck with me, Carmichael. I know you. Everybody does. The second you get tired of Grace, you'll dump her." Coach's expression turned dark. "And you'll break her heart. *That* I won't stand for."

"Again, you're just making assumptions."

Coach pointed a finger at me. "Either leave my daughter alone," he threatened, "or I'm trading you to the shittiest team in the league. Far, far away. I'll send you to fucking Saskatchewan."

"Do they have a hockey team?" I couldn't help but quip.

"You're on thin fucking ice, Carmichael." Coach leaned forward, his voice lowering. "You and I both know why you're not the guy for Grace. If she found out the truth, do you really think she'd stay with you?"

The breath whooshed out of me. It took every ounce of strength not to run out of that office—or punch Coach in the face.

Which wasn't fair, because I'd brought this on myself. All of this had been my fault. I knew it, and I needed to accept that and stop trying to fight against fate.

"Let her go," said Coach quietly. "It's not worth it. I don't want to see either of you hurt. You're like a son to me. You know that, right? And because of that, I'm not going to spare you from the harsh truth."

I nodded tightly. I couldn't defend myself. I'd only been trying to deny what was right in front of me. But reality would always come back to bite you in the ass, no matter how hard you tried to keep it under lock and key.

Later that afternoon, Grace texted me. It was a sweet text, full of heart emoji. It made my own stupid heart soar.

But as I was about to type out a reply, I could hear Coach's voice in my head. I deleted what I'd typed and stuffed my phone back into my pocket.

I'd text her later. Right now I needed to go home and think.

I stayed up nearly half the night, wondering what the fuck I was going to do. Even as I acknowledged that Coach was right, I still didn't have the strength to break things off with Grace. Not yet.

Aren't you just prolonging the inevitable? Why make this worse than it could be?

I snarled and swore. I punched a few pillows. I paced like a caged lion. I stared at Grace's text and felt like I was going to lose my goddamn mind.

Finally, in the early morning, I replied to her.

Hey, I need some time to myself. Just a few days. Don't take it personally. It's just me, not you, I texted her.

I was surprised when she immediately texted me back. I hadn't thought she'd be up this early. I wondered if she'd been waiting all night for my reply, which only made me feel guiltier.

Okay. I love you, was her reply.

I swallowed hard. I told her that I loved her, too, and hoped against hope that maybe, just maybe, we could work this out.

And maybe pigs will fly, and Coach will buy me a sparkly unicorn.

When I sat down on Mac's couch and he handed me a beer, he said, "Are you okay?"

I shook my head. "Not really."

"I'm really sorry to hear about your mom. I wish I could've been at the funeral, but with you being out for the game—"

"It's fine. Honestly, I didn't really want lots of people there. My relationship with my mom was . . . complicated."

"I get it. I do." Mac shook his head. "Going to Caroline's funeral was a mindfuck. Seeing all the people almost made it worse, which I know makes me a selfish piece of shit."

"Nah, man. That just makes you human," I replied.

Mac gave me an odd look. "And do you apply that statement to yourself?"

I looked away. I didn't need my best friend psychoanalyzing me.

"How was your meeting with Coach?" Mac asked.

"Christ, it was a disaster. He told me to break up with Grace, or he'd trade me to the shittiest team in the league."

Mac's eyes widened. "Damn. I mean, I knew he'd be pissed, but this seems like an overreaction. His daughter is an adult. What does Grace have to say about all this?"

I couldn't tell Mac everything about my past. I knew it made me a coward, but I couldn't. Not right now.

"I told Grace I needed some time to myself," I admitted.

Mac groaned. "Dude, seriously? Do you want her to freak out?"

"Hey, she didn't freak out. She said she loved me and has given me space."

"She's a good person. And she's nice. You're lucky. I'm not sure Elodie would be that nice. She'd track me down and give me a piece of her mind, and then probably drag my ass back home."

Did I want Grace to freak out? A ridiculous part of me did. Grace seemed too calm about all of this. As if me potentially breaking things off with her wasn't a big deal.

What the hell do you want her to do? Burn your house down?

"It doesn't matter." I sighed. "I mean, it does. I don't fucking know. I'm a mess."

"We all already knew that one, my dude."

I glared at Mac.

"Look," said Mac, "I can't tell you what to do. But I do know that it comes down to this. Which is more important to you, your career or Grace?"

"Grace," I said without hesitation.

"Well, there you go."

Saying the words out loud was freeing. I'd been so concerned about Coach that I hadn't realized that, at the end of the day, who gave a shit about hockey?

Grace was who mattered. Grace was the person I loved. Hockey was important to me, of course, and I didn't want to be traded to the shittiest team ever.

But if I had to live in Saskatchewan, well, at least I'd have Grace. And maybe we'd like it there. At least it'd be an adventure.

"Enough about my pathetic life," I said, shaking my head, "tell me what's new with you and Elodie."

As I listened to Mac gush over his fiancée, I couldn't stop the wave of jealousy crashing over me. Mac didn't have anything to hide—not anymore. And he could be with the woman he loved. Nobody was trying to split them up or convince Mac that he wasn't good enough for Elodie.

"Elodie wants to get married a year from now," Mac said, "but I don't want to wait that long. She wants a huge wedding and says there's no way we can plan one in a few months."

"Are we seriously talking about weddings now?" I joked.

Mac rolled his eyes. "How the mighty have fallen. But seriously, why can't we just go down to the courthouse? I don't get it."

I held up my hands. "Dude, that's between you and Elodie."

"Are weddings really that complicated that you need an entire year to plan them?"

Right then, I heard their front door open and close. "I'm hoooome!" Elodie yelled. When she came into the living room, she stopped in her tracks when she saw me. "Oh, Brady. I didn't know you were coming over."

I shot a look at Mac. "Uh, I don't want to intrude."

"No, no, sorry. I was just surprised." Elodie cocked an eyebrow at her fiancé. "I had other plans for this evening."

Mac looked chagrined. "Sorry, baby. But Brady needed to vent."

"Vent? Now I'm intrigued."

I sighed, but I also knew that Elodie wasn't going to let me be vague. I gave her a rundown of what Coach had said to me.

"Yeah, those photos were something else." Elodie's lips twitched. "You two really weren't thinking ahead, were you?"

"I didn't think the paparazzi would follow me to Vegas," I groused.

"When everybody knows you've been hanging around the coach's daughter?" Mac slapped me on the shoulder. "I'd tell you to get your head out of your ass, but I was an idiot with Elodie. I can't really judge."

"I appreciate the support," I said. Desperate to change the subject, I added, "Mac here thinks weddings are stupid, and you guys should just go down to the courthouse."

Mac gaped at me. Elodie glared at Mac, clearly outraged.

"Seriously? I already told you why I want a wedding!" Elodie said.

"I never said weddings were *stupid*." Mac glared at me. "I don't get the point of them, that's all. And why do they take so long? You just pick a venue and send invitations. The end."

Elodie sighed deeply. "Oh my God. Men. You do know it takes a year just to get a dress ordered and altered, right?"

We both stared at Elodie. "Seriously?" I said, dumbfounded.

"That's bullshit. A whole year?" Mac said.

"I don't make the rules." Elodie got up and wrapped her arms around Mac's shoulders. "And anyway, don't you want to see me in a gorgeous gown, walking down the aisle toward you?"

"Pretty sure that happens at the courthouse, too," replied Mac.

Elodie smacked his shoulder. Then her gaze moved to me. "Talk some sense into your friend. And if you do, I'll make sure to support you and Grace, no matter what Coach says."

Elodie went upstairs, leaving Mac and me to stare at each other.

"Well, shit," I said, shaking my head. "I guess you guys should definitely have a wedding now."

Mac snorted. "Fuck you, dude."

Chapter 26

Brady
Six Years Ago

Returning to Vegas after spending the last few months at the University of Wisconsin was like entering a new world. I sighed with relief when I felt that blast of hot desert air outside the airport. Back in Wisconsin, it'd just snowed ten inches and was below zero. My roommates had bitched and moaned that I'd gotten to go back home to the desert.

"Brady!" Mr. Dallas gave me a hug when I came into the living room. Mrs. Dallas did the same, patting me on the arm.

"Where's Ben and Grace?" I asked, trying to sound casual.

Mr. Dallas huffed. "Grace is out with a friend." When Mrs. Dallas shot her husband a wry look, Mr. Dallas sighed. "Okay, boyfriend. She has a boyfriend. Happy? I said the word out loud."

I'd had no idea that Grace was dating somebody. Last I heard, she'd been too focused on studying for her SATs to get involved with anybody.

"And Ben . . ." Mr. Dallas shrugged. "Where did he go, anyway?"

"He went to the store to get some things for dinner," Mrs. Dallas said crisply. She turned to me and rolled her eyes. "You know what the secret of success to any marriage is? Listening to your wife when she tells you to pick up stuff from the store before it's the day before Christmas Eve."

Mr. Dallas just grumbled to himself. Mrs. Dallas gave me another pat on the arm and went into the kitchen, telling me we'd catch up soon.

I hadn't planned on coming back to the Dallases' for Christmas break. I'd gone to a teammate's house for Thanksgiving, considering how long the flight was. But when Mrs. Dallas had heard that I'd been planning to spend my Christmas on campus, she'd put up such a fuss that I'd given in and come.

It didn't help that I didn't want to see Grace. Something about that girl never failed to mess me up inside. Despite hooking up with a few different girls at UW, I still couldn't forget Grace.

It was fucking annoying, like a virus I couldn't shake.

"Did you hear the good news?" said Mr. Dallas as he sat on his favorite leather chair. "I thought Elise told you. Well, it doesn't matter. I got a coaching job for the LA Blades. We're moving there in three months, if we can't sell this place sooner."

I sat down across from Mr. Dallas. "Seriously? That's amazing."

The Blades were one of the best teams in the NHL. They were also my favorite team. I followed them religiously, watching every game. I could name all the players' stats, to the point that my teammates at UW made fun of me for it.

"Thanks, son. I'm pretty excited myself." Mr. Dallas nodded happily. "Now, the missus isn't thrilled about moving, but we'll manage. It doesn't help that LA is so damn expensive."

"Well, you'll be making good money, won't you?"

Mr. Dallas grinned. "You bet I will be."

"And maybe I'll be one of your draft picks in a few years." I said the words lightly even though internally, I was all nerves.

Mr. Dallas assessed me. "You might be right on that one. But we'll see what happens. Things can change. Besides, you might end up being drafted to a Midwest team closer to Wisconsin, especially if you like the place."

"And freeze my balls off? No, thanks."

Mr. Dallas chuckled. "I'm surprised you haven't died out there yet. Did you figure out how to drive in the snow yet? You know, it's driving on ice that's the worst. I did it once when I was in Maine for a business meeting, and I nearly shit myself as I did a one-eighty on a highway."

"What in the world are you talking about?" Mrs. Dallas asked. She then beckoned to me. "Brady, I could use your help."

I nodded, knowing full well that Mrs. Dallas was the one who ran this family. Even Mr. Dallas wasn't brave enough to say no to his wife.

"Now, help me with these dinner rolls. You remember how to fold them, right?" she said.

"Yes, ma'am."

"Well, I'm excited to hear all about your first semester of college. A lot has changed around here, too. I'm sure Mr. Dallas told you about his new job." Mrs. Dallas sighed. "I'm sad to sell this house. We've lived here since the kids were small. But it's such an amazing opportunity. Besides,

Grace will be going to college here soon, so we'll be empty nesters."

"How is Ben?" I asked even though I really wanted to ask about his sister again.

"Oh, he's great. He'll be here later tonight. He and his old high school friends are having a bonfire down by the lake. You should go, if you want to. I know you just got here, though."

"He's not coming home for dinner?" I looked at the piles of food that Mrs. Dallas was preparing.

She laughed. "This is for tomorrow. Well, most of it is. Some of this is for tonight. I might've gone a little overboard, but I was excited to have all my kids back home."

I smiled, pleased at her words. Although I'd been reluctant to come back home for Christmas, I was glad I had. It would've been depressing to wander around the deserted campus while everybody else went off to celebrate with their families.

"And Grace should be home soon. She's with her new boyfriend, Sean. He seems like a nice boy. We've only met him twice," said Mrs. Dallas as she stirred a pot on the stove.

I gritted my teeth. Well, Grace must've gotten over her crush on me. I wondered whether this was the same guy I'd seen her kissing at the movie theater a year ago.

"Does she know where she'll apply for college?" I asked, needing to change the subject.

"Oh, she has a whole list. I'd love it if she could go to UCLA or USC so she'd be close by, but she might end up staying here to go to UNLV. As far as I know, she wants to stay west of the Rocky Mountains."

Ben was attending the University of Vermont, both for their hockey team and because, as he'd told me, he wanted to get as far away from his parents as possible. Ben had always found his parents rather overinvolved in his life. To me, they'd just seemed like parents who actually gave a shit about their kids, unlike my own parents.

After Mrs. Dallas thanked me for my help, I decided to go for a swim. At my last game, I'd gotten rammed by a huge dude, and my shoulder was still feeling the hit. After changing into my trunks, I waded into the pool.

I couldn't help but remember when Grace had taught me to swim in this very pool. I'd been such a lost, angry kid back then. It was a wonder that a young girl like Grace had been brave enough to talk to me, let alone teach me to swim.

And now Ben, Grace, and I had all gone our separate ways. I wondered if the Dallases would keep asking me to come back after I'd graduated from college. Or would our connection slowly fade away, and we'd only exchange a phone call once or twice a year going forward?

But then again, if I actually did get drafted by the Blades, I'd still be in their lives. Which also meant I could keep tabs on Grace.

I shook my head and dove under the water. I did a few laps, trying to clear my head.

"Brady! Braaaady!"

I stood in the shallow end of the pool to see Grace waving at me.

Not only waving at me but also wearing the tiniest bikini I'd ever seen. My jaw nearly dropped. I couldn't believe her parents would let her wear something like that.

"I didn't know you'd be home already," she said, smiling.

God, she looked fucking amazing. Her blond hair was longer than I'd ever seen it. It blew gently in the wind as she stood over me. Her body was tan and lithe, her breasts small but firm. Even worse, she had freckles all over her cheeks and shoulders. I was a complete sucker for freckles.

I forced myself to stop staring at her. "Yeah, I'm back," I said weakly.

"Wow, you sound thrilled." Grace jumped into the pool, making sure to splash me. "Come on, toss me!"

She threw herself into my arms like we were little kids. I froze, mostly because there was no place to put my hands that didn't feel inappropriate. I lightly clasped her around the waist and tried to toss her as far as I could.

Grace laughed and launched herself at me again. This time, she tried to climb onto my shoulders, but I wouldn't let her.

"You're too heavy," I groused.

She didn't seem offended. "God, you're so boring now." She splashed me, trying to start a water fight. "Since when did you turn into such a grumpy old man?"

I wasn't going to fall for her bait. I knew she was trying to get a rise out of me.

Well, she was—just not the rise she was expecting.

I forced myself to think of icebergs to stop my traitorous dick from betraying me. Grace, though, wasn't helping. All her jumping and swimming just served to show off her body. Everything about her was so *bouncy*.

It was painful to watch her.

Finally, I got out of the pool after Grace tried one last time to get me to toss her.

She surfaced, frowning. "Where are you going?"

"I have to be somewhere. Sorry."

I knew I was being an asshole, but I didn't care. I almost sprinted upstairs to my old room and locked the door. There, I dried off, got dressed, and got out of the house before any of the other Dallases stopped me.

I spent the rest of the afternoon and evening at the rink. When Mrs. Dallas called to ask if I'd be home for dinner, I lied and said I was meeting up with old friends. I felt guilty, mostly because I knew she'd been expecting me to eat with the family.

But I couldn't be around Grace. She posed too much of a temptation.

I managed to get back into the Dallases' house without Grace noticing. I took a shower, sweaty after skating for so long, and was about to return to my room when the bathroom door opened.

"Shit, somebody's in here!" I yelled. I must've forgotten to lock it.

Grace, though, wasn't deterred. She stepped inside the steamy bathroom and shut the door behind her. She took in my appearance—I only had a towel wrapped around my hips—and I could see a blush creeping up her cheeks.

"Uh, if you need the bathroom, I'm almost done," I said.

She shook her head. "I wanted to talk to you."

"And coming into the bathroom was your best idea? You should go to your room."

If Mr. or Mrs. Dallas realized Grace was in here with me and I was basically naked, they'd kill me. I was about to make Grace leave when she said, "I want you to take my virginity."

I dropped the razor I was holding and stared at her reflection in the mirror. Had I heard her correctly?

"What the fuck?" I growled, turning around.

Grace lifted her chin. "You heard me."

"Are you drunk? High? Get out of here. And don't you have a boyfriend?" I was horrified. I was . . . aroused. I didn't know where to fucking look.

"I realized tonight that Sean isn't who I want. He's a boy." Grace stepped closer, nearly touching me now. "You're a man."

Oh God. Fucking, fucking hell. Was this some kind of erotic dream? It had to be. There was no other way this could be happening.

"You're insane," I said hoarsely.

"You're not saying no, either."

We gazed at each other, the tension building. My body was on fire. Grace was so close; it'd be easy to kiss her. I leaned toward her, my lips nearly brushing hers—

I heard something. Someone coughing? But it was enough to make me jump away. I had to grab my towel so I didn't flash Grace.

"This isn't happening," I said, turning back to the mirror.

Grace's expression was mulish now. But when she seemed to realize I was serious, she deflated. "We'll see," she said and finally left the bathroom.

I let out the breath I'd been holding once the door clicked shut. I locked it quickly, terrified that Grace would try something else.

Terrified? Or excited? I didn't know the answer any-more. I was panting like I'd been running. Desperate, I hopped back into an ice-cold shower to get my brain in order.

After asking Mrs. Dallas if I could take her car, I headed off to the bonfire Ben was attending. There was no fucking way I could stay in that house tonight. Not with Grace about to beat my door down.

I couldn't believe she'd done that. Had she seriously asked me to take her virginity? She'd lost her mind.

Had somebody dared her? Now I wondered whether the whole thing hadn't just been a prank. I gritted my teeth, anger rising inside. If it had been a joke, Grace had seemed completely serious.

I pushed all thoughts of Grace aside when I got to the lake. It was easy to find the party. About thirty people were hanging around, and the huge bonfire was bright in the desert night. A few people recognized me and said hello, asking me how college was going.

I found Ben on a log by himself. It didn't seem like he was drinking, unlike everybody else.

"Brady," said Ben, smiling. He got up and gave me a hug. "Nice to see you, man."

"Same." I grabbed a beer from a nearby cooler. "Want one?"

"Sure."

We drank in companionable silence for a bit before we started talking about college, hockey, and any other interesting updates. Ben told me all about his last hockey game and how his team had lost to their rivals. He seemed depressed about it.

"I can't believe I missed that goal," he said, shaking his head. "Fucking rookie mistake."

I decided not to mention how my team had just won their latest game. It seemed like rubbing salt into the wound. Instead, I told Ben all about Wisconsin and a few of the crazy fraternity parties I'd attended.

After we'd finished our beers, I went to talk with a few hockey guys I'd played with back in high school. An hour later, we were reminiscing about our high school days when Ben came over.

"How did you get here, anyway?" Ben asked.

"Your mom let me borrow her car. Why?"

"Oh, good. I need to use it for a beer run."

I hesitated, but then shrugged. Ben wasn't the type to drink and drive. He'd had only one beer, as far as I knew.

"Here," I said, handing him the keys.

"Thanks. I owe you one."

When people started going home, I decided to catch a ride with Jordan, one of my friends from high school. He lived nearby to the Dallases. I texted Ben, wondering whether he'd just decided to go home, too. Or maybe he'd decided to go to another party.

Ben had always been like that. He tended to fly by the seat of his pants. As teenagers, we'd party-hopped on weekends. Sometimes we'd end up in the most random places and houses, making me wonder how Ben had even heard that this random house in the middle of nowhere was going to have a huge party.

I was tired, not paying attention to what Jordan was saying, when Jordan slowed his car down. In front of us was a huge group of fire trucks, police cars, and ambulances, their emergency lights bright against the night sky.

"Damn, what happened?" Jordan said, craning his neck. "The entire highway is blocked."

"I think we might have to turn around," I said.

"No, they have somebody directing traffic." Jordan pointed.

We were slowly making our way through the maze of vehicles when we passed by the wreck. We both looked, of course, and I grimaced when I saw the car was basically wrapped around a tree. I had a feeling whoever had been in the car wouldn't have made it.

As I looked more closely, though, I noticed a decal on the back left bumper: a red hibiscus from Hawaii. It was a decal Mrs. Dallas had gotten when the family had gone to Hawaii a year ago.

I froze, time seeming to crawl to a standstill. "Pull over!" I yelled at Jordan.

"What the hell? Why?"

Jordan hadn't even fully stopped the car when I jumped out. I jogged over to a police officer. He held up his hands, scowling at me.

"Son, this is an active scene. Get out of here," said the cop.

I didn't listen to him. I just ran toward the car, ignoring the cop's shout. Right then, somebody raised their flashlight to illuminate the back of the car.

On the bumper was the decal I'd recognized. And most definitive of all was another sticker, this one that said PROUD HOCKEY MOM.

"What happened?" I asked. I whirled around. "What happened?"

"Some kid was drinking and wrapped his car around the tree. He didn't make it," said the cop.

I fell to my knees.

Ben. Oh God, Ben.

What have I done?

Chapter 27

Brady
Present Day

The day Grace stopped texting me, I knew something was wrong.

She'd given me space for about two days. Then she'd started texting and calling me, telling me she wanted to be there for me no matter what was wrong.

I didn't reply to any of her messages. I felt like a complete piece of shit, ignoring her, but I didn't know what to say. Every time I started to text her back or call her, I could hear Coach's words in my head.

It didn't help that I kept dreaming of the night Ben had died. Sometimes it was just the actual memory of seeing Mrs. Dallas's car wrapped around that fucking tree.

Sometimes it changed into where I was in the car with Ben. I kept begging him to stop driving, that he was drunk, but Ben would just laugh and tell me to chill.

The worst dreams were the ones where I was the one driving. Sometimes I was drunk; other times, I couldn't get control of the car for whatever reason.

Ben would be in the passenger seat, and then we'd slam into the tree. Sometimes Ben would fly through the windshield; other times, he'd have his seat belt on, but he'd be unconscious.

I always woke up not knowing if Ben was dead or alive. Maybe that was actually the worst part, because I'd wake up hoping that Ben was still alive.

Then reality would crash in, and I'd realize that he was still dead. And it'd been my fault entirely.

I'd given him those keys. I'd seen him drinking. I'd told myself he'd be fine, even when I'd been around my mom when she'd try to drive after she'd been drinking.

I'd known better. I could've stopped Ben from dying, but it'd been easier to say nothing. I'd taken the easy way out because I'd been a coward.

When I was awake and no longer dreaming, my mind still replayed that night over and over again in my mind.

Sometimes I'd be driving, and I'd see a tree that looked like the one Ben had hit. Panic would overwhelm me, and more than once, I'd had to pull over to get myself together to keep driving.

Why had I thought Ben wouldn't drink and drive? I knew the signs. I'd drunk a beer with him, for God's sake, which meant he'd probably been drinking all evening.

And I'd seen Ben drunk before. We'd been high school kids, experimenting with drugs and alcohol on occasion. I'd caught Ben stealing his parents' booze, and he'd sworn me to silence before inviting me to whatever party he was attending that night.

All the hockey guys partied, me included. So seeing Ben drinking at the bonfire hadn't been out of the ordinary. Although he wasn't yet twenty-one, he'd somehow managed to get a fake ID that had miraculously worked when he'd go to buy booze.

It was a Friday evening, and I was home alone, trying to distract myself. I'd considered going out, but nothing appealed to me. Mac had texted me about doing something, but I'd declined.

I'd then considered going to the Scarlet Rope, but that only reminded me of Grace.

What are you doing right now, Grace?

Did she miss me? I missed her, that was for fucking sure. It was like a physical ache in my chest not being around her or talking to her.

With my previous relationships, I'd never really missed them. Sometimes I'd get bored and text them for a hookup, but once they'd left, it was like they didn't exist.

But with Grace, she was present even when she wasn't around. It was like she was haunting me.

"God, I'm getting so pathetic," I muttered to myself after I'd turned off a show that I couldn't get into.

I never would've thought a woman would bring me to my knees. I guess Mac had been right: I was in for it with Grace.

I went back and forth, but my resolve finally broke. I texted Grace, asking her to meet me at my place.

To my relief, she agreed. My heart beat with anticipation that I'd see her soon.

After she arrived, though, I knew something was seriously wrong when I saw her tearstained face. A wave of guilt slammed into me.

Had she been crying over me? That thought nearly sent me to my knees.

As she stepped inside, I went to hug her, but to my surprise, she just shook her head and even put up her hands to stop me.

"I need to talk to you," she said, her voice hoarse.

A chill went down my spine. I knew she'd be angry, but something was wrong.

"I'm sorry I've been radio silent," I said. "Your dad talked to me and freaked me out. I didn't know what to do. I had to think about it by myself. I shouldn't have stopped talking to you."

I knew I was rambling. Grace was just staring at her feet and biting her lip.

"I didn't want you to get hurt," I added, at a loss now. I desperately wanted to hold her, but I could tell she still had a wall up.

"Did you give Ben the keys to Mom's car? When he was drunk?" Grace asked, her gaze direct and searing.

I couldn't breathe. I felt a whooshing sound in my ears.

"Grace . . ." I whispered.

She just shook her head. "Don't. Just tell me the truth, for once in your life. Please."

"At least sit down first."

Grace hesitated, but then she sighed and sat down. When I went to sit next to her, she shook her head. "Please. I need space," she said.

I did as she asked. Then I said heavily, "Yeah, I did. I'm sorry I never told you."

Grace's eyes filled with tears. "Oh my God. Why would you let him drive?"

After the accident, I'd gone to Coach and confessed that I'd given Ben the keys. I'd seen him drinking, but I hadn't thought it was a big deal. Coach looked grim and told me to keep that information to ourselves.

"It'll just hurt the girls more," he'd said. "Because they'll never forgive you for it. And the last thing we need is to lose another son."

So I'd kept that secret. I'd kept it and buried it like we'd buried Ben. When I'd held Grace at the funeral, I'd reminded myself that telling her that I'd been responsible for her brother's death would only cause her pain.

And if it hurt me? So what? I deserved worse. I didn't deserve absolution or forgiveness.

"Why didn't you tell me?" Grace cried. She was sobbing now. "How could you not tell me? All these years, and you said nothing!"

I wanted to die. I wanted to pull her into my arms. But all I could do was watch as she cried.

"Who told you?" I asked.

"Does it matter? Because the person who should've told me was *you*."

"I'm so sorry," I murmured. I closed my eyes. "Grace, you can't know how sorry I am."

"That's it? You're sorry? You're sorry that Ben is dead and you're not?"

The words were a punch to the gut, but I couldn't deny them, either.

Grace wiped at her eyes. "You knew he was drunk? You knew, and you gave him the keys? Why?"

I didn't have an answer for that. I wished I did.

"I don't know," I said.

"That's not good enough. You should've called him a cab. You know about drinking and driving, so don't tell me you don't know what to do. I guess you thought it'd be okay if my brother hurt somebody or if he hurt himself? That's fucked up, Brady."

Grace rose and went to the front door, but I stopped her. "Wait, you can't leave like this—"

"So, what? Are you going to hold me hostage?" Her eyes glittered with rage and hatred. "Maybe you should've been more concerned about stopping Ben instead of me."

I held on to her for a moment longer, but then I let her go. I had no right to keep her here.

I had no right to her, period. I'd known that since Ben had died. Why had I been stupid enough to think I could change fate?

"Are you okay enough to drive? Should I get a taxi or Uber for you?" I couldn't help but ask. I knew that driving while sobbing wasn't a great idea, especially in LA traffic. And it was getting dark, too.

Grace laughed, but there was no humor in it. "Seriously? Now you care about getting an Uber for somebody? Fuck off, Brady. We're done."

Then she left, slamming the door behind her.

I stared at my front door for what felt like hours. I couldn't move. I couldn't breathe.

I couldn't believe that'd just happened.

Then the pain hit, and it was unbearable. I staggered up, grabbed my wallet and keys, and started walking.

I had to get out of that apartment. But as I walked, I could only see the anguish on Grace's face. The way she wouldn't even let me touch her, or console her, or explain myself.

What is there to explain? You killed her brother.

I grabbed a tree and forced myself to take a few deep breaths so I didn't vomit all over the sidewalk.

I'd feared this day for so many years, and it was worse than I could've imagined. Had I really hoped that Grace would understand? That she'd tell me she didn't hate me for what I'd done?

I had to get away from this feeling. I found the nearest open bar and collapsed onto a stool. The bartender gave me a strange look but didn't balk when I ordered three shots of whiskey.

"Hard day?" the bartender asked as he pushed the shot glasses toward me.

I downed one, then another. "You could say that," I croaked as I finished off the third.

I was drunk within ten minutes. It didn't numb the pain completely, but it helped. It made it feel like I might survive this ordeal.

I didn't care that my mom had just died from drinking herself into oblivion. I didn't care that Ben had died because he'd been drunk and gotten behind the wheel.

I didn't care that alcohol seemed to be the cause of every hurt in my life. At that moment, it was my savior. It was the only thing keeping me from falling into a dark pit that I was terrified I'd never get out of.

I somehow ended up in a nearby booth. I'd lost count of how many shots of whiskey I'd drunk. It got to the point that the bartender actually cut me off, the asshole.

"Should I call you a ride?" he'd asked.

I had my head on the table, and it took all my strength to lift it. "Nah," I slurred. "I didn't drive, anyway."

"Well, that's good, at least." The bartender sighed and took away the empty glasses.

I was about to order from a bartender who'd just started her shift when a guy came up to my booth. He leered down at me, reeking of cigarette smoke.

"Is that you? Carmichael? Shit, never thought I'd see you in a place like this," he said.

"Whaddya want?"

"Man, aren't you dating your coach's daughter? Damn, she's a fine piece of ass. I can't blame you there. I'd fuck her, too." He laughed like he'd made the most hilarious joke ever.

Grace. He was talking about Grace. Red filled my vision. Before I knew it, I'd grabbed the guy by the collar and was punching him. I punched him again, not caring that blood was running from his nose, not caring that there were hands trying to pull me away from him. I just wanted to keep punching him until he knew he could never, ever talk about Grace like that again.

The cops arrived soon after. I'd been unlucky, apparently, because a cop car had parked across the street after pulling somebody over for speeding. Then I was on the ground and being handcuffed, my head whirling, feeling like I was going to vomit and desperately hoping that I wouldn't. The last thing I needed was to puke all over myself and be stuffed into a police car.

I was in the back of the police car for a while, my arms aching as much as my head. I tasted blood on my tongue.

Then one of the cops returned, opened the door, and said, "We're taking you in for assault and drunken and disorderly conduct."

I didn't protest. I didn't even give a fuck that I was being arrested. I just sighed and closed my eyes.

I was processed, fingerprinted, read my rights, and tossed in a cell to await my bail hearing. The only thing fortunate about my situation was that the judge could probably see me later that afternoon.

I knew I needed to call somebody. The Blades had an attorney on hand. But I was too drunk and tired to care. Besides, until I saw a judge, I wasn't going anywhere.

By the time I'd gone before the judge, I'd sobered up enough to know I was in deep shit. Sure, I could afford almost any bail the judge set, but my reputation with the team was already hanging by a thread.

I also realized that I didn't know anybody's phone number. Who did when everybody had a cell phone these days?

Ironically, the only number I could remember was my mom's landline when I'd been in foster care. I'd called her often right after I'd been placed in that first foster home, but eventually, I'd stopped trying when she never picked up.

I was too tired to care after that. I ended up puking up the rest of the alcohol in my system and fell into a fitful sleep.

"Carmichael," a man barked, jerking me awake. "Somebody's here for you."

It took me a second to remember where I was. "Who is it?"

"Some woman. Come on, she just bailed you out. Lucky you."

Chapter 28

Brady

When I saw that it was Julia, not Grace, waiting for me outside the county jail, my hopes plummeted.

"Hey, Brady," said Julia. She didn't look happy to see me. "Let's get you out of here."

I considered telling her no, that I'd walk home if I had to. But Julia didn't look like she'd take no for an answer. I gritted my teeth and followed her to her car outside.

"How did you know to bail me out?" I asked.

"I guess you wouldn't have seen all the news stories about you getting arrested," she replied, her tone scathing. She started driving after asking me for my address.

Shit, shit, shit. "Sorry," I muttered.

"Sorry? That's all you have to say?" She glanced at me, incredulous. "You just spent the night in jail after assaulting somebody! Did you even call somebody to get you out?"

I shrugged. I didn't feel like explaining that I hadn't remembered anybody's numbers.

Julia sighed. "Never mind. I'm just glad I could figure out where you were easily enough. Oh, and you owe me five hundred bucks."

"I'll pay you five hundred thousand if you can drive me home without lecturing me," I said.

"No way in hell." Julia got onto the interstate. "Look, I know you've been having a hard time lately. I'm very sorry to hear about your mom passing. When I lost my dad, it was really, really difficult. So I get it.

"But that doesn't mean you can throw your life away, either. You're digging yourself into such a deep hole. It's getting to the point that Silas is talking about having you off the team, and I don't think Coach is far behind him. Is that what you want? To ruin your career?"

"Of course I fucking don't."

"Then you need to pull yourself together. I don't care what it takes. Do you need to go to therapy? Go to some nature retreat? Go volunteer at a shelter and play with puppies? Whatever it takes, Brady. But you need to do *something* other than self-destruct."

I knew she was right. I knew it, but I didn't want to hear it.

Besides, she didn't know the half of it. She had no idea how I was feeling, how the woman I loved wouldn't even let me near her now. That I'd ruined my life way before last night.

"Did you hear what I said?" Julia asked, her voice rising.

I hadn't, so I just shrugged. "I know you're pissed at me. And so is everybody else in my life."

"They're pissed because they care about you. Even I care about you. I know you think I'm just around to make your life more difficult, but it's because I want you to succeed."

I snorted. "You only care about making sure the Blades look good."

Julia's expression was the definition of *if looks could kill.* "Yeah, I care. It's my job to care. Your behavior hurts not only yourself but also everybody else on the team. And I know you're not so selfish as to not care about that."

I sank down in my seat, pulling up my jacket to my ears. "I have a headache," I groused.

"Shocking, with how much you've been drinking. But I don't care. I just want you to hear me."

"Of course I fucking hear you! I hear all of you. I'm a fuckup, and I know that. You don't have to keep telling me over and over again." I groaned as my head started pounding for real. "Can't you just let me figure this out on my own?"

"And let you set the entire organization on fire? No damn way."

Julia parked her car in front of my apartment and gave me a strange look. "Is this where you live?"

"Yeah. I don't need a huge place."

She was silent a long moment. Then she gave me an awkward pat on the shoulder. "Call me if you need anything, okay?"

No way in hell. I just nodded and got away from Julia as fast as I could.

I had a game that night, and I couldn't miss it. Not since I'd missed our last game because of Mom's funeral.

When I showed up, everybody refused to look at me, like they were embarrassed for me. Mac, at least, took me aside and asked me if I was okay. I just shrugged him off and told him I'd talk to him later.

I probably should've called in sick, because we ended up having one of our worst games of the season. I couldn't concentrate, not with my mind going every which way. It didn't help that seeing Coach made me think about Grace, and then I couldn't stop seeing Ben's car wrapped around that fucking tree.

We lost—spectacularly. I missed more than one goal, to the point that Coach pulled me from the game early. But at that point, we were too far gone and couldn't regain the ground we'd lost.

Coach was so pissed that he didn't even speak to us after the game. We were all exhausted and pissed at each other. I knew that if one person said something to me, I'd probably start punching like I'd punched that random guy at the bar last night.

"Carmichael!" Coach yelled as I left the locker room. He motioned at me. "My office. Now."

Mac shot me a look. "Good luck, man," he mouthed at me.

At this point I didn't even care what Coach had to say to me. How could shit get any worse?

Coach was just shaking his head when I came into his office. "I don't know what's going on with you, but this ain't it," he said. "You won't have a job or a girl if you keep acting like this."

I was flabbergasted. "That's all you have to fucking say to me?"

Coach pointed a finger at me. "Don't swear at me, Carmichael."

"What do I care about this team or my career when I don't have Grace?" I felt like everything around me was crumbling before my eyes. "And you know whose fault that is? Yours. You were the one who said I could never tell her the truth."

Coach reared backward. "I did it for your own good. I did it for my daughter's own good. How can you not understand that?"

"Well, Grace knows everything now. She knows I gave those damn keys to Ben, and now she won't speak to me. I guess that makes you happy since you never wanted us to be together anyway."

Coach was silent. His lower lip trembled. I wondered whether he was going to start crying. I almost wished he would. At least I wouldn't be the only one feeling this kind of pain.

"You have no idea what you're talking about," said Coach, his voice hoarse. "Get out of my office. Now."

I didn't need to be told twice. Coach could be pissed at me all he wanted.

If he wanted me off the team? Fine. Who gave a shit? I had nothing if I didn't have Grace in my life, anyway.

I ended up at a bar not far from the rink. I knew I should've gone somewhere farther away where I wouldn't have been recognized, but I didn't care anymore.

Eventually, fans realized I wasn't interested in being friendly and stopped coming up to me for autographs. I sat at the bar and drank the night away because that seemed like my only solution.

I was plastered when the old man next to me said, "You okay there, son?"

I shot him a smile without any humor in it. "No. But that's okay. I have all this." I motioned at my empty glasses of booze.

The old man shook his head. "You're too young to be drinkin' like that."

I couldn't help but point out the irony that the old man was also knee-deep in his own drinking.

"I ain't got nothin' left," the old man said, shrugging. "I'll go out and sleep on the sidewalk and do the same thing tomorrow. Nothin' really matters. But you're too young for that shit. I can tell."

"You don't know anything about me."

The old man chuckled. "Why do I get the feelin' you're gonna tell me?"

He was right. I spilled my guts to this random old man, who nodded and just listened without comment. It was freeing in a way that I would never have thought possible.

Of course, by the end, I asked him what I should do next. The old man had kept drinking through my spiel, and now he was nodding off and about to fall asleep.

"I told ya," he kept saying, his eyes rolling back into his head. "Nothin' really matters."

I laughed, but it sounded like sobbing. I groaned. How the hell had I ended up like this?

But to my surprise, the old man roused himself enough to say, "I let my demons get to me. It ain't worth it. There's a lot more to life than drinking it away."

I snorted. "Tell that to my mom," I said darkly.

"Your mama? She loved you. Mamas always love their kids."

The old man wiped his eyes. "My mama, God bless her soul. My daddy died, and then she was stuck raising six kids on her own. She married a bastard because she needed the money. He beat her up all the time. When I'd tell her we could run away, she'd tell me it'd be all right and just went back to takin' care of us all."

"That's awful," I said, unsure what to say.

"Only good thing my stepdaddy did was die. Anyway, what was my point?" The old man stared off into the distance for so long I assumed he'd forgotten what he'd even been talking about.

"I remember now." He wagged a finger in my face. "Your mama loved you. Even when she drank. My mama drank because it was better than feelin'. I don't blame her for it. Now, I do it, too. It's shitty, but it is what it is. But don't be like us, hangin' on to the past. That's what I'm sayin'."

I nodded. I was already too drunk for any philosophizing, although I sort of understood where the old man was coming from. That didn't mean letting go would be easy—or if I could even do it.

My phone rang, interrupting this strange conversation. It was Mac.

I answered, trying to sound sober, but it took all of five seconds before Mac realized what was wrong.

"I'm coming to get you," he said before hanging up.

Mac showed up shortly after. He took one look at me and hauled me up. "I'm driving you home," he said.

I laughed because this felt like Julia all over again. "Don't lecture me, though," I mumbled as I staggered to Mac's car.

"I'm worried about you, man." Mac helped me into the passenger seat. "What is going on with you? You get arrested for assault and drinking, and now you're back to drinking again?"

The world was spinning. I knew it was from the alcohol, so I closed my eyes and hoped it would stop soon.

"I don't know what's wrong with me," I admitted.

Mac hadn't started his car. My head lolled to the side as I looked over at him. My body felt so heavy all of a sudden.

"Brady, talk to me. Please. You're freaking me out," said Mac.

Even in my drunken haze, I could tell my best friend was genuinely worried about me. That realization made me feel worse about myself.

Why did I keep causing the people I loved so much pain? They didn't deserve that.

I didn't even realize that I'd started crying. And then I was sobbing and bawling like a baby. Mac just sat with me and let me cry, not saying a word but simply being there when I needed him.

I told him everything: about Ben, the car crash, the keys, Coach's demand that I keep my part in the tragedy silent. How Grace found out and wouldn't talk to me now. How I didn't know how my life had fallen apart so quickly.

Mac sighed. "God, man. I'm sorry. I had no idea."

"I don't deserve my career, or Grace. I know that." I swiped at my face, tired of crying. "So why do I keep hoping things will change?"

Mac frowned. "Whoever said you didn't deserve those things? That's bullshit. Besides, does Grace know that Coach made you keep that whole thing secret?"

I shook my head. "I don't think it'd make a difference at this point."

"Uh, yeah, I do think it would." Mac's gaze was intense now. "Grace thinks you were lying to her because you were a coward, not because you wanted to respect her dad's wishes. She needs to know *everything*."

I wanted to believe Mac, but at this point, I didn't know what to believe. For all I knew, telling Grace about her dad swearing me to secrecy would only make things worse.

"Coach was the closest thing you had to a dad. Of course you listened to him. I mean, it sounds like he didn't even give you a choice," Mac pointed out.

"You didn't see Grace or hear what she said. She wouldn't even let me touch her. It was like she was looking at a stranger."

"Well, maybe things won't change. But what do you have to lose at this point?"

I sighed. I was exhausted. I just wanted to sleep until my life felt normal again. Maybe if I just gave Grace some time, she'd come around.

"You're coming home with me," said Mac as he started the car.

"I'm sure Elodie will love that," was my wry remark.

"Elodie will understand. But I don't want to leave you alone right now. And the last thing you need is to get into another fight and end up arrested again."

I didn't have the strength to protest. If Mac wanted to tuck me into bed at his place, fine. It wouldn't change the fact that my life was in pieces, the woman I loved hated me, and that I didn't have the wherewithal to give a shit anymore.

Chapter 29

Grace

A month after I'd broken up with Brady, Kelly and Elodie persuaded me to go out to dinner with them.

"You've been a total shut-in for weeks now," Kelly had said gently when she'd called me a few days prior. "I'm worried about you. It's not healthy."

I hadn't realized it'd been almost a month since I'd walked out of Brady's apartment. Time had seemed to flow both quickly and too slowly. I had barely even noticed.

"This isn't a blind date setup, is it?" I'd asked, suspicious.

"Would I do that to you?" Kelly paused. "Okay, I would, but it's not. I'm inviting Elodie, too. I know you guys are friends. I reached out to her, and she thinks it's a good idea."

I'd wanted to ask how Kelly had managed to get in touch with Elodie, but I hadn't had the energy. Knowing Kelly, she'd probably stalked Elodie at her favorite café and had managed to get her phone number without seeming like a total creeper.

But after some more persuasion from Kelly, I agreed to go to dinner.

I knew I needed to get out of the house. I could tell that my parents were worried, too.

Dad kept acting awkwardly around me, clearing his throat and then asking me inane questions. Once, he'd asked me in all seriousness what my thoughts were on the upcoming demolition of some famous building down the street from our house.

"Why would I care about that?" I'd asked him, confused.

"Uh, well, it's a historical building. You like history, right? Maybe you should read about it."

Then he'd grabbed a drink from the fridge and headed out. Mom had just shrugged when I'd asked her about it.

"You know your dad," she'd said. "He's terrible about talking about his feelings."

Dad's behavior got only stranger. I'd find random treats in the kitchen that he thought I loved: from barbecue chips to brownies to bags of Snickers. One day, I came home to freshly cut flowers that I'd thought were for Mom but were, in fact, for me.

For a quick moment, I'd thought they were from Brady. But then I'd read the card and realized my dad had gotten them for me.

For my favorite daughter, the note had said in his familiar scrawl.

I'd had a feeling Dad felt guilty about the Brady situation. But it was Brady whom I was angry with, not Dad. Brady had been the one to give Ben those car keys that night.

Ironically, my dad admitted that Brady had given Ben the keys after I'd pressed him about it. That was how I'd found out in the first place before going over to Brady's to confront him.

Ultimately, it was Brady who'd kept that secret from me for six years. After all we'd been through, he'd kept that from me.

Had Brady ever planned to tell me the truth? I had a distinct feeling he'd never planned to tell me. He'd held me, kissed me, made love to me, and all that time, he'd never once thought, *I should tell her the truth.*

It disgusted me. Hadn't I told him that I couldn't stand liars? And I didn't care if it wasn't exactly lying. He'd deliberately omitted a key detail to the story about Ben dying. Because it also meant that if Brady had been a decent person, he could've saved Ben's life.

I spent that month without Brady thinking about Ben. I remembered both the good and the bad—how he'd been protective of me but had also teased and annoyed me, as older brothers did.

Once, when I'd been about six years old, Ben had found out an older kid had pushed me off my bike. He'd marched straight down to that kid's house and had punched him in the mouth.

And then, later that day, Ben had stolen my bike and ridden off with it, laughing as I'd yelled after him.

That had been our relationship. We'd loved each other, but we'd fought, too.

Now I wished that I'd told him how much I'd looked up to him, how proud I'd been of his hockey career that was advancing at breakneck speed.

I also wished I could tell him how mad I was at him for driving that night. One stupid choice, and he'd ruined so many lives.

It wasn't fair. It just wasn't.

The night of my dinner with Elodie and Kelly, I arrived at the restaurant after Elodie but before Kelly. Elodie waved from a booth, a big smile on her face.

"I'm so glad you came," she said as she hugged me. "How are you?"

I shrugged. "Not great, to be honest."

Elodie's forehead creased. "I'm sorry. Hopefully, we can get your mind off everything tonight. Oh, there's Kelly." Elodie waved again.

Kelly was dressed to the nines and was somehow more cheerful than ever. I had a feeling she was trying extra hard for my sake.

I wanted to tell her there was no point. It didn't matter how many jokes she told or ridiculous stories she recounted.

My mind and heart were still far, far away.

"Soooooooo," Kelly said after we'd ordered drinks, "how's the internship, Grace?"

"It's fine."

Elodie glanced at Kelly. "I thought you were enjoying it?" Elodie questioned me.

"I am. It's just awkward right now." I didn't feel like I needed to clarify.

Kelly sighed. "Okay, well, let's change the subject. What have you guys been watching lately? I just binge-watched this Turkish drama, and now I'm on to this Korean one where she's secretly dating her grumpy boss, but his evil mother can never, ever find out. The heroine just got hit by a car, too."

Kelly chattered away, Elodie asking questions, with me mostly just listening. I stirred my drink and stared out the window at the traffic.

I knew I was terrible company right now. I felt guilty about it. When I'd told Kelly I wouldn't be much fun to be around, she'd told me that that was fine.

"Do you think I only care about my friends when they're happy?" she questioned. She'd sounded a little hurt.

When Elodie asked me a question, I realized with chagrin that I'd stopped listening a while back.

"Grace," Kelly said with a sigh and a shake of her head, "you can't keep going on like this. You've broken up with Brady. That sucks. But are you really trying to move on?"

Hearing Brady's name was like a punch in the gut, which was silly because I heard his name all the time at work. I'd even seen him at least twice, although we hadn't said a word to each other.

And although my parents tried not to bring him up, it was nearly impossible that his name was never mentioned around me.

"I do want to move on. I just . . . don't know how."

Elodie took my hand and squeezed it. "If it's any consolation, Mac says that Brady is a hot-ass mess. He hasn't even been to the club to get his mind off you. As far as Mac knows, he just goes home to his apartment alone every night."

I swallowed. I hated hearing that Brady was hurting, but it also made me feel strangely good. I wanted him to be in as much pain as I was.

It was petty and selfish, but I didn't care.

"Okay, well, you're going to have to show us that you want to move on," Kelly said. She pulled out her phone. "Let's get your dating profile up. Getting some new dick is your best course of action."

I was about to protest but stopped myself. Maybe Kelly was right. Maybe I just needed to purge Brady Carmichael from my system.

Kelly began typing and then put her phone down so we could all see the screen. "Put in your deets, and then we'll get started. What photos do you have? We should look through those to pick some good ones."

Elodie was nodding along as Kelly asked me questions to fill out my profile. What were my hobbies? What kind of a guy was I looking for? What was my ideal first date? What were some of my favorite shows and movies?

I answered her questions, but even I could tell I didn't have much enthusiasm behind my answers. When I answered, "I don't know," Kelly sighed and began typing an answer for me.

"I thought you wanted to move on," Kelly pointed out, frowning.

"I do. But . . . ." I bit my lip. "Maybe that doesn't mean I'm ready to start dating. Maybe I should be single for a while."

When Kelly looked frustrated, Elodie said, "That's probably a good idea. I think everybody should be single rather than jumping from one relationship to another."

She grinned. "I say that as somebody who was already dating a guy when I started having feelings for Mac, whoops. So maybe do as I say, not as I do."

Kelly looked a little mollified. "Well, maybe you're right. We can wait on the dating thing. Although I think new dick is always a good thing."

We ate our food, then Elodie had to leave. "I forgot that Mac and I have something going on tonight," she said as she hugged me and then Kelly. Her gaze now on Kelly, she added, "Behave yourself, all right?"

Kelly chuckled. "Of course, of course."

After Elodie left, though, Kelly gave me a grin that could only be described as evil. Then she was on her phone, clearly messaging somebody.

"What are you doing now?" I asked, my eyes narrowed.

"Being a good friend. Now, did I tell you about the time I nearly ran over a goat in Pasadena?"

Kelly and I were enjoying a piece of chocolate cake for dessert when two guys came up to our table. Kelly got up and hugged them both before gesturing for them to sit down.

"What are you two doing here?" she asked, her smile wide. "Grace, this is Cal and Darren. They're professors I work with in the program. Actually, Darren, I need to talk to you about a class I'm going to TA in the summer . . ."

I watched in awe as Kelly skillfully pulled Darren aside to give Cal and me privacy. I blinked over at Cal, which made him laugh.

Cal was dark-haired, bearded, and tall. He had an easy smile, and when he chuckled, I could tell he was probably a decent guy.

"Well, I guess it's just us now," Cal said. "Kelly said your name was Grace?"

"That's right."

"Actually, I have a confession to make. I recognized you before Kelly told me your name." His eyes crinkled. "I'm a huge Blades fan, you see."

I blushed. "Oh."

Seeing my reaction, he held up his hands. "Sorry, is that not kosher? I didn't mean to make you uncomfortable. But I know that you and Carmichael were dating and that you're Coach Dallas's daughter . . ."

I smiled grimly. "I guess that's what I get for dating somebody famous."

Cal spun the straw in one of the water glasses sitting on our table. "So you and Brady aren't together, though, right?"

"No, we're not."

Cal seemed to take that as an invitation to flirt. I didn't mind, really. I knew that Kelly meant well in trying to get my mind off Brady. And Cal seemed like a decent guy.

When he started asking me questions about the Blades, though, I felt myself getting tense.

"I mean, what's it like? Being around the team? Does your dad talk strategy with you?" Cal asked.

Is he more interested in me because of the Blades or because I'm a woman? I wondered.

"My dad usually keeps the nitty gritty to himself. My mom doesn't like when he brings work home," I said.

"That makes sense. I'd bet you and your mom get tired of hearing about hockey sometimes." Cal chuckled. "I used to play as a kid, but I was never very good. Which is why I ended up in academia. I'm hoping to get tenure in the next few years."

I sipped my water. "Awesome."

"It's really difficult to get tenure nowadays, but through an act of God I got this tenure-track position. But it doesn't pay like being on the NHL does." Cal leaned forward. "Tell me, what's the craziest thing you've seen a player do? I mean, we all heard about Mac going to that weird sex club. Anything crazier than that?"

I shook my head. "Nothing beyond the usual," I lied.

Cal looked disappointed. "Well, Brady has been in the news a lot lately. Seems like it's affected his playing, too."

I flinched. Cal seemed to sense he'd said too much, because he hastily apologized.

"What do you do for work?" Cal asked. "I realized I didn't ask you."

As we chatted, I realized that all my answers seemed to be linked back to hockey, the Blades, and Brady. My internship, my dad, my ex-boyfriend. Nothing in my life was my own, was it?

Even my brother had played hockey. And now a new guy was interested in me simply because of my link to the Blades.

When Kelly finally returned to our table, I almost jumped out of my seat. "I remembered I have a work project due," I lied, grabbing onto Kelly's arm. "Can you drive me home?"

Kelly blinked, but to her credit, she didn't call me out on my lie. We both said goodbye to the guys and headed out.

After I'd gotten back home, I knew I needed to make some changes in my life. If I really, truly wanted to get over Brady, I needed to have my own life outside of the Blades. And that also meant I needed to carve out a new life that didn't include Brady Carmichael.

When Julia called me into her office on Friday morning, I expected bad news.

"We'd like to offer you a full-time position with us," she said. "We've all been impressed with your performance during your internship, and we think you'd be a great addition to our team."

I stared at her, shocked. I'd been barely pulling my weight in the last month since I'd ended things with Brady. I hadn't even wanted to apply for a full-time position.

"That's . . . awesome," I said, not sure how to respond.

I couldn't help but wonder if Julia was doing this just because I was the coach's daughter. Had my dad talked her into doing this? Because I hadn't exactly been giving my all lately.

Thinking of Dad interfering in my career reminded me that I needed to untangle myself from this world. I couldn't be my own person if I stayed in the Blades ecosystem.

And how could I expect to move on from Brady if I was reminded of him constantly at my job?

I folded my hands, trying to calm my pounding heart. "I appreciate the offer, but I'm going to have to decline," I said.

Julia raised her eyebrows. "Are you sure?"

Saying the words made me feel calmer. It felt like a heavy burden was slowly being lifted from my shoulders.

"I think I need to figure out what I really want to do with my life," I admitted. "And I don't want it to seem like I've only gotten where I am because of who my dad is."

"Well, I'll admit, I'm disappointed, but I understand where you're coming from. If you ever change your mind, please reach out."

We shook hands, and then I left after saying goodbye to Garrett and the rest of the team. I didn't mention that I'd been offered a job, though. I just hoped that Garrett got a job offer: he was the one who deserved it, not me.

I went to my car and sat, staring at nothing for a while. I waited for the inevitable feelings of regret or fear, but there were none.

I just felt lighter. And I thought that I might have the strength to get over Brady Carmichael once and for all.

Chapter 30

Grace

"I need to talk to you about something," Mom said to me the Sunday morning following my internship ending.

Mom had gone out for doughnuts and coffee, something she rarely did, which made me wonder whether something was up. Dad had gone to the gym—he'd wanted to start losing weight after his doctor had lectured him about his high cholesterol and blood pressure—so it was just Mom and I that morning.

I bit into a doughnut, not caring that it was my third one already. "What?" I asked, my mouth full.

Mom handed me a napkin. "It's about Brady."

When I groaned, she added, "And don't tell me you don't have time to talk about him. You haven't been doing anything since your internship ended. You've just been moping around the house. Have you even talked to Kelly? Or other friends?"

I made a face. "I haven't been moping," I muttered.

"And you decided not to take a full-time job with the

Blades." At my surprised look, Mom just smiled. "Honey, there are no secrets safe from me."

"Who told you?"

"Your dad."

"Meaning he was the one who tried to pull strings to get me an offer." I scowled.

"And if he did? He knows you'd be great at the job. He wouldn't have done it if he didn't care about you, either. We both knew how excited you were about getting the internship."

I sighed. "I was excited. I thought it would launch me into something even better, if not a job at the Blades, then with another amazing company."

When I'd graduated from college and gotten the offer for the internship, I'd been over the moon. Not just because I was going back to LA and would thus be closer to Brady, but because I'd genuinely enjoyed my marketing and PR classes at UNLV.

But that'd changed. Suddenly my career had been put on the back burner. I'd gotten so focused on Brady and our on-again, off-again relationship that the internship seemed unimportant.

I wasn't proud of that fact. It wasn't very feminist of me, either. I grimaced inwardly. But I also knew that love could make a person go a little crazy.

"I just hate to see you throw away a potentially amazing opportunity," said Mom.

"It's not throwing it away." I struggled to explain. "I just need some time away from everything. And everyone. I've never had a life that didn't revolve around hockey."

Mom gave me a pointed look. "I know you're sad about Brady, too. We all are."

That made me scowl. "You are? Since when? You were the one who told me that I shouldn't date him. I would've thought you'd be happy that we broke up."

"I'm never happy seeing you unhappy." Mom was playing with her wedding ring now. "Your dad came to me and told me something that you should know. Not just about the job offer thing. It's about Ben and Brady, about the accident."

I set down my doughnut, my stomach twisting. "I already know what Brady did. He told me himself."

"No, you don't. Did Brady ever tell you that your dad is the one who made him keep silent? That he forced him not to tell me or you that he was the one who gave Ben my car keys?"

I couldn't breathe. I stared at my hands, feeling like the world had just tipped on its axis.

I'd been so angry with Brady for lying to me about Ben and his car accident. Why hadn't he told me this?

"Your dad regrets making Brady not say anything," Mom said. "But at the time, he was doing it to protect us. You know your father. He tends to think he's the strongest of us all and has to shoulder all of our burdens."

Mom took my hand. I realized I was shaking.

"Brady didn't lie to you. At least, not because he wanted to. He had to. Your dad gave him no choice," Mom said.

I felt like the ground shifted under me. I'd always known Dad was the type to meddle, but this? This was on another level entirely.

I shook my head. "Oh my God. But I don't understand why Brady didn't tell me anyway? Was he really that afraid of Dad?"

Mom gave me a hard look. "You know that Brady looks up to your dad like a father. Brady feels like he owes us for taking him in, so is it that surprising that he'd respect your dad's decision?"

"Owes us? You guys took him in because that's what you did. You took in foster kids. Brady wasn't the first one you'd fostered."

"No, but it's complicated. Brady probably always felt like he was a burden. Not just for us, but for every family he was placed with. Even when your dad and I did everything to show Brady he was *not* a burden. That's the type of thing you can't just let go of, with the instability he'd experienced as a kid."

Mom's expression was sad. "You're lucky, sweetheart. You've never had to doubt that we wanted you, or that we loved you. Can't you see that Brady sees relationships as transactional instead of unconditional?"

I felt silly that I hadn't realized that. Silly, and naive, and sheltered.

Of course Brady would see relationships as transactional. And because of that, he'd do anything my dad asked to still be part of our family.

All my anger toward Brady was slowly being siphoned away. Regret was all I could feel at that moment.

Regret that I'd been so closed-minded. Regret that I'd made assumptions and decided not to have them challenged. Regret that I'd shown Brady his belief that relationships were transactional was true in his case.

"And I would bet Brady never told you that your dad also threatened him with trading him to another team if he didn't stop dating you." Mom sighed. "Did I mention your dad can be overbearing? And a hothead who drives me insane?"

I smiled, but it was a sad smile. I swiped at the tears that had gathered in my eyes. "I was so angry with Brady.

I said horrible things. I just couldn't believe he hadn't told me about Ben. It felt like a betrayal. Now I don't know how to feel."

"Did you know that Brady called your dad's bluff? Told him to trade him if he wanted because he loved you too much to care about his career."

Now I was really crying. Mom pulled me into her arms and held me as I wept.

How could I have been so oblivious? How could I have ever thought Brady didn't love me? I'd let my own fears and other people's opinions overshadow what I knew about him.

"Even if he still loves me," I said quietly, "how can we ever get back to where we were? I don't think he'll ever forgive me. I wouldn't blame him either. He probably just wants to move on from everything."

Mom was silent for a long moment, then she sighed. "I never told you about this, but I was actually engaged to another man when I met your dad."

I blinked. "What? I thought you and Dad were high school sweethearts?"

"Kind of. We dated briefly in high school, then I broke up with him. I dated another guy in college, and when he proposed, I said yes. His name was Daniel. He was a good guy and from a good family. My family loved him, and I knew they wanted us to get married."

Mom's expression turned wry. "My parents never liked your dad. They said he was too wild. It didn't help that his job prospects weren't so great at the time. He was playing hockey while working at a grocery store. He hadn't started coaching yet. While Daniel already had a good job at his dad's insurance business.

"But then your dad moved into the same apartment complex I was living in. We reconnected." Mom smiled fondly. "He was respectful. I told myself we were just friends, but I found myself missing him when I was with Daniel. Every time Daniel said or did something, I wondered what Mike would do."

Mom blushed a little now. "I'm not proud to say this, but your dad and I kissed before I broke things off with Daniel. I realized that I didn't really love Daniel, at least not in the way he deserved. Marrying him would've been more about security and pleasing our families. When I took them out of the equation, I knew I couldn't stay in a relationship that had nothing to do with my own feelings."

It took me a second to fully comprehend what Mom was telling me. It was hard to believe that my mom had once been a young woman, caught between two men and breaking off an engagement to be with my dad.

"I even moved out of that apartment building. I only had six more months on the lease and was going to move in with Daniel after the wedding, of course. So moving didn't make sense. But I knew I had to do it. Even then it wasn't enough. I couldn't let your dad go."

"How did Daniel take it? When you broke up with him?" I asked.

"He was kind about it, which, honestly, made it worse." Mom chuckled. "I wanted him to yell at me so I'd have a better reason to break up with him. But no, he just said that he understood. And that was that. I gave him back the ring he'd given me, and we called off the wedding."

Mom's mother, my grandma Annie, had died when I was young, my grandpa not long after. "Granny must've freaked out," I said.

"Oh, your grandma was so mad at me. She didn't speak to me for six months, especially when she found out it was because of Mike. She threatened to cut me out of her will and everything. Fortunately, your dad is so charming that he eventually won her over.

"I guess what I'm trying to say is that time will allow you to forget about Brady doing something stupid like handing keys to your brother that night. But time will not allow your heart to heal from losing the love of your life. Believe me. I almost made the worst mistake of my life in marrying Daniel instead of your dad."

My heart was pounding. I wanted so badly to believe that Mom was right. Would Brady forgive me? And could I forgive him?

There was so much between us, so much hurt, betrayal, and anger. It felt insurmountable.

"What if love isn't enough?" I whispered.

Mom shook her head. "Love is always enough. You just have to be brave enough to embrace it when it comes your way."

I didn't let myself think too hard about what I was about to do. I knew it was reckless, and I knew it was a gamble. But Mom's words pounded in my brain.

How could I let the love of my life go without a fight?

I drove over to Brady's, my palms sweating with anticipation. My mind went through all the scenarios of how he'd react to me showing up on his doorstep.

Maybe he'd be happy, or angry, or maybe he'd be so confused that he wouldn't know what to say.

I hoped he'd be happy. He'd pull me into his arms, kiss me, and tell me that he still loved me no matter what. Butterflies filled my stomach.

I'd missed Brady so much. It'd been torture not to speak to him or touch him or hear his laugh. The few times I ran into him at work, it'd taken all my strength not to launch myself into his arms.

I parked my car and took a deep breath when I reached Brady's apartment. I was afraid I'd faint before I even got to his front door.

I had gotten out of my car, locking it behind me, when I spotted a woman: a curvy brunette who looked eerily familiar.

It took me a second to realize she was wearing a flight attendant's uniform. And then I recognized her: the woman on the plane who'd been flirting with Brady.

Tatiana. That was her name.

Brady hadn't known I'd seen her flirting with him since I'd been sitting in the back. But I'd come up with aisle to talk to my dad when I'd seen Tatiana nearly shoving her tits in Brady's face. It hadn't taken much for me to find out that he'd hooked up with her previously.

And now I was watching her go into his apartment.

Feeling sick, I got back into my car and drove all the way back home.

Chapter 31

Grace

It was the next-to-last day of my retreat up in Ojai. It was just after dawn, and I was spending it doing yoga and meditation until we ate breakfast.

"Take a deep breath in, and let everything go," our instructor said in her calming voice. "That's it. I can tell some of you are still hanging on to things that are heavy. Release it."

I focused on my breathing. I'd had a dream about Brady last night, and it was difficult to let go of the memory of that dream.

It'd been a happy one, at least. Sometimes I had dreams where I went into his apartment and saw him sleeping with that Tatiana woman. And then he'd just laugh in my face and tell me to get lost.

The happy dreams, though . . . they stuck around longer. They were worse, in a way, because they reminded me of what I'd lost.

I exhaled and moved to child's pose. My body was stiff, and it took all my willpower to let my muscles relax.

By the time our yoga session ended, I was sweating and starving. The nine other people attending the retreat and I went to the outdoor area where we were served a breakfast of green tea, some kind of healthy protein, and loads of organic fruits and veggies.

When I'd booked this retreat, I'd wanted to get away from LA—and from Brady. I'd never been much interested in yoga or meditation, but it'd promised a respite from reality. So I'd booked it and driven up here, hoping against hope it'd help.

And to be fair, Ojai was a gorgeous area. We weren't far from the ocean, and some of us had gone there to meditate more than once. We also had the opportunity to go hiking in the mountains. The weather was always gorgeous: warm and dry with bright-blue skies.

I could see why this was a popular place for retreats. It truly did feel like another world.

But my mind and heart were back in LA. Every night when I lay in bed, I couldn't help but think about Brady.

I wondered if I could ever trust him again. I wondered whether I'd been seeing things, that maybe that woman hadn't been Tatiana. I wondered whether he'd been sleeping with her, and if so, did I really have a right to be hurt?

We'd broken up. He was as single as I was. If he wanted to distract himself with another woman, did I have a right to get angry about it?

But it still hurt. It made me feel sick to my stomach that he'd moved on that quickly. It was the principle of the thing.

Then, in my darker moments, I thought about finding a guy and just getting some dick, as Kelly would say. Purge Brady from my system. Show him that if he could sleep around, I could, too.

"Are you going to the cooking class this afternoon?" Trina, one of my fellow students, asked me as she began eating a grapefruit.

"I think I might go for a hike," I replied.

"Oh, that's a good idea. I might join you."

I nearly told her not to since I wasn't in the mood for company, but I bit my tongue. Trina was harmless. Although she tended to go on and on about other people's auras and loved to practice tarot readings on everybody, she meant well.

I was just bitter that, when she'd done my tarot reading, she'd pulled Death, the Ten of Swords, and the Four of Pentacles. In her interpretation, the cards meant I needed to let go of my anxiety and start opening up to people.

"You're going through a big transformational phase," Trina had said. "The Death card could mean the death of a phase in your life, or the death of a relationship. It's painful, but necessary. I always tell people not to fear the Death card. You can't have darkness without light, of course."

I didn't want to hear those things right then, because all it told me was that I needed to let go of Brady. And I just couldn't bring myself to do that.

No matter how far I went, no matter where I ran to, he'd follow me. If not physically, then in my heart. It was like he'd taken root inside me, and now it was impossible to decipher where I started, and he began.

That afternoon, I managed to sneak out before Trina noticed and tried to join me on my hike. I pushed myself until I was panting and sweating like crazy. I'd never taken this particular trail. My calves and feet were burning by the time I got to the top. I stood there for a while, taking in the view, breathing deeply.

When I returned for dinner, Kris, one of our instructors, took me aside.

"You seem far away," she remarked. "Are you all right?"

I forced myself to smile. "I'm fine," I lied.

"Mmm, you don't seem relaxed after a retreat where the point is to, in fact, relax."

Kris gestured for me to sit down. I took her invitation, knowing that she was right.

"I could tell you had a lot of baggage hanging over you on your first day," Kris said, "and I hoped you could start to unpack it. But it seems like you haven't even started to unpack your feelings. What's holding you back?"

I sighed. "I don't know. I just can't let go of him. Brady. I still love him, even when I know it's not meant to be."

"How do you know it's not meant to be?"

I gave her a shorter version of our story, including me seeing Tatiana going into his apartment that night.

"It sounds like this is all unresolved. What would happen if you talked to Brady? Knew for a certainty that he's moved on? Because you don't know if he and that woman were sleeping together," Kris pointed out.

I shook my head. "I can't get my hopes up," I whispered.

"Hope is never a bad thing. But not resolving what's bothering us, never getting closure when closure is possible . . ." Kris's gaze was direct now. "I think you're afraid of hearing an answer you won't like."

"Of course I am. Who wouldn't be?"

"Or maybe you just need to forgive this man. It sounds like you're holding on to a lot of anger toward him. But what does that accomplish? You'll never be able to heal your own body if your mind is imprisoned with anger."

I knew Kris was right. I also knew that I was afraid. I was afraid of a world without Brady. That thought alone made me want to cry and scream in anguish.

"I think you need to talk to Brady. Have everything out on the table. And let go of blaming him for something that wasn't his fault. Your brother was the one who decided to drive that night, not Brady," said Kris quietly.

Tears sprang to my eyes. I realized I'd been misplacing my anger onto Brady, when who I should be angry with was Ben.

He'd been drunk that night. He'd been the one to go for that drive. What if he'd hurt or killed somebody else? Was it really Brady's fault that he just handed my brother the keys?

I blew out a breath. "I don't even know where to begin," I admitted.

"Just one step at a time. I know you can do it." Kris put a hand on my shoulder. "And then, once you have that conversation with Brady, you can come back here again to start the real healing."

I was itching to get back to LA by the end of the retreat. I could tell that Kris was amused by how distracted I was, but I didn't care.

I knew I wanted to forgive Brady. I wanted to tell him that I wasn't angry with him anymore. I wanted to tell him I still loved him, and that I wanted to fight for our relationship.

And if Tatiana was still around, I'd fight for Brady anyway. At this point I'd fight anyone who stood in my way.

I tried calling Brady before I started the drive down to LA, but he didn't pick up. I texted him, then left him a voicemail. As I drove, I kept glancing at my phone, hoping he'd call me back.

But he was radio silent. That hope I'd been clinging to was slowly slipping through my fingers.

"No, you can't give up now," I muttered to myself. "You're going to find him. Brady Carmichael, I will hunt you to the ends of the earth if I have to."

I drove to his apartment and knocked on his door, but there was no answer. I called him, and still—no answer. When one of Brady's neighbors came outside, I asked her if she knew where Brady was.

"Brady? I don't think he's been home for a few days now."

That made no sense. Where would he be? I racked my brain. The hockey season had ended, so he shouldn't be away for a game. But maybe he was traveling somewhere? For all I knew, he could be in the jungles of the Amazon.

I got back into my car and drove to Mac's house. I'd been there only once for a party.

When I got there, though, it was empty. No Mac, no Elodie, and no Brady.

I called Elodie, staving off panic. When she picked up, I didn't even say hello. "Do you know where Brady is?" I asked.

"Uh, no, I don't." I then heard Elodie ask Mac if he knew where Brady was. "Mac doesn't know, either. Why? Is everything okay?"

"He won't answer my calls, and he wasn't at his apartment. I'm actually at your house right now."

"Oh dear. No, he's not there. We've barely seen him in the past few weeks. Mac keeps trying to get him to come over, but he always says no."

"When did you last talk to him?"

Mac got on the phone. "Grace? Yeah, I texted with him this morning. I don't know where he is, but he's alive, at least."

I blew out a breath. It wasn't absolute confirmation that Brady was okay, but at least he'd talked to somebody recently.

I said goodbye to Mac and Elodie and headed over to the Scarlet Rope. Fortunately, it was now later in the evening, when the club would be busy. I went inside wearing just yoga pants and an oversize T-shirt, gaining a few strange looks as I went around asking if anybody had seen Brady.

But nobody had. Then again, the club was all about anonymity. Unless people recognized him as a Blades player, they probably didn't even know Brady's name.

I wandered through the club, going to each public viewing room to see whether Brady was there. In one, I caught sight of a man with Brady's build and hair color.

Oh God, is that him? It looks just like him.

But the man was wearing a mask, so it was hard to tell whether it was Brady. But maybe it was him? Maybe he'd come here and that was why he wasn't answering his phone.

I sat down, breathing hard. Brady—if this man really was Brady—now had a woman tied up as he whipped her. She was moaning and writhing, her body a canvas of red marks.

I watched as Brady put nipple clamps on the woman. She screamed when he started whipping her harder with a cat-o'-nine-tails.

Brady had never used that on me, but maybe he'd wanted to try something different. Maybe he wanted to do more intense BDSM than I'd ever wanted to do. It made sense, if he'd come here to distract himself.

I felt sick. I watched the scene as it turned into one of rough sex. Brady let the woman down and tossed her onto the bed. He roughly parted her thighs and plunged into her. She squealed and bucked as he fucked her hard, the sound of their bodies slapping filling the room.

I couldn't watch this. I was about to leave when Brady removed his mask to wipe his face. I realized with a jolt it wasn't actually Brady.

I bit back a cry. I ran from the room and into a bathroom, locking myself in a stall. I couldn't stop the tears of relief.

It wasn't Brady. It wasn't him.

I was in the stall for so long that someone knocked on the door. "You okay in there?" a woman asked.

I wiped my face and opened the door. "I'm great," I replied, a wide smile on my face.

The woman gave me a strange look, then shook her head. I rinsed my face and headed home.

When I got to my parents' house, it was late. To my surprise, though, the first-floor lights were still on.

When I opened the front door, I saw my parents first, sitting in the living room.

And then I saw him. Brady sat on the couch, like he'd been waiting for me to return.

Dad cleared his throat. "Uh, we'll let you two talk."

My parents grabbed their things, which only confused me more. "Where are you going?" I asked.

Mom gave me a kiss on the cheek. "A late movie and maybe we'll go to a bar. We haven't done that in forever." She patted my arm. "Be nice to him," she whispered.

Then my parents were gone, and it was just me and Brady.

Chapter 32

Grace

We stared at each other for what felt like an eternity. I drank him in like I hadn't seen him in years. He was as handsome as ever; his hair was a little longer, and he had scruff on his cheeks. He also looked a little thinner, and I wondered whether he'd been taking care of himself.

"Grace," he said at the same time I said, "Brady."

We both smiled. Then Brady said, "You first."

I sat down next to him, but not quite close enough for him to touch me. I wasn't sure if I could handle that right now. I realized I was shaking, and I had to hide my hands under my thighs.

"I've been looking for you all day," I said.

Brady's brows rose. "Really?"

"Why didn't you answer your phone? I thought something was wrong."

Brady pulled out his phone from his back pocket and grimaced. "Shit. The battery's dead. I hadn't even realized. I'm sorry for freaking you out."

I took a deep breath. Then I looked more closely at

his phone, taking it from his grasp. "How old is this thing, anyway?"

"It still works."

"Um, clearly not." I handed it back, trying not to laugh at Brady's grumpy expression. "I'm glad you're okay. Were you waiting here long?"

Now Brady looked uncomfortable. "Yeah, but I needed to talk to your parents. We hashed things out. Your mom really told your dad off. I'm sorry you missed it. She was pissed about him making me stay silent about Ben."

I closed my eyes. "That's what I wanted to talk to you about. I have so much I need to say. I don't even know where to begin."

"I'm just glad you're talking to me."

I opened my eyes again. Brady was looking at me like I was an oasis in the desert. My heart soared. That dangerous, dangerous hope bloomed inside me again.

"I want to make things work. I don't even care about Tatiana," I said.

Brady looked confused. "Tatiana?"

A blush climbed up my cheeks. "I saw her going into your apartment a week ago. I wanted to talk to you, but then I saw her, and I just couldn't do it."

Brady gaped at me, and then he groaned. "Oh Christ, it's not what you think. Tatiana was at my place, but nothing happened. I swear."

"How did she know where you live?"

Brady grimaced. "We've hooked up before. At my place. But that was a long time ago. She just showed up that night because her flight was delayed, and she was bored. I sent her away."

I could tell by the intensity in his expression that he was telling the truth. I let out a sigh of relief.

"I was about to go fight her," I admitted, laughing.

"You have to know—the only woman I love is you. It's always been you, Grace. I know you're angry with me, and I won't tell you that you should forgive me—"

I scooted closer and pressed a finger over his mouth. "There's nothing to forgive. I realized that I was taking out my feelings about Ben dying on you. I was mad that you hadn't been honest, yes. But my mom told me that it was all because of my dad interfering."

Brady closed his eyes. "So you know everything."

"I do. And you know what? It doesn't change how much I want to be with you."

Brady pressed his forehead to mine, and we breathed each other in. "I hoped you'd say that to me, but I never thought it'd happen," he murmured.

"I'm so sorry for everything I said to you that night in your apartment. The guilt has ate away at me."

"About those damn keys . . ." Brady moved so he could look into my eyes. "I should never have given them to your brother. It was a stupid, split-second decision. I'd seen him drinking a beer earlier, but I assumed that he was sober enough to drive. I thought he'd never drink and drive and put himself in danger, or anyone else. I've lived with the guilt of that mistake. It haunts me."

I could see that in his eyes. I hated that for him, that he'd had this terrible burden on his shoulders for so long.

"I think Ben would want us to let go of the past," I said. "Can't you see him rolling his eyes and telling us to stop moping around?"

That made Brady chuckle. "He'd definitely tell me to stop being a 'bitch baby,' as he'd like to say when my hockey playing sucked."

"My brother was so motivational." I chuckled, then

sobered. "I also get why you listened to my dad. I can't keep wishing you hadn't because if I'm being honest, I would've done the same thing."

"I was so afraid of losing all of you." Brady looked away. "I'd already lost Ben. If you and your mom knew the truth, your dad was sure that you'd never speak to me again. I couldn't bear that. Especially you. I could've lived with that guilt for the rest of my life if it meant I could still be in your life."

"Well, I know you didn't ask for it, but I do forgive you. I love you. It's always been you. You're the only man I'll ever love."

I then took a deep breath. "I also want you to know that you're enough. You don't have to be some amazing hockey player to prove that you're worthy of love. I know you've been through a lot, especially with your mom. I know you felt like you didn't belong with us, but you do. I think I knew that the day you first arrived at our house."

Tears filled Brady's eyes. "Shit. I don't know what to say. I wish I could believe you."

"I hope someday you will believe it. Until then, I'll just keep saying the words and showing you how much I love you."

He hugged me close, and I could feel him shaking. I rubbed his back as I waited for the multitude of emotions to move through his body.

He finally pulled away and wiped his eyes. "Jesus. I didn't even realize I wanted to hear somebody say something like that. All my life, nobody wanted me. I was always a burden, another mouth to feed. My mom couldn't even stop drinking long enough to bring me home. I wanted to be a part of your family so badly, but it scared the shit out of me, too."

He looked away. "Then Ben died, and I thought, *This is it*. This is the end. I'll lose the Dallases, too. Just like I'd been kicked out of every other foster family I'd been in. So, yeah, I did whatever your dad wanted me to. I'm not proud of that, though. I should've been stronger."

"It doesn't matter. All of that is in the past." I cupped his cheek. "We're here, together. And I'm not letting you go, Brady Carmichael."

Brady groaned. He pulled me into his arms, and it felt like I was finally coming home. He kissed me; I clung to him like he was a lifeboat amid a storm.

"I love you so damn much," he said between kisses. "Not talking to you for a whole damn month was too fucking long. It almost killed me."

"I thought about you every day." I grinned. "And every time I masturbated, of course."

He growled. "Don't tempt me or I'm going to fuck you right here in your parents' house."

"They're not coming back for a while." I grabbed his shirt and then led him to the large leather chair. "And if you don't fuck me right now, I'm going to lose my damn mind."

Brady didn't need to be told twice. He kissed me as he ran his hands down my spine. He stripped me out of my shirt and bra in record time. When he palmed my breasts, I gasped. It'd been so long since he'd touched me that it felt like the first time all over again.

"I thought about you all the time, too," he admitted. "I loved to think about you playing with your sweet pussy when I jerked off. But then I'd always end up feeling worse afterward because I couldn't really touch you."

"I felt the same way. Sometimes it felt better not to touch myself, but then I'd always give in."

He kissed me, the stubble rough against my face. I rubbed a hand across his cheek. "This is new," I said with a laugh.

"I haven't felt much like shaving. Or getting a haircut. Or really living, because I didn't have you around."

"Well, then I'll definitely have to take you to a barber after we're finished."

Brady's eyes darkened. "And you think we'll be done before every barber in this town closes? Think again."

I squealed when he pinched my nipples in tandem as he kissed me. I humped his lap, desperate for more contact. But Brady seemed content to make me suffer.

"You're going to get my jeans soaked," he said with a chuckle. He slicked his hand through my folds. "Damn, baby. You really want me to fuck you, don't you?"

I nodded. He began rubbing me—slowly, ever slowly—and I had to bite back a scream. I didn't care that I was humping his hand or that I was probably leaving marks on his shoulders from my fingernails.

Brady kissed the side of my neck; then he swore. "I don't have a condom," he said, frustrated. "Shit. I wasn't thinking."

"It doesn't matter. I'm on birth control."

His eyes widened. "You sure?"

"Absolutely. I trust you."

He sighed and wrapped his arms around me tightly. "I love you. How could I have ever thought I'd be okay without you?"

"That's all over now. You're here, and we're never going to be apart again."

I helped Brady out of his jeans and boxers, needing to feel his cock again. He was hard and hot in my palms.

I stroked him as we kissed, loving the way he pushed into my hands for more friction.

"Put me inside you," he said in a low voice, his eyes narrowed.

I did as he bade. I slowly sat on his cock, loving the way he filled me. We both moaned when he was entirely inside me. I was stuffed full. I leaned forward and pressed my face to his shoulder.

"Ride me, baby." He gripped my hips to start me moving.

I felt a little awkward at first, unsure of what to do. But it didn't take long to find my rhythm. I bounced on Brady's cock and discovered how amazing it felt when my clit brushed against his pelvis.

"That's my girl. God, you're gorgeous." Brady played with my breasts as I increased my pace.

We were both panting now. I felt my climax creeping up on me. I watched as Brady clenched his jaw.

"Baby, you better come soon. Otherwise—" He groaned when I swiveled my hips.

I laughed, but my laughter devolved into moans when Brady thrust up against me. Then, before I realized it, he'd taken control. He used my body to fuck himself, and it was so hot and erotic that it took all of ten seconds before I yelled in orgasm.

I shook and writhed on top of him. It took all my strength just to hold on to him. And then Brady came, and I could feel his cock pulsing inside me. He filled my pussy with his hot cum until I could feel him dripping out of me.

"Fuuuuuuuuck." Brady kissed me as he bucked under me for a few more seconds. "Holy shit, Grace."

I could only shake my head. I didn't have the power to say anything.

We kept kissing for a while longer, not wanting to lose our newfound closeness. When Brady finally pulled away, I blushed when his cum gushed out of me.

"I'll get a towel," he said with a grin. He returned, and we cleaned each other up.

It was only as we were making sure the leather chair was also clean that I started laughing like a lunatic.

"What?" Brady gave me a strange look.

I pressed my hands to my cheeks. "Oh God. Brady, that's my *dad's* chair. I wasn't even thinking earlier."

Brady looked at me, then he looked at the chair. Then he started laughing so hard he was nearly choking.

"Oh my God. Oh, shit." He had to sit down, he was laughing so hard. He wiped his eyes. "Baby, you should've said something."

"I was distracted!"

Brady pulled me onto his lap. "You make me lose my mind, clearly. But you know we'll have to keep this a secret until we die, right?"

"Uh, duh. We should maybe think about taking the chair out back and burning it for good measure."

"And get your dad a new chair without him putting two and two together? Good luck."

I sighed, leaning my head against Brady's shoulder. "I love you."

"I love you, too." He kissed my forehead. "And I think it's time you moved out of your parents' place."

Chapter 33

Brady

It'd been a month since Grace and I had taken our relationship public. Even Coach, to my surprise, had been supportive. When he'd come around the corner to find us kissing after practice, he'd just raised an eyebrow and told us jokingly to get a room.

I'd never realized how freeing it was to be open about how much I loved Grace Dallas. I'd kept that love hidden and buried for so long that it was like a thousand-pound weight had been lifted from my shoulders.

Grace had essentially moved in with me after that day we'd had sex in her dad's chair. Her parents hadn't been thrilled, but they'd let her go without further comment.

I was just glad Grace and I could be alone, because not a day went by when I didn't want her: under me, over me, and every which way in between.

Near the beginning of spring, the Blades had one of the last games of the season. Buoyed by Grace's love and support, I had one of my best games of the season. When we won by three points, it was like a bomb had gone off in the arena. Everyone exploded with excitement, and my entire team converged on me to celebrate.

Even Coach hugged me. I couldn't believe it. I was so shocked that it took me a second to realize what the hell he was doing.

"Carmichael," he said, slapping me on the back. "My boy. Wow."

I swallowed, feeling stupidly emotional. "Thanks, Coach. For everything."

Coach shook his head. "Get out of here and get cleaned up."

Afterward, I came out of the locker room to find Grace. She held a large bouquet and was positively beaming. I didn't even stop to let her give me the flowers. I pulled her into my arms and kissed her.

When we parted, she was breathless. "Oh goodness. What was that for?"

"Because you're my good luck charm. None of this would've happened without you."

"I think you're just a good hockey player, but I'll take the compliment."

I smelled the roses and then handed them off to one of the team's assistants to find a vase for them. That was when I realized Grace was acting a little cagey.

"What is it?" I asked, concerned.

She was blushing now. "Um, I have an idea. A fantasy, really, that I wanted to run by you."

"Go on."

"I think we should go to the club and act like strangers who've never met. And then we have fun . . . in front of people. If you catch my drift."

I stared at her, a little shocked. Then I laughed. "Damn, baby, you're full of surprises. But I'm game if you're game."

"Excellent." She kissed my nose. "I'll see you there at nine p.m. I'll be wearing red lace." Then she winked and left me to stare at her gorgeous backside.

When I arrived at the Scarlet Rope, wearing a black suit and a red tie to match Grace's outfit, my heart pounded in anticipation. It was a few minutes before 9:00 p.m. Would Grace already be here? I scanned the foyer, but I didn't see blond hair and red lace. Not yet, anyway.

I went to the bar to order a drink. The bartender took one look at me and said, "Shit, Brady Carmichael? Amazing game tonight."

"Thanks," I said, meaning it.

The bartender poured my drink and handed it to me. When I tried to pay, he waved a hand. "It's on the house."

"Well, then, thank you, again."

"It seems like you're getting back into the groove. These last few games have been great for you."

I smiled. "Well, finding the love of my life definitely helped. I call her my good luck charm."

The bartender nodded. "Makes sense. Love looks good on you. Congrats, man."

We had chatted for a bit longer, mostly about hockey, when I spotted a woman in red in my peripheral vision. After I finished my drink, I went to find my prey.

Grace was wearing a red-lace number that made my blood pound just seeing her in it. She had her hair up, with only a few tendrils falling to her shoulders. She also wore a matching red mask and red stiletto heels that I couldn't wait to see up in the air as I fucked her.

"I've never seen you here before," I said. I gazed from the tips of Grace's toes to her face, lingering on her breasts. "With tits like those, I would've remembered you for sure."

Grace laughed lightly. "Is that supposed to be a pick-up line, sir?"

"Well, it seems to be picking you up."

She grinned, then looked over my shoulder. "There are lots of men here I could choose from. What makes you so special?"

"I know how to make a woman scream. I bet you like to be spanked, tied up, and gagged. You want a man to take control of you." I leaned closer, inhaling the scent of her hair. "You look like you cream your panties whenever you imagine being used."

Grace was breathing hard now. "You sound so sure of yourself."

"I can see your nipples hardening already. Your cheeks are flushed. I bet if I reached into your panties, my hand would be soaked."

She swallowed, then turned away. "It sounds like you need to show me first. Words are easy. Lots of guys say they're amazing in bed, but then they end up being two-pump chumps."

I growled. "You're playing with fire, my dear."

"Oh good. Sounds fun."

I leaned her head back and nipped at her throat. She shuddered. When I palmed her breasts and rubbed her nipples through the lace fabric of her bra, she moaned.

"I want to show everybody how I can make you scream," I said.

Grace nodded. "Yes. Please."

"And you remember the safe word?"

"Galoshes. Let's go."

We got a room where others could watch us. My blood thrummed, my excitement increasing as we went into the room. We couldn't see anyone on the other side of the double mirror. In other rooms that I'd been in, you could see who was watching you, but not in this one. Knowing there would be voyeurs was erotic enough, though. I didn't need to see anyone's face but Grace's this time.

I came up behind Grace, squeezing her breasts as I kissed her neck. I pushed her bra up, wanting people to see her pretty little tits and how bright red her nipples were.

I cupped her pussy, groaning when I felt how hot she was already. She panted as I rubbed her.

But I was getting ahead of myself. I made her sit down and then went to where the whips hung. I chose a riding crop, testing it and smiling at the sound it made.

I then bound Grace's hands, blindfolded her and gagged her. I had her kneel on a couch and pulled her panties to her ankles. Her ass in the air, I began using the riding crop on her.

She squealed when the first crack of the whip smacked against her ass. Red bloomed across white skin. I rubbed the spot I'd hit before whipping the other cheek.

God, seeing her covered in red marks turned me on like nothing else. Grace kept trying to look back at me, but with her blindfold, she never knew where I'd be. I made sure to keep my slaps a surprise, making her think I'd stopped before using the riding crop on her.

I whipped her until she collapsed onto the couch, her body boneless, her moans turning hoarse.

I tossed the riding crop away and undid my pants, taking out my cock. I pulled Grace up by her hair, making her cry out. I slapped her crimson ass until she was begging me just to fuck her.

"Stay on your knees," I growled.

With her ankles bound, it was a tight fit to thrust inside her. She groaned as I filled her to the hilt. Then I fucked her, relentlessly, filling the room with the sounds of flesh slapping together, accompanied by Grace's moans and squeals. She pushed back against me, desperate for everything I could give her.

"My sweet girl," I crooned as I pounded into her. "I'm going to fill up your pussy with my cum. Is that what you want, baby? Me to fill you up?"

Grace just moaned. I dug my fingers into her hips and thrust a few more times before I felt her starting to come. Her pussy was a vise around my cock. She was so tight that it made me come. I roared, spilling everything I had into her.

We were a sweaty, panting mess by the end. I was trembling as I slowly untied Grace. When she could see me again, there were tears in her eyes.

"Did I go too far?" I asked quietly, instantly worried.

She shook her head. "No, no. It was just intense. But I'd like to be alone now."

I nodded. I picked her up to carry her to the back room, where there was a tub, sink, and couches to receive aftercare. I gently cleaned Grace's body and then rubbed ointment where I'd whipped her.

I then wrapped a blanket around her and held her close.

"How are you feeling?" I asked, kissing her temple.

She blew out a breath. "Exhausted, but in a good way. That was amazing." She looked up at me and smiled. "Thanks for indulging my fantasy."

"Your fantasy? I thought you were just indulging *me*."

"I'm coming around to what you like. It's fun, that's for sure. I've never had better orgasms."

"Well, thank you for being so accepting."

Grace chuckled. "It's hard to believe that we'd be bonding in a sex club years after meeting. Who would have thought? Life is so strange. We're trying out all sorts of things."

"Well, I'm okay with experimenting, but I do have a hard limit," I admitted.

"What?"

"I never want to see you with another person. That one time I saw you kissing another guy . . ." I shook my head. "I nearly lost my damn mind."

Grace looked confused. "Was this recent?"

"No, it was years ago. I picked you up from the movie theater, and you were outside kissing some kid. I never told you I saw you."

Grace's face turned red. "Oh my God, so you *did* see us! I always wondered." She cleared her throat. "Uh, I have something to tell you. I set that whole thing up to make you jealous. Kenny, the guy you saw me kissing? I paid him to kiss me that night. Come to find out later that he was actually gay, so go figure."

I stared at her. "Seriously?"

"That's why I asked you to come get me."

"So nobody was drunk?"

"Well, there were a few drunk people, but Meredith could've still taken me home. Yes, I know it's crazy. But I was desperate for you to notice me. And I guess it worked."

I growled. "You drive me insane, Grace Dallas. You know that, right?"

"Oh, I know. It's why you love me." Her expression turned amused. "You know, I guess I awakened something in you that night."

"What is that?"

She grinned. "Voyeurism. So I guess you getting into this kinky stuff is actually all my fault."

Epilogue
Grace

"Congrats on moving into your new house!" Kelly said as she raised her glass in a toast. After much finagling, we'd finally found a time to get together at one of our favorite restaurants.

Both Elodie and I raised our glasses. I hadn't had time to hang out with my girlfriends for the past few weeks after Brady and I had closed on a house. We'd finally moved in, although we barely had any furniture between the two of us. We'd laughed like lunatics when we'd realized we'd have to sleep on a mattress on the floor until we got an actual bed.

"How is everything going?" Elodie asked.

I smiled, feeling my cheeks heat. Sure, buying a house with your boyfriend and then moving in with him was stressful—but mostly it'd been amazing.

"We're still together," I joked.

Kelly snorted. "I lasted a week when I moved in with my first boyfriend. He didn't believe in doing the dishes, so he'd literally throw away ceramic bowls instead of washing them. Oh, and he never did laundry. He just kept buying underwear. He had more underwear than anyone I've ever known."

"Oh my God." Elodie covered her mouth, stifling a laugh. "I can't even imagine."

"When I tried to wash the dishes one night, he got mad at me. Said I was 'wasting water.'" Kelly rolled her eyes. "Anyway, when he tried to get me to stop flushing the toilet except for once a day, I bailed."

"Great story, Kels," I said.

"Please tell me that Brady lets you flush the toilet," said Kelly.

I assured my friends that Brady did, in fact, let me flush the toilet. He even knew how to put the seat down and wash dishes. His laundry skills were to be determined, though.

"I mean, he doesn't need to do laundry much," I admitted, stirring my drink. "He loves to be naked. It's pretty nice."

"One of the perks of living together, huh?" said Elodie.

"I mean, we lived together before, as kids. But not like this. Sharing a room, a bed . . ." I sighed happily. "It's better than I could've imagined."

"Aw, you make me want to puke." Kelly patted my shoulder. "I'm happy for you, kid."

"You don't mind living near your parents?" Elodie asked, raising an eyebrow.

When I'd suggested that we buy a house near my parents, I'd expected Brady to protest. But to my surprise, he'd loved the idea. And so had my parents.

I'd loved seeing how my parents had really embraced Brady like a son in the past six months. I had a feeling it was more because Brady was allowing them in. He was also on the path of forgiving himself.

"It's kinda nice. We'd like to get a puppy, but we'd need help, obviously. So my parents can come over a lot when we're at work or Brady's out of town," I said.

"You know what they say about getting a puppy . . ." Kelly gave me an amused look. "It's just the first step to having a baby."

I nearly choked on my drink. "Oh God, it's way too soon for that!"

"If I were you, I'd be poking holes in the condoms ASAP. Lock that man down," said Kelly.

I snorted. Elodie was just staring down at her drink, a shy smile on her face. I had noticed that Elodie hadn't ordered alcohol tonight. Now I couldn't help but wonder . . .

"Elodie," I said, narrowing my eyes at her. "What's that smile about?"

Elodie's smile just widened. "Um, what?"

Now Kelly was staring at Elodie. "You've been awfully quiet. What's up?"

"Nothing. I mean, yes, there is something." Elodie sighed. "I'm botching this terribly. I'm pregnant, you guys."

Kelly and I both erupted into squeals at the same time. We were so loud that a few nearby restaurant patrons shot us dirty looks.

"Seriously? How far along? When did you find out?" I asked.

"I've known for a little while now. I know, I know. I was being paranoid. I made Mac keep his mouth shut, and he almost exploded. After the first sonogram, I had to stop him from telling every person he ran into."

"That's adorable," said Kelly.

Elodie lowered her voice. "He'd kill me if I told you this, but he cried at that first appointment. Full-on crying, even a few sobs. I was worried he regretted the baby, but no, he was just so happy."

I felt tears rise in my eyes. "I love that."

"He even wants to get a tattoo of the baby's heartbeat over his heart." Elodie sighed happily. "And don't even get him started on strollers and car seats. He keeps sending me articles and videos of reviews. He wants to buy a few and test them out himself, even though it's not like he's a certified tester."

"You guys are so lucky," Kelly moaned. "How did you manage to find the two guys in the world who are completely obsessed with you?"

We talked a little longer about what softies Mac and Brady were, despite their outward appearance of being big and strong. Moving in with Brady had shown me another side of him. He'd often kiss me on the forehead whenever he'd leave early for practice or a game, and he'd tuck me in at night before I fell asleep. When he'd found out I loved a particular brand of yogurt, he nearly bought an entire case because it was on sale somewhere.

He'd tried cooking dinner last night, but that was still a work in progress. He'd burned the grilled cheese and then had forgotten to put water in the tomato soup, so we'd had burned sandwiches with ketchup. I'd tried my best to eat it with a smile, but Brady had caught on quickly how bad the food was. We'd ended up ordering takeout.

"So does this mean you guys are moving up your wedding date?" I asked Elodie.

"No, I just have to make sure I get a dress that can be altered easily. I was worried about Mac's parents being upset since they're so conservative, but Mac refused to act like we'd done anything wrong." Elodie shrugged. "He'd be fine if I were nine months pregnant and walked down the aisle in a bikini."

Kelly laughed. "Now that sounds like an awesome wedding."

Once we'd discussed Elodie's wedding, I finally found a moment to question Kelly about her dating life. "I thought you were dating that guy from your PhD program?" I asked her.

"Oh, that's been over for a while. I'm trying a different kind of guy lately," she said.

"What does that mean?" Elodie asked.

Kelly shrugged. "Just something different, that's all."

Kelly was never the type of girl to be coy. "Okay, now you're sounding extra sus. Spill, woman," I demanded.

"It's not that big of a deal. You know you gave me a pass to the Scarlet Rope? Well, I went last Saturday."

Both Elodie and I raised our eyebrows. "You know neither of us are going to judge you for that," Elodie pointed out.

"No, it's just . . ." Kelly sighed. "I had a good time. Great, even."

Now I was just confused. "So what's the problem?"

"I might've met someone."

I gestured for Kelly to continue.

"It's weird because you know it was my birthday last week, right? That's why I went. Well, this guy's birthday happens to be the day after mine." Kelly was almost rambling now, which wasn't like her. "And then we got started talking, and I realized that I knew who he was. He had a mask on, though. That's why I didn't know who he was at first."

"Who was he?" Elodie asked.

"Roman Gentry."

My jaw dropped. Roman Gentry was one of Brady's teammates, but he hadn't played as much lately because he attended law school part-time. It'd been quite the coup when he'd stepped down from being a main player three years ago. I'd met the guy only a few times, since I'd been in college during the height of his fame.

"Holy shit." Elodie let out a laugh. "Mac must've given Roman a pass. Roman called Mac up a few weeks ago, and they're planning on going out for drinks soon."

Kelly lowered her voice. "I also had some fun. Before I met Roman, that is. Or knew who he was. I went to one of the rooms where they blindfold you. I thought it'd be freaky in a, well, freaky way. But it was sexy as fuck. Not knowing what the other person was going to do, or how they were going to touch you."

Kelly shivered. "Man, I never thought I was a kinky bitch, but I guess we all have a little kink in us, huh?"

I looked at Elodie. Elodie just blushed, and I burst out laughing.

"So are you and Roman going to see each other again?" I asked.

"I have his number, but I haven't texted him yet," Kelly admitted.

"Why the hell not?" I said.

"Because—I don't know!" Kelly groaned. "I've always been confident around guys, but Roman . . . He was so hot, and confident, and a hockey player. That's like the trifecta for me. And when I told him all about my PhD program, lo and behold, he's going to fucking law school? So he's smart, too? Anyway, I'm too afraid he'll just ghost me."

"Kelly." Elodie put a hand on Kelly's arm. "You're being ridiculous. Just text him. I bet he's dying for you to message him."

"You think so?" Kelly asked.

"Duh," I replied. "You're hot, too. And everything else you just listed. And wait, didn't you just say he was one of the guys in the blindfold room with you?"

Kelly nodded. "That's how we started talking, afterward. He was the one touching me the most, apparently. And he knew what he was doing, I can say that. The man has magic hands. Fuck, I'm getting turned on just thinking about it."

Elodie fanned herself. "Goodness, it's getting hot in here. Or maybe it's just my hormones."

We then talked about Roman and figured out everything we knew about him. Elodie revealed that Roman was also involved in a charity that taught underprivileged youth how to play hockey and pushed legislation to build community centers where kids could skate, among other things.

Kelly then mentioned that he had eight brothers. Eight!

"His poor mother," I commented.

"I googled his family," Kelly said. "And all of his brothers are hot. It's insane, the gene pool in that family."

After dinner, we linked hands as we walked to the parking lot nearby. "I can't wait to have a triple date with all of you and our hot hockey players," Elodie said with a grin.

"All that sexiness in one place? We might die," Kelly said, laughing.

"Six people for drinks and dinner? Good luck finding a table for that in LA," I said.

"Hey, seven people!" Kelly looked over at Elodie. "Soon to be seven, at least."

Elodie patted her stomach. "And if this kid is anything like their dad . . . I'm definitely in for it."

When I arrived home, I sat outside in my car for a few minutes. Mostly because I hadn't really known what our new house looked like at night yet.

I'd left the porch light on, so it illuminated the front enough that I could see the bright pink bougainvillea blooming near the entrance. It'd been one of the first things I'd noticed about the house, making Brady chuckle. "Baby, it's a pretty bush, but we need to make sure the house itself is decent," he'd teased.

Our home was built in the thirties, and it had a vintage charm that we'd both loved. It was a Spanish-style house with white stucco exterior and red clay tiles for the roof. It had a gated entrance with a nice-size front and backyard for the city. Inside, there was original, brightly colored tile throughout, and an open, airy floor plan.

It also had a pool out back, which was lovely for hot summer days. Palm trees bordered our backyard, along with loads of huge succulents that soaked up the desert sunshine.

Right now, though, I was surprised to see only one light on inside the house. I wondered whether Brady was outside in the pool tonight. I'd wanted to surprise him by getting naked and sliding into bed, but if he was already wet and possibly naked outside . . . I'd take it.

I went through the house, turned on a hall light, and then went out back. To my surprise, Brady wasn't in the pool.

That was when a light near the edge of our backyard caught my gaze. As I went to inspect it, I realized it was coming from the two large oak trees—and it was coming from inside what looked like a tree house.

A tree house? That hadn't been there three hours ago and definitely hadn't been there when we'd bought the house. How had Brady managed to get a tree house up there this evening?

"Brady?" I called. I yelled his name a second time.

I laughed in surprise when his head popped out of the side window. "Grace! Come on up!"

I climbed the ladder, grabbing Brady's hand as he helped me inside.

My jaw dropped when I saw that he'd already furnished it inside. Granted, it was tiny, so it could fit only a few things, but I was shocked to see a working wine fridge with two comfy seats and a small table. He'd lit a bunch of candles, adding to the romantic ambiance.

"You even had this thing wired?" I shook my head. "How did you manage this?"

Brady looked like a kid in a candy store. "Oh, I've been planning this for weeks. I was just waiting for you to be gone long enough to get everything installed. But there's no wiring in here. The fridge is battery-powered, believe it or not. I tried to get the contractors to put electricity in here, but they told me that wouldn't be up to code or something."

"An extension cord running from the back of our house might be a little gauche," I said with a giggle. I looked around more closely. "This looks just like the tree house at the Vegas house."

"I know. I did that on purpose." He pointed at a notebook on the table. "I even got you a fresh journal. I know you liked to write in the tree house back home."

"Oh, good. I needed a new notebook to write all my complaints about my terrible, evil boyfriend." I grinned. "How he's so nice to me, and builds me a tree house, and gives me orgasms every single night—"

Brady growled and pulled me into his arms. "You're damn right. I'm a terrible boyfriend. You wouldn't have it any other way."

"No way in hell."

He kissed me until I saw stars. I was half tempted to test out one of the chairs for sturdiness, but Brady stopped before things got too heated. To my surprise, he almost seemed nervous. He gestured for me to sit down like he needed to give me bad news.

Now I was nervous. Had something happened? Was he having second thoughts about moving in together? Had I teased him too hard about burning dinner last night?

"Grace," he said, his voice low, his expression serious. "I wanted to tell you how much I love you and admire you. And how happy I am we're on this journey called life together."

Brady leaned forward, taking my hand. "I can't believe you're crazy enough to be with me, but I wouldn't change it for the world. You're an amazing human being. Kind, thoughtful, smart, gorgeous—"

I let out a laugh. "Brady, now you're making me blush."

"I meant every word." He let go of my hand and fumbled with something in his pocket. Then to my shock, he went down on one knee and opened a ring box, a diamond glittering in the candlelight.

"Grace Elizabeth Dallas," he intoned, "will you make me the happiest man alive and marry me?"

I was so stunned that I didn't say anything for a long moment. When Brady looked like he was about to burst, I finally yelled, "Yes! Of course I'll marry you."

Brady sighed. "Damn, you were making me sweat there."

"I'm sorry. I just didn't expect this." I realized I was shaking, and I could feel tears on my cheeks. When Brady put the ring on my finger, I started crying harder.

"I love you so much," I said, throwing my arms around him.

He kissed me, pulling me onto the floor of the tree house. Then we were laughing like idiots because there wasn't remotely enough room in here for us to have our usual fun.

"Come on," Brady said with a wicked smile. "Let's go inside, and I'll show you just how much I really love you."

THE END

Guess who also has a story? Mac and Elodie!
Read *The Player's Club* Now!

The *Player's* Club
by Fallon Greer

It was supposed to be a simple assignment: stake out the golden boy hockey player Cole "Mac" Mackenzie as he exited the arena after a Los Angeles Blades game.

Follow him.

Get dirt on his personal life—something salacious to please the money-hungry gossip rag I worked for.

But I missed the moment Mac left the building. Or so I thought...

Twenty minutes later, I saw actual Mac exit after the media left. Apparently, he'd used a decoy to throw off the press—waiting until everyone left to make his getaway in private.

I started following the real Mac, and got more than I bargained for.

He led me to a mystery building tucked away in the middle of the suburbs.

Turned out, he was going to... a private club.

A club that wasn't for the faint of heart—as I'd soon find out after sneaking in.

I wasn't expecting to connect with Mac inside. Nor did I anticipate him to invite me back as his personal guest.

What started as a simple assignment turned into something much more—my biggest fantasy I never knew I had.

This wasn't about the tabloid story anymore. I lied to my boss, told him there was nothing to see.

Meanwhile, I kept returning to the club.

I was addicted to unraveling the mysteries of Mac's world.

Addicted to the man who lit a fire inside me.

But—with my own secret—it was only a matter of time before I got burned.

Connect

WITH FALLON ON SOCIAL MEDIA!

www.facebook.com/people/
Fallon-Greer-Author/61553397643622/

www.instagram.com/fallongreerauthor/

https://www.tiktok.com/@fallongreer

Sign up for my mailing list
https://fallongreer.com/
to stay in touch!

About the Author

FALLON GREER is a twentysomething lover of romance novels, coffee, and bookish t-shirts, of which she has far too many. She lives in Miami with her Persian cat, Mortimer, who loves to sit on Fallon's laptop when she's trying to write.

Fallon first discovered her love of reading when she'd steal her mother's Lisa Kleypas novels. That led her to start writing the types of books she loves to read.

When she's not daydreaming through conversations with people and pretending to listen, she's putting those daydreams to good use, writing novels as hot as the Florida sun.

www.ingramcontent.com/pod-product-compliance
Lightning Source LLC
Chambersburg PA
CBHW032006310726
48972CB00002B/288